...way he felt the tug of reg...

...about that," she said.

He wasn't sorry, but how could he say so?

"That's okay. Happens sometimes." It never happened, actually.

She stared up at him and, bang, there it was again— that ache in his chest and the zing of attraction that crackled like the glass glaze Mrs. Yeager used on her white pots. Ray dropped his arm from her shoulder down to her waist.

"Oh," she said. Morgan inched away and met the resistance of his arm as he tightened his hold.

"My daughter is in the other room," she said.

That broke his concentration. His arm fell away and Morgan rose to her feet. She backed toward the door, pausing just inside the threshold with one hand on the doorknob, as if preparing to slam it shut and flee. It was the kind of chase he'd enjoy, only if she would, too.

EAGLE WARRIOR

BY
JENNA KERNAN

First Published in Great Britain 2017
By Mills & Boon, an imprint of HarperCollins*Publishers*
1 London Bridge Street, London, SE1 9GF

© 2017 Jeannette H. Monaco

ISBN: 978-0-263-92860-0

46-0217

Our policy is to use papers that are natural, renewable and recyclable products and made from wood grown in sustainable forests. The logging and manufacturing processes conform to the legal environmental regulations of the country of origin.

Printed and bound in Spain
by CPI, Barcelona

Jenna Kernan has penned over two dozen novels and has received two RITA® Award nominations. Jenna is every bit as adventurous as her heroines. Her hobbies include recreational gold prospecting, scuba diving and gem hunting. Jenna grew up in the Catskills and currently lives in the Hudson Valley of New York State with her husband. Follow Jenna on Twitter, @jennakernan, on Facebook or at www.jennakernan.com.

For Jim, always

Chapter One

Most folks wouldn't trust Ray Strong to look after a houseplant let alone a woman and a child. But that was exactly what had happened. Ray watched the woman in question as she served a complimentary drink to one of the customers on the floor of the tribe's casino—she dipped as she set down the glass to avoid showing too much leg in her skimpy skirt. A shame, really, because she had great legs.

Detective Jack Bear Den, one of his friends and a fellow member of the warrior sect of the Turquoise Guardians medicine society, told him that they had all gone to high school with Morgan Hooke. But honestly, even after observing her several times over the past five days, Ray didn't remember her. That meant that she did not look like this back then.

Morgan was not beautiful, but compelling in a waifish sort of way. She had dark cautious eyes and a generous mouth. For reasons unknown, her thick shock of black hair was cut short on the sides and back and long on the top in a style favored by adolescent boys. He liked that cut on some actresses. But Morgan's hair lacked the product to make it look sassy, so it fell thick and straight in a bowl haircut that looked practical but not sexy, unless you noticed the long curve of her neck. Which he did, and that slim column of sensitive flesh gave him all kinds of bad ideas.

Some of the servers had released their top few buttons to reveal more of their breasts. But not Morgan. She wore the uniform in as conservative a manner as possible. Judging from her tip glass, he was not the only man in the room that rewarded less clothing and more skin.

He watched her retreat to the bar for more drinks. She did look good walking away. Not that it mattered. Ray was not here to pick Morgan up. An outsider had been asking about the shooter's daughter. The Anglo had even been at the casino last Sunday, Morgan's day off. A coworker had furnished Morgan's name, but not where she lived and the stranger had vanished. The woman had called their shaman, Kenshaw Little Falcon, who shared her concern, so he'd sent Ray to watch Morgan's back and see what she knew about her father's involvement in the crime. His shaman had been very specific. Keep her safe and find out if she knew who hired her father. Kenshaw believed that her father had not acted out of some need for justice but had been paid to shoot Ovidio Natal Sanchez. Why was obvious. But who—now that one was a puzzle.

Not as big a puzzle as why his shaman had chosen him for this job. Real dark horse he was and he knew it.

Morgan finished her shift and Ray trailed her out to the parking lot. Morgan stopped to pick up milk and processed cheese. Ray took the opportunity to buy beer and pork rinds. She didn't notice him. She never did because she kept her shoulders rounded and head down all the time. He didn't like it, wanted to shout at her to stand up straight.

Ray gazed across the space that separated them. She didn't seem the type for secrets. But she had at least one. No one seemed to know who fathered her child, Lisa. Everyone had secrets. That made it hard to tell about a person from what you saw on the outside. And no one ever got a look at the inside.

Next Morgan drove home to the small house that she had shared with her father and still shared with her ten-year-old girl. No sign of a man in her life though. A shame. She seemed fragile and Ray wondered why no man had responded to the compulsion to look after her. Not that he was that sort. Not at all.

She stopped again at the neighbor's to pick up Lisa. Her daughter was as skinny as a split rail with hair that flew out behind her when she ran, which she did often. In her features was the promise of beauty and none of the slinking posture her mother adopted. Lisa was bright-eyed and curious. She'd made eye contact with Ray a time or two and even thrown him a generous smile. He liked her. She was outgoing and a little crazy like him, judging from the way she climbed and swung and jumped on the playground at school during recess. But today was Saturday so no school.

When Morgan reached her dark and empty house, Ray waited on the road as Lisa charged toward the door.

April in the Arizona mountains meant that Lisa still wore a heavy coat, though it flapped open as she ran. Ray lifted his field glasses. He had the house behind hers. But this spot on the road gave him a better view of the kitchen. She never shut the curtains over the sink, so he could peer right in as she made dinner.

From his place on the shoulder, he could see both the kitchen on the front corner and one side of the house, including the back window where Morgan's father's bedroom was located. He caught the flash of movement in the bedroom. She left the shades up during the day; he suspected she did this for her cat, who liked sitting in that sunny window on the back of a worn upholstered chair.

Seeing a man pass the window, Ray shifted the direction of his gaze. Redirecting his field glasses, he saw that the contents of the room had been tossed about and there was someone searching the bookcase.

An instant later, Ray was out of his truck and running for the house.

Chapter Two

Morgan Hooke unlocked the front door and her daughter, Lisa, charged inside. One step took Morgan to the small rug just beyond the threshold. She exhaled, glad to finally be home. The day shifts were long and the guests were older, drank only the complimentary beverages and tipped almost nothing. Night shifts paid better, but without her father here at home, she needed to look after Lisa. That meant fewer hours and less pay. She'd picked up the Saturday hours only because a friend agreed to watch Lisa. Money had always been tight, but it had become stretched like the head of a war drum since her father's arrest.

Morgan flicked on the light, chasing off the late-day gloom and looked to the recliner where the cat usually slept. Finding the cushion empty, she scanned the tiny room for Cookie, the cat Lisa had dragged out of a Dumpster behind the school when it was only a kitten.

Lisa had tossed her backpack by the door and now called a greeting to her pet as she entered the eat-in kitchen and switched on the light. Cookie was usually there to greet them, meowing loudly for dinner. Morgan kicked off her shoes, retrieved Lisa's empty lunch bag from her backpack and carried both pack and bag into the kitchen. Lisa had already dropped the sack of groceries on the dinette before making her way down the hall that led to their three small bedrooms on her hunt for the gray cat with the startlingly green eyes.

Morgan frowned at the first prickling of unease. She hoped Cookie was all right because a vet visit was not in the budget.

"Cookie! Coook-key!"

Lisa sang the name and then made a familiar sound proven to lure the cat. The only noise Cookie responded to with greater frequency was that of the electric can opener.

"Mom!"

The alarm in Lisa's voice brought Morgan around. She glanced down the hall where Lisa stood motionless with her hands lifted slightly from her sides as she stared into her grandfather's room.

"Lisa? What's wrong?" Morgan was already moving and had cleared half the distance separating them as she prayed that nothing had happened to Cookie. Then she saw it. Her father was in Phoenix awaiting trial. No one should be in his room. But his overturned dresser now blocked the door.

A small gray cat could not do that.

"Lisa, honey," she whispered as the dread flooded over her suddenly clammy skin. "Come here to me right now."

"But what happened to…" Lisa took one step forward and threw her hand over her mouth. Then she turned and ran.

Morgan did not ask what she had seen. She asked nothing as she grabbed her daughter's wrist and ran for the closest door on bare feet. She heard the footsteps pounding down the hall and pushed Lisa ahead.

"Hurry!"

They cleared the hall and Lisa nearly reached the kitchen door when someone grabbed Morgan by her hair and tugged so hard she saw stars.

Lisa turned back. "Mom!"

A low male voice growled in Morgan's ear. "Where's the money?"

"Run!" she shouted to Lisa.

But her daughter hesitated.

"Get help," she said.

That sent her daughter off. Lisa rounded the table as the kitchen door flew open. Another man stood on the back step. Lisa screamed as the man lifted her off the ground, spun her in a circle and set her behind him on the back step.

"Run," ordered Morgan. The last thing she saw was her daughter's wide dark eyes before her captor tugged her backward into the hall.

"Where is it?" he asked, punctuating his question with a little shake.

Morgan grabbed hold of his wrists and twisted to face her attacker. Then she punched him in the bicep as she'd been taught by her dad. The man released her. Morgan staggered back, right into the second man.

The next instant she was behind him as he continued toward her attacker.

She saw the wide shoulders and clenched fists. Short black hair, a dark hoodie and long legs clad in new blue jeans. The man beyond him was now on his feet.

There was nothing said between them but she could tell by the way that the second man stalked the first that these two were not comrades.

"Listen, buddy," said her attacker, holding his hands up.

He didn't get a chance to finish. Morgan winced at the cracking sound of a fist striking the man's face. Blood sprayed on the white paint and the school photos tacked up in the hall. Morgan balled a fist before her mouth to stifle a scream. From outside Lisa shouted her mother's name.

Her rescuer thumped her captor's head on the hall runner as Morgan turned and fled.

RAY THOUGHT HE should have dropped the guy when he stopped fighting but gave him just one more shot for making him blow his cover. He'd been happy watching Morgan and Lisa from a distance. Experience had told him that things looked better that way. Now they'd seen him and he'd have to come up with something.

Damn.

He released the limp intruder and noticed that the housebreaker was bleeding all over himself but more important he was bleeding on Morgan's hall runner. Ray knew women despised mud or blood on carpets.

Once on his feet, Ray gave the guy a poke with his boot and the guy's head lolled. He retrieved the man's wallet and drew out his license.

"Andrew Peck." Ray glanced from the image of the smiling well-dressed man to the bloody, slack-faced Anglo with the rapidly swelling nose.

"You live in Darabee. Right up the road," Ray said.

A little searching of the billfold yielded several business cards. Mr. Peck was a manager at the Darabee Community Savings. Home invasion seemed a strange thing for a bank manager to be doing. He clearly was not very good at B and E or at personal defense. Ray kept the business card and tossed the wallet back on Mr. Peck's rising and falling chest where it bounced to the ground at his side.

Ray made a call to Kenshaw Little Falcon, reporting in. Little Falcon was his shaman, his spiritual leader, the head of their medicine society and the man who had hand selected the warrior sect called Tribal Thunder. Ray was proud to be among the newest members of the elite group of two dozen Tonto Apache men all selected from within the larger medicine society known as the Turquoise Guardians. Tribal Thunder recruits came from the men who completed the rigorous warrior training required to be considered a candidate. The newest inductees also included his friends Dylan Tehauno and Jack and Carter Bear Den. Like him, all three men were former US Marines but only he had a criminal record and a stunning proclivity for screw-ups.

His shaman told him to contact Jack Bear Den, who was also a member of Tribal Thunder and, conveniently, a detective with the tribal police here on Turquoise Canyon Reservation.

Their tribe of Tonto Apache was small, only 950 members but large enough for a casino and a manmade recreational lake, thanks to the Skeleton Cliff Damn. Their tribal police force totaled seven, including their dispatcher.

When he finished with Jack, he moved to the open back door to call to Morgan and Lisa. They didn't reply. The night was closing in but he could see that Morgan had them both locked in her car. Pitiful place to hide as he could break the glass with any number of rocks lying nearby, but at least he'd found them. She'd obviously left her keys inside the house.

He shouted to her that the police were coming and to stay put. Then he went to check out the damage the guy had done inside. He stepped over Mr. Peck to find a huge mess in the bedroom that had recently been occupied by Morgan's father. The mattress lay askew, bedding stripped, dresser drawers all emptied out.

Ray looked back at the intruder. "Aren't you ashamed of yourself?"

A glance in Lisa's and Morgan's rooms showed the man had either not looked there yet or chosen to focus on Karl's room.

Her father, Karl Hutton Hooke, had shot and killed the mass murderer who'd killed nine people down at the Lilac Copper Mine near the border last February. Ovidio Natal

Sanchez had been apprehended in the town right outside the reservation boundary. On the very day the suspect had been delivered into custody, Mr. Hooke had walked right up and shot Sanchez twice through the heart. Nobody could explain why Karl had done it and, according to Jack, Morgan's dad refused to speak to anyone, including his court-appointed attorney.

Ray heard a sound in the hall and returned to find his captive make a failed attempt to rise.

"What were you looking for, Peck?"

Peck groaned and rolled his head from one side to the other. His hand went to his nose. He coughed blood and opened one eye.

"You want to tell me why you're here?" asked Ray.

"Do I know you?" Peck tried to staunch the copious amounts of blood issuing from his nose with his index finger and thumb. This forced the blood in a new direction and he began to cough.

"We only just met. Why are you here?"

"I was just…" His eyes shifted toward the kitchen, judging the distance to freedom and finding it too far. "I…it…"

"Yes?" Ray asked, lifting his brows and affecting a look of interest.

"I'm not saying a thing without a lawyer."

Ray smiled. "You have me confused with a law-abiding citizen. So let me explain." Ray squatted on his haunches and grabbed Mr. Peck, lifting him by the front of his bloody shirt. "I'm Apache and on *my* reservation." Ray showed him his empty hand. "I could kill you with this.

"Plus I have a criminal record and a bad temper. I'm not calling you a lawyer. So once again. Why, Mr. Peck, are you lying in Miss Hooke's hallway?"

Mr. Peck started to cry. "Please. You got to let me go."

Ray sighed and then shook his head. "No. I don't."

"I can pay you."

"Pay me?" Ray snorted. "This lady is a friend of mine. You scared her. So it's gone past money." Ray lifted Andrew's index finger and gave it a shake. "I expect a bank manager needs these."

Peck tried and failed to recover his hand with a weak tug. When he reached with his opposite hand Ray slapped him in the forehead with the heel of one hand. Peck's head thumped on the carpet and his hand fell away.

"I'm about to break this. Fair warning."

"All right. I was looking for the money."

The obvious question was what money, but Ray didn't do obvious.

"Yeah. Me, too. Why do you think it's here?"

Andrew's mouth quirked and a little of the fear left his expression. His pale twitchy eyes reminded Ray of a rodent.

"He didn't have much time between when he cashed the check and shot that man. Maybe twenty-four hours." He pointed toward the kitchen. "She doesn't seem to have it. Or she's real smart. So I figured I'd start here."

"And you chose a time when Ms. Hooke would find you. Why?"

"No. I thought she worked nights at the casino. Somebody at the bank said so."

"She did. But her father used to watch her daughter. Now she's alone so…"

Andrew absorbed that. "Oh, yeah. Right. So what do you say? Fifty-fifty?"

"How much we talking here, Andy?"

His mouth clamped shut and he sniffed. Ray selected which digit to break and Peck writhed and whined.

"Okay. Okay. It was two hundred thousand. A bank check. He asked for cash. We had to make him come back.

I don't keep that much on hand. So he came back, you know, the next day and the check was good. So I cashed it. And he walked right out of there with that money in a cardboard box. Just folded over the top flaps and tucked it under his arm."

Two hundred thousand? No wonder Kenshaw Little Falcon thought Morgan and her girl needed protection.

"You cleared the check?" asked Ray.

Peck nodded. "Sure did, after the bank in Phoenix cleared the funds."

How long had this twerp been watching Morgan, Ray wondered.

"Karl went away two months ago. Why now?" asked Ray.

"Because people are asking questions now. They're after it, the money. So, I thought I'd better get moving. I'd asked Ms. Hooke personally on two separate occasions when she came into the bank if she needed help investing. She declined. Seemed kind of puzzled. I think she's got it tucked in a mattress or something." Peck coughed blood and sniffed. "Say, mind if I sit down?"

Ray ignored the request. "What people?"

"A detective from Darabee came back in February, the one that got shot."

"Eli Casey?"

"Yes, so I figured he was out of the picture. But then a man came right to my church last Sunday morning and right during fellowship hour he asked me if I was the one who cashed the check for Karl in the amount of two hundred thousand dollars. I was so shocked I said, yes." Peck moved his hand and sniffed. Blood continued to flow down his face and neck. "Can I get a paper towel or some ice?"

"No. Who was he, the one from church?"

"I never saw him before. He didn't give me his name."

"You tell him anything else?"

"I may have said that the daughter's name was Morgan and she worked nights at the tribe's casino."

Last Sunday, Ray thought, the day before Kenshaw called him in to watch Morgan.

The sound of sirens reached him, still a ways off. He turned his head and then looked back at Peck, noting the moment he heard the approaching police.

"You called the cops?"

"You're trespassing on sovereign land."

"What about our deal?"

"Only deal I'll make is that if I ever see you on tribal land again, I'll break this." He set Peck's hand on his chest and gave it a little pat. "And, if I see you near Morgan or Lisa Hooke again, I'll kill you."

Peck trembled. Somehow the man sensed Ray wasn't bluffing. He was surprised to recognize that he wasn't making idle threats. He knew himself capable of killing this man for daring to touch Morgan. Why did this woman rouse every protective instinct in Ray's body? That question troubled him more than this miserable excuse for a burglar.

And who was the man at the casino asking questions? Ray set his teeth as he realized the threat to Morgan may have only just begun.

Chapter Three

Peck's eyes widened. As Ray stood over him, the bank manager rose to his elbows.

"You want it for yourself. Did you find it already? Is it gone?"

"Yeah. Gone." Ray made an exploding motion with both hands.

Ray left him to meet the police, passing Morgan and Lisa still sitting in the shabby white Honda with the windows rolled up and fogging. He noticed the gray duct tape securing the driver's side mirror and shook his head. She needed someone to look after her.

Morgan looked up at him with big wide eyes and in that moment she didn't look much older than her ten-year-old. He wondered two things simultaneously. How old had she been when she'd had Lisa and who was the bastard who left her all alone?

He gave Morgan a smile as he passed and belatedly noticed he had a bloody hoodie.

He knew the young officer who'd arrived first and directed him to the intruder. The next one he sent to speak to Morgan and Lisa.

"Tell her I'm her neighbor. I live right there." He pointed at the house behind hers.

"I thought you lived in Pinyon Forks," said Officer Cox.

"Looking after a friend's place for a few days while he's away."

Ray waited a few minutes for Jack to arrive. It didn't take long to tell him what he'd learned.

"He might press charges," said Jack.

Ray shrugged and made a hissing sound of dismissal. "So?"

Jack left it at that. He spoke to Morgan and her girl and oversaw the removal of the crying mess that Andrew Peck had become as his dreams of riches turned to the real possibility of jail time.

Peck went into a police unit and Jack waved Ray over to make introductions. Morgan stood with an arm resting protectively on her daughter's narrow shoulders. Lisa stayed close and very still, watching them.

"Ms. Hooke, this is an old friend of mine, Ray Strong. Ray and I served together in Iraq. I'm sure you have met him at some point. We were only a year ahead of you in school."

Jack didn't mention that Ray had dropped out and had to take his GED in order to join up with Carter, Dylan, Jack and Hatch.

The awkward pause coupled with Jack's scowl made Ray realize that Jack wanted him to chime in.

"Oh, yeah," said Ray. "Nice to see you again, Morgan. Long time." He rubbed his neck and glanced to Jack who lifted his chin as if silently ordering him to continue. Ray hated small talk. "I'm staying in Felix's place while he's away."

Morgan's expression brightened and she glanced toward her neighbor's house.

"Felix Potts? He told me he was going to Waco to visit his daughter and the new baby. It's her third."

Her voice was musical, like a flute, full of light air and sweet tones.

"Oh, yeah," said Ray, his skin prickling now. "Isn't that something?"

Ray's customary position with women was that they either turned him on or they didn't. If they did and they liked men with a bad reputation, and a surprising number did like that, then they were off to the races. Now he found himself in the awkward position of having to chat with a woman he had no intention of sleeping with.

He knew enough to stay clear of single mothers for a lot of valid reasons. And beyond that, it was a bad idea to mix work and play.

"He didn't tell me you'd be watching the place," said Morgan.

Because Kenshaw had called Potts after he'd left to ask if a fellow Turquoise Guardian could stay in his place. The answer, of course, was yes.

"Well, I'm watching it but he's helping me out. I lost my place recently so..." He looked to Jack to take over. Because he was terrible at making stuff up. Not at lying, he was very good at lying, convincing to a fault.

Morgan held her smile and she now did look beautiful. The pause stretched and her smile faded.

"Ray is a hotshot," said Jack. "One of our captains."

Morgan looked impressed and well she should. Their forest-fighting team was nationally recognized and much requested. They flew all over the country battling blazes. Seemed the Apache men were good at fighting anything, including fires.

Morgan gave Ray a long, speculative look and he could almost feel her gaze like a caress. His skin tingled and his palms began to itch. That wasn't good. Now he was staring at her mouth and *his* gaze had become speculative. Her lips and cheeks seemed especially pink.

She cleared her throat and he met her curious expression with a grin. That grin had gotten him into more trouble than his fists. Her brows lifted as if reading the vibe he was sending and not knowing what to do with it.

"He'll be back next week. Will you be staying on when he comes home?" asked Morgan.

Ray squinted, wondering how to play this. "I need to find a place. I'm looking around."

Her gaze swept over him and he wished they were alone. He thought of Morgan's bed and imagined her stretched out naked on that the white coverlet. Clearly the sexual part of his brain had re-emerged. He shifted his position at the unwelcome ache that began below his belt.

"You were in the casino today," she said.

And yesterday and the day before that, he thought.

"Guilty," he said.

"Did I get you a drink?" she asked.

"No. I just come in to watch…"

Her frown deepened.

He grinned wider. "To watch the games on the big screens."

"Oh!" Her cheeks went bright pink.

Shame on her for making assumptions, he thought.

"Baseball," she said and smiled, the tension easing out of her shoulders.

Her daughter wiggled out from beneath her mother's arm to take a step closer to Jack. She was staring up at the detective who was six-five in his stocking feet and now wore boots. If she didn't quit she'd get a crick in her neck.

"Are you Apache?" she asked him.

Ray's gaze shifted to Jack whose mouth went tight.

Most folks didn't come right out and ask, but Lisa was ten and ten-year-olds were as blunt as dull axes.

"Yeah. Sure am. Roadrunner Clan. You?"

Lisa was still eying the mountain of a man that Jack had become. He looked more Samoan than Apache and it was a constant sore spot for Jack.

"I'm Butterfly Clan," said Lisa. "Why was that man in our house?"

Ray watched Morgan to see what her reaction might be and found her looking as curious as Lisa. Had working in that casino taught her to bluff or was she in the dark?

Was it possible that her father had not told her about the money?

He had other questions, chief of which was what in the wide world had Karl Hutton Hooke done to receive a bank check for two hundred thousand dollars with his name written on it?

The answer seemed obvious. Her father had been paid to kill the Lilac Copper Mine Gunman. That meant that Karl Hutton Hooke was a hitman and whoever paid him had not wanted the mass gunman to stand trial. It also meant that there was a whole mess of money missing.

Jack escorted Morgan back inside and together they checked the house. Only her father's room had been disturbed, but Andy had even gone so far as to slice the pillows and mattress.

"What a mess," Ray said from the doorway.

Morgan directed her question to Jack. "What was he looking for, Detective Bear Den?"

Chapter Four

"Not sure what he was looking for, Morgan," said Detective Bear Den. "Did your dad have anything of special value?"

Both Jack and Ray watched Morgan who seemed to be considering the question while lightly rubbing her fingertips over her lips. The small gesture sent an unexpected shot of longing straight to Ray's groin.

He lifted his brows in surprise. He didn't go for this sort of woman, the "attached with child, daughter of a murderer who might be involved with some very bad people" sort. But there it was, Ray Strong making the worst possible choice, as usual.

His attention now became speculative. What kind of a woman was Morgan in bed?

"He had some of those state quarters," said Morgan. "Turquoise jewelry. Not a lot."

She convinced Ray. If he was a betting man, and of course, he was, he would say dear old Dad had forgotten to tell his girl that he'd had a payday that might just get her and her daughter killed.

They all moved inside and gathered in the kitchen in a loose circle between the dinette and the worn Formica counters.

"You have somewhere you can stay tonight?" asked Jack.

Morgan drew Lisa in beside her, and her daughter

hugged her mom around the middle. Morgan stood in bare feet still wearing the cocktail outfit that looked garish in the drab little kitchen.

"Lisa could stay at her best friend's. The Herons live right next door. But I... I think I'd better stay here."

"You have someone to call, maybe help you clean up?" asked Jack.

"I can help," said Ray.

Morgan's face scrunched up in a way that told Ray that he was less than smooth in her eyes.

"That's not necessary," she said, her smile all tight and dismissive now. That made Ray want to remind her who had removed the vermin from her house.

"I'll have an officer escort you and Lisa to the Herons'," said Jack.

Jack left them and called from the door into the yard. Ray clasped his bloody hands behind his back and gave Morgan a half smile that he hoped made him look less threatening. Jack returned with a young man that Ray knew.

"Ms. Hooke, this is Officer Wetselline," said Jack, sounding all professional now. "He'll walk you over to the Herons'. Maybe you want to wait over there until we finish up here."

She nodded her head and took hold of Lisa's hand. "I'll be back."

Ray watched Morgan go and wondered what she'd look like in tight jeans and a thin white T-shirt. Ever since he'd started watching her, he couldn't stop these images from creeping into his mind. Why her? He didn't date women with children but he liked Lisa and Morgan had the sort of appeal that seemed deeper than physical. She was such a dedicated mom and supportive daughter. Many women would have distanced themselves from a father who committed such a reprehensible act. Not her. According to Kenshaw, she visited her father, often. Respectable, up-standing, devoted, yeah…not his type.

Jack snapped his fingers in front of Ray's face, bring-ing his attention away from Morgan. Jack filled Ray in on his conversation with their shaman.

"He wants you here on site with Ms. Hooke."

"What? How am I supposed to pull that off?" asked Ray.

"I'm going to suggest Morgan not be alone. That her father's arrest might have repercussions for her and Lisa."

"You're not going to tell her about the money?"

"You said that Peck asked her about the money," said Jack.

"That's the first thing I heard when I came in. But she thinks we're talking about state quarters." The image of Morgan being dragged backward by that cowardly little branch manager made Ray want to punch him in the face all over again.

"I can ask her a second time, suggest that her father might have some additional money."

"Don't suggest. Tell her the truth. Her father might have been paid to shoot Ovidio Sanchez. He cashed a huge check the day before he went to jail and that pecker Peck was in her home, looking for the loot."

"This could be very dangerous for her. So I'm going to recommend strongly that she consider hiring a bodyguard. Then I'm putting your hat in the ring."

"I'm no bodyguard."

Jack seemed to know where his mind was going. "You couldn't get to him, Ray. There wasn't time."

Ray never missed a beat as he skipped to Iraq and the night that none of them would ever forget.

"But I could have let him ride with Mullins. Mullins

wanted him. But I stuck him with Tromgartner." The prank had not been funny. Instead it had cost his best friend his life. If only that had been all.

"I didn't get to them either," said Jack. In fact, Jack had held Ray back and let go only to grab his brother Carter. Then he'd run them both out leaving Hatch behind.

Ray blew out a breath. Jack scratched at the stubble on his jaw and smoothly changed the subject.

"She doesn't seem to know anything about the money."

"Who knows what she knows," said Ray. You would think a detective would be more suspicious.

"Let me talk to her when she gets back and you wash the blood off your hands."

"This is a mistake. Kenshaw should call Dylan Tehauno. He's clean-cut, responsible. And he's not crazy. That's for sure."

"Maybe she needs crazy to protect her from bigger crazy."

Ray sighed. He'd never felt less prepared for a job.

"One thing I know," said Jack. "Morgan Hooke will be in danger until that money is found."

Ray couldn't dispute that because it was true. Her father had made a mistake going to a bank so close to home. Maybe it didn't matter. That kind of money would bring trouble even if trouble had to travel long distances.

"Fox guarding the hen house," muttered Ray.

"Yeah, well that hen got plucked a long time ago."

Ray was interested in this conversation. "Who?"

"Don't know. No rumors even."

Ray frowned. In a small place like this, there were always rumors. "See if you can find out."

"Because?" asked Jack.

"Because I'm curious, is all."

Jack raised his eyebrows. "Really?"

He sounded so shocked it pissed Ray right off.

"Yeah."

"Not your type, Ray."

"I know that, Jack."

"Fine, I'll see what I can find out."

Jack followed his officer, leaving Ray in Karl Hooke's empty bedroom. Ray ducked into the bathroom to wash his hands and then returned to set Karl's room in order. First, he righted the dresser. Jack returned as Ray was sliding the mattress back in place.

"Where would you put it?" asked Jack.

"Not in the room beside where my granddaughter slept." As if he'd ever have a granddaughter, Ray thought, which he wouldn't. He was actually shocked he'd lived this long.

"You think Kenshaw knows?" asked Jack.

The two shared a hard look. He understood what Jack was asking. Detective Jack Bear Den wondered if their shaman knew about the money when tribal law enforcement did not. Ray knew Kenshaw had some information because he'd asked Ray to find out if Morgan knew who hired her dad. That meant Kenshaw either knew or suspected that Morgan's dad did not act of his own volition. Did Kenshaw also know about the money?

Is that why his shaman had sent him? Was it more than a stranger's interest in Morgan that caused Kenshaw to send Ray to her? He couldn't send a detective to investigate this because Jack had an obligation to uphold the law and investigate crimes. Meanwhile Ray was blissfully free of such responsibility—any responsibility really, including taking care of houseplants.

"Don't jump to conclusions," said Ray. "Might be that Kenshaw saw Hooke make the withdrawal at the bank or Hooke contacted him to look after his girls."

Jack made a face. "Or maybe Carter was right."

Jack's twin brother, Carter, was currently in federal protection with his new wife, Amber Kitcheyan, who was Kenshaw Little Falcon's niece. They were witnesses in a federal case involving an eco-extremist group called WOLF. Carter had been sent by Little Falcon to deliver a message to their shaman's niece. As a result, his niece had survived the slaying that had killed everyone else in her office, and Jack's brother was now gone from the rez as the Feds prepared their case. Jack feared Carter might have to enter witness protection after the case settled because of possible threats from the extremists. Jack believed the timing of Carter's mission was evidence that their spiritual leader and head of their medicine society had foreknowledge of the mass slaying. If he did, Jack was obliged to arrest him.

"I'm back," called Morgan from the open doorway.

"Wait here," said Jack to Ray.

He did as he was told, setting the drawers back in the dresser and then piling the scattered clothing on the bed. He wondered about Morgan's father. He understood the need for a payday. But he did not understand risking his freedom and his daughter's life in the pursuit of money. Whether it had been his intention or not, Morgan's life was now in danger because Ray just knew that branch manager Andrew Peck was not the sort of man who could keep a secret. The minute he figured out he needed help to get his greedy mitts on the loot, he would tell someone—someone more competent and more dangerous.

More would come for the money and when they couldn't find it, they'd come after Morgan and her daughter. Their troubles were far from over and Ray wondered again if he was up to the task Kenshaw had set for him. Keeping Morgan safe just became a full-time gig.

Chapter Five

Morgan felt suddenly unsure about entering her own kitchen. Officer Wetselline had accompanied her from the Herons' home back here. And she knew her attacker was gone. But still her heart hammered as she stood poised to cross that threshold.

Flashes of the attack exploded like fireworks in her mind. Lisa's scream. Her own voice. *Run!* The man growling as he yanked her backward against his fleshy body. *Where is it?*

"Ma'am?" asked the young patrolman behind her.

She glanced back at him, enfolding herself in a hug and rubbing at the gooseflesh that lifted on her arm.

"Getting cold," she said, making excuses for her chattering teeth.

"Would you like me to walk you in?" he asked.

She smiled and was about to tell him that was unnecessary, but her stomach tightened and she felt dizzy at just the thought of walking down that hallway.

"I'm fine," she lied. "Thank you."

His skeptical look told her she hadn't fooled him.

She glanced about the empty interior. Her daughter's checked nylon lunch bag sat on the counter with the sack of milk and groceries. The red-and-white soup can had rolled halfway across the dull surface. Otherwise everything looked normal. She stepped gingerly inside and felt the terror close in as she realized how close her daughter had been to the intruder. Her shoulders gave an involuntary shudder. She swallowed and then called out to Detective Bear Den.

"I'm back."

Morgan glanced out the door, past the officer to the lights of her neighbor's kitchen. She knew that Lisa was safe with Trish and Guy Heron. Her neighbors had naturally been concerned about the break-in, but she assured them that the guy had been caught and that she just needed to clean the place up before retrieving her daughter. They had been wonderful, as always. The Herons' daughter, Ami, was Lisa's best friend and the two of them had disappeared into Ami's room moments after their arrival.

Where is it?

The chill climbed up Morgan's neck.

Where was what? she wondered.

Ray Strong was nowhere in sight, but Detective Bear Den stepped out from the hallway and paused in the eat-in kitchen beside the oval table. His tread was light for such a big man. She had known him since elementary school when he had begun growing early and fast. Lord, he was big. She also remembered his brother, Carter, because his twin did not look a thing like Jack. None of the younger Bear Den boys had Jack's build or looks either. It had caused Jack trouble all his life.

She vaguely remembered that Ray Strong had been connected with something bad.

"How is Lisa?" asked the detective.

"Scared. But all right. What was he looking for?" she asked. *Where is it?* Was that voice going to haunt her dreams?

"What makes you think he was looking for something?"

"He broke in. Tossed things around in my father's room. I thought…" She stopped talking. Should she tell Bear Den what her attacker had asked?

"Have there been any repercussions from your father's involvement with Ovidio Sanchez?"

What a polite way to ask if her father assassinating the prime suspect in a mass slaying had affected them.

"Lisa has been having a hard time at school. Kids can be mean."

"And you?"

"I had to switch to days because Dad isn't here at night anymore." And her daughter had lost the only father she'd ever known and Morgan didn't understand why her father had done such a thing. It was like standing on the shore of a river only to discover that the water had undercut the bank. She and her daughter had tumbled and were still falling toward an uncertain future. Morgan knew that soon she would have to petition the tribe for assistance and the prospect shamed her. She didn't say any of that aloud, however, and only just managed to mutter that it had been hard.

Bear Den's brows dropped lower over his pale eyes. "I am asking if you have received any threats."

She shook her head. "No. Nothing like that."

"Did you know what your father was planning?"

"The police at Darabee already asked me that. I was interviewed over there."

"By Jefferson Rowe?"

"Who?"

"Police Chief Rowe?"

She shook her head. "I don't think so. A detective. I don't remember his name. He asked me if I knew beforehand, too. I didn't." And she felt stupid that she had noticed nothing unusual…and sad that her father had not confided in her and angry at what he had done. She glanced toward the door. "Have you seen a gray cat?"

"No."

She tried calling Cookie from the back door but with the strangers about and the flashing lights, she didn't expect to see the cat until things calmed down.

Her interruption did not distract the detective from his line of questioning.

"Did your father leave you anything? Instructions. A letter."

"Like a suicide note?" Morgan was still hugging herself. The April air turned cold at night in the mountains so she moved to close the kitchen door. Ray Strong anticipated her actions and got there first. Her hand brushed his before she could draw back. The contact was quick so she could not understand why her insides tightened and her breath caught. The door clicked and she met Ray's dark compelling eyes. One of his brows quirked.

Bear Den cleared his throat, snapping Morgan's attention back to the detective's question. Did she have foreknowledge of her father's plan to commit murder?

"He didn't say anything. The morning before the shooting he took his truck. He's not supposed to drive anymore. I was sleeping when he left. I get home from work about eight a.m. and Dad usually gets Lisa up and I get her ready for school. Then I usually sleep from nine to about three. He wasn't here when Lisa got off the bus but he was here before my shift. He wouldn't tell me where he had gone. The next day he…" She hesitated, tugging at her ear. This topic still made her feel nauseous and baffled all at once. "He left and afterward they arrested him in Darabee. I was waiting for Lisa's bus when tribal police and the FBI got here. They searched the house. They took some things. Maybe they found something like that."

"They didn't. Usually when someone is planning such a thing, they make preparations. Say goodbye."

She thought back to the evening before when she saw him last. "He asked me to pick up a chocolate cake."

Bear Den scowled. "Cake."

"He wanted cake. Gave me the money."

"What money?"

Now she scowled. "For the cake. I don't buy that junk and he shouldn't have it either. But I bought the cake and we had that after dinner on Thursday night for no reason." She stared at the detective. "Was that it? The cake? Like some kind of going away party?"

Jack Bear Den shook his head. "I don't know."

Morgan stared at her kitchen tiles and tried to keep from crying.

"Ms. Hooke, my friend Ray spoke to the guy who broke into your house. The man indicated he was searching for money. He said your father cashed a bank check for two hundred thousand dollars in Darabee."

She snorted at first, thinking he was kidding and then her jaw dropped open as she saw he was deadly serious.

"I have to report that to the FBI. So what I want to know from you is, did you know about this money?"

She couldn't even speak, so she shook her head.

"Do you know where the money currently is?"

"No." Her words were a whisper. "I don't. You think he actually had that much money?"

Jack nodded. "I believe your father was accepting payment."

"Payment? What could he possibly do that was worth that kind of…"

Morgan's knees buckled and Bear Den caught her, drew out a chair and guided her into it. Her fanny hit with enough force to jar her gaze to the detective.

"This can't be happening."

Bear Den looked down the hall. "Ray? Can you come out?"

Her protector emerged from the hall. The front of his shirt was soaking wet and stuck to his chest, revealing the ripped muscles of his abdomen. Morgan's breath caught at the perfection of his form.

"Why are you all wet?" she asked.

Bear Den followed the direction of her gaze. Ray shrugged. "Washed off the blood."

The detective groaned and Morgan blinked, finally forcing her attention away, but took one more long look because a sight like that should be committed to memory.

Bear Den took a seat across from her and Ray retrieved the one between them, spun it and sat, his long legs straddling the back. Then he hugged the top and rested his chin on his hands. At least she couldn't see the wet spot or his tight abs any longer.

Bear Den cleared his throat. "I was just relaying what the intruder told you."

Ray's gaze flicked from the detective to her. "You have some problems, Morgan."

"What are you two implying exactly?"

Ray deferred to the detective.

"It appears that your father cashed a check twenty-four hours prior to his attack on the prime suspect in the Lilac Copper Mine shooting."

"I don't understand."

Ray tucked in his legs and lifted his chin from his hands. "Your father was a paid hitman. Now word is out about the payday, and that means you can expect more like that nitwit I found in your hallway."

Morgan's stomach heaved. She pressed a hand over her pounding heart.

"More."

"More and more competent."

"Competent?"

"Dangerous. The kind of men that don't pull hair. And they won't stop until you deliver that money."

"What money? I don't have it."

"Well I suggest you find it fast. The trick will be to keep you safe in the meantime."

She sat back in the chair. "How am I supposed to do that, exactly?"

"That's where I come in."

Morgan looked from Ray to Detective Bear Den.

"You need a bodyguard, Morgan. Someone tough, resourceful and capable of protecting you."

Her gaze flicked back to Ray Strong.

"Ray has agreed to act as your bodyguard," said Detective Bear Den.

He stood there watching her like a hungry wolf in his transparent T-shirt rippling with contained potency. He was just the sort of male to cause a woman all kinds of trouble.

"I can't afford to put gas in my car," Morgan said. "How am I going to pay for…" She let her traitorous eyes caress him and his mouth twitched. His eyes glittered as if he knew what she was thinking. "I couldn't afford to even feed him let alone pay him."

"You can't afford not to," said Bear Den.

Morgan regarded Ray Strong. The man was tough, powerful and had already shown himself capable of protecting her and Lisa. He also ignited in Morgan an unwelcome burst of lust coupled with a rational sense of fear. The man was dangerous and the threat he posed was more than physical.

She shook her head. "This is a bad idea."

Bear Den spoke again, his voice deep and resonant. "Are you familiar with the Turquoise Guardians?"

"My dad's medicine society? Sure."

"There is a sect within that organization called Tribal Thunder. This is a warrior band."

Morgan didn't think they still had warriors, not the real kind that defended their families to the death, made war on their enemies and took what they liked. She found her gaze slipping back to Ray like a thief on a night raid.

"I don't know of Tribal Thunder."

"Ray is a member of that sect. So am I. We've sworn an oath to defend our tribe."

Now Ray took up the conversation. His voice did funny things to her insides.

He thumbed over his shoulder at her closed back door. "That little twerp is going to spill his guts. Word will get out. There is no calling it back. If you won't do this for yourself, do it for your daughter."

Word will get out.

Lisa. Her gaze went to the back door. What had she caught while her mother was attacked? What had she overheard the officers say afterward and most importantly, what had she told their neighbors?

"I need to get Lisa back." Was that her voice? It didn't even sound like hers.

"I'll have one of my officers fetch her," said Jack.

"No!" Morgan headed out the door at a run and Ray caught her easily. He didn't grab her or try to stop her, just jogged along beside her across the dirt and gravel that separated her door from the Herons'.

She burst through the back door to find Guy Heron alone in the kitchen with Lisa. He had a hold of each of her daughter's shoulders. Every hair on Morgan's neck lifted. At seeing Morgan, his expression changed from eagerness to guilt. His gaze flashed from her to Ray Strong, now standing behind her. Now she saw fear.

"Oh, hey," said Guy. "Everything all right?"

Morgan glanced to Lisa. Her daughter looked frightened and she did not need to call to her. Morgan just lifted a hand and Lisa ran to her mother. Their hands clasped and Morgan drew herself up as she tugged Lisa behind her.

"We were just talking about what happened tonight. Just your dad's room, huh?" Guy's voice held a note of force levity but the room had gone deadly quiet.

"Take Lisa home," said Ray.

Morgan turned to go and then paused as she recalled the man Ray had beaten in her house. She'd seen him dragged out by two officers. His face had been swollen, raw and bloody. Morgan glanced at Mr. Heron. The man had been interrogating her daughter. Morgan knew it and so did Mr. Strong. The fury and fear mingled into a hard lump in Morgan's stomach. Then she looked at Ray Strong, who had dipped his chin and fixed his gaze on Guy in a way that seemed like anticipation. The muscles at his neck bunched in coiled potential energy.

He tore his gaze from Guy to meet hers.

"You're hired, Mr. Strong."

Chapter Six

Ray returned to Morgan's kitchen to find Jack alone at the dinette taking notes on a notepad.

Ray's head swiveled. "Where's the girl?"

"Bedroom. Morgan's with her. Lisa was crying."

Ray's fists clenched and he considered taking Lisa's distress out on Mr. Heron.

"Everything okay?" asked Jack, lifting his chin in the direction of the neighbor.

"He's not bleeding, if that's what you're asking."

Ray briefly related the high points of his chat with her dorky, slimy neighbor.

"He knows from the girl that Karl had money. Not how much. But he's already put two and two together."

Ray hoped he had reached an understanding with Guy Heron. But in his experience, the one thing that trumped fear was greed.

"We're done here," said Jack. "You'll be staying in her father's room."

Appropriate, he thought because her father and he shared certain things. They were both Turquoise Guardians, Apache men and they both had a tendency to break the law. The downside of the room choice was that Karl had a big bed and it was right across the hall from the tempting Morgan Hooke.

"You staying while I get my kit?" asked Ray.

Jack nodded and laced the fingers of his massive hands on the dining room table.

"Be back as quick as I can."

RAY MOVED QUICKLY, scouting once around the perimeter before returning to Felix Potts's home to retrieve his belongings. He returned from Potts's house and moved his truck, parking prominently in the driveway beside Jack's tribal police SUV. Then he pulled his olive green gunnysack over one shoulder and lifted his small duffel, which held mostly weapons.

When he reached the kitchen stoop he was greeted by a gray cat that meowed loudly. Then it stood and rubbed against his leg.

"You live here, too?" he asked.

He rapped on the door and let himself in. The cat scooted past him.

He found Jack leaning with his back to the sink beside Morgan who stood at the stove. The aroma of tomato soup and cooking macaroni greeted him. Morgan stopped stirring the contents of one pot and held the dripping spoon poised over it as she watched him drop his things beside the door, wipe his feet and step into the space. Maybe he should have knocked.

Jack pushed off the sink, which was good because Ray thought there was only one reason to stand that close to a woman. Jack was single. So was Morgan. It shouldn't have mattered because Morgan was a job and a burden, yet her boyish looks had unexpectedly hit him down low and deep. So it did matter.

He glared at Jack, who lifted his brows in surprise and moved out of the kitchen.

"Need any help?" asked Jack.

Ray shook his head.

"I'll check in tomorrow. Let you know what else we get from the bank manager."

Since Jack wasn't allowed to use his fists with the same liberty as Ray, he doubted he'd get much. Little dweebs like that always lawyered up.

Jack called a farewell to Lisa and then to Morgan.

"You're in good hands, Morgan. I'd trust Ray Strong with my life. You can do the same."

She thanked Jack with a sincerity that made Ray scowl all over again. He could see them together—naked. Ray rubbed his eyes. Jack shook his hand and headed out into the night. Ray locked the door behind him and found satisfaction in the click.

The cat rubbed against his leg and meowed loudly again.

"What?" Ray asked it. "If you want food you're at the wrong human."

"Cookie!" Morgan ran to the feline and lifted the boneless ball of fluff. "Where did you find her? Lisa will be so happy."

In Ray's experience cats never needed finding. Morgan squeezed the cat, which now hung over her shoulder, its green eyes watching Ray. Morgan carried the cat to Lisa's room and was met with squeals of delight from the interior. When Morgan came back, her smile eased away at the sight of him still in her kitchen.

"How's your girl?" asked Ray.

"Better now that she has Cookie." Her smile was so sweet and so compelling, Ray took a step toward her before he realized he had moved.

"Detective Bear Den said that you would work for room and board as a favor to my father." He'd work for nothing, but staying on site would make it much easier to guard Lisa and Morgan.

Morgan poured the macaroni into a colander in the sink, sending steam billowing upward.

If Morgan Hooke knew the location of the two hundred thousand dollars, would she be eating condensed soup for dinner?

"And on behalf of your medicine society."

He nodded and tugged at his drying shirt, wishing he could avoid this chatting.

"Tribal Thunder," said Morgan. "I never heard of that sect."

He really could not speak of his medicine society with a woman, even an Apache woman like Morgan. But he did say that it was a warrior sect.

"We've vowed to protect the sovereignty of our heritage, resources and tribe."

"And I fall under tribe," she said, flipping on the hot water and engaging the sprayer to give the limp pasta a shower. Deftly she dumped the noodles back into the pot, added milk, butter and the envelope of fluorescent yellow cheese-like product. Then the pot went back on the stove on a low flame.

"I added another box because—" she waved a clean wooden spoon at him "—you look hungry."

Wow, she shouldn't have said that. He stepped closer. Her eyes rounded. He closed in on an impulse so strong he didn't even question it.

He wrapped her up and found that slippery cocktail dress made her glide up his chest as if she wore satin. When he angled his head to kiss her she pointed the clean end of the wooden spoon into his chest like the butt end of a nightstick.

The mac and cheese was sizzling as the milk boiled away.

"Bad idea," she said, but then licked her wide lower lip, sending him mixed signals.

"That's what I'm best at."

She pulled away and he let her go.

They faced off.

"Listen, you might have some ideas about me because I have a child and no husband. And because I serve drinks. So let me set you straight. I'm not interested in casual sex."

"Great. Because sex is one of two things I take very seriously."

She lowered the spoon. "What's the other?"

"Protecting you and Lisa."

MORGAN STARED UP at her protector. He stood only an arm's length from her with his hand still resting on her shoulder. His face was clean-shaven, revealing the hard line of his jaw and his prominent chin. It looked like the kind of jaw that could take a punch and the kind of chin that dared you to try. He had tousled thick black hair that needed a trim and a wide square forehead with heavy brows. His brown eyes now seemed to hold a hint of green and shone with mischief. He wasn't done with her, they seemed to say. Not by a long shot. His mouth quirked, confirming her suspicion. The man was imposing as all get out, but right now that was what she needed. A man capable of taking care of things as well as her and her daughter.

Morgan understood the seriousness of her situation. It was bleeding into her consciousness like dye into fabric.

"You going to be able to do this?" she asked.

He never took his eyes off her as he nodded.

Ray Strong cocked his head, lifting a hand to trail his fingertips down the sensitive skin of her neck and on to the hollow at her throat. She shivered as sensation rocked her.

"I've been wanting to do that," he said.
His grin promised devilment.
Trouble.
"Mom?"

Chapter Seven

The man was a chameleon, Morgan thought.

Ray now stood at a respectable distance from Morgan, his powerful arms folded and his posture relaxed. Even his smile was different. His expression held none of the banked desire she'd witnessed. Instead she saw only a benign hint of a smile that made him seem, if not exactly safe, at least not imminently dangerous.

She cleared her throat and forced a tight smile.

"Lisa honey, dinner is ready."

Lisa had halted on the bare floor where the carpet runner had been pausing at the place where hallway gave way to the worn floor tiles of the kitchen. The cat sat at her heels, tail tucked around its front feet. They both stared at Ray with curiosity. Lisa's eyes were focused on Ray as if seeing a rattlesnake coiled in her path and calculating her way clear. Her dark eyes seemed to assess a new potential threat. Her girl had more sense than her mother, thought Morgan.

"Lisa, this is Mr. Strong. He will be staying in Pop-Pop's room for a while."

"Why?"

While Morgan debated how much to tell her, Ray stepped forward as Lisa slid a foot backward, preparing to retreat.

"Because the man who broke in here was looking for something of your grandfather's. You have friends at school?"

Lisa nodded.

"Anyone ever have a big secret?"

Lisa nodded again.

"What happened to that secret?"

Lisa looked to her mother and then fixed her attention on Ray. "My friend told our other friend and she promised never, ever to tell, but she must have because I didn't tell and then Bobby Farrow knew and he told all the boys."

"Exactly."

He didn't draw the connection. Just waited. Morgan waited, too.

"So that man, the one who grabbed my mother, he's going to tell Pop-Pop's big secret?"

Ray nodded. "Smart girl."

Lisa's eyes widened in understanding. "And Mr. Heron. He knows because I told him that man asked Mom for the money."

"Yes."

"I shouldn't have said anything."

Morgan went to her daughter and brushed her thick black hair from her face. "It's all right, sweetheart."

Lisa kept her attention on Ray.

"How did you know that the man would hurt us?"

"I didn't. But I've been watching over you two for a while now."

That made Morgan's attention snap from her child to Ray. How long had he been watching them?

"I've seen you at the store and other places."

Ray nodded. "That's right. I got asked by a friend of your grandfather's to watch over you and your mama."

"Do you know the secret?"

"Just that it's about money. Hidden money."

Morgan didn't think Lisa should know that. Didn't want her at risk. But she was at risk, whether she knew or not.

"It's here?" asked Lisa.

"Nobody knows where."

"Except Pop-Pop, so let's go ask him."

Ray glanced back at her and Morgan nodded. That was the logical next step.

"Tomorrow," said Morgan, knowing there were visiting hours then. "Wash up. Dinner is ready."

Lisa moved to the kitchen sink and washed her hands. Morgan eyed him and he followed Lisa, but he had already washed his hands when he'd removed her intruder's blood. Morgan fed the cat some mush from a can. Cookie, apparently, ate first.

They sat down to a meal of tomato soup with mac and cheese. Ray finished his portion and glanced around for more, finding the only remaining pasta on Lisa's plate. He glanced at Morgan who shot him a stern look. She was such a fierce feisty woman it made him smile.

After supper, Lisa drew out her school books and mother and daughter sat together. Morgan read the paper and helped Lisa as needed. Ray took the opportunity to bring his things into Karl's room and to peer out all the windows on the back of the house.

He heard someone enter the room and turned to see Morgan standing with a mound of folded sheets in her arms.

"I thought I'd change these," she said, lifting her arms slightly to indicate the linen.

"Thanks." He stripped off the lovely Pendleton wool blanket that had bold black stripes on a field of red and had the top sheet off before she reached the bed.

"I can do this," she said.

"So can I. I was in the US Marines for a while. One thing I learned was how to make my bed." He'd also perfected his aim with a rifle and handgun. Ray had already known a thing or two about hand-to-hand combat and had more practical experience tracking than most men gleaned in a lifetime.

"My father fought in Vietnam."

Ray knew that. He'd shared a few stories with Karl at their medicine society.

"Sharpshooter," said Ray.

Morgan's jaw dropped but she recovered. "That's right."

She pulled free two corners of the fitted sheet and he released the corners on his side. Morgan began replacing the linen and Ray worked on the two pillowcases. They worked in silence with a fluidity that made their motions seem almost like a dance. They leaned over the bed from opposite sides to place the pillows and their eyes met. Morgan flushed so Ray guessed she was thinking of him stretched out on these clean white sheets…alone…possibly naked.

She straightened and threw out the top sheet so that it fluttered to his side. The blanket followed. She placed a clean sage-green towel on the foot of the bed.

"There. You're all set."

"Thank you again. And for letting me stay."

"I have great respect for Kenshaw Little Falcon and for my father, despite what he has done." She sat on the bed, her hands splayed on the red wool, her shoulders slumped again in that whipped-dog posture he despised. She glanced up at him. "Do you think people deserve second chances, Mr. Strong?"

He sat beside her. "I've already tried to kiss you, Morgan. I think you should call me Ray."

He wanted to try again.

"Fine. Ray. My father killed a man. Probably for money. I can't get my mind around that."

He'd killed more than one man, Ray knew. More than Ray had killed. Karl had been very good at his assignment in Vietnam.

"I can think of two reasons he might want to earn money."

She looked at him. "You mean me and Lisa. I would much prefer to have my father here with us. You might not believe this, but he was wonderful with Lisa. Very kind and patient. He's been with her since she was born, more a father to her than a grandfather, and she doesn't understand any more than I do why he would do such a thing."

"We'll ask him tomorrow."

Her sigh was heavy and Ray felt an unexpected urge to comfort her. That wasn't his forte, holding women who were wearing their clothing. But he wrapped an arm around her and tried to ignore the flowery fragrance of her hair. It took a few moments and his remembering being rocked back to sleep by Mrs. Yeager during one particularly vivid nightmare, but he finally remembered a long-forgotten skill, one he'd learned without realizing. Comfort was not something that women came to him for. Never before, actually, but Morgan hadn't come to him. He'd been forced on her. He had to remember that.

She sagged against him and rested her head on the hollow between his shoulder and collarbone. Funny, the rocking and the warmth of her little body against him made him close his eyes to savor the sensations. And suddenly she was comforting him.

This was what it must be like, he thought, to have a woman not just to sleep with but to hold. The awkwardness eased and they sat there quietly. When she pushed away he felt the tug of regret.

"Sorry about that," she said.

He wasn't sorry but how could he say so?

"That's okay. Happens sometimes." It never happened, actually.

She stared up at him and, bang, there it was again, that ache in his chest and the zing of attraction that crackled. Ray dropped his arm from her shoulder and down to her waist.

"Oh," she said. Morgan inched away and met with the resistance of his arm as he tightened his hold.

"My daughter is in the other room," she said.

That broke his concentration. His arm fell away and Morgan rose to her feet, perhaps belatedly realizing it is always unwise to enter a tiger's cage even if it appears docile. She backed toward the door, pausing just inside the threshold with one hand on the doorknob, as if preparing to slam it shut and flee. It was the kind of chase he'd enjoy, but only if she would, too. He smiled as images of Morgan, playful and laughing, danced in his mind. They'd roll on the couch and onto the floor, where he'd let her sprawl on top of him, pink cheeked and giggling.

"So…we'll go see my dad tomorrow at the jail? Ask him about the money."

Ray let the daydream end as reality encroached. He wanted to go right now but he could see that Morgan was done in. And he knew that Lisa's bedtime varied only slightly on the weekends. And federal authorities were very strict about rules like visiting times for prisoners.

"Yeah. First thing."

Morgan looked scared all over again but there was no helping it.

"I have to put Lisa to bed."

He heard Lisa complain and the television snap off. Lisa slowed at his door and stared at him before her mother pushed her along. Lisa's room and his shared a wall and hers was at the end of the hallway. A few minutes later Lisa walked past his room again wearing pink pajamas that made her look about seven instead of ten. Who was that girl's father?

Had he died like Ray's or simply slipped away? He couldn't imagine having a child...or a woman like Morgan. They seemed so normal and unprepared for the chaos that had swept them up. Why would Karl do this? Money didn't seem like enough reason to leave these two to the wolves. He hoped like heck that Karl hadn't planned on abandoning them and taking the cash. It would be hard to keep his temper if that was the case. Ray had always been in loose control of his temper and there were many places to lose it. One place he had never lost his temper was with a woman or a child. Never had. Never would. Was that why Kenshaw had chosen him?

Ray checked his mail and texts. Lisa appeared in the door with her mother at her back.

"Good night, Mr. Strong. Thank you for saving my mom tonight."

Ray stood to face the child, feeling as out of place as a war club at a child's tea party. He shrugged by way of a reply.

"Mom says you were an army man."

Ray winced. "Marines."

"I'm glad you know how to fight. Do you have a little girl, too?"

Ray glanced at Morgan whose expression told her that Lisa had gone off script.

"No. I don't."

"A wife?"

"Not one of those either."

Lisa's smile seemed satisfied and her eyes glittered with

devilment. Ray knew when he was being set up. Normally he'd be saying good-night, which he was, but this time he'd be staying under the same roof with Morgan right across the hall.

"I'll see you in the morning." Lisa strode forward and offered her hand.

Ray hesitated. She was thin and tiny and her hand was so very small. But he shook hers as if sealing some deal.

Then she surprised him again by thanking him formally in perfect Tonto Apache.

"My grandfather taught me that," she said.

He watched Lisa pad from the room on bare feet and wondered what else Karl had taught her.

THE NEXT MORNING Ray woke to the sound of a shovel rasping against gravel and earth. He headed for the window that faced the backyard. The sun wasn't even up and there was Guy Heron digging up the tire planter in the backyard. The ceramic toad lay on its side next him, one eye staring up at the sky. Ray swore and then tugged on his jeans. He hoped the guy didn't have a job that required him to see out of both eyes.

Ray was out the door a moment later. The day was gray and the air temperature lower than crisp. Heron took another shovelful of earth and dumped it on the ceramic frog. Then he knelt to check inside the hole.

Ray's approach was soundless, not just because of his bare feet whispering over the ground but because of his training here on the reservation and with the US Marines. But still Heron spotted him before he reached him. The man sprang to his feet, gripped his shovel and ran across the driveway that separated the Hooke territory from the Herons', but there was no distinction as all land here was communal. There Heron stopped as if protected by some invisible boundary, the kind that Anglos drew all over the earth. He expected better from a member of his own tribe.

"I didn't find anything."

Ray kept coming. Heron made his second mistake of the day. He held his ground.

"This here is my property." He motioned with the shovel at a line that was not there and then lifted the shovel as if he intended to use it like an ax.

Third mistake, thought Ray as he came to a stop.

"This here?" he asked, marking the line that didn't exist with an index finger.

Heron nodded.

Ray did a fair impression of a mime meeting an invisible wall. Heron's brow knit as Ray seemed flummoxed by the barrier. His big finale was jabbing Heron in the eye.

Heron's knees buckled but Ray grabbed him by the collar before he fell to his face. Then he dragged him back across the driveway and to the hole he had been digging.

"You taking up horticulture?" asked Ray.

Heron struggled, choked and dropped his shovel.

Ray threw him onto the freshly dug soil.

"He just planted these," said Heron. "Right before the shooting."

Ray placed his fists on his hips and admired the speed with which Heron's eye swelled shut.

"Last night I told you that you should stay away from Morgan and her girl."

"And I didn't go near them."

Ray pointed at the ground. "This counts."

"I just thought, you know, maybe I could help her find it." He motioned toward the hole.

Ray grabbed Heron's wrist. A moment later he had that wrist behind Heron's back and the man's cheek pressed into the earth to the edge of the hole.

"Don't help her anymore because if you do, I'm going to use your shovel to bury you in this hole." He forcibly turned Heron's head so he got a mouthful of the dirt. "Do we understand each other?"

Heron spat and wiggled but stopped when Ray increased the pressure on his wrist and shoulder.

"All right!"

Ray held him a breath longer by pressing his knee in his back, using it to stand back up. Then he offered his hand to Heron who ignored it as he drew himself up, glared at Ray and moved toward his home in a gait that was as close as a man can come to a jog without jogging.

Ray followed him to the driveway, carrying the shovel Guy had abandoned in his haste. When Guy turned back, Ray sent his shovel after him. The man made a squeak of alarm and broke into a run. There was nothing like the satisfaction that comes from doing what you love, thought Ray.

When he turned toward the house, he saw the shocked faces of both Morgan and Lisa in the window of Lisa's bedroom. He dusted off his hands and headed toward the house. He tried not to let their looks of shock and horror affect him. He was doing what he'd been sent here to do, but frightening Lisa didn't sit well and Morgan now looked at him as if someone had let a wild animal loose in her home.

In fact that was exactly what had happened, but until someone found that money that was just the way it was going to be.

Chapter Eight

Morgan gasped as Ray pursued Guy to the driveway and tossed his shovel after her neighbor like a spear. The blade bit deep into the earth and the handle vibrated. Morgan blinked at the bunching muscles of Ray's back and the ease with which he tossed his captive aside.

He turned toward the house and his gaze flicked to hers. He stared at her and then stalked toward the kitchen door.

"Get dressed," Morgan ordered Lisa as she headed to the kitchen.

A moment later Ray was there, filling the room, and the sight of him, shirtless and glistening with sweat, was enough to make even the weakest heart pulse faster.

Earlier, while she'd been making coffee, she couldn't help reliving Ray's embrace. Just his arms about her caused lightning strikes of excitement to rip through her. She'd never felt anything like that. Not even with Larry, Lisa's father. She tried not to think of Larry but Lisa sometimes reminded her of him, affecting a mannerism she could not know her father had used. Morgan admitted she had been crazy in love with Larry, foolishly, wholeheartedly, but even when they had been intimate, her body had not churned and trembled as it did with Ray Strong, whom she barely knew. How was that even possible?

She wasn't the sort of woman who took chances, especially on a man as compelling and dangerous as Ray. But she wished she'd let him kiss her, just once. Just for herself. She knew that he was the complete opposite of the sort of guy she and Lisa needed. She needed safe, steady and solid. Ray was none of those things. But he was sexy as all get out. And the truth was that she was attracted to him.

"What are you doing?" she asked now, trying to stop the direction of her thoughts.

He explained what had happened.

"Dad's hummingbird garden?"

She managed to tear her gaze from all that naked male flesh and retreat to her bedroom for a view of the backyard. Sure enough, the bushes were lying on the ground.

"Why that…" She didn't say the word, but she thought it. She turned back to see Ray, now wearing an olive green T-shirt, thank goodness, filling the gap in the open door.

"He was looking for the money," he said.

Her mind flashed her a perfect image of Guy holding Lisa by the shoulders with that guilty look on his face. Morgan found her own fists clenching as the urge to protect her daughter ripped through her like a wave.

Ray glanced toward Lisa's room.

Lisa had told the Herons and that was enough to make the man she had known all her life dig up her dad's newly planted butterfly garden. She'd thought she knew her neighbor and it seemed she didn't know him at all. She felt adrift without the anchor of her father's presence and with the lost money making friends unrecognizable, she did not know who to trust. And poor Lisa had just lost her best friend because Morgan was not letting her visit the Herons any time soon. It was just devastating all around.

"He thought it was out there," she said. "I need to see Dad."

"Visiting hours are nine to three today. I checked."

"I should call ahead." Morgan noted that Ray was now staring at her freshly made bed. His gaze flashed to her next. He didn't say anything, just performed a military-style turn and disappeared down the hall.

With his disappearance, Morgan found she could breathe again. She checked on Lisa, already dressed, and quickly braided her hair as Lisa fired questions at her. Morgan left Lisa in the bathroom before returning to the kitchen to make a call to the corrections facility in Phoenix. It had taken over a month for her to get their names on the approved visitors list for her father. Now she told them she would be visiting and gave them her father's name. She'd learned that sometimes her dad was not available and once he had been moved temporarily before seeing the grand jury.

She had been prepared to hear he was unavailable, but when they told her why she would not be seeing him at the facility, she felt sick. Morgan pressed a hand on the counter for stability.

Ray set aside his coffee and moved to the opposite side of the counter. Morgan had gone pale and he knew something was very wrong.

"But why?" she asked.

Ray was beside her, clasping her elbow. She used her free hand to clutch his, her grip tight and her fingers cold.

"And the reason?…Yes." She nodded. "I can find it. May I see him?"

She listened, thanked the speaker and then disconnected. Her eyes were tearing up when she looked at him.

"He didn't tell me," she whispered.

"Tell you what?" asked Ray.

"The cancer. He said he was in remission. But it's back. It's been back but he never said. And it's really bad now. He's in the hospital." She sagged against him and he gathered her up, trying to feel guilty that Karl's illness had brought Morgan into his arms and failing.

"Shouldn't they have called you?" asked Ray.

"He told them not to. They said it was up to him."

Ray found himself in the unfamiliar position of organizing what needed to be done. Lisa would spend the day with Morgan's uncle, Agustin Tsosie, and his wife, Melouise. Ray called Kenshaw, who encouraged him to go visit Karl and report back on anything he might tell his daughter. He told Morgan to pack an overnight bag and any cash she had on hand.

Then he drove them to the hospital in Phoenix. On the drive, Morgan told him that her father had been diagnosed with prostate cancer. But he had been treated and had been in remission for six years. She had lost her mom, Adril, in a single-car accident with a deer. Lisa was only seven when she lost her grandmother.

Ray thought of his own accident, completely his fault, in Darabee when he'd been so drunk he'd totaled his car. Thank God he'd been the only one hurt. Living with a criminal record was preferable to causing injury or death to someone like Morgan's mom. He'd always felt stupid for his recklessness. Now he felt lucky. He hadn't killed anyone and he'd survived to learn something. Still, he wasn't proud of his behavior. He'd just been so angry.

It had been the day after they heard Hatch's body had finally been found and that he had likely died while being tortured in Iraq. He thought of his own parents' deaths. Was it better to have time to say goodbye or to be torn from this world without warning? Ray somehow thought that Morgan was lucky. At least she had time to tell her father goodbye.

What was a good death, anyway? He didn't know. But

he knew a bad one. Hatch Yeager's death had been long and painful. Ray bore his part in that death on his soul.

They reached the hospital in Phoenix and were shown to her father's room to discover him recovering from surgery. He was unconscious and restrained, his wrist punctured with an IV and fixed to the metal bed rail with a thick plastic zip tie.

The nurse on duty suggested they step outside and explained that they had believed he was suffering from a gallstone until they went in and saw that the systemic cancer from his prostate had spread. Metastasized they had called it. Hospice care had been considered and rejected because her father was in his final days.

Morgan was a weeping mess when they went back into her father's room. She sobbed on her father and he did not rouse. The nurse came back in to check on him and said they had given him something for the pain.

Ray leaned against the window frame as Morgan settled in a vinyl chair at her father's side.

"I don't understand any of this," she said.

"Why he did what he did and why he never told us he was so ill." Morgan pressed a hand to her forehead. "I'd been after him because he was losing weight." She stroked her father's arm and Ray wondered if anyone would be there to sit with him as he passed from this world to the next.

The room was quiet except for the blip and beep of the machines monitoring Karl's IV and his heart. Karl had a strong heart, Ray knew, and a good one. But he'd miscalculated when it came to the payoff. Perhaps he had thought no one but Morgan would know. That he would have time to tell her where it was hidden.

"He took the job because he was dying," said Ray.

Morgan glanced back at him, the frown forming a line between her brows.

"He's the perfect choice. Dying and with a family to support."

"So you believe he was paid to shoot Sanchez and he did it for me and Lisa."

Ray nodded.

"Who paid him?"

That was what everyone wanted to know. Ray shrugged. A better question was who knew her father was so ill? That person might be the link between her father and whoever hired him. Ray thought a man like Karl might tell his army buddies or possibly his shaman. Ray decided to call Jack about that one.

"This makes no sense. Ovidio Sanchez was already in custody. He was going to prison, probably to get the death penalty, so why bother to kill him?"

Ray wondered how anyone could be so innocent and yet a mother. She ought to know something of how the world worked. Sometimes he wished he didn't.

"He was going to be interrogated by the FBI. They were there to take him into federal custody," said Ray.

Morgan blinked at him and he saw the moment she understood.

"The mine shooting. It wasn't a random act of violence. Was it?"

Ray shook his head.

"Sanchez was paid, too?"

"No evidence of that. But he was tied up with some fanatical extremists. Survivalists and..." Ray did not want her to know more than she had to. "Crazy folks with crazy notions. Ones willing to use violence to make a point or get what they want."

"But that mine. It was a giant hole in the ground. Just

a horrible scar on the earth. That mining company should be ashamed, but what did that shooting do besides take human lives?"

Ray knew from Jack that it had also eliminated the man who had been stealing an unknown quantity of explosives from the mine and who had been delivering them to the extremists in an outfit called BEAR. This was from Jack's brother, Carter, whose wife, Amber, had noticed the thefts and nearly died in the mass shooting as a result.

"That mass shooting wasn't random," Ray said. "There were a lot of explosives stolen."

"I didn't hear that."

"You wouldn't. But that was why Sanchez killed those folks. To shut them up. Your father stopped the FBI from interrogating Sanchez."

Morgan shook her head. "No. He didn't do that."

But Ray saw by the horror in her expression that, despite her denial, she believed him.

Her hands covered her face and she wept. Ray rubbed her back and stared down at her father, dying in his hospital bed.

Morgan reined herself in and Ray thought it might be better if she had cried herself out. She now sat still and quiet with her thoughts. Ray left to buy them some sandwiches. Morgan didn't eat much. The doctor came in and gave her a dismal report on details that boiled down to the fact that the cancer was systemic. He did not offer an opinion of how long Karl had left.

Later, Morgan called her daughter to check on her and to report that "Pop-Pop" wasn't doing well. Lisa wanted to see him and Morgan said they'd try to arrange it.

Kenshaw Little Falcon arrived in the evening and he sat with her father so Ray could take Morgan down to the cafeteria for dinner. When they returned, her father was speaking to their shaman but Karl was only semiconscious and seemed to think he was back in Vietnam.

Ray watched his shaman with Karl and wondered if this was the man who had enlisted Morgan's dad for his deadly mission.

Kenshaw left at around ten and Morgan sat a vigil while Ray stretched out on the couch in the lounge. He checked on her in the night, seeing her still in the chair with her head on the bedding. She woke when the nurse came in to check on her dad. His heart rate was slow and his breathing even worse.

The doctor arrived around six to make rounds. He asked Morgan to step out for a few minutes and said he would come find her in the lounge. He met them shortly thereafter and said he was uncertain if her father would wake again. His organs were shutting down.

There was a commotion in the hall and the doctor left them. Ray and Morgan discovered the staff rushing into and out of her father's room.

Ray knew before Morgan. They kept them out of the room but were unable to revive Karl. He had chosen the one moment he was alone to leave them, taking with him the answers that his daughter needed so desperately.

Chapter Nine

Ray took care of contacting Karl's pastor at the gospel church where he was a member. He spoke to the tribal council chairman who would send the necessary paperwork to get assistance for Karl's burial. He drove Morgan to the Phoenix detention center to pick up Karl's personal belongings from the deputy warden at the prison. They didn't amount to much. Just his wallet, an old phone, a few dollars, his medicine bundle and the turquoise ring and bracelet he always wore.

During the following four days, Morgan's house became a magnet for families bearing casseroles and friends of her father but far too many of them wanted to ask Morgan the same questions. Ray only had to physically toss out one persistent guy who did not have the manners his parents taught him.

He helped Morgan work with the funeral parlor to make arrangements for the viewing and funeral, which was scheduled for Friday afternoon.

Thursday night Morgan stopped him in the hall before he could escape to Karl's room. He was finding Morgan more and more distracting from his job here.

"I want to thank you for all you've done," she said, her delicate hand resting on his bare forearm. The contact made him twitch in all the wrong places.

"Well, that's why Kenshaw sent me."

"He sent you to protect me. But you've done so much more. The flowers, the casket, the funding through the tribe. I'm very grateful."

How grateful? he wanted to ask as his gaze fixed on her pink mouth. Instead he said, "It's nothing personal. I'm doing a job. When it's over, I'll be leaving." He met her gaze and held it. "You know that, right?"

Some of the gratitude left her and now he read worry or perhaps indecision there. *Be wise*, he wanted to say. But another part of him wanted to kiss her. She'd had Lisa with no husband. He'd learned that much from Jack. So she was not always wise and she was not always shy.

"I understand."

She didn't move away.

"Do you? Morgan, I'm a mistake. You know it and I know it."

Her fingers splayed over his bicep, lifting the tiny hairs on his forearm as she moved to stroke his bare skin. She lifted the sleeve of his gray T-shirt, pushing the fabric up and away to expose the tattoo there. The symbols had been chosen for him by his medicine man. Eagle Warrior, his shaman had called him. It was a spirit totem that could not have been further from Ray's personality. Perhaps that was why Kenshaw had chosen the eagle.

"What's this?" she asked.

"Kenshaw told me to get this when I joined the Turquoise Guardians."

"Your medicine society," she said. Her father had been a member. He wondered what she knew. "My father has something similar only his animal totem is the puma. I did not know it was related to the Turquoise Guardians."

His brows lifted. A lion was a powerful totem, a clever dangerous hunter. Karl had been all that.

She traced the outline of the medicine shield branded in colorful ink upon his upper arm, pausing at the turquoise and the cross that appeared tied to the outer hoop.

"He doesn't have this."

Morgan's fingers grazed over the five feathers hanging from the hoop and reaching nearly to the junction of his elbow.

"Five," she said as she stroked the final feather.

Ray winced at the pain that cramped his insides.

They had added, one for each of them, the inductees, the best friends, but only four had returned from Iraq. Hatch had come home later in a box draped in an American flag.

"Why an eagle?" she asked, referring to the image in the center, the crying head of a bald eagle in profile, it's yellow eye and yellow beak both bright and sharp.

"Eagles have good sight. They can see things a long way off," said Ray. And Kenshaw said that Ray needed help with that, needed to see things before they happened. Needed to have better judgment. Like now, for instance, when the heat of her body clouded his thoughts.

He told her then about the feathers, one for Jack and Carter and Dylan and him and Hatch. He watched her brows crease at the mention of Hatch Yeager. This reservation was too small for her not to know that Hatch had been reported MIA and then, four years later, his body had come home to be buried in the tribe's cemetery. Did she know he had been held captive for years before they killed him and dumped him in the desert?

He wasn't sure. But he knew Morgan understood loss. Her mother, now her father and before that a brother. Ray heard about that, of course, even in Iraq—such news traveled fast.

"I remember Hatch," she said. "You two were best friends."

"Yes."

She traced the final feather again. It was the only one turned backward. "You must miss him terribly."

He didn't talk about Hatch. Not even with the men who were there that night. Especially not with them, though they all carried the visible tribute to his memory drawn in ink upon their bodies. But he found himself talking again. Morgan did not interrupt. She just stood there in her skimpy tank top and the flannel shorts she slept in with one hand pressed over his heart while Ray spoke in words that came slowly at first. He explained about how the perimeter needed to keep insurgents from attacking their convoys. The two Humvees and how he had tricked his way in by adding his name to their commanding officer's orders before he finished. He never expected SFC Mullins to actually let him ride in that first Humvee. Everyone knew that Mullins preferred Hatch because he was easygoing and followed orders. But Ray had gotten away with it, sending Hatch into the second vehicle with Tromgartner, who had an annoying a habit of clicking his tongue incessantly on the roof of his mouth. Hatch had grinned at him, knowing what Ray had pulled, as he climbed into the second Humvee with Tromgartner, Carter Bear Den and their translator.

"It drove Hatch crazy," said Ray. The memory made him feel physically sick. If not for that joke, it would have been his body flying through space, landing on the hill too far away to reach before the insurgents got him.

"And so he was in the truck that got ambushed?" asked Morgan.

"It was an insurgent attack. The second Humvee was closer to the enemy position. They threw explosives. Two of our men were captured. One was killed."

"The lucky one," she said.

How did she understand that?

"Yes."

"Have people told you this wasn't your fault?" she asked.

He gritted his teeth and nodded.

"It doesn't help, though, does it?"

He met her gaze and couldn't believe what she had said. No one ever said that.

"Not at all."

"Everyone said things to me after my brother's suicide. Instead of helping, it made me so angry."

That was exactly how he felt, too.

Ray looked away before replying. "They mostly said things about the nature of war, like they had been through one or about fate. But that's not true. I'm here and Hatch is dead because my sergeant clicked his tongue and because I let Hatch endure it rather than suffer myself."

She didn't say the next most obvious thing—that he hadn't known. Couldn't have known what that one small action would reap. Because that didn't help either. It just made him angry all over again. He lifted his gaze and waited for her to speak. When she did, she surprised him again.

"That must be a heavy load to bear." She slid her hand away.

She understood him because she'd had to deal with the aftermath of her brother's suicide. But her younger brother had been four years behind Morgan and five behind him, so Ray had been in the service when he had jumped. Ray didn't know him. Now he never would.

How many nights had she lain awake wondering if she could have stopped him? Now she had lost her dad, too.

"How do you bear it?" he asked.

"Some days are worse than others. I spend a lot of time

thinking how old Mateo would be now and what he might be doing."

Ray now found himself in the uncomfortable position of wanting to express his sympathy but not say something predictable.

"I wish I had known him."

That made her smile. "Me, too. Come on. I have beer in the refrigerator."

They sat at the kitchen counter and drank the one can of beer in two small glasses sitting side by side.

Morgan picked up the conversation. "My biggest mistake was trusting Lisa's father, which is a lot easier to bear than yours. And as it turned out, it was the luckiest bad luck I ever had. Like you, I never talk about it."

"You don't have to," he said.

"I know that."

Ray studied his nearly empty glass and swirled the foam that clung to the bottom. She had listened to him. He should do the same. But he found he wanted to slip out the back door instead. Morgan's secrets were none of his business.

"Is it the secret you are wary of or the intimacy?" she asked.

He sipped his beer. "Both," he admitted.

"I was seventeen when I met Lisa's father. He was handsome, employed and madly in love with me. I was young, foolish and mistook infatuation for love. He was very good to me and made promises. He even gave me a ring." She held out her bare left hand as if to show him the ring that had once circled her slim finger.

Had he broken it off or had she?

"When I told him I was pregnant, things changed. He grew restless and preoccupied. Then he disappeared. I was worried. It was so unlike him and it reminded me of the time before they found Mateo.

"But he wasn't missing." Her laugh was harsh and her flush showed embarrassment. "I even reported it to the police." She shifted to face him. "Do you know what they told me?"

He didn't.

"No such person. He didn't exist. So whose child was this?" She laid a hand on her flat stomach. "I found him in one of the places we used to meet. He was with another young woman, dark like me. Mexican, I think."

"Did you bust his nose?" ask Ray.

"No, I followed him home. He lives in Darabee, works for the city sanitation department and has a wife and three young children."

Ray slapped an open hand on the counter so hard the glasses jumped. Then he used some language he'd learned in the sandbox. Morgan smiled.

"Yeah, exactly. I came back home to my parents and told them everything. They helped me raise Lisa. She's turned out to be the best thing in my life. So I'm not sorry. Just ashamed at how naive I was back then."

"You could have him arrested."

"No. It's too long ago. Statute of limitation is up. And I'd rather raise her alone than have her anywhere near him."

"Child support?"

"Not worth the risk."

Ray nodded. "Would you like me to…"

She shook her head.

"I can be discreet. He wouldn't know."

"Ray, you are my protector. Not my avenger."

He looked down at the swallow of beer at the bottom of the juice glass, really wanting to punch that guy.

"You know eagles don't just look down to see what others cannot," said Morgan. "They also fly higher than any other living thing. They carry our messages to the creator and they are holy. Deeply sacred. Perhaps your shaman wanted you to remember that you are also blessed."

"Or to carry his messages for him," said Ray.

"I don't think so. He wants you to see yourself as other see you."

"As a badass? Screw-up? Poster boy for regret?"

"Look around, Ray. Not backward. That's not where we live. We live here now. In this time and place."

Live in the moment. See what was all around him. Ray settled back on the kitchen stool and pushed away his glass.

"You better get to bed. Funeral tomorrow."

He rose. She touched his cheek and he let his eyes slide closed for a moment as he considered pursuing what she seemed to be offering. Then he flicked his gaze to hers. She was not looking for a one-nighter, and she sure didn't deserve a guy dragging an entire boatload of baggage. She was making a connection and instead of welcoming it, he was shutting it down because he already liked her too much to be her next mistake.

"We do live in this moment," he said. "And you are right. I spend too much time in the past. But you have a daughter, Morgan. That means you must look forward to a future that won't include me."

Her hand dropped and she let him go. It was hard to walk away because he knew she was the best woman he'd ever known. But she was a mother, not a plaything. And he had no idea how to be a husband or father. You didn't need eagle vision to see that.

THE FUNERAL WAS better attended than it should have been, considering Karl's recent actions. But there were friends and members of his clan, his tribe and the VFW—Veterans of Foreign Wars—not to mention an unfortunate number of curiosity seekers from Darabee and the surrounding area. It was hard to know how to celebrate Karl's life. He had been a basket man. In the long-ago time, weaving baskets was a man's work while the women typically made the pottery. There were few left—male or female—who wove baskets like Karl. He was a veteran of the Vietnam War, a father and grandfather, a brother and son. He was also a paid assassin.

Ray wondered how many attendees sought clues to finding the missing two hundred thousand. That kind of money had a long tail. Ray had organized the funeral, his first, with the help of the family's pastor and Kenshaw Little Falcon. No one wanted to speak or sing, so Ray asked the other two remaining members of Tribal Thunder to make a drum circle and sing some of the old songs as they had done before joining the US Marines. He missed Carter Bear Den but not half as much as Jack did. Dylan Tehauno was in fine voice and offered his help to watch over Morgan in the days to come.

That was the kind of friendship money couldn't buy.

After the funeral, neighbors and family gathered at Morgan's house. They ate much of the food they had brought and stayed too long. Guy Heron had arrived with his wife and two girls. Lisa and Ami had disappeared into the bedroom with the cat. Guy remained on the opposite side of the room from Ray and no matter where Ray moved, Guy moved in opposition. Morgan sat in a dining room chair now in the living room with her uncle Agustin Tsosie as Agustin's second wife, Melouise, wrapped up leftovers and put them away.

Lisa returned from the bedrooms with Ami trailing behind. Lisa was carrying the bag that had come from the deputy warden and held it out to her mother.

"What's this, Mama?"

Morgan turned to Lisa and looked at the bracelet she held. The sterling silver had a nice patina and the large center piece of turquoise was made more stunning by the black spider web pattern and bright sky blue color.

"That's your Pop-Pop's bracelet, Lisa. You know that."

"No. What's this?" Lisa pointed to the inside of the bracelet.

Ray moved closer and so did Mr. Heron. Morgan's uncle leaned forward.

"It's a maker's mark," said Morgan.

"Next to that. These scratches," said Lisa and pointed.

Heron now stretched his neck to see, spotted Ray watching him and stepped back.

Morgan sensed the audience and took the bracelet. "You shouldn't be in your grandfather's room or touching his things. Put it back."

Lisa did and all eyes followed her as she made her way down the hall and out of sight.

A piece like that had once been the only form of collateral accepted for loans to their people. Loans made in trading posts via pawning the silver jewelry. So, it was called old pawn. It seemed this piece had come to Karl through his family and Lisa knew it well enough to spot something new. And if what Lisa said was accurate, then this would bring more trouble. It didn't take very long.

Ray watched Guy excuse himself to use the bathroom. Ray asked Jack and Dylan to watch Morgan as he headed after him. When Guy left the bathroom and turned the wrong way he was surprised to find Ray already in Karl's room.

"Looking for something?" asked Ray.

Guy said nothing as he reversed course.

Ray remained in the bedroom and was disappointed

to see Morgan's uncle also make his way in there. Two
men left the gathering by the front door but detoured past
Karl's window and peered inside. It was well past dark
when Jack returned to tell him that the last of the guests
had left the grounds.

But Ray knew that some of them would be back.

Chapter Ten

"Do you know why Amber is in protective custody?" Kenshaw Little Falcon asked as Ray walked him to his car.

"She's a witness to the mass shooting," said Ray.

"Shooter is dead."

And she and Carter had not left protective custody. As far as Ray knew, not even his twin brother, Jack, knew where they were.

"Amber still has to testify against that crazy brother of the dead cop from Darabee, Orson Casey."

"Yes. But also she overheard a man's name down in Lilac. That's all. She was just standing in the hallway outside her boss's door and heard him speak a name into his telephone. Now her supervisor is dead and that man, that very dangerous man, wants her to disappear just like Ovidio Sanchez."

"What name?" asked Ray.

"Theron Wrangler. He's a documentary filmmaker out of Phoenix."

"That doesn't sound dangerous."

"He is also an activist."

"Like me?" Ray thumbed his chest and then extended a finger in Kenshaw's direction. "Or you?"

"More like me. He's a founding member of PAN."

Protect All Nature. Ray had been a member, too, at one

time, back before Iraq and Hatch's capture. Back when he thought he could make a difference.

Kenshaw told Ray that the FBI were now watching Wrangler and searching for any clues that could lead them to the explosives.

"You think Karl knew this?"

"Karl told me they spoke to him. He wouldn't tell me anything more."

"But you put his name in the hat. Right?"

Kenshaw stared up at the glittering stars. When he spoke, it seemed as if he spoke to the wind.

"I didn't know what the job was until afterward. Just that it paid well and they wanted a man who would not pose a risk like Sanchez."

"A suicide mission," Ray clarified.

"A chance to serve the cause. I didn't know they selected him or that he'd agreed until after his arrest."

Ray had a sour taste in his mouth.

Kenshaw still stared at the heavens. "He wouldn't tell me who hired him or what he had done with the money. Karl said they didn't tell him why they wanted Sanchez killed although he assumed that they wanted Sanchez silenced before he could speak to the FBI. Whatever Sanchez knew, it threatened someone and Karl took that information to his grave. I don't know who hired Karl."

"But you know who you spoke to when you suggested him."

"I do."

"You have to tell that to our tribal police."

"I do not have to."

"The FBI. They need to stop them before they use those explosives."

Kenshaw heaved a heavy breath.

"You are supposed to protect our tribe."

"That is what I am doing. You keep Morgan safe. That's all you must do."

Ray suddenly did not know who was really giving him orders. Was it his spiritual leader or a man who worked with terrorists?

"Did Karl speak of this when you visited at the hospital?" asked Kenshaw.

"He was unconscious, so he didn't say anything."

"You were with Morgan the entire night?"

"No, but…" He didn't like the way Kenshaw was looking at him. "She doesn't know anything."

"You can't be certain. He was awake when I got there."

"And he thought he was in Hanoi."

"Yet he asked me again to look after his girls."

Ray glowered at Kenshaw. Jack had expressed his doubts to him already. Was their shaman looking out for Morgan or just himself?

"You need to find out what she knows," said Kenshaw.

"Why?"

"Because if you don't, some very bad men are going to consider Morgan a threat. If that happens even you won't be able to protect her."

But damned if he wouldn't try. This time he was not going to mess up.

"I could turn you in," said Ray.

"Yes and that would cause immediate concern to these men."

Stalemate, Ray realized.

"If we can't convince them that Morgan is in the dark, then I'll have to pull you. I don't want you to die with her."

"No one is dying. You sent me to protect her and that's what I'll do."

"The best way to protect her is to find that money and find out if she knows who hired her father."

A shiny black Escalade with tinted windows pulled up in the street before Morgan's modest home, looking as out of place, in a neighborhood of used cars and late-model pickups, as an alien spacecraft.

"Feds," said Kenshaw. "Stay with her during questioning if you can."

"What if they try to take her?" asked Ray, already bracing for a fight.

"Can't. She's on sovereign land and has committed no crime. They can't even be here without tribal council escort."

As if cued by Kenshaw's words, a silver SUV pulled in behind the FBI. On the side of the vehicle was written: Tribal Police Chief. The driver exited first. Out stepped their police chief, Wallace Tinnin, who paused to retrieve his cowboy hat. The opposite door slammed and tribal council member Zach Gill appeared rounding the hood.

"And there they are," said Ray.

"Tinnin is a fair man. Can't see anyone better to have with her." He gave Ray a long look. "Except you."

Kenshaw had a lot of faith in him. Too much, Ray thought.

MORGAN HAD NEVER even seen a real FBI agent—let alone one that was Apache. But here he stood in her kitchen amid the many dishes neatly covered in plastic wrap. Field agent Luke Forrest introduced himself as Black Mountain Apache. He was tall and lean with short black hair sprinkled with a few gray hairs at the temples. His hollow cheeks showed he did not eat enough, but his wide shoulders spoke of power contained in a tailored gray suit. With him was field agent Cassidy Cosen. She was his opposite, short, blonde and fair. They shared a serious expression along with the matching badges and pistols clipped to their belts.

Cassidy took a long look at field agent Cosen. She had taken the name of her husband, a tribal council member of the Black Mountain Apache tribe. This woman Morgan had heard of because she had a friend on Black Mountain who told her of the Anglo who adopted an Apache girl, thinking she was Brule Sioux. She was now married to the brother of the child she adopted. It was like having a celebrity right here in her home.

She offered coffee and one of the many plates of cookies but the agents declined. They didn't look the type for cookies, she realized.

"We are sorry to have to disturb you so late," said Forrest. He had a military bearing and was slender, cutting a fine figure in his Anglo suit. The shiny gold badge flashed as he placed a hand on his trim hip.

"And on the day she has buried her father," said Ray, his voice a growl.

Councilman Gill was a gentleman, and he and Chief Tinnin both accepted a mug of coffee.

Agent Cosen did not observe the custom of speaking some pleasantries as a prelude to the purpose of their visit. He went right to the heart of the matter with the precision of a diving hawk.

"We now believe your father was paid to kill Ovidio Sanchez. We know your father cashed a bank check for two hundred thousand dollars. Are you currently in possession of this money?"

Morgan looked from the fierce blonde woman to Ray who gave the slightest incline of his head.

"I am not," said Morgan.

The questions continued with the FBI obviously not receiving the answers they would have liked. Did they expect her to reach into a casserole dish and pull out wads of cash? She didn't have it and didn't know anything about it except what she had heard from the bank manager. Agent Forrest relayed that the bank manager was now in federal custody. If she did have it she wouldn't keep it. That was blood money and it tainted all it touched. But she had a sinking feeling that until the money was found, she and her daughter were in danger. Where could her father have hidden it? Her mind trailed to the days before the shooting. His disappearance in his truck. She was sure he'd used that time to stash the cash somewhere. But where?

"Tell him about Guy Heron," said Ray.

She did and about the many guests at the funeral that she did not know.

Forrest rubbed his jaw, thinking. Then he spoke to Ray.

"Your friend Carter Bear Den saw Sanchez down in Bisbee right after he left the mine. And his new wife, Amber Kitcheyan Bear Den, overheard her employer mention a man just after she reported an overage in a delivery."

An overage? Was that what the FBI called missing explosives now?

Her supervisor attempted to make a phone call to a certain party.

"Theron Wrangler," said Ray.

Forrest's brows shot upward.

"Carter told his brother who told me."

"Your medicine society," said Forrest. "I understand Morgan's father was also a member."

Kenshaw took that one. "Our society is a religious and cultural organization. We have no affiliation with eco-extremists."

"But you do," said Forrest to Kenshaw. "You protested in Sedona in the 1990s with PAN and were a known associate of Walter Fields, now in a federal detention center for acts of terrorism."

"We were protesting misuse of tribal water rights."

"Yes," said Forrest. "I am aware. But you were and are a member of PAN. And Fields is believed to have headed the eco-extremist group known as WOLF."

Kenshaw's mouth clamped shut.

"That's not an extremist group," said Ray. "They have members all over the country."

"Yes. I have one of their wall calendars, too. Has a buffalo for April this year. But here is the trouble. That Jeep tour outfit in Sedona that went up in flames two years ago, Crimson Excursions? Their fuel tanks caught because they were rigged with explosives. The residue left at the scene in Sedona from the explosion—the same explosion that resulted in the death of the owner, Warren Cushing—is a match for the ones taken from the mine in Lilac. Seems WOLF has moved up from selling calendars."

"But that happened two years ago," said Morgan.

"Exactly. Which means it was not arson, as reported to the public. We knew at the time that mining-grade explosives were used. Now we know the source and we know that the eco-extremist group claiming responsibility has been stealing explosives for at least two years prior to the mass-shooting at the Lilac Mine. It also means that we have no idea how much material they currently have in their possession or what they intend to use it for."

The implications settled over Morgan like a wet wool blanket. She had to remind herself to breathe and when she did it came as a gasp.

"WOLF does not condone the taking of human life," said Kenshaw.

"But BEAR does," said Agent Cosen. "They not only

condone it, they encourage it. Exterminate the species that threatens the planet—us."

"Your father was hired by WOLF or BEAR," said Forrest to Morgan.

"I don't know what that is," she said, shaking her head in dismissal even as the implication bit into her bones.

"WOLF is *Warriors of Land Forever.* They like to destroy property that infringes on natural places. Then there's BEAR. That stands for *Bringing Earth Apocalyptic Restoration.* Now these guys, they mean to end us. Bring the earth back to what they see as the natural order by any means possible. In other words they make no attempt to preserve human life."

"Why don't you shut them down?"

"Have to find them first," said Forrest. His gaze went to Kenshaw and held.

Morgan watched the unfolding drama. How had she ever gotten tangled up in all this?

Councilman Gill blew away a heavy breath and straightened. Everyone turned to give him their attention.

"Although we are alarmed to hear of the missing explosives, our prime concern is our tribe. I fear that stories of this money will cause a rush of treasure hunters onto our sovereign land."

That was already happening.

"I would remind you, Ms. Hooke," said the Anglo agent, "that it is illegal for you to keep any of the money tendered to your father for the purpose of murder for hire."

Morgan met her pale blue eyes, glassy and cold.

"I understand."

"Withholding evidence of a crime is also a violation of federal law," said Agent Cosen.

"I am not withholding anything. I didn't know what my father was going to do and I don't have the money."

It was clear from the hardening of the woman's mouth that she did not believe a word.

Chief Tinnin stood and thanked Morgan for the coffee, signaling an end to the meeting. He ushered the federal agents out and paused to say goodbye to Morgan in Tonto Apache. Then he turned to Ray.

"Find it quick," he said and then he was gone.

Just how were they supposed to do that?

Chapter Eleven

When Ray returned from speaking to Kenshaw it was to a quiet house. That made his heart jump as he called out.

"Morgan!"

She answered and Ray could breathe again.

He found Morgan on the bed in her father's room beside Lisa. Ray leaned against the door frame, watching them. The cat sauntered past him, flicking her tail against his leg before jumping up on the coverlet. Cookie then curled at the girl's side but the feline kept both ghostly green eyes on Ray.

"That's the last of them," he said.

Morgan nodded to Lisa who went to the closet and retrieved the small bag of her grandfather's effects. Lisa drew out the bracelet and handed it to her mother. Her father wore this bracelet every day and removed the ornament only when he slept. Yet suddenly it seemed a foreign object, out of place without him here to wear it. The grief made her throat ache and her hand began to tremble.

"Look inside," said Lisa.

He went to the window and closed the blind then came to stand at the foot of the bed.

Morgan borrowed her father's reading glasses from the bedside table where he had set them the morning he'd left and never come back. She had brought them with his medications, to the prison, but officials would not let him have the glasses because of the broken frame but did supply him with a free pair from the canteen. His glasses magnified the marks Lisa had found.

"It looks like a stick-figure man holding a medicine wheel," said Morgan.

A medicine wheel was a hoop, divided into four sections. Each section had multiple meanings. The first one, yellow, also meant east, youth and spring and the break of day, among other things. Morgan looked at the second figure. "This looks like a rabbit."

Ray looked next. There were two figures. One human. One animal. He could determine nothing else.

He handed the glasses and jewelry to Lisa who held the bracelet in one hand and the glasses like a magnifying glass in the other as she studied the scratches in the silver on the inside of the cuff bracelet. The entire image was only a half-inch high.

"Were they there before?" he asked Morgan.

"I'm not sure. I've never noticed them, but now I can't remember if I've ever seen the inside of this bracelet."

Lisa lifted her head. "I have. These are new."

Ray held Morgan's gaze and a chill made her shudder. She could tell he saw the danger in this and was assessing the risk.

"He knew it would come back to us," Morgan whispered.

Ray nodded.

Lisa continued to study the inside of the cuff. "This can't be a medicine wheel. It's not divided. And rabbits don't have long legs like that. The circle has a little dash inside and some dots at the bottom."

Morse code? wondered Ray.

Lisa stiffened and the hand holding the bracelet dropped to her lap.

"What?" asked her mother.

"I know what this is." Lisa's eyes twinkled as she looked from her mother to Ray and then back to her mother. "Pop-Pop made it for me! Don't you remember? When I was really little. He was sick and he was in that place."

"The clinic?"

"And he had to sit so long with the…" She tapped the junction of her elbow.

"The chemotherapy."

"And his hair fell out and came back white. He couldn't weave his baskets."

"He said it was too tiring," said Morgan, thinking back. Her daughter had been only four but she seemed to remember more than Morgan did.

"When he came home he started painting with those little brushes."

Morgan thought back, remembering the card table and the paints and brushes.

"Ceramics. He took a class at the community center."

Lisa set aside the bracelet and glasses and sprang to her feet. Then she ran to her room with Morgan and Ray in pursuit. From her bedside table, she lifted a six-inch ceramic statue of a gray-bearded prospector standing with an arm across the back of his mule. She passed the figurine to her mother.

In one of the prospector's hands was a circular gold pan painted the same leaden color as his beard. In the pan were tiny flecks of gold paint to represent specks of precious metal. Also in the gray pan was a solid rectangular area painted yellow with some tiny characters painted within that.

Morgan stepped forward, her brows knit. "That wasn't there before."

"What?" Lisa leaned over as her mother pointed to the yellow rectangle. "Get the glasses."

"I can read it," said Lisa, peering at the gold pan. "It says 12311989."

Morgan straightened and nearly dropped the statue.

"What does it mean?"

"It's a treasure hunt," said Ray, studying her. "And your mama understands the first clue."

RAY EASED THE statue back onto Lisa's nightstand. "He knew you'd receive his bracelet with his effects. And, failing that, he knew that Lisa would eventually notice the addition to her statue."

"But what does that mean," said Lisa. "It's just a bunch of numbers."

"It's my birthday," said Morgan. "December thirty-first, 1989."

"But that's not a clue," said Lisa.

Morgan's eyes rounded. "Lisa, you can't tell anyone at school about this."

"Mom, there is no school tomorrow. It's Saturday."

"You can't phone or text or chat. Nothing."

Lisa rolled her eyes. "Fine."

Ray dropped to a knee and took hold of Lisa's shoulders. "Lisa, there are a lot of people after your Pop-Pop's money. If they have this clue, they might hurt your mom to get her to tell them what it means."

Lisa's eyes grew wide. Morgan tugged at his hand.

"You're frightening her."

"She should be frightened. She told Guy Heron about the money and he dug up the backyard. Then tonight, right after Lisa brought out this bracelet, he tried to sneak into your dad's room."

Morgan sank to the bed. "Everyone at the house saw the bracelet."

"And heard her ask what the marks meant before you told her to put it away."

"Oh, no."

Lisa tucked in close to her mom. "Mama, did I do something wrong again?"

Morgan wrapped an arm about her daughter's narrow shoulders. "You have to listen to Mr. Strong. He's here to protect us."

Lisa lifted her head to stare at him, her eyes seeming to judge his strength and his will.

"What do we do?"

"Right now we get some sleep," said Morgan to Lisa. "Tomorrow can take care of itself."

Lisa did not rise from her grandfather's bed.

"What do I always tell you?" asked Morgan.

"We live in this moment. Everything else is illusion," Lisa recited by rote, but Morgan could see her heart wasn't in it.

Morgan rose and offered a hand, seeing Lisa out and to her bedroom to change for sleep. The cat followed Lisa like a duckling after its mother. Once Lisa was tucked in, Morgan did what she could to assure her daughter that everything would be fine, trying not to let Lisa see the real fear she had about their safety. She understood now why her shaman had sent Ray to them and she thanked God for it.

When she left Lisa's room, she found Ray in the hall. He had changed into the snug white muscle shirt he preferred for sleeping and the gray sweatpants that hugged his magnificent backside. Morgan cleared her throat but her heart continued to accelerate. It was difficult to be faced with so much temptation. She knew that he was here on an assignment and that he would leave when the trouble did. But she also knew how good he smelled, with his hair wet from a shower and his skin damp.

Morgan looked up at Ray standing watchful as an eagle, his arms folded.

Here was the only person she had told about her daughter's father and he had not been shocked or judgmental. But he had warned her off when, in a moment of weakness, she had really considered sleeping with him. She was considering it again and only her daughter sleeping in the room behind her kept her from offering herself. This was so bad. She wasn't that kind of woman. But it had been so long and she was attracted to Ray, not just because of how he looked, but because they had both suffered losses, made mistakes. He wasn't a bad man. He was all that stood between her and the bad men. She knew he was dangerous but not to her and not to Lisa.

It was only her need for his protection and her weeping heart that made her feel this desire to experience his hands on her body. She had just buried her father. It was normal for her emotions to be erratic.

"She asleep?" he asked.

"Nearly. It was a hard day."

Morgan stepped toward her bedroom and paused. It had been so long since she had been with a man. Ray wasn't perfect. But he was honest and he was a strange blend of vulnerability and toughness she found irresistible. But she needed to be wise, didn't she? She knew he would not be staying. What she didn't know was if that was a reason to resist her desires or one that meant she should act on them now before it was too late.

"I want Lisa to go to your uncle Agustin's tomorrow. I'm sending Dylan Tehauno along to keep watch over her."

Fear washed away the temptation as she met his serious expression with one of his own.

"We need to find that money and turn it over to the FBI."

"Will that stop all this?"

"We could just give them the clues and let them figure it out," she said.

"Yes, but they won't mean anything to them. They wouldn't have known what that symbol meant. And your birthday—that won't help them find the money. But I have a feeling you know what that number signifies and where to look next."

"I do."

"Then tomorrow we get Lisa somewhere safe and then we try to find this money."

She nodded. "Do you want some coffee?"

It was too late for coffee, but she wasn't ready to face her empty bed just yet. It never felt so lonely before Ray moved in. Whether because of her father's company or because she was busy raising Lisa and with work, Morgan had never really wanted a man in her life—until now. Now the nights were long and sleepless as she fought the urge to slip across the hall in the darkness.

"Water." He followed her down the hall to the kitchen.

The living room was suddenly illuminated with red and blue lights that spun around the walls.

"What's that?" she asked, moving to the living room to peer out the front door.

"Detective Bear Den set up a patrolman in front of your house."

He moved to stand behind her. His breath brushed her neck, lifting the hairs. She wanted to drop her head back against his chest, close her eyes and feel his body against hers. Instead she leaned forward to watch a tribal police officer emerge from his patrol car, flashlight in hand as he approached a dark pickup he had pulled over before her house. This housing development was on a loop that led in a half circle back to the road. The only reason to be on it was to get to one of seven houses.

The officer spoke with the driver and then the truck pulled out. The officer returned toward his unit and Ray slipped past her and out the door. She heard him ask and the officer answer. They were not from the tribe, but were Anglos. There was no need to ask what they wanted.

Ray stepped back inside. Morgan had her arms about herself because she couldn't seem to stop shivering. He took one look at her and drew her in, his arms rubbing up and down her back. She started crying of course. After today she was surprised she had any tears left to cry.

He ushered her to the sofa and they sat side by side.

"We have to find it. Make it stop," she said, and she looked up at his handsome face, seeing an expression of yearning mirroring her own.

Her hand slipped around his neck and she pressed her lips to his. He kissed her with a sweetness that defied everything she knew of his reputation. This kiss was full of comfort and tenderness. His hands were gentle as they gathered her in and rocked slowly with her. He kissed her cheeks and her neck and then he whispered in her ear.

"I'll keep you safe, Morgan. I swear on my life that nothing will happen to either you or Lisa."

She believed him. And suddenly she knew why their shaman had chosen him. It wasn't because he was a warrior or a former US Marine or a member of Tribal Thunder. It was because of Hatch Yeager, the friend he could not save. Kenshaw must have known that Ray would do anything to keep from losing another person he had sworn to protect. Morgan felt a terrible weight of responsibility pressing down on her. She needed to stay safe in order to protect Ray because she was certain he would dive on a grenade to protect her and her daughter. And she also knew that she could not live with that.

He stroked her hair and pressed her head against his chest so she could hear the steady thumping of his strong heart. She splayed a hand across his chest, trying to absorb just a little of that power, for she felt sure she would need it.

Ray took hold of her shoulders and eased her away.

"I have to ask you about your dad."

"All right."

"That day you took your father to Darabee, what do you remember?"

She thought back to that day in February and relayed what she recalled. The drive to the shopping area. Parking in the strip mall. Her dad telling her to meet him in forty-five minutes at a restaurant. Errands and her return to pick him up.

"Did he say who he was meeting?"

"No."

"Why he was meeting this person?"

"He just said he'd arranged to meet an old friend. A vet from his unit."

Ray made a face.

"That was a lie. Wasn't it?"

"Probably." He raked his long fingers through his thick hair. "Where did you go?"

"Grocery shopping. It's right across the highway from that restaurant."

"Was he waiting outside for you?"

"No, I came in and he was alone at a table near the windows."

"See anyone you knew?"

She thought. "I don't believe so."

"Think, Morgan."

She did. "Just some customers. Someone held the door for me." His face had been familiar but she couldn't place him. Where had she seen him before? "I saw the woman behind the counter and another filling the coffee carafes. It wasn't very busy. After breakfast and before lunch. There was a young mother with two kids. I asked their ages. But I didn't know her."

Ray did not seem relieved. This was important, but she really could not come up with a single name.

"I didn't know any of them."

His mouth twitched in what might have been an attempt at a smile.

"Okay. Fine," he said. "What then?"

"He asked me to drive him to the bank. I ran to the drugstore for a few personal items. When I came back he was already waiting in the car."

"Couldn't you get those things at the grocery store?"

"They're less expensive in the drugstore and I had a coupon."

He nodded.

The bank, she thought. "That was the money wasn't it?"

"Did he have a bag or case?"

She shook her head.

"Two hundred thousand would take up some space, so I don't think so. Unless he had it already hidden in your car."

She pressed a hand to her forehead.

"This is unreal."

Ray kept going, not giving her a minute to think.

"Now what about at the hospital, when I left to get us some food. Did your dad wake up?"

She shook her head.

"Did he say anything to you?"

"He was unconscious until our shaman arrived and then, well, you heard. It was just babbling."

Ray blew out a long breath. His shoulders relaxed. "All right. So the number, the one on the statue your dad gave Lisa."

He was clever and she wondered for just an instant if Kenshaw had sent him to find the money, which would make him just like everyone else. A part of her wanted to believe it because it was preferable to the alternative. That she had feelings for her protector that went beyond longing and gratitude. Was it better to be taken advantage of or to harbor foolish thoughts of a future with a man who had told her bluntly that this was a job to him?

Ray cleared his throat. "Why paint your birthday on a yellow rectangle in the middle of that gold pan?"

"It's not just a rectangle. Didn't you see the black circle before the numbers?"

He nodded, clearly not making the connection. Perhaps he had been right when he told her that her father had intended the message only for her.

Morgan hesitated. She knew exactly what that symbol meant and she knew where they needed to go next. The only question was whether to tell Ray or try to get to follow her father's clues alone.

She looked at the man who still held her in his arms. Could she trust him with what she knew?

Chapter Twelve

"Do you own cattle, Ray?" asked Morgan. She made her decision. For better or worse, she would trust the man her shaman had sent her.

Many of their tribe did. Some had been given land to ranch by the tribe, but most kept their cattle in the tribe's communal herd overseen by the tribal livestock manager.

Ray massaged the muscles at his left shoulder with his left hand as if suddenly developing a crick in his neck.

"Not anymore."

But he had. Most folks kept their cattle like money in the bank as insurance against a rainy day. She gave him a curious look.

He glanced away but answered her unspoken question. "They were sold when my parents died."

"I'm sorry."

"We needed the money to settle their debts. And for the headstones."

The stillness in the kitchen and the silence between them buzzed. She told herself not to ask but then she did. He laced his hands on the countertop, seemingly relaxed until she noticed his knuckles going white.

She thought back. She had been young. But she remembered the boy in school who had lost his parents. It had frightened her to know that parents could be lost.

"It was an auto accident. Is that right?"

He nodded. "A trailer hitch failed. It was attached to a pickup truck coming in the opposite direction down Apache Trail, one of the steeper grades. They still don't know why it let go. But it did."

Morgan winced at the image her mind furnished.

"They were killed instantly. Both of them."

"I remember something about it." She'd been in second grade, so Ray had been in third. An eight-year-old, two years younger than Lisa and orphaned. This man knew exactly what Lisa would go through if anything happened to her. So did Morgan—they'd both lost parents in auto accidents. She marveled at Kenshaw Little Falcon's selection for her protector. The man had every reason to fight for her.

"I remember hearing. You lived with the Hatch family afterward." Yeager's mother and father and their son, who had died in Iraq. "I'm so sorry for your loss." She placed a hand over his joined ones.

"It was a long time ago."

"That doesn't matter. I lost my mom almost four years ago and I still miss her every day. There are so many things I want to ask her, about Lisa and..." She stopped talking, met his gaze and they came to a silent understanding. Who among the living ever escaped this kind of loss?

"I don't trust life anymore and live accordingly."

"You mean you don't take it for granted?"

"No. I mean that it's unpredictable and vicious. I don't plan for a future because I don't expect to ever see one. I know people think of me as reckless and impulsive. Maybe I am."

She had heard of his reputation but she also judged by what she saw. With her and with her daughter Ray had been nothing but stable and thoughtful. With her, Ray was a man to be trusted with precious things, like her life and the life of her daughter.

"That's why Kenshaw chose me. Because he knows I will do whatever it takes to keep you safe."

"I believe that."

He moved his hand to capture hers. His palm was warm, dry and callused. She imagined those rough hands skimming over her body and just managed to resist the shiver of longing.

"What does this have to do with the painted yellow rectangle with your birthday?" he asked.

"It's a cattle tag. The kind that goes in their ear. One of our new heifers has a marker with the same number as my birthday. My dad named her Morgan II."

Heifers were young females who had not yet calved. Morgan recalled that this particular girl would be bred for the first time this summer if she put on enough weight.

Ray squeezed her hand and then drew back, a satisfied smile on his face. "So we look there in the morning."

"But how could my father have chased down that heifer. He was weak."

"Yearlings go into the chute for vaccinations between four and twelve months. Your dad is always there to help. He could have gotten to her then."

"When is that?" she asked.

"January."

"A month before the shooting. He was still getting around then. He didn't seem ill." But he had been ill. She frowned at the thought.

"Timing is right," said Ray.

Morgan had another concern. "We don't have a chute. How are we getting to her? Just wander out in the herd?"

"I have a better idea. Jack and his brother Carter used to be fair at calf roping. I'll ask Jack to meet us."

Jack Bear Den looked big enough to drop a full-grown cow on her side, and in a year, this heifer should be nearly 800 pounds.

Ray stood and tucked his stool at the counter. "We best get some rest."

She was certain she would get little. Between her father's death, the distraction of knowing this virile man slept under her roof and the notion of an honest to goodness treasure hunt looming.

They couldn't go tonight because she would never leave Lisa alone and she did not wish to endanger her by bringing her out into the night.

"How will we be sure we are not followed?"

"Tribal police will help." He set his empty water glass in the sink and followed her down the hall. She told herself to just say good-night and make a hasty exit, but instead she paused by her door, wondering what he would say if she invited him in. But she wouldn't ask, not with her daughter there in the next room.

"Well, thank you, Ray, for everything."

"Sure." He lifted a hand and stroked her cheek, pausing for an instant to cup her jaw. Did he want her, too?

His hand fell away and he backed into her father's room. The one her father would never return to again.

She just managed to get into her room before the tears started again.

What a mess, she thought and tumbled into her bed alone.

THE NEXT MORNING, after dropping Lisa and Cookie off with her uncle Agustin and Ray's trusted friend Dylan, she and Ray headed to tribal police headquarters. There they found Jack, who had abandoned his blazer and turquoise bolo in favor of jeans and a flannel shirt, boots and a gray cowboy hat with a colorful turquoise and silver hatband. He stood before a red pickup hitched to a trailer containing two horses.

"Ready to ride?" he asked.

She and Ray climbed in the truck and they headed out away from the tribe's cattle.

"It's the wrong direction," she said.

"Yup," said Jack. Then he lifted the radio on his hip. "Anything, chief?" he asked.

"You got company. I got them."

Jack turned onto a road that would loop back in the direction they needed to travel. They passed a tribal police car and Jack waved out the window. Then he turned to her.

"In case we have more company."

They rode in silence to the tribal cattle herd. Finding Morgan's heifer would be like finding a particular rock in a stream. Except her heifer had not yet calved. That should narrow the search.

The radio at Jack's hip sounded as tribal police chief Tinnin started talking.

"Guy Heron. Neighbor of Ms. Hooke's."

"I got one, too," said another voice.

"That's Wetselline. The officer we passed," said Jack to Ray.

"Friend of yours, Ray," said Wetselline. "Name's Andrew Peck."

Ray growled. "How's he out already?"

"No priors. Anglo. The judge set bail and he posted."

"He broke into her house," said Ray.

"And he'll be tried. Until then he's out."

"I'm going to have to crack open his skull."

"Arrest him for trespassing," said Jack into the radio. "Hold him until I get there."

"I'm escorting Heron home," said Chief Tinnin. "Out."

Jack turned to Morgan, wedged between his massive thigh and Ray's muscular one.

"You are a very popular woman, Ms. Hooke."

And she would be until they found that money. At the grazing area for the castrated males and the unbred female yearlings, Ray and Jack moved like the military unit they'd once been a part of. The horses were unloaded, bridled and mounted. Her job was to help spot Criollo cattle as they drove them by. She'd been given a can of red marking paint and been stationed at the gate between pastures. The plan was to move the cattle through the narrow gate, giving her a chance to see her heifer and use the can to mark her. The men got the herd moving and she ignored the cows with calves and the young males, easily spotted because of their trimmed horns, as she watched for the familiar numbers of any heifers. There were three that had the number twelve on their tags and had a calf. She marked them all. By the time they were done, she was covered with dust but they had three possible heifers. Ray scouted the candidates and found the correct one. Then Morgan sat back and watched in appreciation as Ray easily roped the bovine's head and Jack got a loop around a back leg. The two of them brought her down to her side, neatly hobbling her front and back hooves. When she was down, they called Morgan over. They all inspected the tag and found nothing unusual.

"Dead end," said Jack.

"No," said Ray who had squatted and got his face nearly on the ground. "Flip her."

The two men rolled the struggling heifer to her opposite side and they all looked at the horn, spotting the marks that had been etched in the smooth pale surface and then made distinct with some kind of ink.

"My father must have known that I couldn't locate this alone," she said.

"So he wanted you to find help," said Jack.

Male help, she knew. Her father's way of ensuring that she would have a man, possibly of her choosing, to assist her. Her track record in that department left much to be desired, which was why her dad had enlisted Kenshaw's help. And they had found Ray.

"What does it say?" asked Jack.

They all stared at the marks. There was a capital letter *B* followed by a vertical line and then another capital letter *B*: B |B

"What is that supposed to mean?" asked Ray.

Morgan smiled because she knew exactly where to go next.

Chapter Thirteen

"A brand?" asked Ray, hazarding a guess as he looked at the mark etched in the horn of the struggling bovine.

They were still thinking cattle and in a way they were right.

"Yes and no," she said.

Morgan took Ray aside and told him what the clue meant. The B Bar B was the brand of a ranch here in the 1920s. It had been part of the land swap that had granted them their reservation, allowing them to leave the Salt River Apache Indian Reservation where their people had been forced in the 1870s. In 1910 and again in 1930 they were granted land. But the chimney of one of the more famous rancheros remained on the reservation.

"I used to camp there with my parents. My dad collected willow and devil's claw by the stream there."

Ray knew that Morgan's father was a talented basket man weaving bulbous olla baskets, trays and storage containers of white willow with figures of animals and men crafted from strips of black made from the pods of devil's claw. His work had been sought after by collectors and had supported his family until his illness made it impossible for him to collect materials, let alone weave.

"So this is the mark on a chimney?" Ray asked, clarifying.

"Yes. Up along the stream. All that is left is the chimney and above the mantel is a letter *B* and a bar and below that another *B*. B Bar B."

"And he stashed the money there?" asked Ray.

"I think so." Morgan looked at the calf, bawling beside its struggling mother. "When could he have possibly done this?"

Ray motioned to the calf. "Fresh brand and ear tag on that little fellow. Branding is in March. Was Karl here for that?"

Morgan shook her head. "He was arrested that day in February. So when did he etch that horn?"

"Does he help out with the tribe's herd?"

"Yes. He's good friends with our livestock manager. Or, I mean, he was." She felt the weight of her father's death like a blow.

"Well the calves are branded and tagged in September. He'd have had a chance then."

"So long ago?" She couldn't believe he had planned a murder and all this way back then.

"Or in January when they give the yearlings vaccinations."

That was more likely. She found herself nodding. "Possibly."

She wondered how long ago he repainted Lisa's statue and when he etched that first clue in his bracelet. Perhaps she'd never know.

"How far a walk up the canyon is that chimney?"

"Three or four miles and uphill. It's past the lower ruins in the box canyon."

"I've never seen it."

"You have to know where to look."

Ray helped Jack release the Heifer before returning

to her. "We'll use Jack's horses. I need to get some gear, food, and extra water."

Water was the most important of supplies, as the canyon had only one spring and that was above the remains of the ranch.

He glanced at the sky. The morning was long gone and the afternoon had now crept toward evening. "Gonna be close."

"I'd like to check on Lisa."

He nodded and they headed for the trailer, already loaded and ready to roll. They drove away from town, deeper into the reservation backcountry, off-limits to outsiders without a permit. Near the top of one hill they pulled off because this was one place they all knew had cell-phone service.

She got a hold of Lisa, who had been baking with her aunt, helped take care of the baby goats with Uncle Agustin and Dylan Tehauno had apparently taught her daughter how to throw a Frisbee, of all things.

"We used to do that in Iraq," said Ray. "Ask her if he can still catch it behind his back on his index finger."

Yes, he could, Lisa reported. Morgan spoke to her uncle, who assured her that Lisa could sleep in the guest bedroom and would be waiting for her in the morning. Then he told Morgan to be careful. She planned to do that.

They continued on to the drop-off point where Morgan was surprised to see their shaman waiting with camping gear and supplies. Jack gave Ray a radio.

"You might make it before dark," said Jack. "But best not to take the horses down after sunset. Dangerous. We'll leave my truck and trailer here. Radio in to let us know your status, not your location or anything else you don't want the world to know. If we don't hear from you every few hours, we'll send in help."

The reminder that they were faced with dangers far beyond rattlesnakes and potential falls sobered Morgan and took away the joy she had felt at the prospect of riding out alone with Ray.

Morgan checked the girth of her borrowed mare and found it tight. She needed no help to mount. Behind her in the saddlebags were their food, water and cooking kit. A tightly rolled wool blanket had been tied behind the saddle's cantle. She would be sleeping under it and the stars right next to Ray Strong. Now that was a thought that stirred her up more than strong coffee mixed with whiskey.

A campfire, starlight and a long, cool April night. She glanced at Ray who met her speculative gaze with one of his own.

"You ready?" he asked.

"You bet."

HAD RAY BEEN imagining the desire blazing in Morgan's deep brown eyes? He sure hoped so, but his mind would not let him rest and his body made it difficult to sit in his saddle. He took point and glanced back often, mostly just to enjoy the sight of her, hips swaying with the rocking movement of the saddle and the sunlight caressing her flushed skin. Had he really ever thought she looked like a lost child?

She seemed all woman now, with her chin up and her mouth curved in a knowing smile.

"Almost there," she promised.

They rode along the gradual incline of the wide stream past the towering oak trees that shaded their way. This was good grazing land with plenty of water. He spotted the remains of the fence posts still visible and still clinging to the rusting coils of barbed wire. He might have missed the place that had once been a wide road, had Morgan not brought it to his attention. He had been to the ruins, farther up the canyon, but somehow he had never seen the chimney she mentioned. When they reached it, he understood why. Wild grapes nearly engulfed the standing masonry. Just the top eight feet of the chimney showed—exposed red brick of what had once protruded from the roof of a ranch house. The hearth itself was wide and open.

They dismounted and Ray used Jack's radio to call in, reporting on the weather. Morgan tied their horses, drank some water and then offered the canteen to Ray. He accepted the vessel and lifted his head to drink. She was mesmerized by the rhythmic up-and-down movement of his Adam's apple and the way he used the back of his forearm to wipe away the moisture that clung to his mouth. By the time he stowed the canteen, Morgan's skin tingled all over and there was a steady, insistent throbbing low and deep.

She gave herself a mental shake and left him to search the chimney. It had been years since she had made this trip, before Lisa was born, she realized. Back when she was no more than a girl herself and life seemed richer and more full of promise.

Morgan tugged back the hearty vines to reveal the marks as Ray made his way to her. In the redbrick column, the maker had added a gray-stone *B*. Beneath was a four-inch piece of similar stone and below that another capital letter *B*.

"Never saw this before," he said.

They looked in the chimney and felt around but found nothing that could be a secreted box of money. Finally, sweating and with bits of grapevine clinging to their hair, they stepped back.

Morgan spotted it first and gave a little cry of surprise.

"There!" she pointed at the side of the chimney. The stones inside the hearth had been blackened from many fires. But someone had used a stone to pound away a design in the same manner by which the petroglyphs had been created on the face of the dark basalt stone cliffs by ancient people.

Ray examined the images. They were just the right height for someone sitting in the hearth and the rounded stone used to make the pattern still lay in the hearth.

"They look recent," said Ray.

Morgan lifted the stone tool and gave a gasp. "My father's mark."

She held the stone and he saw the capital *K* and the shape of a fishing hook. Karl Hooke. Ray recognized the insignia that her father had included on the rim of all his baskets using a banded pattern of black devil's claw and white willow. And there was the same mark scratched on the side of the pestle Karl had used.

"He made this," she said, her fingers reverently stroking the mark. Then she turned her attention to the petroglyph her father had knocked into the wall of the hearthstone in a series of taps so that the pattern seemed to be created with a machinist's ball-peen hammer instead of a stone. Ray studied the engraving, thinking it looked like many he had seen in various places on the reservation and elsewhere in the southwest. The symbols showed two turtles and a crane. Morgan nodded and a smile played across her mouth.

"I know these marks."

"It's a location?" he asked.

"The upper ruins. It's on a stone in the cliff dwelling."

On the ride in, they had passed the lower ruins, which were a series of stone mounds and the walls that once formed the lower rooms of red stone and oak-framed communal homes. This was all that remained of a pueblo people who came before them. Ray knew the place, of course.

Then there were the upper ruins left by the ancient ones who had lived here a thousand years before the Apache and left for reasons of their own. Their home had been built of stone that had been carefully laid into the natural cave. The water came from the spring at the foot of the cliff, which was hauled up the cliff face in clay pots tied with cordage made from willow. There were pots still up there, untouched by their people and yet undiscovered by pot hunters, the looters who saw only money when they looked at the possessions of the ancient ones. Perhaps her father had left her the money in one of those pots. Ray hoped so, because his next call confirmed that the treasure hunters were becoming bolder.

They checked in again and Jack told him that the patrol had turned away two more vehicles. One of the shops in Darabee was selling maps with the location of Morgan's home and the museum where some of her father's baskets had been available were now sold out. Jack reported that the one large olla basket in the tribe's museum, also made by her father, had been stolen and recovered. Ray stowed the radio and they prepared the horses to resume their journey.

The upper ruins resided high in a natural cave in the rock face. Reaching it took climbing skills and a complete absence of the fear of heights. He gave Morgan a speculative look.

"What?" she asked.

"You've been up there?"

"Of course. Many times."

"Into the kivas?" he asked, referring to the circular chambers built high up on the cliff face into the natural cave by the ancients for religious ceremonies.

"What are you asking, Ray?"

"You seemed like the both-feet-on-the-ground kind of girl. Risk averse and definitely not a pot hunter."

"I'm no pot hunter. But I'm a good climber. If you are careful, it doesn't have to be dangerous."

He grinned. "Keep telling yourself that. Everything is dangerous. This stream cut these canyons. Those logs were thrown up on the bank during flash floods from storms farther up. Lightning strikes. Rattlesnake bites. Horses can roll on you." He patted the side of the Appaloosa who did not slow his steady gate.

"Trail hitches fail," she said.

He met her gaze, seeing an understanding of him that gave him a chill.

He nodded. "Deer in the road."

"You never expected to make it this far, did you?" she asked.

Ray shook his head. "It's freeing, in a way. Not expecting to survive. It gives you a kind of courage to try things. From the outside it might look like recklessness or bravery. But it's really a lack of faith and an understanding that none of us can expect a future. Planning for it seems counterintuitive."

"I couldn't live like that. I have a child. So I don't take risks and I plan for her future."

He nodded. "I can understand that."

"You're good with her, you know? My daughter."

What did that mean? Was she trying him on for size as a potential father to her girl? Ray surprised himself by not feeling an immediate rejection of the thought. Instead he was gripped with something unfamiliar, a kind of ache behind his breastbone. He wasn't staying around to play house. She must know that. So why was he picturing her waiting for him in the welcoming kitchen of her small home?

Morgan was more than appealing and Lisa was a wonderful kid. But he wasn't the sort of man a woman chose for a husband and father. He knew what women wanted from him and up until now that had been just fine. So what was with the ache in his chest?

He was more the sort you brought home to terrify your parents and impress your friends. The wrong kind of man for a good girl who didn't like risks.

"Lisa is a sweet kid," he said.

"And she's been through a lot."

That must be true. No father, but Ray knew that Karl had adequately filled those shoes. But he could do so no longer. Ray's mind shot him an image of his parents' graves and the single headstone they shared.

People you loved left you. Not by choice. But they were just as gone. Lisa deserved a dad. Someone like Jack or Dylan. The idea of him trying to be a father to Lisa terrified him more than his nightmares of the insurgent attack where they lost Hatch.

"We better get moving," he said.

Chapter Fourteen

Ray retrieved the horses and held her mount as she swung up into the saddle. She was a fine sight astride a horse. Made his own withers twitch as images that had no business in his mind continued to pop up like prairie dogs in a meadow.

Ray's radio crackled and he spoke to Jack, explaining their decision to spend the night. He did not give their location or any other details. Jack promised to check on Lisa and radio back. Then they were on their way. They followed a Jeep trail cut in the tall yellow grass. They rode abreast, each in one of the ruts left by the tires.

"Seems someone has been up here recently," said Ray, studying the tread marks left in the sand. Too small for a pickup, he realized. "Do you think your father was well enough to make this ride?" said Ray.

Karl had been in the last stages of his cancer. Riding up to a cliff dwelling seemed impossibly difficult to Morgan.

"He might have used his four-wheeler for most of it. He has one as well as ramps to drive it right up into his truck."

"You said he couldn't drive."

"He wasn't supposed to drive. But the day before the shooting, he took his truck. I was on nights then. He was gone when I woke up but back before my next shift."

"You ask where he went?"

"I did. He said it was personal."

"When do you get home from work?"

"In time to get Lisa on the bus."

Ray paused, thinking. "So he was gone up to ten hours?"

"Possibly."

The sunlight now shone just on the eastern wall of the canyon, painting the rock a dazzling orange, but shadows were slowly climbing up the rock face as the sun sank.

"Do you want to camp at the base of the cliff or up in the caves?" he asked.

"Caves are better for defense," she said.

Ray lifted his brow. She was thinking like a strategist. "Sounds good. We should make it by dark. Be close though."

They took the turn along the stream past the willows that grew so thick he did not see the elk until it darted out from cover to charge up the opposite bank. They dismounted and led the horses away from the stream, taking them up the dry canyon and pausing to water them at the natural spring. Ray admired the green vegetation here by the water. There were pinyon trees and oak and an abundance of wild grape growing with broad leaves and the buds that would soon flower. But just past the spring and in all directions to the canyon walls, the ground was thirsty and the vegetation sparse, dry and yellowing.

He tied the horses and loosened the girths, but left the bridles for now. He let the horses drink as he refilled their water bottles and his canteen. They each took a few minutes alone to relieve themselves. They met by the water and washed away some of the dust from their faces.

"Your father was wise not to leave the money with you, but the clues make it unlikely that anyone could find the cash without you. That puts you and his granddaughter at risk. I know Karl well enough to know he never intended that."

"But did he really think I would keep it?"

Ray cocked his head as if this never occurred to him.

"It's blood money. If all that you and the FBI have told me is true, then he was paid this ransom to murder a man."

"A mass murderer."

"A human being."

"Who shot nine other human beings dead, including women, one of whom was pregnant."

"Sanchez was a disturbed man. But my father, he wasn't a killer."

Clearly Karl had not shared any of his war stories with his daughter. That was for the best. But Karl *had* been a killer. A darned good one. A killer and a man who wove baskets.

"Even if it wasn't illegal to keep the money, I could never spend any of it. It's just morally wrong."

"Your dad was trying to look after his family. He used what he had, a talent for shooting and the knowledge that he was not long for this world."

"I love my father, Ray. But that does not mean I condone his actions."

"He was a good man."

"But he deceived me and he knew…" She stopped talking and looked at the rock face rising to their left.

"Knew what?"

"He knew that I hate deception. After what happened to me with Lisa's father. I just can't bear people lying. He knew that and yet he did not reveal a word of his plans."

Ray's stomach clenched. He was here to protect Morgan, but that was only part of his assignment. Kenshaw had also instructed him to discover exactly what Morgan knew of her father's business. This had not bothered him when he accepted, but now that he knew her, everything was different. She'd hate him, too, when she discovered his lie of omission.

"He was protecting you."

"He hasn't protected me. He's put me and his granddaughter in danger. All because of a lie. He knew if he told me what I would say."

"You'd have tried to stop him."

"Of course I would! I'd have gone to Chief Tinnin and had him locked up. Isn't that what you do with those you love? You keep them from making mistakes—even if for the right intention, his decision was wrong."

Ray knew that he wouldn't have told her either. And he would have been a lot more careful about how he collected that cash. But then, it would not have mattered. Because Morgan would just give it all back.

"So you want to turn the money over to the FBI," he said.

"As fast as humanly possible."

"That's probably a wise move. Once they announce the recovery of the money, the wolves will leave your door. You and Lisa will be safe."

"But still broke." She laughed. "I need to get back to work at the casino or I'll need to apply to the tribe for temporary assistance."

Medical care, such as it was and Lisa's education were paid for by the tribe. Morgan might be paying rent on the tribal housing, if she could afford it. Without Karl here, the tribe might reassign them to a smaller place. Lisa would lose the only home she had ever known. Ray thought of the day he left his home to move in with Yeager's parents. He didn't know what happened to his parents' things. The adults had taken care of that.

"Ray?" Morgan asked. "Are you all right?"

"Why?"

"You just look sad."

"Karl didn't want you to lose your home."

She straightened her spine and lifted her chin. "It's just a house."

That was an admission that Morgan knew exactly what was coming. He realized that there were many challenges ahead for Morgan and her girl, small everyday struggles with everyday issues. But that was only if they could find this money. He looked at the sky, still blue but fading now with bands of yellow and orange creeping in from the west. They needed to get to the ruins. He glanced back.

"You think we are being followed?" asked Morgan.

"I wouldn't be surprised."

They continued along in silence, Morgan falling behind his horse as the path narrowed. If Karl had driven, he would have had to make these last two hundred yards on foot, carrying the money. Then he would have to hide it before walking back to his vehicle. And that was if he hid the money at the base of the cliff dwelling. Ray hoped they would not find another clue turning them back the way they had come.

Here the banks grew steep with red rock rising on their left. Cactus and yucca clung to the clefts along the way. And now he saw the cave some one hundred yards up the steep rocky grade. The last fifty feet was a sheer cliff face with niches carved by human hands to assist in the final ascent. He could not picture Karl making such a climb, especially not burdened with anything, like two hundred thousand dollars.

Then he and Morgan scrambled up loose rock and over red stone to the base of the cliff. He retrieved the wooden ladder that was carved in a series of notches up the trunk of a ponderosa pine. The ladder did not reach the lip of the cave, but nearly so. The last fifteen feet was made along a fissure in the rock with the assistance of niches carved by the ancient ones. Together they leaned the beam into the notch that had likely been used for a thousand years for this purpose. She headed up first, leaving Ray to admire the sight of Morgan as she climbed up and then into the fissure in the stone. The woman had not been bragging, for she climbed with the ease of a mountain goat. Once she was out of sight, he released his hold on the beam and tied their packs and saddle bags to a rope, which he tied to himself. Then he followed her.

By the time he reached the crack in the stone, she had mounted the final few feet of the steep incline that led to the cave floor. This dwelling was easy to miss from below if you did not know the location. He wondered if enemies might have walked right below the noses of the people living in the caves above. The place was very defensible. There were poles in the caves cut to a length that could knock the pine ladder away. If an enemy was climbing to the rim of the cave, it would be easy to knock that enemy off the ledge with falling stones or the strike of a club.

But there were two vulnerabilities. First, there was no water in the caves, so an enemy might wait them out. It seemed that a historic drought did drive the ancient ones away. The second weakness was the exposed lip of the cave floor that protruded from the cliff face, making it possible to roll rocks down from above.

Morgan called down from above that she had reached the top. Ray concentrated on placing a hand and then a foot into the notches carved in the sandstone wall. Each had three grooves, worn from the fingers of thousands of men and women who had climbed before him. They, however, were not wearing boots. The footholds were never meant for such footgear or for a man who was over six three and wore a size twelve shoe. In this climb, a woman had the advantage. He reached the top, sweating and thirsty. Morgan offered him a hand and he took it. She hauled and he pushed until he stood on the cave floor beside her. She did not try to retrieve her hand.

"Look," she said, motioning with her free hand.

The light that had vanished from the canyon floor still clung to the lip of the canyon rim, turning the sandstone brilliant orange. His breath, which was already coming fast from his exertions, caught for a moment at the beauty of this place.

"Can you imagine seeing that sight every evening?" he asked.

She moved closer to his side and he looped an arm over her shoulder.

"It's lovely."

Her body felt just right tucked against his and in that moment of calm and peace, Ray glimpsed something he had not seen in many years, a future. He could imagine it now, the long days ahead with Morgan and her daughter, it came to him in a flash and vanished just as quickly. Crushed by his belief that future plans were for fools who did not understand that life was not to be trusted.

He stepped away.

"I'd better get our gear. The light's fading." He hauled their packs up and together they set up camp and had a meal of cold sandwiches and water with the fresh fruit Jack had added to their things. Afterward they went to see the petroglyph Morgan recalled. There in the back of one of the rooms were the animal effigies that were nearly identical to the ones Karl had tapped into the side of the chimney. But search as they might, they found no place nearby where the floor or stone walls had been disturbed.

"A dead end," he said.

Morgan's shoulders drooped. "This means they won't stop coming."

He feared that this treasure might become like the fabled Lost Dutchman's Mine in the Superstition Mountains with entrepreneurs selling maps to treasure hunters who would invade their land as the Spanish and the Anglos had done. But worse than that, they might hurt Morgan in an attempt to find that money.

The sun sank behind them and the sky changed rapidly from orange to deep blue. Stars emerged one after another until, by the time they finished their meal, they were scattered across the heavens.

"Did you ever sleep here?" he asked.

"No. Day trips only. My dad liked to look at the petroglyphs and pottery shards. He studied the cordage to see how the ancient ones made their ropes and baskets."

"I'd prefer to be well away from the edge when we bed down," said Ray.

They had not hauled wood and so they had no fire. They sat on the ledge looking out at the stars and Ray thought this one of the most peaceful moments of his life. A silent contentment filled him as Morgan spoke about coming here with her father as a girl.

"His favorite glyphs are those the ancient ones used as calendars. He used to show us the petroglyphs and explain them. He came here a lot as a boy especially at the equinox. He said there was a mark for each one."

"To mark the solstices and equinoxes?" he asked.

"Yes and the times to plant the crops."

Ray looked back toward the wall of markings. "I'd like to see that."

"It's down below. There's a rock whose shadow points to the markings when the sun crests the eastern canyon wall. It lines up perfectly for each planting time."

"And your father showed you this?"

She nodded.

"Morgan, maybe that's where he left the next clue."

"Should we go down there?"

"You think you can make that climb in the dark?"

She nodded and they gathered up their supplies. Ray lowered them to the ground and went first. Morgan climbed down behind him and they reached the canyon floor in only a few minutes.

"Easier in the dark," she said. "You can still see the hand holds but you're not distracted by the height."

For a woman who loved security and didn't take risks, Morgan was certainly doing a good impression of a daredevil.

MORGAN LED HIM a short distance along the cliff face. Around them, the familiar shrubs and brush cast long shadows in the starlight. There was more than enough light to see and she found the place easily.

Ray studied the swirling spirals and series of descending lines that reminded Ray of a staircase.

"That's the planting schedule. When the shadow from the tip of that rock—" she pointed to a jagged rock that had split from the main canyon wall in some long-ago time "—falls on this mark, it tells the people to plant their first crop. Here's the second and the third, which was cotton. Over there, each of the spirals marks one of the solstices or equinoxes. The whole thing is an elaborate calendar."

"Where does the shadow fall now?" Ray asked.

Morgan turned to him, seeming to know his mind. She smiled. "I guess we will find out tomorrow."

They laid out the bedrolls so that they would be here beside the wall at first light. Morgan moved her bedroll closer to his and settled in. He excused himself and when he returned it was to the soft breathing of a sleeping woman. He tried to tell himself it was for the best. That this woman was special and she deserved a man who could love her for a lifetime. He could protect her. But he was not the sort of dependable man who could help her make a home. He remembered his parents. But they had left him when he was so young. He had no clue how to be a father to Lisa, who would be preparing for her sunrise ceremony in only a year. Morgan should have a dependable, reliable man of honor. That was what she needed. Not one who had a prior for rolling his car in Darabee, an event he could not even remember because he'd been so drunk. Not a love affair. Not another man to leave her. She needed a man who would stay forever.

He lay awake beside her, watching the stars gently wheel across the sky and the moon crest the top of the canyon. Morgan rolled toward him, giving him a view of her sleeping face. He felt blessed that she trusted him enough to sleep beside him. He didn't deserve it, of course. He was to be trusted no more than any man and less than some because he wanted what any male would want, and he'd deceived her. Ray had not told her about his mission from Kenshaw to see what she knew of her father's business.

He felt like a traitor and wished he could be the kind of man she deserved.

MORGAN ROUSED IN the night in a panic, unsure where she was. Ray was there in an instant whispering reassurances and gathering her close. She laid her head on the pillow of his arm and rolled to her back, staring up at the sparkling curtain of stars visible between the gap of the canyon walls. If there was a more beautiful sight, she had never seen it.

"Lovely," she whispered.

He made a humming noise that rumbled through his chest. Then he kissed the top of her head. She lifted her chin and the next kiss dropped on her willing mouth. Morgan slid a knee up over his muscular thigh as the kiss blossomed into something warm and sensual.

Ray's mouth moved to graze his teeth against the sensitive skin of her neck as her hands worked up under his shirt to the strong cording muscles of his back. She raked her nails down his flesh and heard his intake of breath. His mouth met hers and he deepened the kiss, their tongues gliding over each other as his fingers caressed her.

He broke away to lift her blouse and kiss her stomach, each swirl of his tongue bringing her sensitized flesh alive and triggering a pulsing want that only he could satisfy.

"Ray?"

His dark head lifted and he stared up at her, his eyes hooded and mysterious.

"Don't stop."

His grip tightened as if he wanted to possess her, but he did not move, just stared up at her.

"Are you sure?" he asked. He seemed to be holding his breath as he awaited her answer.

She nodded. "I'm certain."

Ray's smile was devilish and now her breath caught as he unbuttoned her blouse and slid it from her shoulders. He followed by tugging off his shirt and T-shirt together. Then he turned his attention to the tops of her breasts exposed above the lace of her white bra. His delicious hot breath fanned her desire and she lifted to unclasp the bra, adding it to his discarded clothing. He paused to look at her and she found his gaze stirred her as much as his touch. He had told her that this was a job to him, but this, what they now shared, she knew it was real. She also knew it would not last. Nothing this good ever did. Not for her anyway.

He stroked the skin at her collarbone as he moved in to kiss her breasts. Her body reacted with heat, growing wet and ready. But he took his time, exploring her thoroughly before moving downward. When he moved back up to take her mouth, her boots, socks, jeans and panties had been cast aside and she could taste herself on his lips. She was ready but Ray rolled away. It gave her a moment to think about what she was doing. It didn't make her change her mind but served only to convince her how much she wanted him, if only once.

When he returned to her it was to offer the slim, slippery foil package that showed either his willingness to protect her or his desire to safeguard himself from unwanted encumbrances. She tore open the packet and together they slipped on the sheath. Her hands shook in her eagerness.

"It's been a long time," she said, nervous and wanting all at once.

He smiled and she knew it had not been a long time for him. Men like Ray were never without female company unless they chose to be. She needed to remember that. But in a moment she was in his arms again and her qualms slipped away. She didn't care about tomorrow. Only tonight and Ray and the heat and the friction and the bliss.

Chapter Fifteen

Ray woke with the birdsong. Morgan lay tucked up against his side, her bare back and bottom pressed against him, warming him. He threw an arm over his forehead and grew aroused all over again at the memories of Morgan in his arms. She was not the sort of lover he'd expected. He assumed she would be subdued and gentle. But Morgan was a hunting puma and her fire thrilled him. He had been with enough women to know the difference. He and Morgan had a rare chemistry and syncopation that made him hungry to have her again.

But now, in her slumber, all the cares and worries she bore faded. He saw the perfect peace and otherworldly beauty that he had no business trying to possess. Even if he longed for this kind of woman, he didn't deserve her and had no faith that she would want a broken man haunted by ghosts.

Ray roused from his bedroll, tossing away the blanket with disgust. He had some nerve messing with a single mother. Some nerve.

Still he glanced back at her, the blankets now at her hips. He reached for her and then stopped, fisting his hand and forcing himself to leave her be.

The sun was up but had not yet risen over the eastern lip of the canyon when Ray had the fire going and the coffee on. That roused Morgan, who yawned and sat up to stretch in a way that made Ray drop one of the tin coffee cups. He caught it on the second bounce and found Morgan smiling at him. The look of satisfaction she held in her dark eyes made him feel only marginally better about his breach of protocol.

"I'm starving," she said. "What's for breakfast?"

"Morgan, I want to apologize for last night."

Her smile faded and the worry lines returned to her forehead. Some of the beauty vanished like moisture into the dry air.

"Apologize?"

"I don't want you to think that what happened last night changes anything between us." In fact, sex changed everything between a man and woman. He knew it and from the confusion in her eyes, she knew it, too. "I'm still your protector. I'll stay as long as I'm needed. But…"

She snorted. "We slept together, Ray. You didn't ask me to marry you."

Now he was wondering what she would say if he did ask. *No* would be the wisest reply. *Hell no*, even better.

"Yeah. I know. But women read things into such encounters. I didn't want you to do that."

"Encounters." She fastened her bra, drawing the lace over her breasts, before yanking on her blouse and finally, tugging on her jeans. Next she slid bare feet into hiking boots and headed for the privacy of the brush. But she turned like a cornered animal to face him. "I never asked you for any sort of commitment, Ray. I'm a big girl and certainly don't need you to explain to me how the world works."

She left his sight and a moment later he heard a familiar rattle that could only come from a coiled rattlesnake.

Such snakes gained a rattle each time they shed their skin and the sound of this rattle told him it was a damn big one.

"Morgan?"

She did not answer.

"Don't move. I'm coming."

He found her standing stock-still facing a coiled rattler that had its back against the rock face and had no way to escape but by lunging at Morgan. Ray had a pistol in his boot, but they were too imprecise. The rifle was back at camp.

Ray drew out his knife. Morgan's eyes moved but she wisely remained motionless. The snake continued to rattle a warning. Ray usually let snakes be, but there was no way to this time because Morgan had inadvertently cornered the reptile and now stood in striking distance. If he got close enough to use a stick to pin the head, it might just lash out at Morgan's leg and hit her above her boot.

"Don't back up. Don't move. Run when I hit it," he said. Ray would have to be quick as a mongoose. He adjusted his grip on the knife, taking hold of the wide, flat blade. One of his favorite pastimes as a boy and then in Iraq was throwing this particular knife. He was accurate at twenty paces. But he'd never had a woman's life hanging in the balance. Not just any woman, but Morgan.

And now she had become so much more.

Don't think. Just do it.

He lifted the weapon. The snake's tongue flicked and the rattling increased in tempo. Ray threw.

"Run!"

Morgan sprang away like an antelope. But it was unnecessary. The snake's head had been severed from its writhing body. Ray watched the blood drain and the snake's body come to eventual rest.

"All I could think of was Lisa," Morgan said as she now

clung to him. "I just want to get that money back to the FBI and go home."

Ray allowed himself to hold her until she stopped trembling. After checking the area to be sure there were no more snakes, he left her to finish her business.

He used the radio to call Jack and then checked on the horses, walking them down to the spring, then back to the camp to find Morgan, pale but composed. Her eyes seemed a little redder than he recalled. He hoped she had not been crying or if she had been that she wouldn't start up again. What the heck had he been thinking last night?

Ray snorted. Thinking was not what he'd been doing. And just like always, this Eagle Warrior spotted trouble too late. He didn't know what to say or do about their little encounter. But in truth, he was already thinking about how to do it again.

Man, he was low.

They ate breakfast and broke camp as the sun rose higher, nearing midmorning and the time it would make its appearance over the canyon ridge.

"This is where we used to sit. My father said that rock was the one that the ancient people used." She pointed to the wall of stone that had separated from the rest of the rock on the canyon's face. The sun had finally reached the ridge, sending rays of light across the eastern wall, gradually inching down the cliff dwelling and closer to their position. They were only a little past the spring equinox but he could see where the one spiral was very near to the place the shadow now fell. The other spirals showed how far the shadow traveled through the year.

"There," she said. "See how it has gone past the first two dots on that line? That means the first two plantings are over and it isn't yet time to sow the cotton seeds. That was the third crop. After that it's beans and squash and pumpkin."

Ray watched the shadow crawl across the canyon wall as he sipped bitter black coffee from his mug and he made a guess as to where the shadow would fall when it met the earth. There he saw a pile of stones that did not look as if they had been arranged by nature. Could Karl have expected them to follow this trail and to be here in the month of April? Did he know so well the shadow's path and when he would die and when Morgan would follow those clues? The small hairs lifted on his neck and he knew that Karl had planned it all.

"Morgan. Look at that pile of stones."

She did and her mouth dropped open as she put the pieces together. Then she shivered. "Do you think?"

"I do."

They moved to the pile, preceding the shadow that moved quickly now as the sun rose higher. They moved the stones, one by one, and found a green plastic cooler half buried in the dry soil. Ray looked at Morgan who sat back on her heels.

"That's it, isn't it?" she whispered.

"Do you recognize this?"

"Yes. My father's. I didn't notice it was missing."

Ray lifted the lid, knowing what he would find. He was not disappointed. The small cooler, designed to hold six cans of liquid instead held stacks of bills, neatly tied with long strands of buffalo grass that had just begun to yellow.

Morgan tilted her head back until she looked straight up at the sky as if she could not look at the money. Ray left the lid open as he watched her. They sat behind the line of shadow but the canyon wall now blazed with light.

She shaded her eyes. "What's that?"

He followed the direction of her gaze and saw something dark in the gap between the two canyon walls. It did not soar like a hawk but hovered like a hummingbird, soundless and three hundred feet or more above them. Ray snapped the lid of the cooler shut.

"Drone," he said.

"A drone? You mean one of those things that fly around and interfere with aircraft?"

"I have to call this in." He was on his feet as the drone veered out of sight.

"Is it from the FBI?"

He sure hoped so. "No way to tell."

Ray radioed in and told Jack what had happened. Jack said he'd call Luke Forrest and that he was on his way with back up.

"Get to the horses," Ray said.

"Are we taking the money?" she asked.

Great question. Because either with or without the money, they were bound to meet trouble.

"I got it." He yanked the cooler free and tied it to the cantle of his saddle. Then he checked his rifle to be sure it was loaded and ready. Morgan bridled the horses and secured their bedrolls. With the horses saddled and the girths tight, the two mounted up to begin the ride down the canyon.

They met trouble before they even left camp.

RAY'S FIRST INDICATION of company came when the bedrock at his feet exploded. He recognized a rifle shot but his horse went crazy, rearing on his hind legs and continuing over. Ray had been on enough horses to know his mount was going over backward and leaped from the saddle, landing beside the rolling horse as the spine of the saddle cracked.

"Ray!" Morgan leaned from her saddle, extending her

hand for him and he was about to accept her hand when he realized the money and his rifle were tied to his saddle.

Another shot sent rock shards up beside his boots. Ray drew the pistol from his boot holster and turned in the direction of fire.

"Drop it, soldier, or I drop her."

Ray didn't, of course and the next shot was fired. Her horse screamed and fell to its front knees, sending Morgan tumbling over the withers and onto the ground. Her horse struggled to his feet, his fetlock gushing blood.

"Next one takes her life," called the shooter.

Ray threw his pistol aside and moved to Morgan.

"Radio," said the shooter.

Ray dropped his only means of communication. Cell phones were useless up here. The man motioned him back and then moved in to smash the radio with a rock while Ray thought about his knife. It was a straight blade, about four inches. The right sort for cutting a rope or throwing at a man's chest.

"Walk this way," called their attacker.

Ray helped Morgan rise and they walked in the direction of the bullets. A man stepped out from cover. He was dressed for riding in a denim jacket, wide brimmed hat, jeans and boots. His hair was dark and he needed a shave. The Anglo was about fifty and had a badge clipped to his belt.

"You're on tribal land," said Ray.

"I know where I am, Strong," came the reply.

Morgan gasped. "I've seen you before," she said.

"I was afraid of that. Avoided you at the station when we brought you in."

"You brought me in?"

"My guys. I'm the chief of police in Darabee."

Ray took another look. It had been a while since he'd met Jefferson Rowe, but he remembered him.

For just a moment Morgan looked relieved while Ray judged the distance he'd need to throw the knife and found it too far. He had to bury that blade to the hilt and he didn't expect that Chief Rowe would allow him close and personal enough to stick him.

"Well, Ray Strong. Been a long time." He laughed.

Rowe had been the arresting officer the night Ray had rolled his truck in Darabee with a blood alcohol level that should have rendered him unconscious which at the time seemed preferable to his grief over Hatch. That was no crime. But then he'd picked up his keys and driven his truck. He deserved what followed—every bit of it.

"Are you here to arrest us?" she asked.

"Not exactly. If you wouldn't mind getting Ray's horse? And please don't touch his rifle or I'll shoot him where he stands."

Morgan left them to do exactly what Rowe ordered.

"You a private contractor now, Rowe?" Ray asked.

"Sure beats a cop's pension."

Morgan returned leading Ray's Appaloosa gelding. Rowe motioned for her to come nearer, keeping the rifle aimed at Ray. She advanced slowly, showing the caution she had said she lived by. But if that were true, then when she had been out of sight up the canyon, she could have kept on going. Instead she had returned with his horse, which seemed uninjured, and placed herself right back in Rowe's sights.

"They're really worried about you, Morgan. What your father told you. What you know. If you can identify the man who paid your dad off."

Ray realized that the chief of police would make a valuable operative for the eco-extremists.

He hazarded a guess. "Would that be the same man who made sure her dad knew exactly when and where he'd have a clean shot at Ovidio Sanchez?"

"Very good, Mr. Strong. I see you are not always pickled in alcohol."

"I saw you in the restaurant that day," said Morgan. "You held the door for me."

"See, I knew you held eye contact a little too long. Did you recognize me from the station? I was careful not to be the one to interview you after your dad's arrest."

Morgan shook her head.

"Well, shoot. But you did spot me after I dropped off the check. You understand my reason for concern?"

"You work for BEAR?" she asked.

"See? You shouldn't even know the name of that outfit. Bears are dangerous, child. So, I can safely report that you do know what organization hired your father."

"Because the FBI questioned me about them."

"And that I was hired by BEAR. You know any of their names?"

She shook her head.

"Not sure I believe you. I know they won't. Skittish as cattle at a slaughterhouse, that group."

"But I don't know them," she said.

"Doesn't matter. What matters is that they think you know them. That you were your father's confidante. They are aware of your visit to your dad the day he passed."

"He was unconscious," said Ray.

"Not all day. They have information. And you were both there. This group doesn't take chances."

"But you stood by while they collected a great deal of explosives," said Morgan.

"That's not true. I protected them. Transported goods and kept them all safe. Now I'm planning a retirement in

Alaska. Should be far enough away to avoid the crater they'll make. They have nearly unlimited funds thanks to all those bleeding hearts who want to restore the wild. They never show the blood on the claws of the tigers in the fund-raising videos or the elk with shredded hamstrings thanks to those newly reintroduced wolves."

"What are they blowing up, Jefferson?" asked Ray.

"Don't know. Don't care. I've got enough money to get while the getting is good. Hope they blow up Las Vegas. I hate that wart on the desert. Or New York. Gray buildings. Cold and rainy most days, and when the sun comes out, it stinks like garbage. We'd be doing them a favor. Believe me. Don't even get me started on LA. They're pampered poodles with affluenza up the ying-yang. Spend $100 K to protect tree frogs and step right over the homeless veterans on their way to their limos." Rowe spat.

"So are you are here for the money or to see what Morgan knows?" asked Ray.

"Both. Kind of a win-win."

"Your drone?" asked Ray.

"Theirs. It's a loaner. They have such cool toys. Been watching you two." He rubbed the top of the barrel with an index finger in a shame-shame motion.

Morgan's cheeks flamed and Ray clamped his teeth so tight they squeaked.

"And here I thought you were a nice girl," he said to Morgan. "You turned me down a time or two at the casino."

Her eyes widened in remembrance. "You were at the casino the night before the shooting."

"That's right. I'd handed your papa a big fat check a few days before and dropped by to see his little girl had quit her job yet. But you were still there. Made me think you two weren't as close as I thought. He didn't tell you about

it before hand. Did he? Must have done that after because he'll never live to spend it. But I sure plan to. Nice of him to cash that check for me." He glanced at Ray. "Now, I figure the FBI is en route and Detective Bear Den is already on his way up the canyon. So I better scoot."

"He'll see you coming down," said Ray.

"See me? Hell, boy, he called me for backup. Your tribal police only got three or four guys on duty on a good day. Plus I'm closer to the ruins than they are up in Pinyon Forks. I just got here sooner."

"How will you explain the money? I told him we found it."

"You think he'll search me or look for your killers?"

Ray knew the answer. Jack would take the lawman at his word and come searching. He hoped that Rowe didn't plan to hurt Jack. He slipped his fingers around the grip of his knife, thinking he was running out of time. Funny, for a long time after he came back from Iraq he really hadn't cared if he lived or died. The unnecessary risks told him he was leaning toward dying. But not now.

Now death had found him and he wanted to live to protect Morgan.

"Pull that knife and I shoot you first," said Rowe. Then he turned to Morgan. "Drop the reins and step back."

She dropped the reins and stepped back. Rowe reached to take hold of the bridle as Morgan threw something. At first Ray thought it was a bit of rope, but as it sailed through the air, he recognized it as a headless rattlesnake.

An instant later the Appaloosa's eyes rolled over white.

Chapter Sixteen

Morgan dove back and rolled across the loose rock and sand, clearing the gelding's flying front feet as he tried to stomp the headless snake. Chief Rowe was not so quick and one of the hooves clipped his chest, sending him staggering back. Ray drew his knife and headed at him on a run. Rowe landed hard on his seat, regained his balance and lifted his rifle, taking aim at Morgan.

Ray threw his blade.

Because Rowe was in profile, he could not aim at his black heart but the knife did sink deep into his right side, slicing between the ribs. Rowe's shot went off target as he screamed and rolled to his uninjured side. Ray was on him a moment later, tearing the rifle from his grip and rolling to his feet above the writhing man.

Frothy blood gurgled from Rowe's mouth and Ray knew he had deflated his right lung. The chief of the Darabee police now breathed fast and shallow.

"Now you've done it," he said.

Morgan collected Ray's pistol and held it on Rowe, as well.

"Might have at least saved your little girl, Morgan. Now they'll use her as leverage to keep you quiet."

Morgan turned and ran toward Ray's fleeing horse. Ray

away to avoid the crater they'll make. They have nearly unlimited funds thanks to all those bleeding hearts who want to restore the wild. They never show the blood on the claws of the tigers in the fund-raising videos or the elk with shredded hamstrings thanks to those newly reintroduced wolves."

"What are they blowing up, Jefferson?" asked Ray.

"Don't know. Don't care. I've got enough money to get while the getting is good. Hope they blow up Las Vegas. I hate that wart on the desert. Or New York. Gray buildings. Cold and rainy most days, and when the sun comes out, it stinks like garbage. We'd be doing them a favor. Believe me. Don't even get me started on LA. They're pampered poodles with affluenza up the ying-yang. Spend $100 K to protect tree frogs and step right over the homeless veterans on their way to their limos." Rowe spat.

"So are you are here for the money or to see what Morgan knows?" asked Ray.

"Both. Kind of a win-win."

"Your drone?" asked Ray.

"Theirs. It's a loaner. They have such cool toys. Been watching you two." He rubbed the top of the barrel with an index finger in a shame-shame motion.

Morgan's cheeks flamed and Ray clamped his teeth so tight they squeaked.

"And here I thought you were a nice girl," he said to Morgan. "You turned me down a time or two at the casino."

Her eyes widened in remembrance. "You were at the casino the night before the shooting."

"That's right. I'd handed your papa a big fat check a few days before and dropped by to see his little girl had quit her job yet. But you were still there. Made me think you two weren't as close as I thought. He didn't tell you about

He hazarded a guess. made sure her dad knew exactly when and where he'd have a clean shot at Ovidio Sanchez?"

"Very good, Mr. Strong. I see you are not always pickled in alcohol."

"I saw you in the restaurant that day," said Morgan. "You held the door for me."

"See, I knew you held eye contact a little too long. Did you recognize me from the station? I was careful not to be the one to interview you after your dad's arrest."

Morgan shook her head.

"Well, shoot. But you did spot me after I dropped off the check. You understand my reason for concern?"

"You work for BEAR?" she asked.

"See? You shouldn't even know the name of that outfit. Bears are dangerous, child. So, I can safely report that you do know what organization hired your father."

"Because the FBI questioned me about them."

"And that I was hired by BEAR. You know any of their names?"

She shook her head.

"Not sure I believe you. I know they won't. Skittish as cattle at a slaughterhouse, that group."

"But I don't know them," she said.

"Doesn't matter. What matters is that they think you know them. That you were your father's confidante. They are aware of your visit to your dad the day he passed."

"He was unconscious," said Ray.

"Not all day. They have information. And you were both there. This group doesn't take chances."

"But you stood by while they collected a great deal of explosives," said Morgan.

"That's not true. I protected them. Transported goods and kept them all safe. Now I'm planning a retirement in

it before hand. Did he? Must have done that after because he'll never live to spend it. But I sure plan to. Nice of him to cash that check for me." He glanced at Ray. "Now, I figure the FBI is en route and Detective Bear Den is already on his way up the canyon. So I better scoot."

"He'll see you coming down," said Ray.

"See me? Hell, boy, he called me for backup. Your tribal police only got three or four guys on duty on a good day. Plus I'm closer to the ruins than they are up in Pinyon Forks. I just got here sooner."

"How will you explain the money? I told him we found it."

"You think he'll search me or look for your killers?"

Ray knew the answer. Jack would take the lawman at his word and come searching. He hoped that Rowe didn't plan to hurt Jack. He slipped his fingers around the grip of his knife, thinking he was running out of time. Funny, for a long time after he came back from Iraq he really hadn't cared if he lived or died. The unnecessary risks told him he was leaning toward dying. But not now.

Now death had found him and he wanted to live to protect Morgan.

"Pull that knife and I shoot you first," said Rowe. Then he turned to Morgan. "Drop the reins and step back."

She dropped the reins and stepped back. Rowe reached to take hold of the bridle as Morgan threw something. At first Ray thought it was a bit of rope, but as it sailed through the air, he recognized it as a headless rattlesnake.

An instant later the Appaloosa's eyes rolled over white.

Chapter Sixteen

Morgan dove back and rolled across the loose rock and sand, clearing the gelding's flying front feet as he tried to stomp the headless snake. Chief Rowe was not so quick and one of the hooves clipped his chest, sending him staggering back. Ray drew his knife and headed at him on a run. Rowe landed hard on his seat, regained his balance and lifted his rifle, taking aim at Morgan.

Ray threw his blade.

Because Rowe was in profile, he could not aim at his black heart but the knife did sink deep into his right side, slicing between the ribs. Rowe's shot went off target as he screamed and rolled to his uninjured side. Ray was on him a moment later, tearing the rifle from his grip and rolling to his feet above the writhing man.

Frothy blood gurgled from Rowe's mouth and Ray knew he had deflated his right lung. The chief of the Darabee police now breathed fast and shallow.

"Now you've done it," he said.

Morgan collected Ray's pistol and held it on Rowe, as well.

"Might have at least saved your little girl, Morgan. Now they'll use her as leverage to keep you quiet."

Morgan turned and ran toward Ray's fleeing horse. Ray

it before hand. Did he? Must have done that after because he'll never live to spend it. But I sure plan to. Nice of him to cash that check for me." He glanced at Ray. "Now, I figure the FBI is en route and Detective Bear Den is already on his way up the canyon. So I better scoot."

"He'll see you coming down," said Ray.

"See me? Hell, boy, he called me for backup. Your tribal police only got three or four guys on duty on a good day. Plus I'm closer to the ruins than they are up in Pinyon Forks. I just got here sooner."

"How will you explain the money? I told him we found it."

"You think he'll search me or look for your killers?"

Ray knew the answer. Jack would take the lawman at his word and come searching. He hoped that Rowe didn't plan to hurt Jack. He slipped his fingers around the grip of his knife, thinking he was running out of time. Funny, for a long time after he came back from Iraq he really hadn't cared if he lived or died. The unnecessary risks told him he was leaning toward dying. But not now.

Now death had found him and he wanted to live to protect Morgan.

"Pull that knife and I shoot you first," said Rowe. Then he turned to Morgan. "Drop the reins and step back."

She dropped the reins and stepped back. Rowe reached to take hold of the bridle as Morgan threw something. At first Ray thought it was a bit of rope, but as it sailed through the air, he recognized it as a headless rattlesnake.

An instant later the Appaloosa's eyes rolled over white.

Chapter Sixteen

Morgan dove back and rolled across the loose rock and sand, clearing the gelding's flying front feet as he tried to stomp the headless snake. Chief Rowe was not so quick and one of the hooves clipped his chest, sending him staggering back. Ray drew his knife and headed at him on a run. Rowe landed hard on his seat, regained his balance and lifted his rifle, taking aim at Morgan.

Ray threw his blade.

Because Rowe was in profile, he could not aim at his black heart but the knife did sink deep into his right side, slicing between the ribs. Rowe's shot went off target as he screamed and rolled to his uninjured side. Ray was on him a moment later, tearing the rifle from his grip and rolling to his feet above the writhing man.

Frothy blood gurgled from Rowe's mouth and Ray knew he had deflated his right lung. The chief of the Darabee police now breathed fast and shallow.

"Now you've done it," he said.

Morgan collected Ray's pistol and held it on Rowe, as well.

"Might have at least saved your little girl, Morgan. Now they'll use her as leverage to keep you quiet."

Morgan turned and ran toward Ray's fleeing horse. Ray

had no doubt that she intended to gallop all the way to her uncle's home, if necessary, to get to her daughter.

"We'll tell them what you did," said Ray.

"Yeah. Go ahead. I'll tell them you stabbed me while I was trying to apprehend you. That you found the money and it made you crazy." A smile hovered on his bloody lips. "Crazier. You've always been crazy. Right, Ray? Plus you've got a criminal record. And Morgan is the daughter of an assassin, who just found her dad's blood money. Who do you think they'll believe? You or me?"

Ray backed away, uncertain now. The FBI could arrest both him and Morgan because they should have reported the information they uncovered instead of setting out alone to find the money. At the very least, they had put her daughter in more danger because with both of them in custody, who would protect Lisa?

"Well?" said Jefferson Rowe. "What are you waiting for? If I'm dead, you're a murderer. Hard to explain away your knife in my side. So you better hope to Christ I don't bleed out before they get to me."

Ray left him, scrambling after Morgan. He needed to get Rowe medical attention and he needed to get Morgan's daughter to safety. It took a few minutes to collect the horses.

The police chief might be right that the FBI would believe his lies. But there were two factors working in Ray's favor. First, they were on Turquoise Canyon Reservation land and that meant that even the federal government had limited authority. And second, Ray had called Jack last night to report the progress of their search and again this morning to relay their discovery and the drone's appearance. It was something Jefferson Rowe could not even imagine, that Morgan wouldn't want even one dollar of that money. He had judged them on his belief system and

Ray was ashamed that he had ever considered keeping what they had discovered.

Morgan's honesty might be the factor that swung the balance in their favor. Or that money might still get them killed.

Ray took charge of the horses while Morgan bandaged Jefferson's wound, leaving the knife in place to help slow the bleeding. It took both of them to get Jefferson mounted. Her horse was lame, so they left it behind. They took the packhorse instead, though his horse's fall left Ray without a saddle. Morgan led them down and he took the position behind Jefferson.

They met a party riding four-wheelers soon after they started. Jack Bear Den lead the group, looking massive on the rugged recreational vehicle, wearing his familiar gray cowboy hat with the badge clipped to the ornate turquoise hat band. Behind him came three similar vehicles ridden by men and women dressed in a particular navy blue jacket with bold yellow lettering announcing that they were FBI.

Ray dismounted and went to meet the welcoming party. Morgan fairly flew off her horse, dropping the reins to rush past him. She headed straight for Luke Forrest, the Black Mountain Apache and FBI field agent.

"My daughter. You have to get her. Right now. Please."

Forrest glanced to Jack Bear Den.

"Your daughter is already at the tribal police station."

Morgan didn't know if she should be relieved or more concerned.

"She's safe," said Forrest.

Morgan drew the first full breath since coming down from the ruins.

The other officers moved past them, heading for the wounded man who started talking fast and loud.

"We're taking these two back to Pinyon Forks," said Forrest to his partner, Cassidy Cosen.

"I thought we were going to Darabee," said Cosen.

"We stay on tribal lands for now," said Forrest.

"Darabee is closer and Rowe needs a hospital." She turned to Ray. "Is that a knife in his ribs?"

Ray admitted that it was not only a knife but his knife.

"You are under arrest," said Cosen.

Forrest stepped in. "You accompany Rowe to the hospital," said Forrest. "Check in with me on his condition. Put a protective detail on him and make sure he stays put until I get there."

"We should bring them all to Darabee," said Cosen.

Forrest shook his head. This man understood the protection afforded Apaches while on their reservation and that those protections would end the moment they set foot off their land.

Cosen scowled but lifted her radio, calling for paramedics. Then she took charge of Jefferson Rowe, seeing him moved from the horse to the four-by-four. She and two of the agents disappeared back down the canyon.

"Now," said Forrest, "We have some questions."

MORGAN AND RAY rode in Jack's patrol car, preceded and followed by FBI.

"They sure seem like they're running the show," said Ray.

"Well they're not, because they can't take either of you unless our tribal council votes to turn you over. And they'll only consider that if you are charged with a crime they think warrants federal prosecution.

"Like stabbing the chief of police of Darabee?"

Jack made a face.

"Why did you move Lisa to the station, Jack?" asked Morgan.

"Dylan suggested it." Jack glanced at her. "You have to stay calm. Your daughter is fine."

This, of course, had the opposite effect. Her heart now hammered so loudly in her ears she could barely think, let alone hear. She held both hands pressed over her pounding heart, trying to assuage the pain and the dizziness that threatened.

Ray wrapped an arm around her and tugged her against him. "She's safe. Jack just said so."

Morgan nodded. "Safe," she whispered and squeezed her eyes shut.

"What happened?" asked Ray.

"Someone tried to grab her from the backyard of your uncle's place. Dylan got to her. She was shaken up but unharmed."

"When did this happen?" asked Ray.

"Between when we called Darabee for back up and you were found."

Ray thought about that.

"Did they catch the perp?" asked Ray.

"No. He got away. Dylan got a partial plate and a very good look at him. Young. Anglo. Hair in a man bun and with a full sandy-colored beard."

"Drive faster," said Morgan.

"We sent out one unit. The rest were with me. They didn't see him."

"Because Rowe is hiding him in Darabee," said Morgan.

"We'll look into that."

Ray knew there was little Jack could do if the neighboring police force was some kind of private army for BEAR. En route Ray told Jack everything he could remember, especially about Rowe's part in giving Morgan's father the access he needed to shoot and kill Sanchez. By the time they reached the station, Jack knew everything Ray did. It made Ray feel better but he also knew he had just put his friend's life at risk. If they were willing to kill him and Morgan on the chance Morgan knew her father's contacts and capture Lisa to ensure Morgan's silence, he had no doubt that Jack's name had just been added to their list of potential threats.

"Be careful," Ray said. "You don't know who they got to."

Jack nodded his understanding and then parked his unit. The minute they cleared the police station doors, Ray was separated from Morgan. Jack stayed with him during the questioning by Agent Forrest and assured him that Chief Tinnin was with Morgan. Ray knew Tinnin was a Turquoise Guardian, but he didn't know him well enough to trust him with Morgan's life.

Kenshaw Little Falcon arrived but Ray was not allowed to see him. Jack was called out to speak to Tinnin and Little Falcon. When he came back he told Ray that Jefferson Rowe was recovering from surgery and expected to make a full recovery. He had engaged an attorney and his room was guarded by both his men and the FBI.

"His attorney is Gaston Wohern," said Jack.

"That supposed to mean something to me?"

"He's out of Phoenix. He is way out of Rowe's league. That means Rowe has friends, the rich kind who hire the best legal counsel money can afford."

"BEAR," said Ray.

Jack nodded. "I'm sure he'll stick to his story that he tried to apprehend Morgan and you and that he was attacked."

"Our word against his," said Ray, knowing whose word would carry more weight.

"We'll keep you here on the rez for now. Best thing."

"You charging me?"

"No, but Rowe will press charges and I'll have to arrest you."

Ray felt afraid for the first time. "You can't. That will leave Morgan unprotected."

"The FBI has the money and they should be preparing a statement to that effect. That should call off all the low-life treasure hunters and opportunists selling her home address and bogus treasure maps."

"But Rowe said that BEAR felt threatened. They're more dangerous than a hundred guys with shovels and dreams of quick money."

"I agree. But I don't know how we can protect her from BEAR."

"We got a look at one of their men. Dylan saw him. The one with the beard." Ray wiped his mouth and thought. "And Rowe. The FBI have to get something out of him. They have to see he's lying."

"You don't have to convince me," said Jack. "You need to convince him." Jack pointed at field agent Luke Forrest. "Because you'll need the Feds' protection to keep Morgan alive."

Chapter Seventeen

Morgan didn't like the deal she'd been offered but she trusted Ray and was beginning to trust Jack. Forrest was another matter. He was too polished and there was a certain hawkish glint to his eyes that made her uncomfortable. Lisa waited with her uncle in the chief's office, but she knew that her uncle was not equipped to protect her daughter.

The FBI was. She glanced from Agent Cosen to Agent Forrest.

"What do I have to do? What exactly?"

They explained it to her. She asked to see Ray and they refused. They would not let her go to Lisa either. But they did promise to release her daughter and her uncle if she didn't agree. That was the deciding factor. She wouldn't let those extremist maniacs at BEAR get to her little girl. And if she had to be human bear bait, then so be it.

"All right. I'll do it."

They had her sign some papers.

In an hour, maybe two, Lisa would be among strangers in protective custody until this was over. But her daughter would be safe. The agents shuffled their papers and excused themselves, leaving her alone with Chief Wallace Tinnin.

She spoke in Tonto Apache, knowing that the agents,

now having a private conversation of their own, could not understand.

"I wish Ray could stay with me," she said.

"No, you don't," said the chief.

She understood. To ask Ray to be involved in this was to endanger his life.

"You're right. I don't want him hurt." She just was not going to say why out loud. She might confess to herself that she had fallen in love with Ray Strong. She might even admit that she was aware that Ray was not the kind of man who made commitments to a woman who had a child. But knowing that did not keep her from trying to protect him.

"That's not the reason," said Tinnin.

Morgan wrinkled her brows as unease tugged at the muscles of her shoulders and neck.

"Why then?"

"Because he wasn't sent just to watch over you, Morgan. Kenshaw also sent Ray to find out what you knew about your father's mission."

Her eye rounded. She couldn't breathe. It felt like he had punched her in the stomach.

"No."

Was he one of them, those eco-extremists who had paid her father to murder Sanchez?

The objection sprang from her lips. "He's not one of them."

Tinnin's brow twitched but his face remained somber. "I hope your faith in him isn't misplaced. Strong has a reputation for trouble. He's a wild one. And Kenshaw has ties to some dangerous people. I know that at least one of them is a member of WOLF."

"That's the nonviolent one? The eco-extremists who don't endanger humans."

"Not intentionally, maybe. But driving a nail into a

tree when you know a logger will be using a chain saw on it isn't respectful of human life. Soaking a car dealership with gasoline and tossing a match isn't respectful. I believe in protecting the earth, Morgan. But I also believe in protecting humanity."

"Are you telling me that Kenshaw hired Ray to get information on what I know?" said Morgan.

"The FBI agents are speaking to him. Ray asked for me to be present. Detective Bear Den told them that Ray related to him that the head of our medicine society sent Ray to be your protector while he discovered what you knew about your father's business, especially if you knew who hired your father."

"So all this time…" She had trusted him. Confided in him. Slept with him. And just like the other important men in her life, he had deceived her.

RAY DIDN'T LIKE his friend's sour expression. You didn't need to be one of Detective Jack Bear Den's best friends to read his mood from the glowering look and furrowed brow. He had just come from the chief's office where Tinnin and the FBI agents had been questioning Morgan. He could see her through the wall of glass windows but she sat with her back to him.

Ray stood to meet Jack. "Is she all right?"

Jack nodded.

"I want to see her."

Jack's mouth twitched and the breath he drew was long and labored. "But she doesn't want to see you."

"What do you mean?" The fear that he had felt when he'd watched Hatch taken by insurgents came back to gnaw on his gut like termites in wet wood. Before Jack even spoke, he knew because it was the only reason that Morgan would refuse to see him.

Ray sat heavily on his friend's swivel chair staring sightlessly at Jack's desktop. "She knows."

"Tinnin told her about your mission, all of it."

"How did he know?" asked Ray. Ray had confided in only one person and that man was standing right before him. Ray leaped to his feet and grabbed Jack by the front of his shirt. Jack didn't lift a hand.

"You're a Turquoise Guardian!" said Ray. "You're a brother in Tribal Thunder."

Jack's mouth twitched. "I'm also a detective for the tribe."

"You told Tinnin," said Ray.

"Also a Turquoise Warrior. Also my boss and the chief of police."

"Your first responsibility is to your tribe."

Jack shook his head. "It's to the law. And if either you or Kenshaw have broken tribal law, I'm the one who will arrest you."

Ray released him, choosing the reply that would cause the most damage. "You are not Apache."

The hurt filled Jack's face twisting it in an expression of pain mixed with grief.

"Perhaps not. But my heart is Apache." His voice cracked and he swallowed before speaking again. "Do you understand what has happened? These men, the ones that will come next are not after the money. They will come to protect their operation, the operation that has secured an unknown quantity of explosives for an unknown target. They sent Sanchez to kill Amber Kitcheyan not because she realized the mining explosives were missing but because she overheard a name."

"Theron Wrangler," said Ray, knowing Jack's brother Carter had told Jack that before they took him into protective custody.

The implications now settled like dust from the bombshell Jack had just thrown. Morgan had powerful enemies. The kind that hired assassins and arranged mass shootings and stole explosives—all in the name of protecting the earth. But who would protect Morgan?

He would. With everything he had and everything he was. Not only for Kenshaw, his medicine society and for his tribe, but because he needed Morgan to live. No one had to tell him that Morgan deserved better or that he wasn't the sort of man she would choose for a mate and a father to her daughter. But he knew that somewhere along the journey, he had lost his heart to Morgan Hooke.

"Did Kenshaw tell you who hired Morgan's father?"

"You want to read me my rights before you arrest me?" asked Ray.

"I'm not arresting you. I'm asking you a question."

"He did not."

"Do you have knowledge of WOLF, BEAR or the contacts that approached Karl Hooke to hire him to assassinate Sanchez?"

"No, again. I need to speak to her."

Jack shook his head. "She's elected to work with the FBI."

"What? No!"

Ray's gaze flicked to Morgan to find her now watching him with eyes that accused him of deceit.

His friend rested a heavy hand on his shoulder. "Ray, she's traded her cooperation for FBI protection for Lisa."

Ray kept his gaze pinned to Morgan as he spoke to Jack. "*Cooperation.* What does that mean, exactly?"

"It means you're not her protector anymore."

KENSHAW LITTLE FALCON spoke to Cheney Williams on a burner phone. His friend was a well-known environmental attorney and the production manager and long-time confidant for the powerful producer, Theron Wrangler. Williams updated him on Jefferson Rowe's condition.

"He's maintaining his position that he was called in by the tribal police as backup and was the first on the scene. He says that when he tried to place Strong and Hooke under arrest that Ray threw a knife at him."

"The FBI buying that?"

"Not sure. It will be interesting to see who they believe. I'd feel better if Rowe hadn't admitted to Strong his part in giving Karl Hooke access to his suspect. It lends credence to Strong's story."

"You know what BEAR will do about him?"

"Nothing yet. But they are worried. They are too close to completion to take a risk."

"What about Morgan Hooke and Ray Strong?"

"Strong doesn't know anything but what Rowe told him, which isn't much. But Morgan has seen Rowe with her father. If they believe her and arrest Rowe, then we lose access to Rowe and he can connect the money to our people in WOLF."

"WOLF made the delivery of funds?"

"Yes, to Rowe. Rowe delivered the check to Karl Hooke. Rowe isn't a member of either organization. Wrangler didn't trust him enough. Seems he was right."

"Rowe must know they'll kill him if he talks."

"He's not a fool. He knows they might kill him either way. If I were him, I'd be working out a deal for witness protection."

"How did he know where to look for the money?"

"WOLF's delivery boy recruited him. Wanted Rowe's help to find the money. Now WOLF is on damage control because it's their man who fouled up. BEAR knows that it was WOLF's delivery boy who followed Karl after Rowe delivered the check. Wrangler told me his people didn't know their man went after the cash and had to hear it from him. I don't expect BEAR will forgive the betrayal. His job was delivery and he got greedy."

Kenshaw wished Cheney had given up a name.

"They found it, the money. Morgan and Ray. But hid it again up there in the canyon."

"I'll pass that along."

"Is BEAR going to try to get it back?"

"They don't need money, friend. You know that. They have more money than Turquoise Canyon has water. I'll let you know if I hear whether they'll send someone for Morgan or Rowe."

"Who will they send?"

"That's up to them. Renzo won't make a move without their say-so. They might send his son again."

Kenshaw smiled. He had a name.

Cheney continued. "But his kid already disobeyed orders and they know it. Tough one." There was a pause and Williams cleared his throat. "Kenshaw, your name has come up, too."

"I'm not surprised."

"They know you spoke to the FBI and that you were with Hooke the night he died. Funny. They don't know whether to promote you or kill you."

"Difficult choice."

"You take care. I'll let you know when I hear."

"Walk in beauty, Cheney."

"Many blessings, Kenshaw."

Kenshaw disconnected and handed the phone to FBI agent Forrest.

"Did you get it?"

Chapter Eighteen

Ray waited outside the station for Kenshaw to be released. He knew that finding the money was not enough to protect her. Now he needed to find out who was coming after Morgan. Kenshaw appeared after dark and Ray met him before he reached his truck.

"Ah, there you are. You have done well, Ray," said Kenshaw.

Ray wondered who was right. Jack who said their duty was to the law or their shaman who said their duty was to the tribe. Was Kenshaw using him as a pawn to do the bidding of the eco-extremists?

"She still needs my protection," said Ray.

"Now more than ever. I have called for Tribal Thunder to meet tonight and have a sweat. We will pray and ask for guidance on what we must do."

"Where's Morgan?" asked Ray. "What are they going to do with her?"

"She is still in there." Kenshaw pointed to the station. "And her girl is in protective custody, according to Chief Tinnin. No one but the FBI knows where."

"It's blackmail, using Lisa. She'd do anything to keep her daughter safe," said Ray.

"Any good mother would. The question is can the FBI keep Morgan safe, or do they need the help of Tribal Thunder?"

MORGAN STARED AT the night through tinted glass in the hours when today became tomorrow. Pinyon Forks lay behind her and the community of Koun'nde just ahead. Luke Forrest rode beside her. His partner, Agent Cosen, had preceded them to make arrangements in Morgan's home.

They had allowed her to see Lisa, giving Morgan a chance to explain to her daughter what has happening before her child was moved to a safe house in Phoenix. Lisa was not reassured by strangers, despite the team of agents having included a seemingly very nice Anglo woman. Their parting had been tearful. Morgan's throat still ached along with her head and her heart.

Ray had deceived her, too. Why did this keep happening to her? The worst of it was that she still loved Ray, despite his deception. But she didn't know if she could forgive him.

Field agent Forrest refused her request to remain the night with Lisa, insisting that the less time Morgan spent with the FBI the more likely outsiders were to believe that she was still on the hunt for her father's treasure. Only Morgan's belief that she could not keep her daughter safe gave her the strength to let her go.

Once away, and much to her shame, she admitted to herself that she preferred the lie and Ray's protection to the cold, honest efficiency of the Federal Bureau of Investigations. Was their interest in her any more conscionable than Ray's? They had both wanted something from her, information that she did not have, but could perhaps get. If she didn't die in the process. She thought of Lisa going to live permanently with her mother's brother. Uncle Agustin was a fine man, but too old to raise a girl. Perhaps one of his girls, her cousins, would take Lisa if something happened to her. She knew her tribe would see to raising her daughter but that did not mean she would lie down and die. She planned to fight for survival and her freedom.

Morgan stared at the familiar fence line and the sparse sprinkling of houses. Most were dark because of the late hour and so no one witnessed her return. Still, Forrest explained that her car was waiting close to home and she would drive herself from Koun'nde in case the route was being watched.

"Jefferson Rowe has already had several visitors. We have his room under surveillance, which is why I know that his food tray included a burner phone."

"A what?"

"It's a phone that is very hard to trace. After use, the phone is destroyed."

"Don't you check his tray?"

"Yes, but it was placed on the tray after the nurse carried it past us. She's being questioned, but it looks like she has no involvement other than making a rather poor choice for a payday."

"She'll lose her job."

"Already has," said Forrest.

"I didn't think you would believe me," she said.

Forrest gave her a look. "Not sure we do yet. It seems unlikely that your father, who was so very ill, could have managed to keep all his meetings secret from you. You were his driver, after all."

"I already told you everything I recall."

"Yes." Forrest looked out the window. "Now we need what you don't recall."

They pulled onto a road she knew led only to the upper pasture of one of her neighbors. The headlights showed her battered white Honda. The large SUV drew to a stop.

"We have every room but the bathroom hooked up with video. There are microphones in every room. Just speak to us and we'll hear you."

"How will you know if they are in that extremist group and not just people looking for the money?"

"Because the treasure hunters will be after the money."

He left the rest unsaid. The eco-extremists did not want the blood money they had paid. They wanted the silence that her father had promised. They wanted assurance that his daughter would reveal nothing that could jeopardize their plans. That meant her removal. She knew it. The Feds knew it. That's why they needed her because you couldn't catch a bear without the right kind of bait.

Morgan climbed out of the large SUV used by the FBI and into her shabby wreck. There were a few moments of panic when her car refused to turn over, but at last it gasped to life and she was on her way.

She pulled into her driveway before midnight. The eerie silence of the house stopped her. She gazed up at the starry night and realized that last night at this time she had slept in Ray's embrace and had dreamed of a future that would never be. This morning she had awoken under that same sky and watched the golden sun paint the canyon wall. Now she stood alone before a quiet house that had once held her family.

It was hard not to call a greeting as she entered. The house felt different, empty, invaded, for she knew the agents had been here with their wires and cameras. Some of their essence still remained. She dropped her keys on the counter and slipped out of her coat, draping it on the back of one of the dining room chairs.

There came a scratching from the kitchen door and then a familiar meow. She opened the door to find Cookie looking put out. Lisa's cat! She had forgotten to ask if they had taken Cookie with her daughter. Had the cat walked the several miles from her uncle's home to here? The feline's coat was dusty. Cookie circled her once, rubbing against

Morgan's legs and then looking about. Was she searching for Lisa?

"She's not here, Cookie."

The cat regarded her with unblinking eyes.

Morgan scooped up the cat and carried her into the kitchen, crying on her soft, short fur. Cookie tolerated Morgan's weeping to a point and then wriggled until Morgan set her down. Cookie paused at the empty food dish, which Morgan filled before sitting on the floor with her back to the cabinet as Lisa's rescue kitty ate. The smell of the cat food and the sticky noise of Cookie's ingestion made Morgan feel ill and she left Cookie to get ready for bed. When she came back, Cookie stood beside her empty food dish. Morgan changed her water and added dry food to the dish, which Cookie snubbed as she turned to the water instead. Though the house felt empty and she appeared to be alone, she knew the video monitors were all in place, and she wore a wire for when she left her house, plus a tracker to ensure the FBI could locate her or her body.

Cookie demanded egress after her meal and then almost immediately howled for readmission. Once inside she glided past Morgan to Lisa's room where she settled on her daughter's comforter and turned her luminous green eyes on Morgan.

"She won't be back tonight," said Morgan and then thought of the agents listening to her conversing with a cat.

Once in her own bed, she did not sleep, but tossed from side to side, wondering if the microphone was transmitting her heavy sighs and the sound of the toilet flushing. They'd left her no privacy. Agent Cosen had mentioned that she might want to consider a fresh start in witness protection. Such a suggestion showed a complete lack of understanding of who and what she was. You might just as well uproot a pinyon pine and plant it in the Sedona Desert. Her people had fought hard through the federal legal system to gain back their land. She was not leaving her heritage or her daughter's birthright because some crazy group was trying to return the southwest to its natural state.

Morgan closed her eyes, kicked at the covers, rolled and finally forced herself to stillness. Now only her mind raced. Finally she left her bed in favor of Lisa's. There, with Cookie coiled at her feet, Morgan finally dozed.

She woke when the duct tape blanketed her mouth.

Chapter Nineteen

Morgan's eyes opened to darkness as cold hands seized her. She writhed, struggling to escape, the duct tape muffling her cries. Something pricked her neck. The injection took her quickly as her mind clawed to remain conscious but her body felt strangely detached as if wrapped in cotton.

The covers fell back and rough hands pushed up her tank top. The cool air brushed her bare skin. A dark shape loomed over her. She tried to scream. The adhesive of the tape tugged at her mouth. The intruder's gloved hands brushed down her sternum and swept along in the darkness down her hip, over her legs but the touch felt a long way off somehow, as if her skin no longer wholly belonged to her.

She could feel herself sliding away. Her eyes slid closed against her command as her hammering heart slowed and she accepted that she would die.

Ray.

Lisa.

She closed her eyes and fought to stay alive.

RAY BREATHED IN the sweet moist air inside the sweat lodge. He sat in his black cotton gym shorts wearing nothing but his medicine bundle. The other men sat in a circle around the fire pit of hot river stones prepared in the sacred fire that sat outside the wickiup beyond the entrance that stood in the eastern portion of the round, domed enclosure.

Whether by design or unintentionally, they had left two places empty. One had belonged to Hatch Yeager, their fallen comrade. The second had recently been vacated by Carter Bear Den.

Outside the sun would soon break the line of mountains to the east, but inside was as dark as the burrow of a rabbit. The three remaining members of Tribal Thunder, Ray Strong, Dylan Tehauno and Jack Bear Den, listened as their shaman spoke of the need to replace Carter Bear Den. Jack was opposed, insisting that his brother would return, but Kenshaw said the group was out of balance with only three. Four was the sacred number in the medicine wheel because there were four directions, four seasons, four stages of a man's life and four characteristics of a warrior. Many things in the world moved in a circle. Jack's objections were assuaged when Kenshaw suggested the inclusion of his younger brother Kurt, now twenty-four and a paramedic for the air ambulance out of Darabee.

With that settled, Kenshaw turned to the matter of Morgan Hooke, now under the protection of the FBI.

"You are no longer responsible for this one," said Kenshaw to Ray. "She has chosen another protector. Your mission now is to help Jack and Dylan protect our land and our tribe."

But Ray still felt responsible for Morgan and Lisa, more now than before. He knew that the moment they had finished their business and prayed their prayers, he would return to watch over her.

The matter of the stabbing of Chief Jefferson Rowe was still under investigation. He now shared Jack's suspicions regarding their shaman's connection to the eco-extremists. But Jack cared about upholding the law and Ray cared about protecting Morgan. Kenshaw's foreknowledge of the attack at the Lilac Mine and the steps he had taken to protect Morgan and Lisa could not be consigned to intuition. Despite their uncertainties, both were respectful of the sweat lodge. This sacred ritual would not be sullied with accusations.

Kenshaw poured water on the hot coals, sending steam through the green cedar boughs. Ray breathed deep and joined in the chanting prayer. The men were a unit of brothers, but now doubt had come into their midst and Ray felt the distrust as strongly as he felt the sweat running in rivulets down his nearly naked body. He looked at the empty place where his best friend should be and for an instant before he blinked his eyes, he thought he saw Hatch sitting among them. Ray stared but there was nothing there. It did not matter, because now every hair on his body stood up.

Ray pointed to the place and told the others what he had seen. There was much said of ghosts in Apache culture and most of it very bad. His ancestors went to great lengths to see that ghosts did not return to this world and Ray could not keep the dread from filling his chest.

"A warning," said Kenshaw. "Something unseen."

"It's a flashback," said Jack. "I get them sometimes, too."

Ray looked at him. Jack had never told him that. In fact they never spoke of the night Hatch was taken.

"Me, too," said Dylan.

Ray's skin itched and the sweat stung his eyes. "Something is wrong. I have to go."

Kenshaw nodded. "It is time for all of us to greet the day with a prayer and blessing."

Their shaman ducked out of the wickiup and into the cool, crisp morning air. Jack followed and then Dylan. They each took a turn sluicing water from the stream over their heads with a bucket. The icy water puckered his skin and washed away the sweat until he felt clean and alive. Soon they were shivering in their gym shorts, which they discarded to tug on dry clothing.

Kenshaw finished last, seeing that the sacred fire was out. When he finished they sat in a circle by the stream. Dylan, their drum keeper, set out the large barrel that had once been a portion of a ponderosa pine, hollowed now and with a cowhide stretched tight over the gap. They used bowed willow sticks to communally strike the rhythm. Kenshaw sang in a high true modulation encouraging many blessings for their people, and the three members of Tribal Thunder repeated the last portion of his prayer together in one voice. This, too, was a vital role of the medicine society, to follow the path walked by those who came before and mark the way for those who would follow.

The sun peeked over the ridge, sending bright beams of golden light across the land. Still Ray found no peace but battled the continuing feeling that he was not where he was supposed to be.

Was she sleeping in her bed or did the FBI have her in some hotel room under guard? Would he be able to see her? Now that she knew of his duplicity, would she even want to see him?

He did not expect her forgiveness but he lived in hope that he could earn a second chance because Morgan's happiness was nearly as dear to him as her safety. Ray prayed louder as the sun's apex crested the trees. Behind them, the hillside flooded with light.

Please keep her safe, Ray thought.

Jack seemed impatient to finish and was on his feet before the drum had gone silent.

Now the detective reemerged as he asked Kenshaw the

questions he had held back during the sacred time inside the wickiup and here in the drum circle.

"How do you know the plans of these extremist groups?"

"Extremist." Kenshaw laughed. "There was a time when the Tonto people were extremists. Enemies to be eliminated."

"Are you one of them?" asked Jack.

"I have been many things in my life," said Kenshaw. "I have taken part in acts of civil disobedience for causes I believe are right. To stop wars. To take back land and water rights. To keep peace with other nations and to protect the earth that is our home. Yes, I am a part of all things as are you."

"How do you know these things before anyone else?" asked Ray.

Kenshaw smiled. "I have lived a long time. I hear things on the wind and from cellular towers." He laughed. "But if you ask me to tell you who speaks to me, I will say what I said to Agent Forrest. It is my right to speak and it is my right to be silent."

"Are you one of them? Of those eco-extremists that call themselves BEAR?"

"I am not."

Jack seemed relieved, but Ray noticed their shaman did not deny membership in WOLF.

"WOLF?" asked Ray.

"If I answer that, my friend Jack here will have to arrest me."

Jack seemed ready to arrest him anyway but was interrupted by the chiming of his phone, which sounded at the same moment as Kenshaw's and Ray's. They lifted their mobiles. The text was from Luke Forrest and was only three words: Important—call me.

The chill Ray had experienced in the sweat lodge and

the vision of his fallen friend now pressed on him. He knew before he was told that something terrible was happening. He issued a prayer as he called Forrest and pressed the speaker button.

"Is it Morgan?" asked Ray.

"Yes. We've lost contact." He told Ray that they had last seen her a little after one in the morning and only with the daylight realized that her bedroom was empty and Morgan gone.

"Did she slip away?" asked Jack. "Or evade your custody?"

"That's the question. We know that Dylan and Ray have tracking experience. We'd like their opinion."

Ray was already running toward his vehicle. The fifteen miles to Morgan's home were the longest of his life. They reached the small home and he and Dylan went to work, conferring as they checked first inside and then outside and came to the same conclusion. Ray took off on the trail, moving carefully. He heard Dylan speaking to Forrest and Cosen.

"She was taken by force out that window," said Dylan.

Ray headed toward Guy Heron's home and tried to keep the rage from consuming him.

"One man," said Ray, his words still clear. "When he left, he was carrying Morgan."

"How do you know that?" asked Agent Cosen.

"Depth of the footprints compared to entry," said Ray. "And nothing else is missing that would weigh enough to account for the difference."

Forrest trailed Ray. He glanced back at his shadow.

"My grandfather had a reputation for tracking," said Forrest. "I was lucky to have known him and to have learned some of what he knew."

Ray pointed at the exposed stretch of sand and the footprints. "What do you see?"

"He has a head start, judging from the sand that has fallen into the tracks. He is wearing boots and, guessing from the size, he's male."

Ray nodded. "And Morgan did not shift her weight as they carried her. These prints are straight and the tread natural."

Forrest met his gaze but did not seem to understand.

"She wasn't moving," said Ray.

Forrest's eyes widened. "But no blood."

That was true. Ray hoped that Morgan was alive.

"You can't get information from a dead woman, at least not the kind that will tell them where to find the treasure."

But killing someone was an excellent way to be sure that no one else got information from them. Ray moved more quickly now.

He had to find her before it was too late.

Chapter Twenty

Morgan woke by slow degrees. First to the pain of her legs, cramped and alive with pins and needles. Next she recognized from the groan that tried to escape her that her mouth had been taped. With her eyes now opened, she found her vision clear but she could see nothing from under the camouflage-patterned vinyl tarp that covered her. The motor sound and the jostling alerted her to movement. Her best guess was that she rode in a cart fixed to a four-wheeler of some sort and that they were on an incline. It didn't take a genius to deduce why someone would steal her from her bed and drag her up a mountain. The trouble was the money was no longer here. Likely her captors would not know that because the FBI had not revealed that the money had been recovered. Instead, they told her, they let word out that she and Ray had admitted to finding the treasure and hiding it again before they were taken into custody.

Her abductor must want the treasure or she would already be dead. The trick would be to lead them to a treasure that was no longer here and stay alive until help arrived.

She was so grateful that her daughter was safely away. But how had her abductor managed to grab her right out from under the FBI surveillance? Or perhaps the FBI had let him take her. Were they following them? Either way,

the sun was well up judging from the light through the
tarp and the heat that made her entire body damp with
sweat. She was so thirsty. The need for water tormented
her far more than the pain in her hip and the tingling in
her legs. Now she had to figure out how to stay alive until
help reached her.

Ray. She spoke to him in her mind. Apologizing for
leaving him without thanks. He had not told her everything, but he had kept his word, protecting her and helping her retrieve the money. Once they found it, many men
would have just helped themselves. Ray had not done that.

Of course it was logical to assume that her father had
told her everything. But her father was wiser than that.
He'd tried to find a way to protect her from the men who
had hired him while still giving her the money. Hadn't
he known her well enough to understand that she would
never keep it?

Would Ray come after her or, with his mission complete, would he leave her to the wolves?

The cart hit a particularly vicious rock, sending her
airborne for just a minute before throwing her back down
to collide with the metal floor. The jolt got her moving,
searching beneath the tarp for something she could use as a
weapon or to cut the ties that secured her wrists behind her.

The forward motion stopped, sending her skidding
along the floor. The motor cut and Morgan held her breath.
Should she be unconscious or try to spring at him? Even
if she managed to knock him down, would she have time
to find something to cut her ties and run?

An instant later the tarp fell back and the brilliant sunlight poured down on her. She managed to look far woo-
zier than she was as her kidnapper lowered the rear gate.
He wore camo from his hood to his boots. Across his face
he had a camouflage mask, likely designed to make him

invisible to prey. Today it served to make him a faceless menace that froze her blood on this hot morning. Was it good that she couldn't identify him?

Perhaps.

She looked about for another attacker but found them alone.

Her captor tugged her out the back of the cart. She did not have to pretend that her legs would not support her and went down so fast he could only slow her descent. He swore and then retrieved a knife from his belt then cut the plastic at her ankles.

"Get up."

She didn't. Instead she sprawled on her stomach, hoping he'd cut the bonds at her wrists. But he used those bonds to tug her to a sitting position.

"Up!"

Morgan complied, but she had managed to rub her face over the sandstone. The tape across her mouth was now curled at one side.

"I know the others didn't find it," he said. He sounded Anglo to her and young. "I'm betting you did. Our man said he could be trusted. But then he goes off with you and finds it."

Ray, he was speaking of Ray. But why would this man think that Ray could be trusted? And who was their man?

"That's right. Your boyfriend was working for us all along. You really think we'd leave you for the FBI to question without knowing what your dad told you?"

Oh, no. That couldn't be. Ray had told her he was assigned by the Turquoise Guardians. Had that also been a lie?

Her captor grabbed her arm in a punishing grip. "You're going to show me where you hid it. No sense in leaving it out here to rot."

Morgan struggled to speak, making a series of muffled sounds.

"You don't need to talk to show me where it is. So get moving." He gave her a shove.

She staggered forward and then looked around. They were at the base of the upper ruins. She was staring right at the spiraling symbol marking the winter solstice. The sun had already reached the canyon floor and the shadow rock now served no purpose. Morgan thought. A plan came to her that was followed immediately by thoughts of all the ways it could go wrong.

But she had nothing better so she walked to the notched log that served as a ladder and she lifted her gaze to the upper ruins.

"I knew it. I was sure because he had me wait down past the turn. I followed your dad after I delivered the check to Rowe and again when he cashed it the next day. He drove down here in that heap of a pickup with the four wheeler in the back, but he was so quick and I was on foot."

Delivered the check? He was one of them, the eco-extremists.

"You're wondering why I didn't just take it from him before he drove up here, right?"

She hadn't gotten to that yet.

"Because he hadn't done the job yet. But really. What does a dead man need with all that money? Can't spend it."

He was one of them. A WOLF or a BEAR. She wanted to ask him what they were going to do with the explosives, the target, the FBI called it. But her mouth was taped shut.

So her father had come here with this man in tow, tapped out the clue in the chimney and they'd driven up here to bury the money at the base of the cliff.

Morgan put her foot on the notched log that lay at the base of the cliff.

"Okay. I gotcha." He lifted the ladder and propped it against the rock face. "Ladies first."

Was he kidding? She couldn't climb with her hands bound. Morgan turned her back and lifted her clasped wrists.

"Just so you know, I hid the only key to the four-wheeler and I'm packing heat. You try anything and you'll be bleeding all over this canyon."

She nodded her head in understanding, waiting. Next came the scrape of the knife leaving the sheath. He wouldn't kill her yet because he needed her to find the treasure but still her breath caught and held. He inserted the blade between her hands and tugged. The bonds fell away and she extended her cramped fingers, then rolled her wrists as the breath she held escaped into the dry air.

"Let's go," he growled.

Morgan marched to the ladder like a good little soldier, tugging at the gray duct tape as she went. Her skin tingled where the adhesive had clung. She was an excellent climber. And she needed to make the climb of her life now. Morgan placed a hand on the notch at eye level and mentally prepared herself. A rush of adrenalin flooded through her bloodstream making her heart pound and her ears buzz. But she held herself back, beginning the climb with a slow and careful focus. Then she felt the ladder shift, as he joined her on the climb. That instant Morgan took off, climbing with a speed that bordered on recklessness.

"Hey! Slow down."

She didn't of course, because she knew that he could not hold the ladder and a pistol. This would be her only chance. The people here before her knew something about defending against their enemies and he had inadvertently sent her to a stronghold perfect for defense.

Morgan reached the top of the ladder and used the niches carved in stone to scramble the last few feet up and over the ledge and onto the wide, flat plateau that formed the cavern floor. She did not pause as she ran to the forked branch resting inside the first room of the honeycomb of apartments. She would have only one chance at this. She dragged the branch behind her as she hurried to the edge.

Morgan threw herself to her stomach and extended the branch over the edge. Her kidnapper was already reaching for the niches in the stone.

"Hey. Don't!"

But she did, catching the top of the log in the notch and pushing. He made a desperate choice then, releasing the niche to scramble downward. Had he chosen to lurch upward he might have reached her. Instead he slid down the log as if it were an enormous fireman's pole. As a result, he was midway down the forty-foot log at something between a fall and a slide when she dislodged the ladder. It toppled with him still clinging to it like an ant on a blade of grass. She had to admire how he was able to get his feet under him and pushed off so that he was falling free and clear of the giant ponderosa trunk for the last ten feet. His landing was hard and simultaneous with the log. The dust rose but she could see him, sprawled on the loose shale and rock. He didn't move.

She took the opportunity to gather several stones from the broken wall, ignoring the thirst that had turned her tongue to sandpaper.

She knew her history. Knew that the upper ruins were known by outsiders as Apache Leap, the stronghold that none could find during the Apache Wars. But the Apache Scouts had discovered her people and brought the cavalry. General Crook had hurled boulders down on her ancestors. There was no room in the cavern for all of them. Caught between the falling stones and the cliff, many of the men, women and children had chosen to leap to their deaths.

Morgan dropped one stone from the wall at the edge of the cavern floor and then another. She checked. Her captor was not moving. Morgan briefly considered throwing them down on the fallen man, but she did not have the stomach for it. Such things marked the soul.

Instead she sat back to wait. The FBI might not know where she was, but Ray and Jack and Dylan would find her. She had confidence in Tribal Thunder. Were they on their way now?

She peered over the edge at the still form and prayed they would come soon.

Morgan missed Ray. True, she had faulted him for doing as his medicine society had asked him. What had he done to her really? Had it been a lie or had he just kept his secrets? She thought of Lisa's father who had deceived her and of how she had never told a soul about him, not even her father, until she had spoken the truth to Ray. But all those years she had kept silent. Wasn't she entitled to her secrets? Wasn't he?

He had been assigned to her protection. He had also been given an objective. And although she had been an assignment at first, she believed all that had changed the night they had slept here in this canyon. At least it had changed for her because against all her best judgment and her past experience, she had fallen in love with Ray. And she planned to tell him so. Now all she had to do was stay alive up here on the hot stone beneath the blazing sun with no water until he arrived.

Chapter Twenty-One

Ray and Dylan agreed on the tracks and followed them to the driveway of a neighbor. Chief Tinnin and FBI rousted the occupants but they had seen and heard nothing.

"We let it out that Morgan found the money and left it up in the canyon by the upper ruin," said field agent Cassidy Cosen.

Ray did not need any more information. He was already running for his truck.

"Wait," said Forrest. "We're getting four-wheelers from Tucson."

How long would that take? The machines were faster, but Ray had a trailer and two good horses that loaded well. Dylan swung up into the passenger side.

"We'll meet them," said Dylan.

It seemed to take forever to load the gear, horses and supplies. But both men knew better than to go into the canyon unprepared. The drive along Turquoise Lake to the lower ruins was only seven miles but it was insufferable to Ray who cursed at every slow-moving truck and each winding turn.

"It's not faster if you put us in a ditch," said Dylan.

Ray gritted his teeth and hunched over the wheel as they bumped into the lot and saw the sign that announced a permit was required to visit the ruins. Permits were necessary for outsiders, not members of their tribe. The lone blue pickup parked here did not display a permit but did have a residential parking permit for Phoenix affixed to its front windshield.

Ray pulled in beside the vehicle and threw his truck into Park and Dylan exhaled loudly as he released his hold on the overhead hand grip. They left the truck and met again behind the trailer. Ray swung the rear gate open.

"Look at that!" Dylan pointed skyward.

Ray glanced up and was rewarded by the sight of a canary-yellow hot-air balloon floating up and over Turquoise Lake.

"Is that today?" Dylan asked, referring to the semiannual hot-air balloon festival that began and ended off tribal lands but drifted over their airspace.

Ray had no time for hot air. The air down here was hot enough and he knew what this kind of heat could do to a person. Did she have water? He backed out the first mount, a gray gelding. Dylan followed a moment later with the chestnut with white stockings. They swung the blankets and saddles up in unison.

"You think about that Indian Relay Race at all?" asked Dylan.

Ray grunted and cinched the girth so tight the gelding groaned. He let the strap out a notch.

"'Cause I don't think those Brule Sioux have anything on Apache when it comes to horse racing."

Ray shook his head and loaded the water and pack on his mount. Next he checked his rifle and then slid it into the sheath and tied it to the D-ring on the front of the saddle. Finally, he swung up. They were off. After the lower ruins the trail wound up giving him glimpses of the dirt lot below. The outsider's vehicle and his truck and trailer were still the only vehicles parked there. If the FBI were coming, they certainly were taking their time. Ray looked forward now. He and Dylan were on their own. The trick would be to find Morgan and her kidnapper before he knew that they were there.

His ancestors had a fierce reputation as warriors. He and Dylan and Carter and Jack and Hatch were warriors, if modern ones. He was well trained and ready for a fight. But he'd never faced a foe with so much fear in his heart. If anything happened to Morgan, he would never forgive himself. He had to reach her soon. He had to bring her home to Lisa. Ray swallowed at the lump rising in his throat as he realized the terrible truth.

Somewhere along the way, he'd ceased to follow his shaman's orders and begun to follow the whispering of his heart. He loved her but with the dry air and relentless sun that might not be enough to keep her alive.

MORGAN SQUINTED AGAINST the harsh sunlight. The urge to move to the shade and relative cool of the cave lured but to do so was to lose sight of her captor. Unfortunately, to remain here at the rim in the rising heat of the day threatened her in other ways. She scanned the canyon floor for rescue but, seeing none, she despaired. The unrelenting heat of the rock rim at midday stole her strength, killing her bit by bit. Her head pounded and her tongue stuck to the roof of her dry mouth. Her pulse was too fast and she now struggled with dizziness. She tried to recall the last water she had tasted. Last night, a small swallow after brushing her teeth. If only she had known.

Morgan forced herself up and to the lip of the cave, where she discovered that the man was not only up but he was also heading to the four-wheeler and retrieving a rifle. If he intended to shoot her out of her cave, he had better have something more than a .38. He lifted the rifle stock to his shoulder and she drew back from the edge.

A moment later bullets pinged off the rock, peppered with some very colorful language. She did not reply to the barrage of bullets or foul names. She did move to the far side of the ledge, affording her a different view and the chance to see him before he spotted her. The man was up on his feet. He had removed the camouflage head cover and looked up at the place where the ladder had rested. She stared at the unfamiliar face. As she suspected from his speech, he was Anglo. His hair was light brown and short, his face fleshy with a jawline obscured in a double chin both of which were in need of a shave. Blood flowed in a steady stream from his cheek. His hands bled, likely from his rapid descent down the log and his clothing was coated in dust.

She did not want to hurt him but she also did not want to die of dehydration up on this ledge. She eyed the orange cooler strapped to the cart behind his four-wheeler. Then she searched down the canyon for any sign of rescue. Was Ray in one of those shiny beetle bright vehicles winding along the ribbon of road that threaded around Turquoise Lake?

Something above her caught her attention. Big and bright and yellow as a summer squash and rising in the blue sky. It was a balloon, the kind they launched for tourists from Goodwin Lake. Another appeared over the ridge of the canyon wall, this one had wide blue-and-red vertical stripes. When the rainbow balloon appeared she recalled the hot-air-balloon festival that took place each April. She and her father used to sit on the back porch and watch them float by. They could even hear the sound of the fire from the tanks that lifted the voluminous nylon up into the sky.

The sound of shoed horses brought her attention rap-

idly back to earth. But the source of it did not make sense.
Beyond this canyon lay miles of Mazatzal Mountains and
no easy access to roads or trails. A person would have to
ride up the parallel canyon and then circle back to reach
this place from the northwest. Morgan pushed up and away
from the lip of the canyon to get a better look at the riders. Hope rose but she knew that most of the tribe's horses
were not shod and she could clearly hear the steady clank
of horseshoes on stone.

Her abductor must have heard it as well because he lowered his rifle to listen and then swung the weapon toward
the two men who rode in line with a pack horse on a lead
following behind.

One rode a large chestnut and the other a piebald with
a white rump and black tail. The pack animal was a lath-
ered dun with a head hanging from fatigue. The riders
seemed easy in the saddle, dressed in jeans, boots and long
sleeved shirts. Their riding gloves and the broad cowboy
hats made it impossible for her to determine their ethnic-
ity or anything other than that they were of average build
and both carried rifles, sheathed and tied to their saddles.

"Gifford, you damned fool. You took off your mask?"

She judged the speaker to be the lead rider. His words
had an odd quality. Not muffled exactly but vibrating in
a way that did not seem quite natural.

Her abductor lowered his rifle and took two steps backward as if struck.

"Bleeding all over himself, too," said the second rider,
coming abreast of the first.

"I—I…" Gifford did not make a winning reply.

"Where is she?"

Gifford pointed and Morgan tensed. She did not draw
back from the lip but continued to stare down. The first
man glanced up at her and then the second. She frowned

as she tried to make sense of what she saw. They wore masks, the molded plastic kind. The first man wore a red fox mask and the second the likeness of a brown bear. A chill slithered up her spine.

"What did you tell her?"

"Nothin'. I swear. I just said she was going to take me to the money."

"What were your orders?" said Mr. Fox.

"Deliver the check to Rowe and return to base," said Gifford. His voice had taken on a tone of contrition showing weakness and submission. "I did that."

"You returned two days late," said Mr. Bear. "And now you're back up here."

Gifford's head hung and he did not meet the gaze of the animal spirit men that questioned him. "But she hid the money up here. I was going to get it back for us. For the cause."

Even from here, Morgan could smell the lie. Gifford had been acting for Gifford and now he was facing his superiors and the music.

"It's not our money. It was payment for a job that was completed," said Mr. Bear, glancing up at her.

Morgan shifted, trying to resist the urge to disappear from their sight.

"Your father wanted you to have that money, Morgan, you and your young daughter, Lisa."

She scowled, hating that they knew her name and the name of her daughter. The tiny hairs lifted on her body and for an instant, the blazing heat of the sun and the broiler that the flat rock beneath her had become were forgotten, as her skin went cold. It was a threat and she recognized it as such.

"Are you the ones who tried to take my daughter?" Her voice sounded strange, hoarse and scratchy.

The bear shook his head. "Not ours. Treasure hunter out of Tucson."

"But she has the money. It's up here," whined Gifford.

"But she doesn't. Kenshaw thinks she does. Not me. She's too honest. If she weren't, the Feds would still have her in custody. She cut a deal, sure as I live." Mr. Bear looked up at her through the two circular holes in his plastic mask. "You gave it all to the Feds. Didn't you? I would think a Tonto woman would have more sense than to trust the descendants of the men who stood on this cliff and hurled rocks down on your women and children." The man lowered his head, returning his attention to Gifford as he drew his rifle and rested the stock on his thigh.

"She didn't give it back. It's here," said Gifford.

"That's what they wanted you to believe," said Mr. Fox. "It's a lie and a lure and you swallowed it whole. I don't expect you to think for yourself—I expect you to follow orders. Did that oath you swore to our brothers in WOLF mean nothing?"

Was she looking down at two members of the extremists' branch of BEAR? Morgan began to tremble. Forrest had told her that these men made no effort to preserve human life in their quest to return the land to its natural state. They had the mining explosives and they had the only man who could identify them, one from among their own ranks, killed by her father's bullet.

"I'm sorry, Mr...." Gifford paused in mid-sentence as the man in the bear mask aimed his rifle at Gifford's head.

Gifford raised his hands in a gesture of surrender and defense. But flesh and bone is no shield against a bullet. The man in the bear mask fired. Morgan gave an involuntary shout as Gifford fell to his knees and then sprawled forward in the sand.

"Check him," said Mr. Bear, still aiming his rifle at the motionless, prone figure.

From her vantage point the scene seemed surreal, the effect amplified by being light-headed. Morgan's heart beat very fast but whether from the shock or from the unrelenting heat, she did not know. She gazed down on the smaller figures as the fox dismounted and checked for a pulse on Gifford's neck, kneeling, waiting and then shaking his head.

"Got him," said Mr. Fox.

"Greedy fool," said Mr. Bear as he sheathed his rifle. "He was about to say my name. They'll be questioning his father now. Have to cut him loose for a while. See if he's really one of us now."

Morgan imagined someone hurting Lisa. She would never give her allegiance to such a man.

Mr. Bear's gaze went to Morgan. She glanced toward the stack of rocks she'd collected. "Hot day, today, Ms. Hooke. I figure you have a few hours at best. If help comes in that time, you might survive. I do not plan to kill you because my sources say you do not know me or any of my compatriots."

She tried to speak but her tongue felt clumsy and thick in her mouth. Her spit was like paste. She cleared her raw throat and exhaled, knowing the dry air stole water from her lungs with each breath. She needed drink and the sight of the water strapped to the men's saddles tortured her.

"I don't know you," she said, her voice a rasp.

"Did your father name us?"

"No."

"He was a smart man and we owe him a debt. I'm sorry for your loss. You can take comfort in the knowledge that your father died for a great cause."

Her father died in a vain attempt to earn enough money

to support her and Lisa when she would have given it all
back again to spend just five more minutes with him.

"Time to go," said the fox.

The buzzing in her ears grew louder. Morgan looked
down at the two men in plastic masks and smiled. Why
did their smiling faces and long snouts seem so funny?

Her head pounded and she just wanted to rest and drink
water and ice tea and pink lemonade.

In her confusion, she almost crawled headfirst off the
cliff. She was also slow to recognize that the sound she
heard was not in her head but coming from down the canyon. A motor.

Mr. Fox mounted up.

"Farewell, Morgan Hooke," called Mr. Bear, touching
the brim of his hat. "I wonder if you will be alive to greet
your friends. Nature is a harsh taskmaster."

Then the two men turned their horses and retreated
back up the canyon.

"That's the wrong way," she whispered, knowing
they'd be trapped up there. That meant the FBI and possibly Tribal Thunder would have to face these two faceless
men in masks. She didn't want that.

Ray. She had to warn him to keep him away from Mr.
Fox and Mr. Bear.

Chapter Twenty-Two

The sound of the shot brought Ray to a halt. He rose in his stirrups to look up the trail but he could see nothing. They had stopped only once, to let the horses drink.

He glanced back to see Dylan looking up the canyon. He met Ray's gaze and nodded.

Ray pressed his heels into his gelding's sides and shot forward. He had the rifle out, gripping the stock as he guided his mount up the steep grade. They were only a few hundred yards from the ruins and Ray knew in his pounding heart that Morgan was there. Hope and dread blended like blood in water as he raced forward, praying and cursing in turns.

He barreled around the curve of the steep canyon wall as another hot-air balloon drifted over the gap in the stone above. Finally he sighted the cave and the ruins. An instant later he saw the still form lying at the base of the cliff. He pulled up on the reins as his heart seemed to rise into his throat, choking him and blurring his vision. Was it Morgan?

He urged his horse forward, the hoof beats landing with the rhythm of his heart. A man lay motionless in the sand, sprawled as if he had fallen from the upper ruins. Ray's head sank in relief as he recognized it was not Morgan.

Behind him, Ray heard the click of a cocking rifle. He

glanced forward and saw two mounted men. One aimed his weapon at Dylan, the other aimed at Ray. Their wide-brimmed hats shaded their faces but it seemed that they wore some grotesque, grinning animal masks. He glanced from one to the other, looking for Morgan.

Where was she?

"Mr. Strong. Mr. Tehauno," called one. "You are early."

"Where's Morgan?" shouted Ray. He gripped his weapon but did not raise it. Ray nudged his horse forward. "What have you done with her?"

"Nothing but stay out of range of her rocks." He pointed up to the cliff dwelling.

Ray saw an arm dangling over the ledge. He watched and saw no movement. He turned back to the men. "What's wrong with her?"

"Carelessness. Mr. Journey no doubt failed to see her properly hydrated. She was red faced when we arrived but I see now she has gone pale."

Dylan spoke up now. "If you've harmed her—"

"The heat has done that." The man in the mask of the bear turned to look through small circular eye holes at Ray. "So you have a choice. You can try and stop us or you can save yon maiden in her tower from the fiery sun dragon."

Ray sheathed his rifle. Then he was off his horse and running for the ladder cut from the pine trunk, water bottle in his hand. Dylan kept his rifle aimed as the two men set their mounts in motion. By the time Dylan joined him, Ray could see the two weaving up the steep grade that he knew led deeper into the box canyon.

"They'll be trapped up there," said Dylan.

The two men rode out of range as Ray reached the top of the ladder. There was a time when he might have thought twice about choosing not to stand his ground. But that was before a certain Apache woman had burrowed into his heart.

When he crested the top, holding the strap of the water bottle in his teeth, he found Morgan lying on her belly with her cheek on the hot stone cave floor. She wore a dirty powder-blue tank top and boy shorts that hugged her hips. Her legs sprawled out as if she had been bracing as she looked over the edge. Beside her was a pile of stones she had likely removed from the masonry of the dwelling walls for defense against the attack from below.

"Morgan!" She did not move or give any sign that she heard his cry.

He sank to his knees beside her and gripped her arm, finding it slack and hot. He rolled her limp form up off the hot stone and onto his lap. Her eyelids fluttered but her eyes rolled back in her head showing the whites. His panic swelled as he struggled to unscrew the wide black cap from the water bottle.

"Dylan! Bring all the water you can carry up here."

His friend shouted an affirmation.

Ray's hands trembled as he poured water over her head and ruffled her hair to be sure the water soaked her boiling head. Then he doused her shirt. Still she didn't move. He stripped out of his shirt, leaving him in only his straw cowboy hat, jeans and boots. He soaked his shirt and laid it across her forehead, soaking her hair. Then he lifted her and ran her back into the recesses of the cliff dwelling. How had she gotten away?

Her shirt was already dry. He soaked it again and then soaked her shorts. Her face remained an unnatural gray. He checked her pulse and his panic rose when he found her heart beat as fast as a captured bird's.

At the time of her birth Morgan would have been given a bead carved from an abalone shell. All Apache girls received such a bead, just as the boys received a similar one fashioned of turquoise. At the time of their death they would fly through the hole in the bead and to the world of spirits in less time than it took to blink an eye. Ray kept his bead in his medicine bundle. He did not know where a woman kept her bead, but he hoped it was now far, far away. He prayed aloud in the language of his ancestors for Morgan to linger here with him on earth. He made her promises that he knew she would not want him to keep, promises for a future together with a man who did not deserve her but loved her with his whole heart.

Dylan appeared wearing his saddlebags like a backpack and with a coil of rope over one arm.

"She's too hot," said Ray.

Dylan checked her by touching the back of his hand to Morgan's cheek. "We have to get her off this ledge."

"Cool her first. Take off your shirt. Soak it and put it on her legs." Together they continued to douse her with water. Her eyes fluttered but she did not rouse.

Dylan looked at Ray with an expression of a man who has not given up hope but is considering it.

"Dylan, I can't lose her, too."

His friend sucked in a breath. But if anyone could understand, it was Dylan. His friend knew Ray had lost his parents and his best friend. And by saying, too, Ray had lifted Morgan into the circle of those closest and most dear to his heart. Dylan's brow furrowed and he nodded.

"Soak her again," said Dylan.

"It's my fault," said Ray. "Just like the last time."

"That wasn't your fault. Neither is this."

Ray shook his head, feeling the moisture well in his eyes and knowing Morgan's poor little body was too hot and too dry to even cry. "If I hadn't deceived her, she wouldn't have gone to the FBI. I would have been there when that creep came for her."

"We got her, Ray. We'll get her down and get her evac'd out."

"If she dies…" He couldn't say it because he didn't know what he would do. What Lisa would do. He pressed one hand to his forehead and wept. "I love her. That's why she's going. Everyone I love…"

Dylan had him by the wrist and gave a jolting tug. Ray glanced at him. "We need to get her down. They'll be here any minute. They have the four-wheelers. But we have to move."

Ray stood, carrying Morgan in his arms.

"Too dangerous to climb. We need to lower her down." Dylan released the ties that held the bedroll from his back. They wrapped Morgan and soaked her and the blanket with the last of the water. Then they tied the rope around her. Ray stood back to brace himself as he wrapped the rope around his back. Dylan eased Morgan over the edge and gradually released the rope, allowing Ray to take her weight. Ray kept the rope around his back and used one gloved hand to slow Morgan's descent by pressing the rope down and around the inside of his thigh. Gradually he let the rope slide through his hands. Dylan called out her progress. When he slid halfway down, Ray pictured Morgan there, wrapped in a brightly colored Pendleton blanket, twisting between heaven and earth. It was a good place for a soul to slip free and that thought made him want to hurry her down, but he forced himself to go slowly, letting the rope go inch by inch.

"I'm going down. I'll tug when I have her." Dylan disappeared over the edge leaving him with his fears and the diminishing coil of rope.

He looked at the unforgiving sky and watched the hot-air balloons floating peacefully past on the currents of hot air. He could even see some of their passengers looking down at the life-and-death struggle visible beneath their baskets. Then he looked higher. There above the tops of a colorful collection of balloons and beneath the burning sun soared an eagle. Where once the eagle had helped him see far and true. Now all he could see was Morgan's hot face and his dreams of a future with her floating away on the currents of hot air.

Chapter Twenty-Three

Ray felt the tug on the rope that told him Morgan was safely in Dylan's arms. He eased off the tension and then moved to the edge to look to the canyon floor.

"She's hot again. And her clothing is already dry."

They needed to get her back to the spring some three hundred yards down the canyon. Ray dropped the rope and hurried down using the niches that angled through the V that formed the last few feet of the climb to the cliff dwelling. As he went he pictured the ancient ones, men, children and women with baskets upon their heads, carrying loads to their sky home. When he lost his grip with one toe, he found himself hanging from his arms only. Ray regained his footing and forced himself to slow down. If he fell, Dylan would be forced into making some tough choices.

He heard the whirring motor of a drone. The flying camera appeared a moment later, looking like a mechanical dragonfly. He did not pause as he continued down the wooden log ladder. The drone hovered, tilted, sank. Then it swooped close to the man that the riflemen shot in the head. Ray did not know if the drone had a microphone but Dylan was speaking to it and using gestures that Jack could interpret and that Agent Forrest likely could, as well. Those gestures had been the way to communicate with other tribes in the southwest when they did not share a common language. Ray's education had included learning these signs and now he was grateful for that. Dylan explained that they needed medical assistance and that the man at the foot of the cliff had been killed by the armed men. He pointed up the canyon and told the heartless flying eye which way they went. The drone lifted and zipped up the canyon disappearing from sight as Ray reached the canyon floor.

"Help should be close," said Dylan.

Ray knelt beside Morgan. Her red face frightened him. The color of her cheeks reminded him of the candy apples sold at fairs and rodeos. Was it better that her skin was no longer gray?

"That's the last of my water," said Dylan. "Are you going to make a travois and carry her or wait for Jack?"

"We aren't waiting," said Ray, scooping Morgan up in his arms and heading for his horse. "Cinch him for me. Will you?"

Dylan readied his horse.

"Your body heat will just make her hotter," he warned.

He knew that. But he'd be damned if he'd let her go. He let Dylan lead and then cursed at the slow pace Dylan set. Always the perfectionist, Dylan chose the safest, but not the fastest, route to the spring. At last Ray spotted the lush green of the grasses and reeds that benefitted from year-round water. He handed Morgan down to Dylan but caught up with him before he reached the spring and relieved him of his precious cargo.

"I won't drop her," Dylan promised.

Ray needed to get Morgan cooled. He splashed into the gurgling water muddying the hole. The horses did not care. They had followed and were now pawing at the mud before drinking as horses did. A survival reflex, perhaps to see the area clear of snakes. Ray sat in the water supporting Morgan. Her arms floated out and her dark hair billowed up around her head. He kept her down so that only her face and hands broke the surface. There he waited, keeping an eye on her.

Thank God this canyon had a spring. Most were dry and he knew what would have happened then. Morgan's blood would have grown thicker and thicker as the dry air stole more moisture from her skin and lungs. Then her organs would fail. First her kidneys and liver and finally her heart. That beautiful, kind and willing heart.

"Morgan, darling," he whispered. "Come back to me. Come back, sweetheart. I love you. Let me have just one chance to prove it to you."

Dylan stood with the horses, watching Ray hold the weightless woman who floated like a water spirit.

"Stay," he whispered. "For Lisa and for me. We need you."

Her fingers moved, curling and then extending. Her limp body regained a more natural muscle tone. His breathing was fast now, nearly as fast as hers. Morgan's eyelids fluttered and this time he saw her beautiful brown eyes as she gazed up at the sky.

"Ahh," she said and lifted an index finger.

He followed the direction of her gaze and saw a hot air balloon with a blue, yellow and red chevron pattern followed by one that was shaped like a gigantic butterfly and a third that resembled the head of the blue Cheshire cat.

She smiled, following the floating parade with only her eyes. Her hand dropped back into the spring water.

"Morgan? Sweetheart?" Ray kept one hand on the middle of her back and swept the hair from her forehead. "Can you hear me?"

Her gaze shifted to him and a line formed between her

brows. Confusion or disappointment? He was not certain but she continued to stare.

"Ray?"

"Yes!" He laughed. He had been so afraid the heat would damage her brain, sending her into that spiral from which there was no return.

"Lisa?" She struggled now to get her feet under her with clumsy, weak thrashing.

"Lie still. Lisa is safe. She's with the FBI. Remember?"

"The men." She continued to struggle, so Ray eased her up, dragging her onto his lap.

Dylan left him and the horses who continued to suck up the water in noisy slurps. Ray listened and heard the four-wheelers but the reeds and high green grass blocked his view of their approach. He heard them pause and heard Dylan speaking but could not make out what was said over the engine noise.

"They're gone," said Ray. "The man who took you is gone, too."

"Dead," she said and pinched her eyes closed. She pressed a hand to her forehead. "They said you...worked for them."

He scowled. He wasn't working for the ones the FBI were chasing. Was this some delusion her confused mind had created?

The motors revved and the four-wheelers moved on. Dylan reappeared.

"Didn't you tell them we need help?" asked Ray.

Dylan gave him a certain look that Ray read as annoyance.

"I did but they barely slowed down. Seems catching those men is a higher priority."

Ray seethed. Morgan had put her faith in those agents and they had failed to keep her safe, had endangered her life, been too slow to get to her and now they left her here when just one of those four-wheelers could bring her into town in less than an hour.

"I'm glad I didn't take the test," said Dylan.

"What test?"

"They recruited me after I left the service. And a few times after that."

"You never told me that," said Ray.

Morgan lifted her hands to brush back her short crop of hair. She looked so different with her bangs swept back to reveal her high forehead and widow's peak.

"How do you feel?"

"Dizzy. Nauseous. I'm trying not to puke."

Her color had changed from hot pink to a greenish gray. Ray had seen enough in Iraq to recognize a person who was at risk of going into shock. He wanted to give her water, but was afraid. He knew she needed to be conscious and the shock dictated against letting her drink.

"Horses," said Dylan. His friend disappeared through the grass.

Ray leaned in and kissed Morgan's cheek. "You have to stick with me. You're strong. Stay awake."

"Vision is funny…like looking down a hole."

Tunnel vision. Her body began to grow slack again as she slipped into the swoon.

"Morgan!" He shook her. Her head lolled forward and against his chest. He had to get her to a hospital. Ray stood, still holding her in his arms, and charged out of the spring to find three horsemen: Jack, tribal police chief Tinnin and Jack's younger brother, Kurt Bear Den. Kurt was a paramedic for the air ambulance, and Ray had never been so glad to see a person in his life.

Kurt was already off his horse and reaching for his bag.

"Put her there," Kurt ordered, motioning to the shady side of the canyon.

Within short order, Kurt had Morgan's arm sterilized and an IV inserted. Ray didn't know what was in the clear sack of fluid that Kurt ordered him to hold in the air. All that mattered was that it was moving from the transparent bag and into Morgan's body. Ray lifted his head to the sky and began to sing a prayer for the return of Morgan's spirit to him.

Above, the messenger to the creator circled on the currents of air.

The golden eagle was back, soaring with his prayers.

Chapter Twenty-Four

Morgan woke in the ambulance and again as they loaded her into the helicopter. Later on, she recalled the emergency room with the blinding white lights and the headache that shot pain behind her eyes.

"I'm her husband."

She knew that voice. But she did not have a husband. *Ray. Of course.* He was so good at lying she almost believed him. Almost believed he cared. Almost believed she would have married him. Almost.

Somehow her past and the deceptions of Lisa's father had taught her nothing.

Her legs cramped and the pain made her cry out. Someone gripped her hand.

"I'm here, Morgan."

Her body ached as if she had the flu. This time when the dizziness came she welcomed it, throwing herself into the darkness to escape the torment of her body.

When she woke again she was lying as still as a corpse with her hands carefully placed on either side of her body, which was draped in a white bedsheet. Above her head a muted light shone down on her. Her body felt cold and something moved beneath her, like water.

For a moment she thought she was on a slab in the morgue.

The sounds flooded in next, followed by the beep of the machine that recorded her heartbeat and the noise from the corridor outside her room. She breathed out her relief.

She had been in a hospital bed once before, after Lisa was born. She had delivered her child herself, alone, in the studio apartment in Tucson. Then called the ambulance because she was afraid for Lisa. Her last visit to the hospital had been the final time she had seen her father. What would he say if he knew what his deed had caused?

The tears slid down her cheeks and she smiled. She could cry again. That meant she was no longer dry as the desiccated bodies of those who venture into the arid wilds without enough water.

Now she heard the sound of a pump and then the sensation of movement beneath her again. Some kind of cooling pad, she decided and closed her eyes. She moved just her arms, bending them to lace her fingers over her middle and the machine beside her started to wail.

She glanced at the upright IV. She shifted and felt the tug that told her she had both a catheter and something else down there beneath the clean white sheets. She winced and something like a growl escaped her.

She caught movement to her left and shifted her gaze. Two men stood in a silhouette against the blue glass of the window. They stepped forward into the light. Ray Strong and Detective Jack Bear Den, she realized.

"Keep that arm straight, darlin'," said Ray.

Darling. She smiled and complied then closed her eyes. Was she his darling? That was good, wasn't it? But no. Her smile ebbed. He brushed away the trails of the tears that fell from the corners of her eyes to soak into the hair at her temples. His touch was so gentle and so sincere, or was that just her trying to see only what she wished to see instead of what was.

She opened her eyes and stared up at Ray.

With Lisa's father, her love had been as foolish and childish and immature as the bud of a rose. An infatuation that would not have lasted even if he had been all he had claimed. But for Ray she had the love of a woman, full and lush and blooming. Despite what she knew of him and his flaws, she had tumbled into a love so strong that it ached to look at him. But now she was faced with a terrible choice. She could love him and protect him, even from his friend who was a detective. Or she could love him and do what was right for her tribe and reveal what he was, a man working for BEAR.

"Hi," said Ray, lifting her hand as if she were made of glass. She felt like that, somehow. Fragile with a heart cold and yet still beating. "You gave us all a scare. But you're doing better. And your core temperature is dropping." He motioned to one of the monitors. Then he drew up a chair and sat on the edge.

Core temperature? She shifted and decided that was one of the intrusions she felt.

Ray seemed so concerned and attentive. She stared at his handsome face. The money was gone. So why was he still here?

Hope flared like a shooting star and just as quickly winked out. The words of her abductor bubbled up like road tar. *"Your boyfriend was working for us all along. You really think we'd leave you for the FBI to question without knowing what your dad told you?"*

She looked at him and wondered if she could just pretend. Pretend she didn't know he had deceived her. Pretend he would stay. Her gaze shifted to the form looming behind Ray. Detective Bear Den loomed like a menacing dark angel, his thick brows sinking over his green eyes.

"I'd like..." She stopped speaking because her voice

was nearly unrecognizable, just the scratching of dry sticks against each other, more rasp than speech.

"Just rest," said Ray. "You're safe. Lisa's safe. I'm so relieved. I was afraid I was going to lose you there."

Either Ray was deceiving her or someone close to him was using him. *Our man*, Gifford had said. Who was close enough to Ray that he would trust him implicitly? Her gaze turned to Detective Jack Bear Den, his grim visage now suddenly seemed a threat.

"Water," she said.

"Not yet. They said they have to be sure you are fully conscious." Ray lifted the call button someone had tied to the raised rail of her bed and depressed the plastic button. In a few minutes, the nurse appeared. Her gray hair was pulled back from her fleshy face and her hot-pink top was covered with Disney princesses in a rosy color repeated in her scrub bottoms and again with her rubber-soled clogs, also pink. Her stethoscope dangled from her pocket and held her ID card.

"Well, look who's awake," said the nurse. "I'm Kathy. We met when you came on my floor."

Morgan didn't remember. Kathy asked the men to step out. Ray refused.

The nurse put her hands on her wide hips and made a face but seem resigned. It seemed to Morgan that they had had this conversation before.

"Ray, please," Morgan whispered.

His eyes widened and his expression changed to something close to pain. She felt the stab of guilt. He was tired, dirty and needed a shave. His clothing was rumpled and he had circles under his eyes. He looked as if he'd been dragged all the way down the canyon behind his horse. But what she saw most clearly was the shock of her wanting his absence.

"Just for a minute," she said, her voice still not seeming her own.

He pressed his lips together and nodded. Then he trailed his friend from the room.

Here was her chance. She could ask the nurse to call Luke Forrest and tell him all that Gifford had told her. She could point her finger at Ray and tell them that he was no better than her father, helping those extremists. Or she could trust her heart.

That heart had been wrong before and disappointed so often. She barely had the courage to listen. But she closed her eyes and tried. And there it was. Against reason and against evidence to the contrary, she believed in Ray and what that horrible man had said changed nothing. She loved Ray and she would give him his due. Love and trust were two inseparable entities. You could not have one without the other.

Kathy checked the monitors and listened to Morgan's heart. Then she raised the bed so Morgan was sitting up.

"Your husband is as stubborn as a potbellied pig I once owned," said Kathy.

"My husband?"

The nurse glanced toward the empty door. "I knew it." She turned pale blue eyes back on Morgan. "Between the FBI and that detective and Mr. Strong, I just didn't have the energy." She snorted. "He's cute though and very devoted to you. I think he'd like to be your husband. You could do worse. That's certain."

Kathy returned her attention to her patient. When she finished, Morgan had been thoroughly mauled but she now had nothing but the IV and heart monitors attached to her body.

"They won't tell me anything, of course. No one ever does. But I have to tell you that I could not get that other one, Mr. Strong, to leave the room. My friend in the ER said that he was impossible in the ER and ignored the Critical Care Unit ICC rules about visiting hours."

"How long have I been here?" asked Morgan.

She glanced at a digital watch with a wide pink strap. "You came in yesterday and onto my floor a few hours ago. It's 5:00 p.m. on Tuesday and you're in Phoenix."

"Phoenix?" She had assumed she was in the small community hospital in Darabee.

"Yep. If you are in pain, I can give you something," said the nurse.

Morgan shook her head. This was not the sort of pain she wanted numbed. It was more a confusion over her feelings for Ray. She knew his reputation and what he thought of himself. But that man and the man she knew were two different people. She drew a breath, filling her lungs with sweet cool air and a sense of hopeful optimism that most would think foolish and others would call reckless. She wanted to tell Ray how she felt and see if she could convince him to stay with her and Lisa, to see if they might grow into a family.

"I need to speak to Ray. Alone,"

The nurse paused and lifted her thin brows.

"I do not want the detective or the FBI back in here," said Morgan.

Her nurse could not have been much over five feet tall but the iron in her expression and the confidence in her smile made Morgan believe that she was up for that challenge.

"I'll have that detective get some ice chips. You have FBI outside your door, too. They might be able to hear you talking."

Kathy offered Morgan ice water from a plastic cup with a straw. Nothing had ever been quite as welcome as that first sip. It soothed her raw throat. She felt it glide down her esophagus and all the way to her stomach.

"Slow at first," said Kathy. "Let's see how that sits."

It seemed to arrive in her stomach like moisture to a dry sponge. She felt no discomfort so Kathy let her have the rest.

"You've had a lot of intravenous fluid, so you should be feeling much better. Are you hungry?"

Morgan nodded.

"I'll see about getting you something to eat. I have lemon ice at my station. Best start with that."

Kathy spun with military efficiency and reversed course past the empty bed beside Morgan's and out the door. Her voice was clear as she ordered Jack Bear Den to follow her.

A moment later, Ray appeared, peeking in at her and then casting her a welcome smile that was as cheerful as a spring bouquet. His eyes sparkled and the smile masked the fatigue on his features.

"How you feeling?"

She motioned him forward, causing the IV in her arm to throb. He moved to her side and took hold of her hand, his thumb stroking her skin. The tingle that followed the simple touch was unexpected and as welcome as July rain.

"That man who took me?" she whispered in Tonto Apache.

Ray's smile vanished and he looked suddenly forbidding and fierce.

"He's dead, Morgan. He can't hurt you ever again."

"I know. I saw those men kill him."

Now his thick brows sank low over his dark eyes. "You saw them?"

"Did they catch them?"

He shook his head and leaned closer, matching her quiet tones. "No. The FBI pursued them to the end of the canyon. They found a lean-to with their horses and a half-full plastic water trough for their livestock but no sign of the men. They asked Jack to go up there with Chief Tinnin to have a look. Best they can figure from the tracks and the spikes they found was that those two had a hot-air balloon waiting. With it, they just drifted up into the hot-air-balloon festival and floated to Phoenix with the rest of the participants.

"Could you identify them?" asked Ray.

She shook her head. "They wore gloves and masks."

His shoulders sagged with visible relief. "Thank God."

"The one who took me."

"Gifford Journey," Ray spat the name. Then he called him a name that made Morgan's ears heat. "May he find no peace in the grave."

"He wanted me to show him where we put the money," she said.

"That's what they wanted, wasn't it? The FBI? To use you to get to them. You could have died." Ray's face flushed and his free hand gripped the bed rail so tight his knuckles turned white.

He'd been against her working with the FBI. She'd shut him out. She hadn't trusted him and as a result she'd almost left her precious daughter an orphan. She might have been just like Ray had been, alone, vulnerable and left to the tribe to place.

"I'm so sorry, Ray."

He sank to his knees. "No. Don't be. You're safe. Lisa is safe."

"But they didn't catch them. It was all for nothing."

"They have their horses. Maybe some physical evidence. They have the Gifford connection. He'll lead them somewhere. They've called in his father, Renzo Journey, for questioning. His father owns a stone and gravel business in Carefree."

Now Morgan squeezed Ray's hand. The weariness dragged on her as her body demanded rest. But she had to tell him the rest.

"Ray, the man who took me, he said that they had a man on the inside. He called him 'our man.'"

Ray loomed over her. For just a moment she reconsidered telling him what Gifford had said to her. What if the inside man was Ray?

"Where?" Everything about him had turned hard and dangerous.

She swallowed back her trepidation but her heart monitor betrayed her, beating at a faster pace. It was not too late to turn back, but she wouldn't. She had to know the truth.

"I don't know who. He just said, *'Our man.'* He said something like that you could be trusted because 'their man' told them to trust you."

"Me?" He pointed a finger to his chest. "I could be trusted?" He glanced past the empty bed beside her to the open door. "We have to tell Jack," said Ray.

Morgan shook her head. "What if it's him, the one they called our man?"

Ray's eyes narrowed. She knew what he was thinking. He trusted Jack with his life. But Morgan barely knew him.

"It's not Jack."

"How do you know?"

"The same way you know it's not me."

She stared at him in silence as her skin prickled with apprehension.

"What else did he say?"

"That you had been working for them all along. And that they were not stupid enough to leave me alive to talk to the FBI without knowing everything my father had told me first."

His eyes widened and his mouth dropped open for a moment before he clamped it shut so tight the muscles at his cheeks bulged. Then he took a step closer before pausing to glance back at the door. In the hallway, his friend Jack waited with the FBI agent stationed to guard her.

"Morgan, I'm not the inside man and if they have one, I don't know who it is." He waited in total stillness as she met his gaze.

She didn't have any special powers to divine the truth. She knew only that she wanted to believe him. But her daughter's safety was also at stake. That made her hesitate.

"I know that you have had some men lie to you, trick you and even use you. Kenshaw Little Falcon did ask me to discover what you knew of your father's dealings with the eco-extremists. He's my shaman, Morgan. I'm sorry if I hurt you."

She wanted, no longed, to believe him.

"I don't know what to do."

"Believe me," he begged. "Believe in me. You won't be sorry."

She wouldn't survive it, another deception, because this time she knew that she loved Ray foolishly and totally. If he broke her heart, there would be nothing left. Before, with that married man who had deceived her, it was her pride that had suffered. She had lost an infatuation and a fantasy. Now she faced much greater stakes. If she didn't believe him, she would lose him. If she did believe him and he was deceiving her, she would lose him, too.

She nodded. "What should we do?"

His eyes closed and he placed his hand over them rubbing outward as if to eradicate the memory of this near miss.

"You believe me?" he asked.

"I do."

He lifted his head from his hands and watched her. "Why?"

She couldn't tell him it was because she loved him. She knew Ray was fond of her and was attracted to her. But neither of those meant that he loved her or that he planned to stick around after this was over.

Morgan cleared her throat and went halfway there. "I believe you because I believe my heart. I have to."

He leaned forward, pressing his forehead to hers. "Thank you. I'll see that you never regret it."

"But if you didn't know, then that means someone very close to you is using you."

The growl began in Ray's throat and leaped out as a roar.

"Jack!" he bellowed.

"No, wait," she said. But it was too late because the big man entered at a fast walk, one hand on his pistol as he swept the room for signs of a threat.

If Ray was wrong and Jack was the inside man, then Morgan was now facing the person that the eco-extremists had placed on the inside.

Chapter Twenty-Five

Morgan blew out a breath, refusing to let the fear gobble her up. She had to trust Ray's belief in Jack because if she didn't, this nightmare might never end.

And once it did, well then she could keep Ray.

Morgan sank back in her bedding. That was it. Her stupid, deluded attempt to keep Ray meant that she couldn't ever be safe. Because once she was, his mission from their shaman was complete and he could leave her.

Morgan squeezed her eyes shut, ashamed at the coward she had become.

Ray met Jack at the door and the two stepped out in the hall before her door. She could hear outside Ray's voice speaking Tonto Apache and Jack's reply, a low gruff whisper. What were they saying?

She needed to tell her tribal police everything. Tell the FBI everything. Help them catch these men, whose plans were unknown but involved a great deal of explosives. Then she would get Lisa back and have to tell Ray goodbye.

The nurse came and went, bringing a tray with Italian lemon ice, gelatin, coffee and apple juice. Morgan closed her eyes to savor that first spoonful of ice.

"How's that?" asked her nurse.

"Mmmm... Thank you."

"I'd like to have you take a walk around the floor in a little while."

"Sounds good."

The nurse promised to order her some real food and left, passing Ray at the foot of the empty bed beside Morgan's. Behind him came Detective Bear Den. Morgan told the detective just what she had related to Ray.

Jack Bear Den cleared his throat. "If it's not you, Ray, or me, then there are only two other possibilities."

"Dylan and Kenshaw Little Falcon," said Ray. "It can't be Dylan."

Jack nodded. "I agree. But if it is not Dylan, then it means that our shaman and the leader of Tribal Thunder is working for these extremists and it's my duty to arrest him."

"I need to speak to field agent Forrest," said Morgan.

"Already on his way," said Bear Den. The detective glanced to Ray. "I've got to go. This is my best shot to bring him in before the FBI gets to him. If they take him while he's not on reservation land, I might never get a chance to get to the bottom of this."

Ray nodded and Jack turned to Morgan. "Thank you for your help, Morgan. I'll be in touch."

Ray walked him out but returned in a few minutes and took a seat beside her bed.

"You're staying here?" she asked.

"Until I know you're safe."

"But the man who sent you to watch over me might be the man they're all after. In which case, you don't have any obligation to stay here with me."

"You're wrong there."

"Am I?"

He nodded.

"Why are you staying?"

"Because you still need me."

Morgan's mouth twisted at that. This was not the answer she longed to hear.

"I'm not your responsibility anymore. The FBI is protecting me now."

He leaned forward in the chair at the side of her bed and gave her a long, hard stare. "Are you asking me to leave?"

"No."

"Good. Because I'm not going. Not anytime soon."

She told her foolishly thrumming heart that Ray was staying out of some sense of honor. Not love, she reminded herself.

"If Kenshaw did what you claim, he'll answer for it. But he was right about one thing. You need someone to watch over you and for now, that someone is me."

THE FBI HAD not wanted Morgan to leave her room but she had been up to use the bathroom a few times. Dinner had helped give her some much needed energy. Ray said the color was coming back to her cheeks.

That evening Dylan appeared with a change of clothing for Ray and some other necessities. His mother had also sent Morgan a simple two-piece camp dress for her to wear home. All Apache camp dresses consisted of a loose long-sleeved blouse and modest ankle-length skirt. The outfit was cool cotton and colorful. This one was royal blue and had a lemon-yellow rickrack on both yoke and which repeated around the skirt.

"She'd heard about what happened and wanted Morgan to have something clean for the journey home. This was my sister's. She wore it when she was mentoring Paula Fields on her sunrise ceremony."

It was a very thoughtful gift.

"That's nice. We'll see it gets back to your mom."

"I'll bring it in to her, all right?"

Ray trusted Dylan to keep watch over Morgan while he stepped out for a few minutes.

"I've never seen him like this," said Dylan.

"Like what?" asked Morgan.

Dylan grinned. "In love, Morgan. Hasn't he told you?"

Her heartbeat blipped louder on the monitor as she shook her head in denial.

"You're wrong, Dylan. He is just worried about me."

Dylan's boyish grin remained. "If you say so."

"Knock. Knock," said a male voice from outside the room. A moment later field agent Luke Forrest entered with his partner, Cassidy Cosen.

Dylan lifted his phone and called Ray who appeared before Forrest had finished the pleasantries of asking how Morgan was feeling. Cassidy told her that Lisa was well and passed on a letter from her.

"I have a daughter. She just turned thirteen," said Agent Cosen.

Thirteen was an important age for Apache girls and Morgan knew Cassidy Cosen's daughter was Black Mountain Apache. Some of Morgan's friends had even attended her daughter's sunrise ceremony because the invitations had been sent far and wide.

Morgan accepted the letter with thanks and was reading the contents when Ray reappeared. She finished and pressed the page to her chest over her heart.

"Can I speak to her?" Morgan asked Agent Forrest.

"You can see her," said Luke. "Just as soon as you're released, which we think will be tomorrow."

"What about protection?" asked Ray.

"Not necessary. We have credible intel that Morgan and Lisa are no longer in danger."

"What intel?" asked Dylan.

"I'm afraid I'm not at liberty to say. But we believe that the men Morgan met in the canyon are satisfied that Morgan is ignorant of their identity and does not know who hired her father to murder Sanchez."

Agent Cosen spoke up. "That means she does not need our protection or the US Marshals Service to provide witness protection. She's not a witness to anything and her father wisely told her nothing."

Forrest took over. "All of the money has been recovered and we have advised the public of this with a press conference. You can see it on the local news again at eleven."

"What about the police in Darabee? Chief Rowe can't have been alone over there," asked Dylan.

"Very good, Mr. Tehauno. I really was serious about recommending you for the FBI. I wish you'd consider my suggestion to apply."

Ray's friend flushed and nodded.

"To answer your question," said Cassidy Cosen, "it's an ongoing investigation. We can't discuss that. But we can say that we are as certain as possible that it is safe for Ms. Hooke to go home. We'll keep the agent here overnight as a courtesy and escort her back to Turquoise Canyon tomorrow."

"Are you still using her as bait?" said Ray.

"Absolutely not," said Forrest.

Ray and Dylan exchanged a look and Ray nodded his acceptance of the FBI's assurances.

Morgan waited for either Dylan Tehauno or Ray to mention their suspicions about Kenshaw Little Falcon. She would not be the first. Accusing a man of such a thing was serious but made more so by the fact that he was a fellow tribe member. She knew that tribal matters were often handled by the tribal courts and Detective Bear Den was on his way to speak to him. It was rare that a member of their tribe was turned over to the state for prosecution and she could not think of one instance where a tribe member was given to federal custody.

The FBI departed and Morgan asked Ray about it.

"I'm giving Jack time to speak to Kenshaw. We'll let the Feds know in the morning and I'll be here until then."

She had Ray for one more night and she was going to be spending it in a hospital bed. What a waste.

Morgan made a promise to herself. The next time she and Ray were alone, she would reveal her true feelings. He had told her that he was not the kind of man to settle down. Morgan prepared to have her heart broken once more but her fears would not muzzle her because the only thing more frightening than telling Ray that she loved him was not telling him.

Chapter Twenty-Six

Ray spoke with Luke Forrest the following morning in the hallway outside Morgan's room while she met with the nurse to sign her release papers. Forrest informed him that Gifford's father, Renzo Journey, was a suspect and under FBI surveillance. "He didn't send his son after Morgan, but we are fairly sure that Gifford got his information from his father and then acted alone."

"How did the other men in BEAR find out what Gifford was up to, then?"

"We believe that Renzo notified them."

Ray digested that. The FBI believed that Renzo had turned over his own son to BEAR. He must have known what would happen. He glanced at Forrest. The lowered brow and the perfect clarity of his expression told Ray that was exactly what had happened.

"I'd never turn over my own son," said Ray. Not that he had a son. He glanced toward Morgan's room and wondered briefly if she wanted more children. Lisa was fast becoming a teenager. Her daughter would be more like an auntie than a sibling. Changing diapers while raising a teenager wouldn't be easy. Ray rubbed his neck.

"Strong?"

He turned his attention back to Forrest.

"I was saying that Morgan is in no danger."

"How can you be sure of that?"

"Not at—"

Ray finished the familiar refrain. "Liberty to say. I know." Ray scrubbed his knuckles over the stubble on his jaw. "Well you won't mind if I stick around awhile to be sure."

"Gifford is dead. The money is gone. A representative of BEAR told her that she's safe. What do you want, a certificate? You're done, Ray. I'm sure your shaman will tell you the same. Go home."

That was just it. He didn't have a home. He had a trailer up near the lake. He had a tribe and friends and the Yeagers who treated him like a son. But until he'd met Morgan, he had not realized that he did not have a home. And he wanted one. With her. Trouble was he had no cause to stick around.

He knew Kenshaw would tell him to lay off it, if Jack hadn't arrested their shaman.

"What about Jefferson Rowe?" asked Ray.

"Awaiting trial. He can't hurt her."

Ray wondered about one other threat. Ironically, it was the very same man who had sent him to Morgan. Worse, he was a fellow member of their tribe. Ray was not going to point the finger at his shaman and the leader of Tribal Thunder no matter what Jack thought Kenshaw had done.

But what if not speaking endangered Morgan?

"What?" asked Forrest.

"Detective Bear Den had some concerns about…" Ray could not believe he was doing this. But if Kenshaw was dirty, he did not deserve protection. And Ray disagreed with Jack on one matter. Jack wanted to keep housecleaning on site. While Ray thought they might need an outside contractor.

"Concerned about?" echoed field agent Forrest.

"About how much inside information Kenshaw Little Falcon has on BEAR and WOLF."

"Concerns?" Forrest's impatience morphed into a look that showed apprehensions of his own.

"Kenshaw sent his brother down to Lilac to fetch his niece before the Lilac mass shooting. He sent me to Morgan just before it became known that her father hid all that money."

"Why don't you let us handle that?"

"Too late. Jack is still angry that he lost his twin brother, Carter, to witness protection. He said he's going to arrest our shaman and bring him to tribal police for questioning."

Luke Forrest had his phone out before Ray had even finished speaking.

"He can't," said Forrest.

"Why not?"

Forrest pressed his lips closed. He lifted his phone and used it to point at the agent guarding Morgan's door. "Gutherie will see you to the border of the reservation." Then he stalked away. Ray heard him issuing orders into his phone. He caught two words—*cover* and *blown*.

His brows lifted. Was Kenshaw working with the FBI? That, however, did not explain how he knew the plans of BEAR and WOLF before anyone else. It did explain why the FBI would want him as an informant.

Ray recalled that in February, after the shooting, Kenshaw and Carter Bear Den had been detained for questioning. Carter had gone into protection. Kenshaw had been released. Now he understood why. And Jack was going to arrest Kenshaw. That would certainly jeopardize any future intel Kenshaw might provide. And it might also endanger Kenshaw's life.

Ray lifted his phone and dialed. Jack picked up on the second ring.

"What?" asked Jack.

"Where are you?"

"Eating breakfast with Kurt at Mom's. Why?"

"You see Kenshaw?"

"Missed him last night. But I know where he'll be today," said Ray.

"Don't go."

"What? Why?"

"Trust me. Leave it for now. I'll explain when I get up there."

Ray heard a chiming tone.

"I got another call," said Jack. There was a pause. "It's Forrest."

"Take it. Call me back."

"Okay." The line went dead.

Ray pictured Jack in his mother's kitchen, putting two and two together. He wondered if Jack had ever sent in that sibling DNA test. Jack had told him that Carter had furnished a cheek swab. That was all he needed to learn for certain if he and his brothers shared the same father. Ray knew Carter and Jack's mother, Annetta, very well. He could not picture the special education teacher cheating on her husband. And the chances of getting pregnant with twins, each by a different father had to be astronomical. But not impossible, Jack had told him. And Jack looked different from any of the other three boys. Carter, Kurt and Tommy were nearly interchangeable in looks, size and personality. But Jack had always been different.

Ray thought about Annetta Bear Den again and decided that you never really knew a person.

The nurse left Morgan's room holding her clipboard. She nodded as she passed him. Ray found Morgan dressed and standing by the bed. He paused to take in the sight of Morgan dressed in so traditional a manner. The bright

blue complemented her skin and the bands of pieced yellow fabric triangles formed a yoke at her neck. The bands
repeated twice more on the skirt.

He switched to Tonto because it seemed right.

"You look beautiful."

Her smile lit him up inside and out. He stepped closer
and she slipped naturally into his arms.

"I can't wait to get home and see Lisa," said Morgan. "I
know she is okay. But she's never been away from home
overnight and I just won't feel right until I see her with
my own eyes."

He knew that when she had been in danger, he'd had
reason not to let Morgan out of his sight. But now? The
FBI said she was safe. She didn't need him.

But what about him, about them?

Had there ever been a them, or was all that he felt and
all that he longed for only what he wanted?

He had no doubts that Morgan deserved better than the
likes of him. If he really loved her, he would let her go.
Then Morgan would be free to find the sort of responsible, caring man who would make her a fine husband and
good father for her girl. Upstanding, decent. A man like
Jack or Dylan or the kind of man Hatch would have been.

Of course, Jack was too serious. Lord, did he ever laugh
or crack a joke? Dylan was too predictable and upstanding
to the point that he never did seem to make a mistake. And
Hatch, well he was dead, so whatever kind of husband he
might have made was lost in that distant blood-soaked sand.

Somehow he needed to do what was best for Lisa and
for Morgan. He didn't know how he would say goodbye
without making a fool of himself. But he was going to
try, because he loved Morgan and he wanted her to have
the best. He knew only one thing with certainty—that
was not him.

THE DRIVE BACK to Turquoise Canyon was uncomfortable. Morgan felt by turns as if she were traveling with a stranger and also someone too preoccupied to even notice her presence. He was preparing himself to leave her. She felt it with the same keenness she had the IV that had punctured her vein.

Morgan had been told that Lisa would be returned late in the day to her home. She wanted to be certain that she was there in time to meet her. Cookie was with Lisa, so when she opened the front door to her home, the house felt empty and far too quiet.

Ray followed her in, checking each room before returning to her where she waited in the kitchen. The look he cast her made her breath catch, for it was full of longing and heat and a pain that she had only glimpsed before. Now it was there, clear and tangible as an electrical storm. He was summoning the strength to leave her. While she needed to gather the courage to make him stay.

"I believe you'll be safe now, Morgan," he said.

"You've done your duty to your shaman and to me," she said, but it wasn't enough. She wanted more. And all she had to do to get it was risk everything by telling him that she was madly, hopelessly and foolishly in love with him.

"Do you need anything else from me?"

She stepped closer, her mouth dry and her palms damp. "Yes."

His brow rose and he cocked his head as he watched her advance in small hesitant steps. She lifted her arms and looped them about his neck. He grasped her waist but she could not tell if he meant to pull her in or push her away.

"I need you, Ray Strong."

He flushed. "You mean you want me to sleep with you?"

"Yes. Every night."

Now his eyes went wide as her meaning began to sink in. "What about Lisa?" he asked.

"She needs a father."

Now he did let go and backed toward the kitchen door, which was the closest exit. With each step he shook his head in denial.

"Ray, if you don't want me. If you don't love me, then you should go. But if you are leaving because of some sense that you are not capable of being a husband and a father, I have hard news. You have been that to us already."

"I haven't even known you two weeks."

"It's enough for me to be sure that you are the one I've waited for all my life."

He pressed his big callused hands to his mouth and squeezed his eyes shut. Gradually he lowered his hands and straightened his shoulders. Then he opened his eyes and met her gaze. The pain was still there, making his eyes glassy.

"It's not me, Morgan. You were under attack. You were alone. So it's natural to turn to a protector. But you're confusing your need with love."

"I'm not confused, Ray. I know what I feel."

"Are you forgetting that I deceived you?"

"You kept your word to our shaman. You did what he asked. I have secrets, too, Ray. I never told anyone but you about Lisa's father because the truth made me feel stupid and used. You are entitled to your secrets. Everyone is. It doesn't change my feelings."

"I'm not husband material. I've been arrested. I've served time. If not for Jack and Dylan getting me help,

I would have been dishonorably discharged from the US Marines. I don't deserve you or Lisa."

"Because you switched seats in that convoy with Hatch Yeager?"

His mouth dropped open and then snapped shut. But he found his voice had abandoned him. It was as if she had shot an arrow right to the heart of the matter.

"I forgive you in Yeager's place. He would forgive you and want you to forgive yourself. It was a prank, Ray. You could not have known what would happen."

"Of course I could. We were in a hot spot. They called that place the Triangle of Death."

She stepped forward and pressed an open palm over his heart, feeling the steady beat in his chest.

"You have been nothing but tender and protective to my daughter. You have been nothing but conscientious and loving toward me. I refuse to believe that you did that as part of your assignment. You have feelings for me, Ray. I know it. And you are allowed to be happy. Allowed to make me happy because you did not die back there. And because you did not die, you have to live with your regrets. But you have to live."

"What if I screw this up, too?" he asked.

She smiled as she realized that he was considering it and it scared him to death.

"Your past makes you who you are, Ray. You're not the kid who joined the US Marines or the man who drank too much and flipped his vehicle outside Darabee. You're the man who protected me, rescued me...loved me. Don't let us go because it scares you, Ray. Be brave. Be the risk taker you claim to be and claim me."

He hesitated one instant more as his gaze swept her face, reading her expression. Did he see the love in her eyes, the willingness in her smile and feel the hope in her heart?

Ray could barely breathe past the hope that rose in his throat. Morgan really believed he could do this. He'd taken so many chances, survived so many foolish risks. But this chance, this risk would involve a child and a good woman. Did she understand what she was asking?

He held her gaze and Morgan nodded. "You can, Ray. If you want to."

The lump in his throat remained despite his attempts to swallow it again. Foolish hope, still alive after all this time. Who could have ever predicted that?

"All right. Let's do this."

Then Ray swept Morgan up in an embrace, spinning her once in a circle as she settled against his chest. Their mouths met in a joining that was so much more than physical. In his kiss, she felt the promise of a future together. When he finally set her on her feet, his hands came up to stroke her cheek and glide down her throat before settling on her shoulders. She felt the weight of his hands as he squeezed.

"You sure?" he asked, giving her one more chance to come to her senses. She hoped she never did.

"I am."

He smiled at her. "I love you, Morgan Hooke, and if you'll have me, I want to marry you. I've never been a husband, never had the optimism to consider it, but if you think I can do it, then I'll try every day and night not to let you or Lisa down. Will you be my wife?"

Her reply caught in her throat and all she could manage was a choking sound and a vigorous nod before she threw herself back in his arms, burying her head against his chest. He stroked her head and chuckled.

"Well, I'd cry at the prospect of marrying me, too."

She slapped him on the shoulder, that same shoulder that held the tattoo of an eagle, a tattoo he'd gotten in the hopes that someday he would be able to see beyond the obvious. Now he felt that he saw farther than ever before. He saw possibilities and a future with this woman and her child. And if he looked very far indeed, he saw more children in the home they would make together.

* * * * *

There is more trouble brewing on Turquoise Canyon as Apache hotshot and war hero Dylan Tehauno saves wealthy documentary filmmaker Charlotte Wrangler from a wildfire, only to find they've been framed for arson and murder. On the run from the killers and the law and battling the fire of attraction burning between them, Dylan and Charlotte must uncover the evidence that will prove their innocence.

Jenna Kernan's APACHE PROTECTOR: TRIBAL THUNDER *series continues in May 2017 with FIREWOLF.*

"What's going on, Casper?" Alexis asked.

"Nothing," Casper said, but his eyes were dark.

"Don't lie to me. What's wrong?"

He glanced over at her and took off his cowboy hat, then set it on the dashboard. He ran his hands over his face and through his hair in exasperation. "I just think it's going to be better if you get away from all this—this investigation."

"What happened?" she asked, trying to stop the hurt from leaking out into her voice.

All she had been trying to do for the past two days was solve this so they both could get their jobs done. Now, after a strange meeting with the Canadian Mounties, she was on the outs. It didn't make sense.

"You didn't do anything, Lex. I promise."

She tried to remind herself they were only friends, and maybe barely that. Sure, they had shared the kiss in the woods, but ever since they had gotten caught he had barely been able to look at her.

"Is this because of what happened. . .you know, back there?" She motioned in the direction they'd come from.

But she was sure he knew exactly what she was talking about.

WILD
MONTANA

BY
DANICA WINTERS

First Published in Great Britain 2017
By Mills & Boon, an imprint of HarperCollins*Publishers*
1 London Bridge Street, London, SE1 9GF

© 2017 Danica Winters

ISBN: 978-0-263-92860-0

46-0217

Our policy is to use papers that are natural, renewable and recyclable products and made from wood grown in sustainable forests. The logging and manufacturing processes conform to the legal environmental regulations of the country of origin.

Printed and bound in Spain
by CPI, Barcelona

Danica Winters is a multiple award-winning, bestselling author who writes books that grip readers with their ability to drive emotion through suspense and occasionally a touch of magic. When she's not working, she can be found in the wilds of Montana, testing her patience while she tries to hone her skills at various crafts—quilting, pottery and painting are not her areas of expertise. She believes the cup is neither half-full nor half-empty, but it better be filled with wine. Visit her website at www.danicawinters.net.

To Lane—
You work miracles.

Acknowledgments

This book wouldn't have been possible without the help of my fans. Thank you for taking a moment out of your lives to leave a review, come to book signings and send me notes, cookies and even the occasional bottle of vodka. You inspire me to keep writing when the going gets tough. Thank you.

Prologue

Seven. Most people thought the number was lucky. *He'd* even thought it had been lucky. This was supposed to be his seventh trip, the last run of the season, the last cleanup before he could head to Mexico and lie on the beach for the winter. Señoritas, sunshine, cervezas...everything he needed to be happy.

Yet now as he stared down the predator, he could have sworn seven was a curse.

The grizzly hopped on its front legs like a dog ready to play, but from what little he knew about bears, it wasn't an action that meant fun and games... no, that was an action that meant danger.

He eased back a step as he held the bear's gaze. Its beady black eyes bore into him, sizing him up.

Not for the first time in his life, he wished he were eight feet tall.

"Good bear," he said, putting his hands up. "Good bear." He turned to look over his shoulder, but the man he'd been sent there to meet was gone. "Damn him."

Without warning, the bear charged. The fur on its shoulders rippled, its gold tips harsh against the white snow. He screamed, the sound echoing through the high mountain valley.

The beast didn't slow down.

He turned to run, but it was too late. The griz hit him like no force he had ever experienced. Its putrid, hot breath seared the back of his neck as he fell to the ground. Heat and pain spread through his body as the predator's teeth met bone.

He closed his eyes, pain burning through him as the gunshot rang out.

The world, the pain, the fear—everything stopped.

Chapter One

Alexis Finch forced her body up the steep trail and toward the location the hikers had described. Ravens swooped through the air above her, calling out secrets to their comrades as they flew west. Even though she hiked nearly every day through the backcountry of Glacier National Park, each step was torturous. The altitude made her breath come faster, but she focused her attention on the thick pines that surrounded them, and she ignored the pain that shot up from her tired calves.

"Ranger Finch," the Customs and Border Protection agent called from behind her.

She was thankful as she stopped and turned back, taking the moment to catch her breath and shift the straps of her backpack, as they had started to cut into her shoulders. "Hmm?"

Casper Lawrence stopped beside her, his cheeks pink and a sheen of sweat covering his tanned face. She found comfort in the fact that after more than three miles of this uphill battle, the handsome agent was hurting just as badly as she was. "According to the GPS, this should be the spot." He motioned around them.

The hillside was covered with thick, frost-bitten grasses, timber and patches of snow that hid in the shadows. No evidence of a struggle. No blood. No fresh tracks.

"Look," she said, pointing toward the ravens overhead. "No matter what the GPS says, we follow the birds. Listen to nature. It'll give us all the information we need." She cringed as she realized how much she sounded like a bumper sticker, but as she spoke the words she knew they were true, especially when it came to finding a body.

If she'd learned anything in working as a law enforcement park ranger in the park for the last five years, it was that the only thing she could trust was Mother Nature's fickle attitude. She did as she pleased, and danger could be found in the moments that a person underestimated her power. It was easy to identify the people who had misjudged her; they were usually the ones Alexis and the other rangers were sent into the backcountry to find—or the ones whose bodies they were sent in to recover.

"I like nature, but don't you get tired of being stuck out here?" Casper looked up, taking off his Stetson and wiping away the thin line of sweat that it had collected. His slightly-too-long chestnut hair hung down over his caramel-colored eyes, obviously blinding him from the beauty that surrounded them.

He gazed toward the birds and slipped the hat back on his head.

"Stuck? Out here?" She laughed. It was hard to imagine being stuck in a place like this, where there was only open sky and rugged earth. "I'd much rather be out here than in some tiny apartment. I had enough of that kind of thing in college." She glanced over at Casper and his tan-colored hat. The wide brim cast his face in shadows, accentuating his firm, masculine jaw.

"Your girlfriend give you that?" she asked, motioning toward his hat.

He looked at her like he was trying to get a read on her. "I bought it in Kalispell a few years back." He took it off again, spinning the brim of it in his hands like he was talking about an old friend.

"Cowboy hats are a lost art," she said as she started to move up the trail.

A lot could be learned about a man by the hat he wore, whether he was a rancher or a weekend cowboy. Each style meant something different, but from the dents, the line of the crown and the sweat marks, it was clear he wanted to look like a cattleman.

"You grow up on a ranch?" she asked, excited that maybe they had some common footing.

He gave her that look again, like he just couldn't make heads or tails of her, but rather than making her feel uncomfortable, she liked the feeling of keeping him guessing. Maybe she spent too much time alone, but being an enigma to this too-handsome cowboy made heat rise from her core.

"No, my family comes from Butte."

"Ah," she said, forcing herself to look away from the agent. "A Butte boy... So you're Irish?"

He sent her a sexy half grin that made her nearly trip over her own feet. "Yep."

"You visit a lot?"

"Last time I was there was for my brother's funeral," he said, his tone hard.

"I'm so sorry."

Casper shrugged. "Robert had a lot of problems."

From his tone she could tell he didn't want to talk about it, so she dropped it and let the sounds of their footfalls fill the space between them. It made sense that he, the man who seemed to constantly be looking at her as if he was digging for something, came from a family of secrets in the rough and tumble mining town.

They crested the hill that led to Kootenai Lake. The crystal-clear water mirrored the snowcapped, jagged outcrops of Citadel Peak; it was an almost perfect picture, like one of the many postcards they sold at their visitor center. A raven cawed, pulling her attention away from the breathtaking view.

The bird sat in an old snag and picked at a bit of meat that it held in its grip.

"I think we're in the right place," she said, motioning toward the feasting bird. "Where did the hikers say they spotted the body?"

"When they stopped at the border crossing to re-port their findings, they said there wasn't much of a body to speak of. All they said they found was a boot. Apparently, they marked the area." As he spoke, an icy breeze blew off the lake. Near the west bank a piece of pink plastic duct tape fluttered on the bough of a tree, catching his attention. "There," he said, pointing in its direction.

She hurried over to the tape, the weariness she had been feeling suddenly dispelled by a surge of adrenaline.

Hopefully the hikers had been wrong. Hopefully this was nothing more than some tourist's castoff and not what they had assumed. If it was, she and Casper would have a mess on their hands and that, at the end of the main season, was the last thing that either one of them needed.

She pinched the tape as if it would give her the answers she needed, yet the plastic remained silent.

There was nothing at the base of the tree except needles and pinecones. No doubt that since the hik-ers had left this morning, the birds and other scav-engers had been at work.

Alexis dropped the heavy pack she'd been car-rying and started searching the ground around the pine. The grass had been mashed, and there was a faint trail of broken stems that led into the forest. She followed the game trail away from the lake and deeper into the timber.

"Ranger Finch?" Agent Lawrence called out, with a hint of panic in his voice.

She looked up from the nearly invisible game trail and turned. Agent Lawrence was nowhere in sight. "Yep," she called. "I'm over here."

There was the sound of breaking twigs and his cussing as he bulled through the timber. He may have been an agent, but he was clearly no ninja. He broke through the grips of the trees and came into view. There was a scratch across his cheek, complete with a speckle of blood.

"Don't run off. I don't need two bodies to recover."

She chuckled. Based on his trail-breaking skills, she was more likely to make it out of the underbrush long before he would.

"Don't worry, city boy, I won't leave you again if you're scared," she teased.

He wiped at his cheek. "All right, I had that coming, but seriously..."

She waved him off as she started moving. "Got it, Agent Lawrence."

"And quit calling me Agent. Only tourists call me that. I'd like to think that since you let me tag along on this one, we're at least kind of friends."

Kind of friends... She smiled at the thought.

In truth, she had been glad when he'd called and, due to the proximity to the International Border, they had decided to work this case together. For the first time since she had started working here, she had been looking forward to the end of the main season so she could find a little more distance from the tension between her and her ex. Until then, this cowboy and their kinda friendship could be her perfect distraction.

There was a scurry of movement as a small brown animal sprinted through the underbrush. Her body tensed as she stopped and tried to see the animal, but it had disappeared through a line of bushes. It could have been a pine marten or any number of other small mammals, but the unexpected movement made her even more wary than she had been before.

There had to be a body around here somewhere if the smaller animals were scavenging. No doubt bears, mountain lions and wolves were in the area. The scent of death would have brought every hungry mouth from miles around. She turned to warn Casper but stopped. He had a gun in his hand; it was half-raised.

"Little jumpy, eh? You can put the gun away, Casper," she said. "If that had been a bear, it wouldn't have done you much good anyway."

"Hey now, I'm a good shot," he said, sheepishly dropping the gun back into its holster.

"I doubt that," she said, thinking back to the days she had spent plinking cans off the tops of fence rails at her family's ranch. Back at home in the Bitterroot Valley, everyone knew her family—and her history. It was nice to meet someone who couldn't judge her for her faults.

She moved toward the brush where the animal had first appeared. There, tucked under the branches, was a man's REI hiking boot. Its sole was worn where the ball of the foot would have been.

"I got it," she called.

Casper stepped carefully, avoiding the dried twigs that littered the ground in what she had to assume was his attempt to be quiet. He stopped beside her. "What is it?"

"See for yourself." She lifted the branch so he could see the man's boot.

"Do you think someone just left it behind?" he asked. "Maybe it dropped out of their pack or something."

"No one just leaves behind their hiking boots, not here. Not when they still have a few miles to get back to the nearest trailhead."

She took a few pictures to document the scene and then gingerly pulled the shoe out by its well-worn laces. The boot's leather had dark brown stains over the toe and around the ankle to the heel. She flipped it up.

Her breath hitched in her throat.

Inside the shoe was the mucky white color of bone and dried dark red strings of chewed tendons and eviscerated flesh.

Whoever had put this shoe on was still wearing it.

She let go of the laces and stepped back from the gruesome object. She'd seen plenty of dead bodies, but nothing quite like this. It was so deformed and mutilated that, if it hadn't been in a shoe, she almost wouldn't have believed it had once belonged to a person.

"What do you think happened to this guy?" she whispered, out of some instinctual response to being around the dead.

"I have no idea," Casper said, shaking his head. "But we have a place to start finding out."

"How's that?" she asked, looking up at him.

"We know the guy didn't hike out." Casper ran his hand over the stubble that riddled his jaw. "Now we just have to find the rest of his body."

Chapter Two

The Flathead Emergency Aviation Resources, or
FEAR, helicopter touched down near the lake, its
blades chopping at the air and making white caps
on the crystal-blue water. Casper always hated this
moment, the instant when the chain of command
shifted and their team lost some of its control. Most
times, he could find his best evidence and the most
answers before a mess of officers showed up. Yet this
time, he had to admit it was different. This was a
death in which the only witnesses were the animals
who had feasted on the remains and the two way-
ward hikers who had found the body. With an incident like this, they needed extra hands on deck—no
matter how badly he wished it could just be him...
and Alexis Finch.

It had been nice following her up that trail, her
tight green pants stretching over hips and her full,
round curves. It had made the brutal hike a little more
bearable—and he'd found a new love for standard-
issue forest service pants.

Alexis stood beside him, lifting her hand to shield her eyes from the dust the chopper's blades kicked up. She squinted as she glanced over at him. "Let the party start," she said with a cynical smile that made his gut clench.

He forced himself to look away from her full lips and the way the fine lines collected around the corners of her eyes when she glanced over at him.

He had to focus on their case.

It was only out of sheer luck that the hikers had come to him and he'd convinced his boss that he was vital to the investigation. His boss had only let him go when he'd lied and told him that there was some evidence that the hiker may have crossed the border—which landed the case squarely in their lap. If they screwed this investigation up his boss had, in no uncertain terms, told him he would be out.

This was his last chance.

His next stop on the career line was a desk job at a DMV somewhere—if he was lucky. Then again, he'd already been sent to the Siberia of the contiguous United States: a tiny stand-alone border crossing station on the side of a lake only accessible by ferry or foot. It was the CBP's equivalent of exile.

Things couldn't get much worse.

The coroner bent down out of the rudder wash and hurried toward them. The man was pale, but when he straightened up as he neared them, Casper noticed the telltale spider veins and reddened nose of a major alcoholic.

"Where're the remains?" the man yelled above the sound of the slowing motor.

Alexis motioned for him to follow her.

As they drew near, Casper stared at the blood-covered leather boot. It was strange, but it looked exactly like one he had bought at REI earlier that summer. He wondered if somewhere along the way the man who'd worn this one had stood beside him in the store, passing the boot from one hand to the other as he decided if it was really the right one for him—just as Casper had done.

He pushed the thought from his mind. He had to remain detached.

It was the moment when things became real that emotions came into play, and emotions had been what had gotten him into trouble with the FBI. They had wanted the Robo-Cop—the man who could run through the blood and muck and then stand there and eat a sandwich without thinking about the residue of life that stained his footprints and constantly filled his reality.

If only he was better at disconnecting his head from his heart—life and work would be so much easier.

"Nothing else?" the coroner asked, like he appreciated the fact that there was so little to transport back to the medical examiner.

Alexis shook her head. "No. As of this time, these are the only remains we've managed to locate."

"We need to get a full canvass on the area." The

coroner stepped out of the timber and motioned toward the helicopter.

Two rangers stepped out of the chopper and rushed toward them. From the puckered look on Alexis's face she must have known the men. She gave a begrudging grunt as the guys made their way over and stopped next to them. The dark-haired ranger kept looking over at her like he was trying to get her attention, but she gave him the cold shoulder.

"Where do you want us to start, Hal?" the dark-haired ranger asked.

Alexis turned to the man. "I have a place you can go, Travis—"

"Travis, you take the northern trail," the coroner interrupted, giving them both a disapproving glance. He turned the other ranger, a blond. "John, you take the south. We only have a couple of hours before nightfall. The pilot needs us out before he's flying in the dark. Make it count."

Though he couldn't say the same of the two rangers, he liked the coroner. He'd always appreciated the type of people who cut the small talk—all business and no bull. Life would be so much easier if everything worked that way; no politics, no favorites, no strings.

"Alexis, you go east and Agent—"

"Lawrence," Casper answered.

"Agent Lawrence, you go west," Hal said, motioning to each of them in the respective directions. He pointed to his radio clipped to his waist. "If any of you find something, I'm on four." He turned away and went to work, going over Alexis's pictures and her notes about the scene and its presentation.

Travis and John moved away through the timber.

Casper started to move west. He didn't make it far before Alexis grabbed his arm and pulled him to a stop. "Let's work together."

Her face was neutral, but he couldn't help getting the feeling that she was frightened.

He looked in the direction of the coroner, but the man was busy with his work and didn't seem to notice the break in his ranks. "Hal doesn't seem like the type who likes rule breakers." He nudged his chin in the man's direction.

"First of all, this is my investigation. He had no business taking control of how I'm running this scene," Alexis said, her voice flecked with anger. "Besides, he'll be happy if we find something, and there's a better chance to find something if we actually work together in canvassing the area."

"You're the boss," Casper said, but in truth he was more than happy to be working with her. He liked being alone—he'd grown accustomed to it over the last year of working at the border crossing—but she made the constant hum inside him grow still and calm.

They walked a few arm lengths apart, moving through the timber and skirting around the lake. Every time she crawled over a bit of deadfall she would sigh, and after what must have been the hundredth tree he was certain that soft moan would be ingrained in his memory forever.

She sighed again and his thoughts moved toward the other moments she would make that noise... How her body moved... How she would look without those green pants and that khaki shirt. Maybe she was the kind of woman who liked lingerie, or maybe not. A girl like her was probably more of the comfort type, real.

She glanced over her shoulder as she was stepping over a downed log, and the leg of her pants caught on a sharp branch. She stumbled, her body moved slowly through the air as she tried to pull her leg from the gnarled grip of the broken bit of deadfall. Yet as she struggled, she lost her balance.

He rushed to her side. "Are you okay?"

He released her pant leg from the stabbing bit of wood. It had torn through her pants, making an L-shaped hole

"I'm fine," she said, trying to move but her body was wedged between two logs.

"I thought you were the expert in the woods, Ms. Ranger," he teased, trying in vain to make the embarrassed look on her face disappear. He held out his hand, waiting for her to take his peace offering.

She stared at his hand for a second. "Even experts make mistakes." She struggled to push herself up.

He reached down and took her hand, not waiting for the beautiful, stubborn woman to accept his help.

There was a surge of energy between them and

her eyes grew wide, her mouth dropping open almost as if she felt it, as well. He pulled her to her feet and quickly let her go. She was gorgeous standing there, her mouth slightly agape as she flexed her fingers.

"Thanks for the hand. I guess it's been a long day." She glanced in the direction they'd come, almost as if she was expecting to catch a glimpse of someone. "I'm off my game."

"Don't worry, I got your back." He felt stupid as the words left his mouth. He wanted to say so much more, ask her so much more. Yet it wasn't the time or the place. The spark he'd felt was probably nothing more than residual adrenaline leftover from their hike, or some misplaced stress from their findings.

She opened her mouth to say something, stopped, and turned away. He moved ahead of her, taking the lead so he could help her through the deadfall. This time her movements were slow, deliberate.

He stopped when he spotted a patch of animal hair on the trail in front of him. It looked like fresh fur, its golden tips still sparkling in the little bit of sunshine that managed to break through the trees. "I think we got something here."

She moved closer. "Look at those tracks," she said, pointing toward the gouges in the earth beside the tuft of fur. The holes were deep and massive, and they littered the ground in the shape of a nearly perfect circle. "There must have been some kind of fight." Bending down, she picked up a piece of the dirt and inspected it, like she could read something from the way the dust felt in her fingers.

The woman was amazing. There was no way she would ever be interested in a man like him—nothing to offer, no place to call home and one screw up away from being unemployed. More than that, she seemed like the kind of woman who liked being on her own—except when she'd seen the other rangers.

She looked up at him, her green eyes nearly the same color as the moss growing on the trees that littered the ground. "These are griz tracks. More than one—the scent of death must have brought them in. I'm guessing it was probably from sometime in the last twenty-four hours."

That's exactly what they needed. Not one, but two hungry grizzlies in the woods near them. In the deep underbrush, it was more than possible that they could run into one. Hopefully it wasn't a sow with cubs. They'd never make it out alive.

Maybe that was what had happened to the hiker—one misstep in the woods; a hike that had started out as some kind of goal or dream and then ended in tragedy.

"Be careful," he said, moving closer to her.

Her mouth quirked into a sexy smirk, but she instinctively reached down and touched the plastic trigger of the bear spray at her waist. "If I go out by bear, at least I'll go out fighting."

He didn't doubt her, but he could have sworn he saw a flicker of fear in her eyes. Then again, anyone who came into these woods and didn't pay heed to the place's ability to take them out at the knees was a fool. And maybe it was just that type of fool whose body they were trying to locate.

A branch snapped and his attention jerked toward the unnerving noise. The sound came from higher up the mountain, as if something was moving through the dense forest in a hurry. He could only hope whatever had made the sound was moving away.

Alexis was motionless, but her body was tense as though she had kicked into fight or flight.

"It's okay," he said, trying to calm her fears while at the same time trying to conquer his own. "Whatever made that sound is long gone." He waved almost too dismissively.

She glanced over at him, and her frown reappeared. "If there's an animal up there, it means there might be more of the body. We need to look."

He paused. The last thing he wanted to do was end up like the victim they were trying to identify, but he didn't want to come off like a coward to the sexy, dark-haired Alexis. "I'll take point. Watch my six," he said, trying not to think about the job he'd volunteered for as he followed the deep gouges up the hillside in the direction of the terrifying noise.

On a small patch of melting snow a square of army-green cloth caught his eye. He moved toward the object, unsure of whether or not the thing was really something worth looking at or just another green splotch in nature's underbelly.

Moving closer, he knelt down so he could make out the square lines and straps of a backpack, the kind that could be found at any of a million surplus supply stores. There was a smear of blood on the bag, near the right shoulder strap. Before he touched it, he motioned for Alexis to take photos. She snapped a few, carefully documenting the scene.

She stuffed the camera back into her pocket and knelt down beside him just as his knees started to grow damp in the snow. She gingerly picked the pack up by its straps and set it upright.

Opening up the bag's top flap, the bag was filled with clear, square packages of drugs. She took out the bricks and one by one laid them on the only dry spot she could find, a downed log, and took pictures of each item with a scale.

"Holy…" he whispered. "How many bricks are there?"

"Ten," Alexis said. "You have any idea about what kind of drugs these are?"

He leaned in closer, and through the cloudy plastic he could make out hundreds of blue pills. "Without a drug test kit I can't be a hundred percent sure, but I know they ain't Viagra." His face flamed as he realized what he had said to her, and he instinctively glanced to the hand he had held.

She giggled, like she had been able to read his thoughts, and the heat rose higher in his face.

He held his head low, fearing that if he looked in her direction she would be able to see how embarrassed he was, but instead of studying him, she reached in the bag and pulled out the last brick and documented it.

She flipped the bag over. At the bottom was a wad of cash, at least a thousand dollars, held together by a thick rubber band.

"How do you think the bag got up here? You think the bears stole it?" she asked with a slight laugh at her twisted joke.

"You know of any bears that need a thousand bucks and some drugs?"

She laughed again, the sound fluttering through the air like a rare butterfly, and just as quickly as it had come, it disappeared.

"But really, either the guy dropped it when he was running or…" He picked up the bag and showed her the claw marks. He flipped it so she could see the dark bloodstains that were speckled over its surface. "This is definitely arterial spray. Which means this guy must have been carrying this when he was mauled."

She shrugged. "It definitely could have been a mauling. It wouldn't be the first and I doubt it will be the last, but something about this whole thing—maybe it's the drugs—it just doesn't feel right. There has to be something more, something we're missing."

He felt it, too, the strange charge in the air that came with a great case. "Do you think someone murdered this guy, Alexis?"

"Call me Lex," she said, interrupting him. "My

friends…they call me Lex." A faint tinge of pink rose in her cheeks.

He smiled. So they were friends, just as he had hoped.

"Anyway…what were you saying?" she asked, her voice soft and coy.

That place deep inside him—that place in his heart he often pushed aside for logic and reason—reawakened.

"I… I guess I was just saying that you might be right was all… I mean, if I was a killer and I wanted to hide a body, this is one heck of a place to do it. It's late in the season. It would be easy enough to bring a person up here, shoot them and leave them to be reabsorbed by nature. Another few days and no one would have been back up here until next year. It could have been a nearly perfect attempt at a murder and cover-up."

She nibbled her bottom lip, and it made him wonder what it felt like to kiss those lips. They were so perfect, pink and full, even a little suntanned from all her hours hiking. He ran his tongue over his lip and gave it a slight suck as his mind wandered to more sultry thoughts of all the places of hers he would like to kiss.

"How do you know that's arterial blood?" she asked, motioning toward the stain on the bag.

He forced himself to look away from her mouth. "Arterial blood spatter tends to have a redder color, and the droplets are small or medium because they are expelled from the body at a higher speed."

Her face pulled into a tight pucker and she looked up the mountain. "You thinking it could be from a bullet?"

He shrugged. "Without having the medical examiner go over the foot, and without more of the body… well, it's hard to say exactly what might have happened. Maybe it wouldn't be a bad idea if we go get Travis and the other guys."

"No," she clipped. "We don't need Travis. We'll be fine."

There was definitely something between her and this Travis guy. Jealousy zinged through him.

She snapped another quick picture of the drugs and the money, and stuffed everything back into the bag before she stood up. "Let's keep moving up the mountain. Maybe we'll find the rest of whomever this belongs to. If we do, it's possible we can get a few more questions answered."

Maybe it was selfish, or adolescent, or whatever his therapist would've called it, but what he really wanted more than to find this body—and open whatever can of questions it would entail—was to spend more time with Lex. Their time together was the first real human contact he'd had all summer. Sure, he'd seen hikers and tourists, but their interactions had been little beyond looking at passports and the normal small talk.

In the deepening shadows, they picked their way

up the hill into larger and larger clumps of snow, which made their tracking easier. A squirrel chirped overhead, making him jump.

"There," she said, pointing toward a reddish patch on the snow. "Look…"

There, half-buried in the snow, was a yellow patch of bone. On its surface were smears of blood. His stomach dropped. Hopefully he'd been wrong about this being a murder. Hopefully this was nothing more than a mauling. A death was always a terrible thing, but if this was a murder the ramifications would play out until the case was solved, and the deeper the investigation would go, the deeper he would be forced to go into his former world—a world he had promised to leave behind.

Alexis carefully snapped a picture and documented the scene. She pulled on a pair of latex gloves, and reached down and picked up the bone that was buried in the snow. The bone was round and, where it wasn't tacky with blood, it was oily from fat.

It could have been his years of seeing the dead, but as he watched her work to gently move the heavy, wet remains from the ice that had formed around it, he wasn't thinking about the life that this bit of flesh had once belonged to; rather, all he could think about was Lex and the way her face had paled the second her fingers had touched the bone.

"You don't have to stay, Lex. You can go get the guys," he offered. "I can handle this."

She shook her head and wiped the back of her sleeve over her forehead.

"Seriously, Lex. You don't have to do this."

"No. I'm fine," she said, but her voice was weaker than what he was sure she had intended it to be. "This is my job. I got it."

Ever so gently, he reached over and took the bone from her.

She gave an appreciative sigh. "Do you think… it is him?"

"It could be," he said. He slowly turned the bone.

Lex gasped.

In his hands, barely discernible thanks to the jagged holes and chew marks, was the partial face of what had once been a man.

Chapter Three

The coroner laid the skull down on the black body bag. There was a patch of hair, dark with dried blood and grease, and an ear that hung limp, tethered by only a thin strip of pale skin. "Look at this mark right here," he said, pointing to a jagged, round wound at the base of the man's skull. "If this was the entrance of a bullet wound, it would be smooth around the edges, and depending on the angle, there would be a large exit wound."

"So this wasn't a homicide?" Casper asked as he leaned in closer to look at the mark on the bone.

"If you look right here," Hal said, "the margins of the wound are jagged. It's the type you normally see associated with a high-pressure compression wound, consistent with that of a bite. However, without the rest of the body, it's hard to say if this wound was the cause of death or was caused antemortem, peri-mortem or postmortem."

She looked away. To get through this she had to

think of him as just another man. A random being. A victim of the fates. It was nature.

"Are you okay?" Casper asked, putting his hand on the small of her back.

She swallowed a bit of bile that had managed to sneak through her resolve. "I'm fine," she said, her voice hoarse.

Hal zipped up the bag, hiding the gruesome head from view. "I'll get this to the medical examiner. Maybe he can tell us a little more, but for now I'm going to rule the cause of death as undetermined. Don't be surprised if this comes back as being likely due to unintentional injuries. This bite," he said, motioning toward the bag at his feet, "would have been fatal." He stood up and wiped off the knees of his pants.

Travis tapped Hal on the shoulder, drawing his attention. "You ready? The pilot is starting to get antsy."

Hal nodded. "You guys need a ride out?"

Casper took a step toward the copter, but Lex stopped him as she looked over at Travis. The last place she wanted to be was sitting next to her ex-husband in a flying death machine. "Thanks, but we'll hike out."

"Are you sure? Alexis, I think you should get back to the station—" Travis started to protest, but stopped as if he had realized, a moment too late, that he no longer had control over her. "Or do whatever. You never listened to me anyway."

It wasn't that she hadn't listened, it was simply

that she wasn't the kind of woman who was ever going to have her actions dictated to her—especially not by someone who had once said that he loved her. "Would you and John let the other rangers know that we have a possible dangerous bear?" She carefully sidestepped his jab. "We're going to need to send up the biologists and a ranger in the morning to track this bear down. We don't need any more tourists getting hurt."

"Maybe you should worry about yourself," Travis grumbled, glancing over toward Casper.

Casper smiled, the motion so wide that it made her wonder if he had misunderstood Travis's tone. "Don't worry about Alexis," he said, motioning toward her. "She'll be safe with me."

Travis gave a tight nod and turned away, muttering unintelligibly under his breath.

Watching him walk away, she was filled with mixed emotions. She thought of the first time she'd met Travis. It had been her first day at work, he had been so kind in showing her around and when she'd gotten a headache, he'd driven three hours to get her Tylenol. At first he had been so good at the little things, the love notes and wildflowers left on the counter. Yet after a couple of years, things progressively got worse and she hated him and what he had done to her, the way he had always put her down and treated her like she was less-than. Then again, such hate could only come at the cost of having once loved.

Casper looked over at her, and she tightened her jaw in an attempt to hide her thoughts from leaking into her expression. She didn't need him asking her any questions about her past. "Thanks for everything, Hal. And please let me know how it all turns out," she said, giving the coroner a quick wave.

"No problem. But wait, what about the drugs?" Hal asked, motioning toward the backpack at Casper's feet.

"This whole thing's going into evidence once we get down," Casper said.

"You sure you don't want me to take them with us? I can drop them off in evidence for you. Would save you a couple pounds carrying it out," Travis said.

She would carry a thousand pounds just so long as she never had to ask for Travis's help. "Nope. We got it," she clipped.

"My team's at your disposal if you need," Hal added and then quickly made his way to the helicopter, disappearing behind its doors. She reached down and took Casper's hand and pulled him, urging him to follow. His hand was hot in hers and she let go, the touch a jolt to her cold, exposed skin. Casper looked at her, a shocked expression on his face like he was surprised that she had touched him, but she pretended not to notice.

Hopefully Travis was watching and could see that no matter how they had left things, she was moving on with her life.

The helicopter lifted off the ground, the wash sending bits of dust and debris in every direction. Travis sent her a look through the copter's window as he said something on his radio.

Casper turned toward her. "You do realize that now we're going to have to hike out…in the dark."

"That's the easy part," she said with a wicked smile.

He raised an eyebrow in question.

"The hard part," she teased, "is that you won't be able to beat me." She took off with a laugh, relieved that once again she was alone with the cowboy.

THE CBP's CHEVY always seemed to list to the left when he drove down the road, and it squealed when he applied the brakes, but as they got to the bottom of the trail, he had never been happier to see his old, beat-up, Fed-issued truck.

"You're crazy. You know that, right?" Casper said between heaving breaths.

He'd thought five miles uphill going in was bad, but basically jogging five miles down steep terrain carrying not only his go-bag, but also the missing hiker's drugs, had nearly killed him.

Even in the light of his flashlight he could make out the beads of sweat that were dripping down Lex's temples. Her hair was damp and her cheeks were red, but she laughed like her body couldn't be aching as badly as his. "Come on, that was fun."

"Having a heart attack is never fun. You could've killed me. I'm getting old, you know."

She lifted her brow, giving him a sexy "come on now" look. Reaching into her bag, she pulled out two protein bars and handed him one. "Here. Eat this, old man. It'll make you feel better."

He took it, dropping his bags on the tailgate of his truck parked at the trailhead. She lifted her bag up and set it beside his.

He looked over at her and tried to guess at her age. She was young; the lines on her face were barely defined in the thin light, but she had the eyes of a woman who had had her heart broken more times than once. "How old are you?"

"Young enough to be okay with it, but old enough to know not to answer," she said, her sexy smirk returning.

He laughed, and some of his tiredness disappeared. "You wanna ride back to Apgar with me or do you want me to drop you off at the nearest station?"

She dropped her hand down on her backpack. "Apgar would be great. I don't want to have to wait for another ranger so I can catch a ride." She looked down at her watch.

"You don't want to have to wait for another ranger, or is it that you don't want to run into Travis?"

Her face puckered at the man's name and he instantly regretted asking her the question.

"Sorry. Don't answer that. It's none of my business. Let's go." He slammed closed the tailgate and the topper. He jumped into the truck before she had a chance to answer.

After a minute she dropped into the seat beside him. They drove in silence for what seemed like an hour.

"How'd you know about Travis?" she finally asked.

"I was in the FBI for five years. Let's just say I've learned how to read people."

"If you're so good at reading people, then how did you end up working at Goat Haunt? I thought only loners and outcasts liked that station. Last year it was manned by some lady... Gertrude or something. I swear the only word that woman ever said to me was, 'Passport?'" Lex's voice was soft, like she was trying to avoid hurting his feelings, but the blade had already sliced.

She was right. Goat Haunt was his own private version of Alcatraz.

"What can I say, I guess I'm just lucky," he said, trying to make light of the situation.

He steered the truck around the sharp corners and down the narrow road of the Going-to-the-Sun Highway. The moon had risen and made it just bright enough that he could make out the snowcapped peaks of the jagged mountains around them. To their left was a steep drop-off; the only thing standing in the way of a car going over and plummeting hundreds of feet to the bottom of the mountain was a short rock wall.

He forced himself to focus on the road and ignore the tight knot of fear that always filled his gut when he came this way. At least the park was closed for the night, so there were only a few other cars—those that dared to spend the night in the park, or were hurrying to get out.

"I'm sorry. I shouldn't have said that," Alexis started. "I… I'm just a little touchy when it comes to Travis. He's my ex-husband. Lately things haven't been going well between us."

He knew all about exes. He'd had more than his fair share, but after the events that had transpired with the FBI, he'd taken the last two years off from dating. It was his way of protecting another person from getting hurt. Yet when he looked at Alexis, he was tempted to break his self-imposed vow of celibacy. There was just something about the tomboy next to him. She wasn't the type of woman who worried about a broken nail. She was the type who would be happy hanging out, reading a book, maybe going for a hike—and no matter how he counted it, spontaneous and real were always a turn-on. No matter how badly he didn't want them to be.

"You want to talk about it?" he asked, trying to avoid looking at her hand resting between them on the bench seat.

She shook her head. "What about you? I noticed you don't have a ring."

"It's a long story," he said, casting a look at her.

"I heard that kind of thing has been going around." She smiled. "Relationships are tricky—when you

think you have a good one, it's easy to get compla-
cent and take things for granted, and with bad ones
you are always struggling to find an escape."

His thoughts moved to his parents and how tricky
their relationship had been. They hated one another
and had fought every day when he'd been growing
up. Though they were still married, the thought of
the relationship they had made the word *marriage*
sour on his tongue.

Though he didn't like the thought of marriage—at
least the type of marriage he'd seen as a child—he
still held hope that one day he'd find something different. Yet from the way Lex spoke, he wasn't sure
if she was attempting to make him feel better, or if
it was a way of telling him she wasn't interested.
Either way, whatever residual hopes he had held in
making something out of their clandestine meeting
were gone.

A roar grew loud behind them. In the rearview
mirror was a single headlight.

Alexis leaned forward and peered into the side
mirror. "Who'd be crazy enough to drive a motorcycle down this thing at night?"

Besides the cliffs and the sheer drop-offs, Glacier
was known for the goats and random assortments of
animals that loved to use the highway as their own
personal travel system, avoiding the steep embank-
ments and treacherous climbs.

"Maybe that's why they want to hug my bumper,"
he said, checking the mirror. The bike was now so

close to their tailgate that he could no longer see the headlight—it was nothing more than a reflective glow.

He moved to slow down, but as he did, so did the biker, moving back so far that he lost track of the headlight around a corner.

"What's that guy doing?" Alexis asked, a whisper of fear creeping into her voice.

"Who knows, but don't worry. We're fine. The guy's probably just drunk or something." Casper had driven this road a few times over the summer, but normally when he got off work he'd just avoid the park and drive home to the tiny town of Babb outside the park, where he had a little apartment on the second floor of a local auto mechanics shop. "Where's the next pullout?"

Alexis shook her head. "Not for a mile or two."

He was blinded as a car turned the corner ahead. It was moving fast and hugging the center line of the narrow road. He gripped the steering wheel, his fingers digging into the hard vinyl.

At the last moment, the car swerved into their lane. He jerked the wheel, running the truck off the road and toward the rock wall.

He reached across the truck, trying to stop Lex from lurching forward, but there was nothing he could do. The old Chevy's tires squealed as the steel body ran against an outcrop of unyielding stone in a mess of metal and sparks.

The truck's tire caught and, almost in slow motion, it twisted. The world shifted and what had once been up was now down. As they slid to a stop, the truck was lying on its roof. Lex was held in place by her seat belt, her body slumped against the straps and her eyes closed. Blood dripped down her hair and fell onto the gray roof.

"Alexis? Lex?" he called frantically, hoping she was still alive. "Lex, are you okay?"

He started to move, but his strap held him in place upside down. The blood started to rush to his head, making his face feel heavy and bloated. Reaching up, he tried to unclasp his belt, but his fingers fumbled as he tried to make them work.

The deafening beat of his heart started to slow and as he looked at Lex his vision distorted, making her look as though she were a picture going out of focus. His vision tunneled until he could only see her face. A wave of peace filled him.

If this was it, the last thing he was going to see— her long hair and full lips—he could think of no greater goodbye.

Chapter Four

Alexis opened her eyes. The world was awash with the sounds of frantic voices. She didn't know where she was; the world floated around her, moving and swaying like she was watching it through a pool of water.

"Alexis?" A man's voice broke through her thoughts. "Are you okay? Lex?"

She blinked and there, kneeling beside her, was Casper with his silver badge on his belt and hair the color of chestnut, reds and browns that reflected the lights that filled the night, and shoulders so muscular that she was certain he did push-ups as a hobby. As he looked at her, his eyes were wide with fear.

She tried to speak, but nothing more than a slight squeak escaped her lips. Her head ached and as she drew a breath, her chest ached. Swallowing back the pain, she tried again to speak. "What…happened?"

Casper leaned closer and moved her hair out of her face. The strands stuck to her skin and she moved to reach up, but he stopped her. Then she tasted the blood. It filled her mouth, giving it the iron-rich taste of spilled life.

"Don't worry. You're going to be okay. The EMTs are almost here. It's just important that you stay awake. Got it?" He spoke in fast, clipped words that she struggled to understand.

"How?" she asked, groping for the words that seemed to jumble in her mind.

"We were in a car accident."

It all came flooding back. The car flipping through the air. The screech of metal on stone. The scent of gas in the air. She drew in a gasp, but was stopped by the pain in her chest.

She tried to sit up, but stopped as Casper shook his head. "Don't move."

A thin bead of blood slipped down Casper's hairline and stopped next to his earlobe. "Are you okay?" she asked.

He nodded, reaching up and wiping the blood away, leaving a streak of red on his cheek. "I'm fine."

In the group of people beside Casper there was a man staring at her. He wore a black leather vest with the words "Madness and Mayhem." Just below them was the word "Montana" and then a black patch with red stitching that read "Filthy Few." On the other side of the man's vest was a patch that read "one-percenter." The man had gray hair and even though it was dark, he had on sunglasses.

The man must have noticed her looking at him, as he lifted his chin in acknowledgment. This must have been the man who had been following them, the headlight in the mirror. Yet before she could speak, someone stepped in front of him and the man disappeared, becoming just another face in the growing crowd.

On the rock wall beside them she could see the glow of red and blue lights. Tires crunched on the side of the road as the EMTs pulled to a stop.

"Everyone out of the way!" the paramedic yelled as she pushed her way through people.

The EMTs poked and prodded Alexis, taking her pulse and checking her reflexes with lights. Even without them telling her, she knew everything wasn't right. She closed her eyes and when she reopened them she was already strapped down to a board, her head and back immobile, and they were loading her into the back of the ambulance.

"Casper…" Alexis whispered as the female EMT stepped up into the back of the ambulance beside her.

"What, honey?" the EMT asked.

"Where's Casper?"

"Your friend?"

Alexis tried to nod, but was stopped by the thick straps on her forehead. "Yes. I want Casper."

The woman jumped out of the wagon and a moment later, Casper was sitting beside Alexis. He smiled. The blood on his temple had dried. "I'm here."

There was so much going on. So much she didn't understand. "Stay with me," she pleaded, suddenly afraid.

"Don't worry, sweetheart, I'm not going anywhere. I'll stay by your side as long as you need."

HE'D SEEN MORE people hurt than he could count, but
he'd never felt as terrified as when he saw Alexis
covered in blood and confused. Hopefully she would
be okay. She was so out of it.

She slept as they waited for the doctor to return
with the results of her MRI. He hated the monoto-
nous, shrill beeps of the machines that filled the
emergency room.

Reaching into the plastic bag at his feet, he pulled
out the little sewing kit he'd bought at the hospital's
shop and grabbed her pants from the foot of her bed.
He pushed his fingers through the L-shaped hole
in her pant leg from where she had caught it on the
deadfall. She probably didn't care about the pants,
but he couldn't sit there with nothing to do but worry.

He pulled out some string, threaded the needle
and set to work as he sat in the pink vinyl seat beside her bed. When he'd been younger, his mother
had told him that good domestic skills were the mark
of a true man.

The stitches were even and as he mended, he kept
looking up, hoping Lex would wake and everything
would be okay.

He hated this. He hated hospitals—it brought up
moments of his past that he never wanted to relive.
The sooner they could be out of here, the better.

Every hospital he'd ever been to carried the same

overpowering disinfectant smell. They could scrub away the blood and the waste products, but no matter how much they tried to hide it, he could still make out the pungent aroma of panic and fear. Yet as he sat there working, he wondered if the scent was carrying in from the patients or from those waiting for their loved ones to be helped.

He reached over and caressed Lex's hand. There was no more fear for her, not now, not with the drugs that filtered through her system to numb her pain. Now the fear was solely his.

His phone buzzed. "Hello?"

"Agent Lawrence, this is Ranger Grant with the Glacier National Park Rangers Office. I was one of the responders at the scene of your accident. I believe you left me a message?"

"Thanks for returning my call. I appreciate it," Casper said. "Did you manage to find the evidence?"

There was a pause on the other end of the line. "We found two large hiking backpacks—which I assumed were yours and Alexis's—and there was an empty green military-style bag."

"Empty?"

"Yep."

"You've got to be kidding me. You sure there wasn't anything in the bag?" He pulled a hand over his face, trying to stave off the start of a headache.

"Yes, sir."

"The drugs were packed into bricks. Were there any that had spilled out? Maybe into the truck bed or on scene?" He tried to sound calm as he thought about what it would mean if the drugs were truly missing.

"I didn't find any bricks of drugs, but your topper took a pretty big hit when you rolled the truck." The man paused. "When we pulled up, the truck's topper door was open. I guess it's possible they fell out and weren't recovered."

"Or they were taken…"

His mind raced. Who'd want to take the drugs? Only a few people had even known that they had them and were taking them back to Apgar. Was it possible that the coroner or one of the rangers had said something? Or was it completely a random occurrence that they had been in an accident and the drugs had been stolen?

He didn't believe in coincidences, but he had a hard time believing that the rangers or the coroner would have any ill-conceived ideas of stealing the drugs. No one had seemed overly preoccupied with them on the scene. If someone had wanted them, Casper would have had some type of clue. He was jumping to conclusions… No doubt the drugs were probably scattered along the roadside near their crash site.

"Can you make a run back up to the site? Take another look around? We can't have thousands of dollars' worth of drugs get into the wrong hands."

"No problem… I'll call you when I get back into cell service and let you know what I find."

Casper squeezed Lex's hand. It had started to chill

under the hospital's air-conditioning and he carefully tucked her arms under the warm blanket.

"Thanks, Grant," he said. "Appreciate your help." He moved to hang up.

"Wait, Lawrence," the man said.

He lifted the phone back to his ear. "Huh?"

"We did find a receipt inside the green bag. It was wadded into a ball and was stuck in the bottom corner."

A receipt? He thought back to everything he'd dumped out of the bag. He didn't recall a receipt. Was it possible it had been there the whole time, or had the person who'd stolen the drugs accidentlly, or purposefully, left it behind?

"What about the money?"

"No money. Just the receipt," Grant said, sounding tired. "I'll take a picture and send it your way."

"Thanks, Grant."

"No problem. We'll start putting out feelers. If the drugs were stolen, maybe we can help you try to get a handle on this before word moves up the chain. Hate to see you get in trouble."

"Let me know if you hear anything." He hung up the phone.

He moved too fast as he pushed through another stitch and the needle jabbed into his finger, making him curse as he pushed his finger into his mouth to stem the blood flow.

He was going to be in deep trouble if the news that he'd fallen victim to a heist hit the Fed circuit.

If it did, within twenty-four hours everyone from his boss to his old FBI buddies would know that he'd lost a vital piece of evidence.

Just when he thought things couldn't get any worse.

He knotted the thread as he finished mending the hole and then put everything away.

He was going to need to get in touch with his boss. He glanced down at his watch. Midnight. No wonder Grant had been tired.

Instead of calling and waking up the captain, he wrote him a bare-bones email that emphasized the fact he was sitting in the ER. It was low, playing the mercy card, but he needed to buy some time and a little leniency. The last thing he needed his boss thinking was that he lost the drugs due to his incompetence.

The door to Lex's room opened, but with the curtain drawn around her bed he couldn't see who was coming in.

"Is this the right place?" a man asked, his voice tight and filled with panic.

"It is, Mr...." a woman answered.

"Yellowfeather. Travis Yellowfeather."

Casper's heart lurched in his chest. What was Lex's ex-husband doing here?

He looked down at her sleeping face and contemplated waking her. Yet she looked so peaceful, her eyes fluttering with REM sleep and her hair, still specked with blood, haloed around her head. She needed her rest.

"Mr. Yellowfeather, I'm afraid she already has a visitor. We only allow one visitor at a time," the nurse said.

"To hell with one visitor," Travis said, pushing aside the curtain.

As soon as he saw Casper, Travis's eyes darkened and his lips curled into a smirk. "I should've known it was you who would be here. I guess it wasn't enough that you got her hurt, now you have to stay here to make sure she doesn't die—all in an effort to save your conscience, I suppose."

Casper went slack-jawed, but he quickly recovered his composure. "Who do you think you are, Travis, walking in here and accusing me of anything?"

"I'm her damned husband," he retorted, moving to the side of Alexis's bed.

"Ex, from what I hear."

Travis's scowl darkened. "She told you?" He snorted. "So she's already on the prowl," he said, half under his breath.

"Why don't you leave, Travis? I know she wouldn't want you here."

"And you think she wants you?" His scowl turned into a dangerous smile. "If you think that, you don't know Lex at all."

Travis wasn't wrong. He couldn't tell anyone Alexis's favorite sandwich or the color of her childhood bedroom, but that didn't mean he was going to leave her here with the man whom, only hours before, she shied away from. He knew fear and hatred when he saw it.

"If you think she would want you here, then I may know her better than you do," Casper said.

Lex's hand tightened in his and he turned to see her eyes fluttering open. "Boys," she said, her voice weak, "don't fight."

Travis pulled his lips into a tight line, but he shut up.

"How are you doing, honey?" Casper asked. He moved to caress her face but stopped as he felt Travis's gaze searing into him. Lex didn't need a fight, and no matter how much he disliked the man standing at the other side of the bed, he had been right—Casper barely knew her. They had talked a lot as they hiked, and there had been playful banter, but they were only friends.

She blinked for a few moments, as if trying to make sense of her world. "What are you doing here, Trav?"

Travis stepped closer to her and took her other hand. "I heard you were in an accident."

He suddenly felt out of place as Alexis said her ex-husband's pet name. Maybe he'd misread the entire situation. Maybe she didn't hate Travis like he'd assumed. He let go. He was the interloper here, not Travis.

"But why are you here?" She moved her hand out of Travis's. Casper hoped she would reach over for him, but she remained still. "You and I are done. You made that abundantly clear."

"We may be divorced, Lex, but that doesn't mean that I can just stop worrying about you."

She pushed the button that moved the bed up. "Actually, Travis, that's exactly what a divorce means. If that's not what you wanted, then maybe you should have treated me like your wife instead of just someone you could use and throw away."

Casper cleared his throat, his discomfort rising. He shouldn't have come here and inserted himself into whatever domestic situation they had going on. "Hey, Lex, I'll see you later."

"No," she said, her voice strong. "You stay here. Travis, it's you who needs to go."

"Are you kidding me?" Travis spat. "You are going to let this son of a—"

Alexis stopped him with a wave of her hand. "Just go."

Travis looked at her and started to open his mouth to say something, but must have thought better of it. He turned to Casper. "You think she's great now, but let me tell you a little something about Alexis Finch. She only cares about two things—the park and how she fits into it. She doesn't care about anyone or anything else. If you think you are going to change her or if you got some notion that you are going to be someone she gives two shakes about…" He snorted. "You got another thing coming." He turned and stalked out of the ER, rattling the curtain rings as he bulled through them.

Casper stood in silence, staring at the curtain. He

had no idea what to say. Divorce was never pretty—especially when it came to navigating the waters of a new relationship. Not that they had a relationship, but things could get a bit hinky when it came to seeing an ex with someone else.

"I'm sorry about that," Lex said. She tried to move her head, but it was still in the confines of a brace and as she moved, she winced.

"Are you okay?"

"I'm fine," she said, the tired edge returning to her voice.

"I'm serious, I can go, Lex. I don't want to…interfere."

Her lips turned into a thin smile. "You made a promise. You said you would stay by my side, remember?"

He moved closer to her bed. He thought about reaching down and taking her hand, but now that Travis had been there somehow it didn't seem right.

"How're you feeling?"

"I feel like I was in a fight… Who won, me or the truck?" Her lips curled into a playful half smile.

There was a knock on the door and the doctor pushed back the curtain. He had a black tablet hugged to his white lab coat.

"Mrs. Finch?" he asked.

"Miss," she answered.

"Right, Ms. Finch, I'm Dr. Tag, the neurologist here at Kalispell Regional. I just got off the phone with your brother, Dr. Paul Finch. He was very concerned about your well-being."

She cringed at the sound of her brother's name. "I'm sorry, Doctor, he can be a bit…overwhelming sometimes."

Dr. Tag didn't smile or nod, rather, he remained unflappable, making Casper wonder if that was exactly what had drawn the man to medicine.

"It was no problem, Ms. Finch, but you should call him back when you get the chance. I think he wishes to speak to you regarding your accident now that you're awake."

She nodded but looked down at her hands.

"As for the results of your CAT scan, you are experiencing a slight bit of swelling, consistent with a mild concussion."

"What does that mean, Doc?" Casper asked, trying to mimic the man's cool demeanor.

"It means that for the time being, I'd like to have you stay here and be monitored for any residual effects. However, I think it would be safe to send you home tomorrow. You will just need to rest and everything should sort itself out." He tapped on his tablet like he was noting something in her chart. "You are a lucky woman. A TBI, or a traumatic brain injury, can have a number of long-term effects, but from what I'm seeing on your scans, you should be okay."

Casper let out a breath he hadn't known he was holding. In a day that had been filled with nothing but death, despair, accidents and blood…something was finally going right.

Chapter Five

Lex took a tentative step out of the car as Casper raced around from the driver's side to help her into her house. He wrapped his arm around her waist and took hold of her arm as he cradled her body against him. He was so…warm. In fact, he was so warm that she wanted to move closer to him, to rest her body against him and let his heat ease the pain that seemed to pulse from her bruised and battered body. He smelled of hospital, but beneath the sharp odor of antiseptic was the heady scent of his sweat and the tangy edge of fresh air. She closed her eyes and took his scent deep into her lungs, trying to remember it for those nights that she would be alone.

"Do you need anything for your house? Groceries? Anything?" Casper asked.

"No, uh, I think I got everything I need." She looked over at him as she spoke and saw his face was tight, just like it had been when the doctor had been in her hospital room last night. It was sweet that he was so worried about her, but he needn't be;

she was strong. "Thanks for giving me a ride—and for keeping the car on the road this time," she joked, trying to make light of the accident.

Her joke fell flat as his brow furrowed and a storm brewed in his eyes. "I'm so sorry, Lex. I... I never wanted you to get hurt—"

She stopped him by pressing her finger to his lips. The instant she touched him, a strange buzz of energy filled her and she quickly lowered her hand. "You—it wasn't your fault. It was unavoidable. That car came at us. Seriously, don't worry. Everything is fine. And hey, at least it was a work truck, right?" She struggled to find the right words to make him feel better, and to quell the surging need to touch him again.

He looked at her and some of the darkness in his eyes lifted. Before he could say anything, she stepped out of his cradling arms and hurried toward her house.

The log cabin was dark brown and its windows were trimmed with white, and like most of the other buildings of the park, it radiated with a cozy, rustic charm that always beckoned her home. She'd spent the last few summers holed up in the tiny building with Travis, often hating its inconsistent hot water and the electricity that seemed to come and go depending on the weather, but regardless of its downfalls she loved the place.

Yet it felt strange walking up the path with a man who wasn't Travis. In fact, the night he'd left, she had sworn that, as long as she lived there, he would be the last man who would ever set foot in this place. Then again, Casper wasn't anything like Travis.

He was handsome…maybe even a little too handsome for her liking. Every nurse who had come into her room had kept their eyes on him a moment too long. It had been tempting to show the women that he was hers, but the truth was just the opposite. He was nothing more than a work colleague…albeit a work colleague who hadn't left her side since the accident.

More than simply being handsome, he had a kind side. Often he tried to act tough, all business, but when he'd stepped between her and Travis in the hospital she had caught a glimpse of the sensitive and caring side that he tried to hide from the world.

She glanced over at him, but his face was hidden in the shadow cast by his hat. Maybe she was wrong; maybe she had an idealized version of who he really was—she had a terrible habit of doing that. She had sworn Travis was her knight in shining armor. At first it hadn't mattered that her friends had warned her off; it didn't matter when he told her who she could be friends with and what time she should come home, and it didn't matter that for days on end he treated her like she was nothing more than his often neglected pet…coming and going as he pleased and not speaking to her for days. All that had mattered was that when he looked at her, the world stood still.

If only she had listened to what everyone had told

her, and that tiny place in the back of her mind that had told her it was all too good to be true.

She couldn't risk being hurt like that again. She doubted she could live through it a second time. "What did you do before you got stationed at Goat Haunt?" she asked as she unlocked the door.

Casper tensed at the question. He was so quiet that she wondered if he had even heard her.

"Casper?"

"Yeah... I was in the FBI. Mostly specializing toward the end—handwriting analysis, that kind of thing." He closed the door behind them and stood there, his back to her as he stared at the door like a trapped animal.

"Look, if you want, you can go. I think I can handle things from here."

He took out his phone and glanced down at his screen. "No...it's fine. Grant hasn't gotten back to me yet. There's nothing more for me to do until I hear from him."

"What all did he say?" she asked as she gingerly walked to the old, tattered brown couch and sat down. There was a threadbare quilt that hung over the back, one her foster mother had made her back in grade school. There was even a bit of purple nail polish she had carelessly spilled ages ago.

"The drugs are missing. He's going to go back to the scene and check to make sure he didn't miss anything." Stuffing the phone into the breast pocket of his jean jacket, he sat down in the recliner across from her. "And he found a receipt."

"A receipt? What do you mean?"

"It was jammed into the corner of the green bag."

"I swear I looked everywhere in that thing... But I guess I could have missed it. Wait, do you think someone planted it, Mr. FBI?"

He cringed, but she wasn't sure why.

He opened up his phone and pulled up the photos of the bag that they had taken on scene. "Regardless of how it got there, because we screwed up the chain of custody, the receipt can't be used in court for anything. We can't prove that it was or wasn't there without reasonable doubt."

"But it could help us figure out the vic's identity, right?"

"I suppose," he said, giving her a weak smile. "Right now though, you need to take care of yourself and just focus on getting some rest." He stood up and grabbed the quilt off the back of the couch, wrapping it around her shoulders.

She caught his familiar scent and closed her eyes. She imagined pulling him down on the couch beside her, wrapping him in the blanket and letting him hold her. They could spend the day together, huddled in each other's embrace and away from the hurt that filled the world around them.

When she opened her eyes to find him looking at her, she started to reach toward him, but he pulled away. She dropped her hand and realized that it was still hidden by the blanket. He couldn't have known what she was thinking or what she wanted, but there was still a pang of rejection.

"Uh, tea or coffee?" he asked with a cute half smile.

By this time of day she was normally on her second or even third cup of the tar-black stuff they brewed at the ranger station. Yet the thought of the melt-your-spoon coffee made her stomach churn. "Tea, but I can get it." She moved to stand up, but he stopped her.

"No. You. Sit. Down," he commanded, pointing at the couch. "I got this."

She did as he asked and he made his way to the kitchen.

There was a bang of cupboards and the sound of water running. She leaned over the arm of the couch, trying to catch a glimpse of what he was doing, but he was just out of sight. "The teapot's on the stove, but if you need a cup—"

"Got it, but where're the tea bags?"

It was her solemn belief the best tea could only be brewed by use of loose leaf teas, but somehow asking him—the man who banged around in her kitchen like a gorilla in its cage—to go to that much work seemed like a stretch. "There's some leftover stuff in the cupboard over the stove," she said as a smile played across her lips.

Somehow it felt right having a man back in the place, someone to share the little space. Then again, over the last year she had found solace in being alone. She could have things her own way and take things at her own pace. There was never anyone there pushing her, making her compromise or check in. She had been truly independent.

Casper poked his head around the corner and lifted up a box of Lipton. "This it?" He smiled, and the simple action made her heart stutter.

She nodded. "Are you sure you don't want help?"

He waved her off. "I got this, Lex. Have faith."

Faith was something she had in limited supply—especially when it came to having faith in a man.

She got up, walked to the kitchen and leaned against the wall, the quilt still wrapped around her shoulders.

Casper had his back to her, and his hips moved with a song that must have only been in his head. She moved to speak, to let him know she was there, but stopped and instead just enjoyed the view of his round, well-muscled derriere shifting under his tight jeans. Maybe she was objectifying the man, but she couldn't help herself. He was a fine specimen.

There was a faint whistle as the kettle started to boil and he turned to grab a cup with string hanging out. He saw her and smiled. "How long have you been standing there?"

"Long enough to know that you might have missed your calling. You should've been a stripper." She laughed, and heat rushed to her face as she realized how bold she sounded. "Sorry…" she quickly offered. "Sometimes the filter between my brain and my mouth malfunctions."

"I don't think my mother would agree with you… at least about the stripper bit." He laughed, the sound rich and thick. "And your filter, or lack of one, is something I happen to like about you. Honesty is always attractive."

The heat intensified in her cheeks. "I…er…" she stumbled as she realized that he thought she was pretty. She didn't know exactly how to respond. "Is the tea ready?"

He poured the water over the tea bag and let it sit for a few seconds before handing it to her.

"Thanks," she said, taking a sip of the boiling hot liquid. The tea was so old it had gone stale, but she swallowed it down. "It's great," she said, her voice so high that she wondered if he could hear her lie.

He lifted a corner of the blanket as it started to slip from her shoulder. As his fingers grazed her skin, she found herself leaning into his hand, wanting more.

"How's your head, filter notwithstanding?" he said, his voice taking on a soft edge.

"I'm good." Aside from the way her head seemed to lighten every time he drew near, she felt fine. "Do you have a picture of the receipt?" she asked, trying to move the conversation away from the way she felt. "Maybe we can pull something from it if the person paid with a card."

The light in his eyes dimmed, like he was slightly disappointed in being drawn back to work, yet she

couldn't be drawn into anything more than a friendship with the handsome agent. It was too soon to
jump into another relationship. It had been a year,
but her heartache was still too fresh to want to step
into something that almost certainly would shatter
her further.

Casper pulled out his phone and scanned through
its pictures. "There's one…it looks like the receipt is
for someplace called The Prince and the Pea."

"Really?" She giggled, stepping close so she could
see the picture of the receipt. "Oh wait, I know that
place. It's on the Waterton side."

Glacier National Park was merely one part of the
first International Peace Park, spreading over the
American/Canadian border and merging with Waterton Lakes Park in Alberta.

"What kind of shop is it?"

She bit her lip as she tried to remember. "It's just
a touristy place. You know, flag cups and Waterton
sweatshirts."

He stared at his phone. "He spent thirty-seven
bucks."

"In a place like that, that wouldn't go very far. Everything around the park is expensive." She glanced
at the phone but the receipt didn't list what was pur-
chased or a credit card number.

"Look," she said, pointing to the time stamp. "It's
from three days ago, kinda late in the evening."

His gaze moved to the door as if he was thinking
about how badly he wanted to go after their lead.

"Let's go," she offered. "If we don't go, we're missing a chance. Maybe we can find whoever was working and they can give us an ID on whoever this belongs to."

He looked back down at his phone and then up again, studying her. "You're supposed to rest. I'm sure Grant is looking into it."

"Grant is a great guy, and he's many things, but he's not the first one I would go to when a lead needs to be investigated."

In truth, Grant was fine—maybe he was biding his time until he was eligible for retirement, but his heart always seemed to be in the right place. He loved the park, maybe even as much as she did.

She took another sip of the steadily cooling tea and tried to control a pucker as bitterness laced over her tongue. Looking over to her closed bedroom door...if she wasn't careful, she feared that she would fall into old habits—habits that led too quickly to that bedroom.

He took her cup and set it in the kitchen sink. "Sorry about the tea."

She laughed. "How about you buy me a cup in Waterton?"

"Why do I have a feeling that this is an argument I'm not going to win?"

Her like for him grew. In her relationship with Travis, he had never pushed her when she'd made up her mind. It was one of the things she had loved about him—his acceptance of her independent nature. But when things had started to go downhill, his love for her independence had turned into hatred of the thing he had sworn he adored. As much as she had tried to compromise and give up a bit of her freedoms, in the end, his possessiveness had only led to irreparable damage.

Maybe things with Casper would be different—then again, who would want to love her? If life had taught her anything, it was that any time she got close, the people she loved fell away. Love, while it started with promises of milk and honey, only ended in immeasurable pain, and pain like that was something she could live without.

IT WAS A long drive to Waterton and they spent most of it talking about the weather and the mundane events of everyday life—not that Casper minded. It was a nice break from the worry and the guilt he'd felt after the accident. Yet every once in a while he still caught himself looking over at her and making sure that she was all right.

She stared out the window as they drove north on Highway 6 on the Canadian side. Waterton wasn't much farther, and the closer they got the quieter she had become. "Are you okay?" he asked, hoping pain wasn't keeping her silent.

"I'm fine," she answered simply.

"You're being quiet. Should I be worried?"

She looked at him with a tragic smile. "Actually, I was just thinking about the accident."

A pang of guilt drove through him. "I'm sorry. Seriously."

"I know. I don't blame you at all." She waved him off. "I was just thinking about the car that came at us. Did Grant find out anything about the other driver?"

He could still see the car's headlights as it came straight at them, and the tiny "H" emblem at the center of the grille. "The car didn't stop. And no one has come forward with any information about who the driver was of the Honda. Why?"

"You remember the biker behind us?"

"Yeah." His hands tightened on the steering wheel.

"You don't suppose they were working together or something, do you?"

He reached up and ran his fingers through his hair, glancing at his hat resting in the middle of the dashboard. "I doubt it. Very few people knew about the accident up by Kootenai. Even fewer knew what we found, and even less knew what we were planning on doing with the evidence."

· She sighed. "I know. But everything about this just feels *off*. You know?" She looked over at him with her big green eyes. As they caught the light, he could just make out the edges of brown at their center.

Travis had been an idiot for letting her go.

He forced himself to ignore the feelings that rose within him.

Lex was right. Something about this entire series of events was amiss. Though it could have been mostly the woman at his side, the woman who had reawakened his heart, the woman who made him question the man he thought he was, that had him the most confused.

He just needed to focus on the investigation. While he wasn't sure that she was correct in her conspiracy theory, he had to admit that there was something wrong with the picture.

"We have to look at this objectively, Lex. Right now there is nothing to prove that there was any real criminal act. For all we know, the drugs flew out of the truck and over the side of the cliff, and the car that came at us...well, maybe the driver just wasn't paying attention."

She gave him a sideways glance. "You know that's crap. If the drugs were still on scene, or even near it, Grant would have found them. Someone took them."

"Okay, let's say that happened. Then what are they planning on doing with the drugs? Why would someone take such a huge risk in stealing them from a Fed?"

"Someone who thought they wouldn't get caught," she said. "Think about it. We're in an accident in a place that is basically off the grid, there's little traffic, at least this time of year, and there's a lot of money to be made."

They had been a perfect target, Fed or not. "Or it may have been nothing more than an opportunistic theft. Maybe whoever picked these drugs up is sitting in their hotel right now, wondering how they got themselves into such a mess. They know that we're going to find them. It's only a matter of time."

"Don't you think you're giving people just a little too much credit in assuming that they feel guilty over this?"

In truth, most days he felt the same way, at least when he'd been deep in the FBI. All he'd seen were the dregs of society. They were everywhere—thieves, con men and murderers. It didn't matter what age, sex or socioeconomic bracket a person found themselves in; human nature and the filth that came along with it didn't change.

Yet what could possibly be behind Lex saying something like that? Who had hurt her so bad that she thought the world was only full of evil?

"All I'm saying is that sooner or later we're going to track down these drugs," she continued. "Either someone's going to talk or the drugs are going to start hitting the streets. If they start moving around Montana, we'll hear about it from the local law enforcement."

He cringed at the thought of more agencies joining the chase. It would be a pissing contest in no time and at the center of it all would be him and what some would undoubtedly call his incompetence. "I hope we can figure this problem out long before we get to that point."

He pulled the car to a stop in front of The Prince and the Pea. The place was definitely a tourist shop, its brightly lit windows filled with everything from books to blankets.

Casper walked around the car to help Lex, but she was standing tall. Aside from the bruise on her cheek, she looked strong—strong enough that she didn't want or need his help.

He opened the door for her that led into the shop. An elderly man stood behind the counter, sipping on a cup of coffee.

"Hi. Let me know if I can help you with anything," the man said with a slight Canadian accent.

"Thanks. Actually, I was hoping to ask you a few questions." Casper reached into his back pocket, pulling out his wallet to flash his badge. "We found some evidence linking a person to this store. We're just hoping to get any information you may have that can help us."

The man ran his hand over his gray hair, which sat in a plastered comb-over across his balding dome. "I…sure. I guess."

Casper pulled up the picture of the receipt on his phone. "We found this. According to the date, it's from a couple of days ago. Is there anything you can tell me about it?" He set his phone down on the counter so the man could take a look.

"Sure…" The man squinted as he leaned in and studied the details. "Hmm, I was working that day, but you know, we get so many people in and out of these doors throughout the season that it's hard to keep track from one day to the next."

"It's important that you remember." He glanced around, looking for some type of security cameras, but there were none in sight. "Do you have any cameras, anything we could look at, anything that could jog your memory?"

Lex stepped closer to the counter and motioned toward the picture on his phone. "What kind of thing would you have sold for that amount?"

The guy looked around the store. "With this cold weather we've been selling a lot of sweatshirts." His face brightened. "Actually, there was a lady who came in that day. Bought a sweatshirt and a Coke. With tax, that puts us right around that amount." He zoomed in on the time.

A woman? Was it possible the green bag hadn't belonged to the man they'd found disarticulated in the timber?

"Let me check my sales." He turned to his computer and tapped away at the keys.

Casper nodded appreciatively at Lex. Of course the man behind the counter wouldn't think in terms of people. Rather, he'd think in terms of the merchandise that had moved.

"Yeah," the man said with a nod. "Here it is." He tilted the screen so they could see his copy of the transaction. "She paid with cash. American. Wasn't very talkative." He pointed toward a rack of blue sweatshirts. "She bought a plain blue sweatshirt, just a small logo of the park on the breast."

"Can you describe the woman?"

The man looked up and squinted, like he could pull the woman's image from thin air. "I don't remember much about her. She was in her midthirties. Had darkish hair?" His tone didn't incite a tremendous amount of confidence.

"You remember what she was wearing?"

The guy nodded. "Oh yeah, that was the weird thing. She was wearing a leather vest thing. Had some patches."

"You mean the woman was part of a motorcycle club?" Lex asked, excited.

The man looked at Lex and shrugged. "I guess. I think she was driving a motorcycle or something. Oh, and she didn't want a plastic bag—which is just fine if you ask me. It might only save me a few cents, but it adds up, you know."

"Why didn't she want a bag?" Casper asked.

"If I remember right, she put the sweatshirt on. And she stuck the Coke in her backpack."

Casper twitched. "By chance, do you remember what her backpack looked like?"

"It was green. Kind of a military-style one."

"Did you get a good look at her leather vest?" Lex asked.

The man tapped on the counter. "I didn't get a real good look. But I think there was a set of green wings and there was a badge thingy that read "Property." He motioned toward the place on his chest, right above his right pec where it would have been.

"A top rocker. Did it have any kind of name underneath?"

"Couldn't tell ya." The guy shrugged.

"Is there anything else you can tell us? Anything at all?" Lex pressed.

"I'm sorry…" The guy shook his head. "But if you have any more questions, you can come around anytime."

They may not have found the identity of their victim, but with the man's help, they'd found their break, a lead that could help Casper save face. And maybe it could keep him from losing another job—or at least let him keep it for a little longer.

Heck, if things went right, he could stick around. If he did, maybe he could give falling in love another shot. Then again, love was far more dangerous than the people he chased.

Chapter Six

The wind blew cold against Lex's skin as she walked out of the shop. Casper's face was pulled tight into a worried expression, one she had come to know so well at the hospital. His grin was much more handsome, but even serious he was so good-looking that he made her uncomfortable.

She sucked in a breath as the icy-fingered breeze brushed over her skin and made goose bumps rise on her arms.

He glanced over at her, and his face grew impossibly tighter. "Are you okay? Do you need to sit down? Damn it. I knew I shouldn't have brought you up here."

Her chill was quickly replaced by annoyance. "First, I'm fine, just cold—you don't need to get worked up over me. I'm a big girl. If I didn't think I should be out here I wouldn't be. I know my limits." She held up her fingers. "And second, do you think this is just *your* investigation? In every way this is my jurisdiction. Your boss called in a favor in ask-

ing to include you on the body's recovery and sub-
sequent investigation."

Casper's face fell. "You talked to Randall?"

"He explained that the CBP wanted to be included
on this as it involved a potential illegal incident that
may blow back on your post."

His cheeks paled. "I didn't let this guy through.
Anything suspicious and I'm on top of it."

"You better hope that's the case." She felt sorry
for him as she watched what little color was left in
his face drain away. "Your boss sounded none too
pleased that you had let an undocumented through—
I can only imagine what he's thinking if he heard
about the drugs."

"I never saw a guy carrying a military-style bag
come through—I would have noticed," he said, an
edge of panic and fear in his voice. "There's no way
I'm responsible for what is happening here—heck,
he might not have ever crossed the border, or he may
have slipped it. Thousands of people just walk over
the border near my post. I can't investigate every
sensor that goes off—in fact, Randall wouldn't even
allow me to investigate ten percent of them. The
only reason he let me this time is in case the press
got ahold of this…"

"Don't worry, Casper, we'll figure this out. In
fact, we're going to do such a good job buttoning
this up that you or I may be the next employee of
the month." She tried to take the edge off, but she

couldn't manage the inflection needed in her voice to sell it, and the joke fell flat.

He quirked an eyebrow as he looked at her. "Somehow I find you getting employee of the month hard to believe. You... You are too independent. Does your boss even know where you are?"

Was he really going to pick a fight? With Travis she normally would have stepped right up to the plate, taken a swing and let the fight commence, but with Casper it was different. He wasn't picking a fight out of a need for control; it felt as if it was more out of the need to protect.

As a former FBI agent it made sense that he would have the intrinsic need to safeguard those around him. Yet that still didn't answer why he'd been sent to the nowhere border. And as badly as she wanted to get the real answer, with them halfway to a fight it didn't seem like the right time to try and pry it out of him.

She sighed in an attempt to compose herself. "I think you're confusing independent with determined. And right now, Casper, I think determination is going to be the only thing that is going to solve this case. Then I can check in with my boss."

As she spoke, her phone stirred to life and belted the song "Born to be Wild." Heat rushed to her cheeks as she thought of how much it paralleled the conversation they were having, and she turned away in order to avoid any sort of self-righteous smirk that was probably playing across Casper's lips.

"Alexis?" She was met with her boss Head Ranger Denver Dragger's voice. "Where are you?"

Speak of the devil.

She caught a glimpse of Casper in the window, complete with that damned smirk.

"Uh…what?" She tried to force herself to concentrate on her boss's voice, but she couldn't stop looking at Casper's wide-set jaw and the stubble that riddled his cheeks. He needed a shave, but something about the scruffy look made a part of her stir to life.

The head ranger coughed. "Alexis, are you listening?"

"Yeah. I'm here. We're just tracking down a lead on the dead hiker case—I think we're close to getting an ID on him, and maybe we can figure out where the drugs were coming from and where he was taking them."

She could almost hear Dragger shake his head. "Lex, I'm calling because I wanted to check on you after your little accident, but if I'd known you were going to use your day off to go traipsing around the world…" He paused. "There's work that needs to be done. As it is, if you're feeling better, I need you to come to work in the morning. I want someone else on this. I need you at the Sperry Chalet. It needs to be buttoned up for the season."

The Sperry Chalet was a primitive cabin only accessible by horse or hike. Normally she liked to help with the winterization process, but this time it didn't call to her like the investigation. She certainly couldn't hand it over to someone else now, when they were so close to finding some kind of answers. "Sir, I'm afraid I'm—"

"If you're not in your bed right now, then I fully expect to see you at the station in the morning." He hung up without waiting for her response.

Normally she and Dragger saw eye to eye on most things and they treated each other with a sort of mutual respect. In fact, he'd once made a point of telling her that she shouldn't look at him like a boss, rather as a comrade in arms. They had always been friends—at least up to now.

Maybe she had simply misunderstood the man. Or perhaps it was that things were winding down for the season and he was just stressing about everything that needed to be checked off the list. God knew there was a boatload of things that needed to be done; cabins that needed to be winterized, chalets that needed to be locked down and prepared for the onslaught of snow that they would undoubtedly receive, and there were the ongoing needs of the thousands of guests that ventured through their park via roads and trails. Truth be told, they were sorely understaffed and underfunded, but that hadn't ever caused a rift in their friendship before. She just couldn't understand why it would suddenly drive a wedge between them—and she certainly didn't understand why he would want her to hand off the investigation.

This was hardly her first investigation into a

death in the park. Every summer a few more people found their ends there. Last summer she and Travis had handled an investigation into a woman who had fallen into McDonald Creek and drowned. After they'd concluded their investigation, Dragger had made a point of commending them.

He liked her work, so why was he pulling her?

She wasn't going to change his mind. Not Dragger's.

She dropped the phone back into her pocket. She'd only have a few more hours until tomorrow morning, and then this case would fall into someone else's hands.

"What's going on?"

She looked up at Casper and their eyes locked. "It looks like I called it down on myself, and my independence just bit me in the ass." Her heart sank as she looked at him. "I'm supposed to go to work on the seasonal projects tomorrow, and this investigation will be taken over by another ranger. You're right, I don't think I'll be getting employee of the month after all."

"If that's the case, we're going to need to work fast. Who's Sherlock without his Watson?"

"You are really calling yourself Sherlock?" Her spirits picked up.

He nodded, straightening his back and pretending to hold a pipe.

At least the man knew how to make her smile. "I should be Sherlock," she said with a laugh. "Regardless, where would you like to begin, my dear man?" she asked in her worst British accent.

His laugh rippled through the air and spread through the quiet street.

A man sitting alone on a park bench turned and looked at them and gave them an appreciative nod.

"Shhh..." She reached over and touched Casper's arm as she giggled. His skin was hot and penetrating on her cold fingers and she drew them back.

He looked to the place where she had touched him. "This could be simple. The man in the shop told us that it's a woman and she was wearing a cut. That may mean she is a part of a local motorcycle club. The Hells Keepers are in control of the territory, all the way out to Washington as far as I know."

"Could she have just been a leisure rider?" They were up through the park all the time, weekend bikers. Often they could be found at the top of Logan's Pass, victims of the stalling effects of the elevation.

"A leisure rider doesn't wear a cut, especially not one with a property top rocker and a wings patch."

"Is that supposed to mean something to me?"

"Women aren't welcomed into the motorcycle clubs, or the one-percenters—the outlaws. Their only way in is by being a turnabout, a Mama, or they can be one of the guys' old ladies."

"Old lady?"

"A woman that's in a serious relationship with one of the men. They don't have to do anything like the turnabouts—selling their body or being a thing that is passed around the club—but even old ladies have to do the men's bidding."

"That makes absolutely no sense to me. What kind of woman would want to be used like that? Or worse, to let their man control every aspect of their lives?"

"I get why you wouldn't understand, Ms. Independent, but there are a lot of women out there who are nothing like you. They like to have the safety net that an outlaw club provides. Sure, they run outside of the rules of social customs, but that kind of life brings danger. In exchange for protection they respect and trust those in their club—it's their family."

She gave him a confused look.

"Their strength lies in the power of the brotherhood, and the women who go out of the way to protect them. The ATF, you know the Bureau of Alcohol, Tobacco, Firearms and Explosives, and other federal agencies are constantly trying to infiltrate their group."

"Because of fear of the power they have?"

Casper took her gently by the hand and helped her back into the car. "They are more powerful than most average citizens realize. These groups, and those like them, are some of the biggest smugglers of drugs and weapons into the United States, and they have well-developed and successful distribution channels."

"Haven't the agencies taken them down? I see the things on TV all the time, where one of you Feds goes undercover and infiltrates their group and brings them to their knees." She buckled her seat belt as Casper walked around, got in and started the car.

He took off his hat and slid it onto the seat between them like it was a physical reminder that they needed to be kept apart. "The government has had some big busts in the past, but truth be told, nailing these guys is a bit like playing Whack-a-Mole. You knock one chapter down only to have another one spring up near them and take over the business they left behind. There's always someone who wants to live outside the norms that society has placed on them—and they use their fringe lifestyle to build a network of those just like them."

"A 'divided they stand' kind of thing?" she asked.

"Exactly. Even for the women."

In a way she could understand a woman's desire to want to be loved, to be part of a group, and find acceptance—especially when the world was against her. Heck, she could definitely understand the world being against her. Ever since she was a child and she had been in the foster system and then shuffled from one house to the next, she had known the fear of being alone and the feelings of powerlessness that followed on its heels. Maybe she wasn't so different from the women after all. Maybe the only difference was in the fact that now she was fighting violence while they were simply fighting the world.

He drove down the shop-lined road that led to a park on the edge of town near the Prince of Wales Hotel. Passing the palatial expanse of green lawns and rows of white and pink roses that adorned the lawn of the hotel, they entered the forest. Large pines poked their heads up from the crowd, each one struggling for a little more sunlight than the one next to it.

"Where are we going?" she asked.

"The trailhead." He dipped his chin, motioning down the road. "It may be a long shot, but maybe we can find something there. The woman has to be involved somehow with the guy and his drugs. If they were coming from the store, then this trailhead seems to be the most likely place where our vic would have started his hike.

"You know what? I bet you money that this guy came through after my checkpoint closed. It makes sense. The time on the receipt was six p.m. From the trailhead it was about a three-hour hike. The guy must have planned this whole thing to avoid getting caught." As he spoke, his eyes brightened and color rose in his face.

He turned and the sunshine glistened off his chestnut-colored hair, making it sparkle, and there was a hat ring where his hat hugged his head. He caught her staring and sent her that sexy grin that sometimes drove her crazy, but right now she wouldn't change it for the world. As he looked at her in that moment, it was as if he was peering down into the very core of her and seeing her for the woman she truly was. The thought made her shift in her seat and she glanced away.

She didn't want him to look at her like that. She

would hate for him to look into her soul and not like what he saw. She'd already had far too much rejection in her life.

Everyone had baggage, and though he knew about Travis and the divorce, he didn't need to know any more about her—or about her past. Some things were just better left unknown.

The road came to an end, looping around, and it was edged with parking spots. Casper pulled to a stop and got out. He picked up his hat from the seat and shoved it on his head, hiding his beautiful hair.

The parking lot had a few cars, most with Montana or Alberta plates, but there wasn't a motorcycle in sight.

"What do you think we should be looking for exactly?"

"Most of the time when it comes down to investigating a crime, there's a few things you generally look for—but in this case, all I can say is that I hope that we'll know what we're looking for when we see it," Casper said.

She hoped he was right. They didn't have much time and she'd hate to waste what little they had on an idea that wouldn't pan out.

Casper walked around the asphalt parking lot, picking his way one spot at a time, looking at the tire tracks like they held some kind of clue. Yet after about the tenth parking space, he ran his hand over the brim of his hat in frustration. "Damn it, I was hoping we'd get lucky."

"It's fine. There has to be something else we can find. Maybe we can get someone else to give us a lead on the girl. Maybe someone saw her coming out of the shop, or meeting up with the man whose body we found." She touched his arm, trying to reassure him, but the same familiar burn returned and she dropped her hand.

Would it be that way every time she touched him?

"Let's just keep looking. Maybe peek over there in the tree line," she said, motioning toward the woods.

She looked down at her fingers and wiggled them as he walked away; maybe she was just imagining the feeling when she'd touched him. Maybe it wasn't real.

She thought back to the first time she had ever come to Glacier National Park. She had been young, and it hadn't been long after she had been moved into her third foster home when her foster mother, Melody Finch, had brought her to Lake McDonald. The waters were so clear that the colored stones made it look like a rainbow had been trapped under the weight of the water. The peaks of the mountains had been covered in thick layers of snow, framing the natural beauty that surrounded her.

For the first time in her life, she had felt truly and absolutely free. In that moment, with Melody holding her hand, she had felt the burn—the love of the place that surrounded her and the love for the woman who could show her such beauty and kindness.

Looking back, she realized the sacrifice her adoptive mother had made in taking her, a child who had been through so much, into her home. She'd loved her and raised her as her own, never treating her differently than Paul, or her sisters Raquel, Treana or Anna. Without her adoptive mother, Lex didn't doubt for a second that she would have become a lost soul—perhaps just like the biker woman they were tracking.

It was strange how one moment in time, one little feeling, could change a life forever.

She glanced over at Casper. He was working his way through a thick stand of timber at the side of the parking lot. Though it wasn't especially warm, there was the sheen of sweat on his face.

"Come here," he said, motioning toward her.

She gingerly made her way through the gnarled and ripping fingers of the pines to his side. On the ground, at the tip of his cowboy boot, was a thin trail, almost like a game trail, but the ground was black with organic matter that had been torn away rather than worn down.

"Someone's been driving through here," he said, pointing his chin in the direction the trail headed.

The trees that surrounded them were too close and too thick for a normal vehicle to fit through. On the other hand, it would have perfectly fit a motorcycle.

Casper followed the path into the woods.

"Wait," she called after him, hurrying to catch up. She took hold of his arm and gently tugged him to a stop. "Wait. What if this is some kind of trap?"

The trail ahead of them was swallowed up by the shadows of the trees, silently disappearing into the foreboding forest.

Her question didn't seem unreasonable; any number of things could have been waiting for them at the end of the path, but Casper looked at her like she was a skittish deer.

"Don't worry, there's probably nothing on this thing. I just need to take a look," he said, his voice soft and low. She wasn't a damned deer. She wasn't weak—at least, she wouldn't ever be again. She'd had too much of that as a child. Her strength was the only thing that would keep her sane.

"Maybe it was just some kids having a good time with their dirt bikes, Lex. Trust me, you don't have to be scared. I'd never let someone hurt you."

Casper reached down and took her hand. His fingers were rough with calluses and his skin was hot, and the burn deep down in her core returned. The movement came so fast and unexpectedly, that before she could stop herself, she wrapped her fingers around his. He led her forward, and her apprehension decreased with each step they took together.

Though she was supposed to be watching for clues, all she could look at was their entwined fingers. She knew it was her hand in his, but she couldn't feel where she ended and he began; rather, it was as if they were one, tightening and loosening as they flexed and moved.

Her breath hitched in her throat as she imagined

what it would be like to feel him in another, more intimate way. Her cheeks warmed and she forced herself to look away from his thick, work-worn fingers.

She closed her eyes and tried to collect her breath and force her thoughts away from the forbidden embers of dreams that he stoked.

Not watching, she took a step forward, colliding with him, and let go. "Whoa, I'm sorry," she said, afraid that if she looked into his eyes again, he might be able to catch a glimpse of her thoughts and the lurid dreams that she was struggling to hide.

He didn't say anything, and she glanced up. His back was turned to her, and he was looking at something she couldn't see. She stepped around him in hopes of seeing what had caught his attention.

There, parked at the base of a tree and poorly concealed by a smattering of broken-off pine boughs, was a Harley-Davidson. A thin layer of dust covered the bike's leather seat and several days' worth of fallen pine needles were littered over its body.

Casper had been right. Sometimes you knew a clue the moment you saw it; and this one had two giant skulls painted on the bike's gas tank that stared right back.

Chapter Seven

The two skulls leaned against each other like they had been set there as part of some kind of Mayan sacrifice to the gods, except the sockets were painted in a red so deep that it reminded him of the color of spent arterial blood. At the base of the skulls was a coiled snake, its diamond-shaped head sitting between them, as if waiting for the exact moment to deliver the fatal blow.

The rear fender was midnight-black, like the base coat on the gas tank, but instead of skulls it had strands of silver razor wire running down its length.

"This thing just needs a danger sign and I think it would be the full package," Lex joked.

He chuckled. "Everything about it just screams *hug me*, doesn't it?"

He motioned toward the Madness and Mayhem motto that was etched into the gas tank's lid and nodded. "I think you nailed it. I mean, just look. He must be a big softy."

"There's no license plate," she said, pointing to

two empty screw holes where someone had deliberately removed the plate. "So, how can we find the owner?"

"There should be a VIN." He searched the bike's frame, but he was surprised when there was nothing more than a series of scratches where someone had scoured away the machine's identification numbers. This was a bike of someone who knew there was a possibility of leaving it behind—and didn't want it to be traced back to the owner.

Casper searched the ground around the bike, but there was nothing, not even a cigarette butt. Whoever had dumped the thing had been clean—too clean. It made his skin prickle.

Even so, they must not have understood the tenacity of a CBP agent on a mission; especially when the more time that went by, the less likely they were to find out the identity of the man who had been running drugs. If they couldn't identify the man quickly, there was no chance they would find the person supplying the Canadian Blue and put a stop to the influx of drugs, at least through Casper's territory.

"Did you find it?" Lex asked.

"It's not there." He kicked the dirt near the back tire as he stood up.

"Is there another way?"

"With no plate and no VIN, there's only one other way we can try and find out who this bike belonged to—we're going to have to go to street level."

"What do you mean?"

He smiled. "I got a friend in the US Marshal Service, Evan Steel—he can put some feelers out in the biker community and the prison system. Maybe he can get a lead on this guy for us. Then we can track down the woman from the store. In the meantime, unfortunately, we're going to have to call in the locals on this one. We're on the wrong side of the border."

He made a quick call to the local Mounties to report an abandoned vehicle and the possibility of its tie into a criminal investigation.

"They're on their way," he said, slipping the phone back into the breast pocket of his blue flannel button-up shirt. As he spoke, the sky above them darkened, sending ominous, skeletal shadows. "They said they'd be here in about an hour. From the looks of things, we may be waiting out here in the rain."

A rattle of thunder echoed through the timber, the sound deep and crashing and so loud that Lex jumped. Casper had a primal urge to reach over and pull her into his arms and shelter her from the storm, but he held back.

"Do you want to go back to the truck, wait there?" Lex asked, jabbing her thumb in the direction of the parking lot.

Her eyes were wide with fear, and the urge in him worsened. Here was this strong, incredible woman… a woman who could handle death and car accidents like they were just another day at the park, yet she was afraid of thunder. The thought was endearing.

Lex stepped beside him and took his hand. He

squeezed her and let their entwined hands fall be-tween them as he slowly led the way back down the trail toward the car. He took his time picking through the timber and weaving around trees in an attempt to keep holding her—it felt so good, her skin against his.

His shoulder brushed hers and as they touched, he could have sworn he heard her breath catch, but he told himself that it was nothing more than the sound of the wind in the trees.

Rain spattered down, kicking up the thick black dirt at their feet and splashing mud against their legs as they walked. Lex was frowning as if she realized that Casper was intentionally lengthening their hike, but she said nothing and instead gripped him tighter.

He led her toward a stand of trees where two could barely fit side by side and, as they moved, she was forced to turn slightly, putting them face-to-face. She blinked slowly as she looked up at him.

The rain fell around them, wetting their faces like spent tears.

Reaching up, he cupped her face in his hands, running his thumbs over the soft skin of her bottom lip. Her warm breath caressed his finger, a hard con-trast against the cold rain, and the feeling only made him want her more.

"You're so damned beautiful." He moved closer, so close he could feel the warmth radiating off her body.

She stepped forward, not waiting for him to make

the first move, and pressed her lips to his. She ran her tongue against his, making a need deep inside him move with carnal hunger. He wanted her. This. Now.

He pulled her against him; her body was soft and supplicating as he pressed her to the bark of the tree. He trailed his fingers down her back, grazing over the intersection of her lower back and the top of her pants and cupping her. She was round in his hands, strong and muscular and even better than he could have imagined.

Squeezing her gently, she moaned softly into his mouth, making him rise with a want so urgent that he felt the urge to growl. There was something so right about this moment and this woman that, as he held her, all of his misgivings slipped away. Maybe they could make something work out. He'd be reassigned to another point of entry over the winter, but he could stay close—anything to be near her.

The tree bark crackled as he lifted her and wrapped her legs around his waist. She was hot against him—her body's response to their kiss. She wanted this. She wanted him.

Breaking their bond, she leaned her head back and sucked in a breath as he trailed kisses down her neck. He pulled back her shirt, just exposing the top of her pale skin. She was so soft. So warm. So his.

"Is that you, eh?" a man with a thick Canadian accent asked, shattering the moment.

Casper let go of her, and she swayed slightly. He

took her hand in an attempt to help her catch her balance, but truth be told, he was unsteady, as well.

He turned at the sound of a man's laugh.

"We didn't mean to interrupt you all. If you want we can all come back a little later—give you some privacy, you know."

He wanted them to disappear, so he and Lex could finish what they had started. But before he could speak, Lex, who was brushing off the back of her shirt, stepped around him. "We were just waiting for you. Glad to see you could finally make it."

Casper gave the sergeant and his man a quick rundown of the case, giving them what little information he had. It ate at him to include more people in the investigation, but it was good to have their cooperation in finding anything on their side of the border.

The sergeant nodded as he spoke, but the man couldn't seem to keep his gaze from drifting to the bike.

"You know anything about the bike? Who it may belong to?" Casper asked.

The officer beside the sergeant leaned in and whispered something about a razor, but as hard as he tried, Casper couldn't hear everything that was said.

The sergeant shook his head and gave the man a look that said shut up in every language. The man shut his mouth immediately.

"I'm afraid we haven't a clue, but rest assured we will be looking into this bike and its owner," the sergeant said.

"We'd appreciate it. Any information we could get would be great. Right now we have little more to go on than a wing and a prayer," Casper said in an attempt to build a little comraderie.

The sergeant smiled; the motion was so tight and high that Casper suspected the man liked to hear about their failings.

Did they think they were better than some silly Americans? Or was it something else that made the man react like he had?

He shook the thoughts from his head. In the end, it didn't matter what the Mounties thought. They just needed to work together to get as much information as possible.

As they loaded the bike onto the flatbed truck to tow it away, Casper made sure to snap a few more close-ups of the bike and scene. He emailed them with a note explaining everything to his friend, Evan Steel.

His phone rang. He turned to Lex. "Will you be okay here?"

She gave him a confused look. "Why wouldn't I be?"

He glanced over at the Mounties, who were busy talking to the tow truck driver. Maybe he had them all wrong, but a gut feeling warned him not to leave them alone with Lex. "I gotta answer this, but stay where I can see you, okay?"

She frowned and gave him a confused grin that he found so sexy. "No problem."

He walked back into the timber and out of earshot from the Mounties, but close enough that he could still keep an eye on Lex.

"Stuck, huh?" Steel said, his words resting in the middle ground between a question and a statement.

"Never said that," Casper said with an acknowledging chuckle. "But I'm glad you called. You ever seen a bike like this one before?"

"I had a chance to run an image search for you in the database. According to what I found, the two skulls and the snake image is used by only one specific motorcycle club, a group called Hells Keepers. It sounds like they do a lot of the club's dirty business."

"Where are they out of?"

"Their main clubhouse is in Calgary, but there are quite a few chapters along the borders."

"You know anybody that has had run-ins with these guys?"

Steel sighed. "They are slippery. From what I've managed to put together about them, they are just like American clubs—they have their own laws, and when we run into them, we have a heck of a time trying to pull any information. They are one-percenters through and through."

"Do you know if they are missing a member? We'd like to get an ID on the body."

Steel's laughter was as tough-sounding as his name. "Trying to find out if there is a missing member would be like trying to find out if ghosts are real—in all honesty, that's basically what these people are. They have nearly perfected a lifestyle out of staying off law enforcement's radar, and when and if they are in it, they know how to disappear."

"Do you think you can at least get me a list of the most recent known members?"

"I'll send you whatever I can get my hands on."

Casper glanced over at Lex, who was leaning against their car. She was staring off into the distance and he wondered what she was thinking. Absentmindedly, she ran her finger slowly over her lip and his body went rigid with the thought of their kiss.

"Do you know anything about their women?"

"That we have a little more information on—we have a few of their names and addresses. I'll send you that, as well."

"Great, thanks."

"And hey, Lawrence, if you need anything else, don't hesitate. I've made it a personal mission of mine to bring down as many of these clubs as possible. They're bad business… They're one of the abhorrent parts of our society. I hope you get your bastards. And who knows, maybe we can use this to help raise awareness of drug running across the Canadian border? Everyone talks about Mexico, but Canadian suppliers are just as dangerous and their drugs are more diversified."

Casper moved to hang up but stopped. "Steel, have you seen any new Canadian Blue hitting the streets in and around Montana?"

"Over the last few years, the DEA has seen a steady stream of Blue coming through Montana and spreading across the Dakotas, Idaho and Washington."

Casper snorted. "I don't know for sure, but if I had to bet, all of it is being run through the park."

Steel remained silent, almost as if he was digesting the information. "If that's true," he finally said, "then you need to do everything in your power to get to the bottom of this."

"Thanks, Steel. 'Preciate your time." Casper walked toward Lex.

"Lawrence, let me give you one more little piece of advice. These guys you're investigating…they're bad dudes. In the last year, we've heard whispers of their involvement in some revolting crimes—crimes involving women and children, even animals. These men have their own sense of right and wrong and what they consider justice. You need to be careful. They'll stop at nothing to keep themselves out of the public eye—even if that means taking out a federal officer or his family and friends."

He slipped his fingers into Lex's. Her hands were cold and she wrapped her free hand around her body in an attempt to warm herself.

There was no way he'd let these bastards get their hands on the only person he cared about.

"Thanks for the heads-up, Steel."

"Like I said, Lawrence, best of luck. Keep your head out of the sights."

Steel hung up, and as the phone clicked, chills ran down Casper's spine. It wasn't his head that he was worried about.

He made his way over to the tow truck where the Mounties were standing around, chatting about the case. The sergeant was talking with his hands, making some point that Casper couldn't quite hear.

"You guys ever heard of Hells Keepers?" he said, interrupting them.

The sergeant stopped and slowly turned. "What about 'em?"

"So you know who they are?" Casper pressed.

"Sure, we know. You think this is one of theirs?" He pointed toward the bike that was strapped to the flatbed and his gaze flickered to another of the officers as though he was hoping for a witness, making Casper's internal danger meter spike.

What did this Mountie know about the club? When Casper had mentioned the club's name it was as if the air had charged around them and they were one spark away from an explosion. The last thing he needed was the motorcycle club finding out that they were a part of an investigation. Steel had made a point of telling him to stay out of their sightline.

"We're not sure," he said, careful to avoid the full truth, but it was a fine line between getting the information they needed and raising flags. "We're thinking it's probably not related to the club," he lied. "By chance, though, you heard of any of them who've had problems lately?"

"Look, if you think this has anything to do with the Keepers, I would strongly recommend that you look elsewhere. Bad things happen to people who stick their noses in places they don't belong, eh?" He looked over at Lex.

Every hair on his arms stood straight at the poorly veiled threat. He didn't know how the man was involved with the club, or if he was, but he couldn't put Lex at risk.

"We'll drop it. No problem. I was just wondering—that's all. The thought stops here."

The man visibly relaxed and he leaned against the flatbed. "Anybody ever tell you that you're a smart man? If you were a Canadian, we'd hire you."

He couldn't even fake a smile. "I'll keep that in mind." As he spoke, the bitter taste of bile rose from his stomach. He'd screwed up in his past. He'd made his fair share of mistakes. But unlike the men who stood in front of him, he'd never be crooked.

Chapter Eight

As they made the long drive back toward her cabin, Lex checked her phone. They finally hit an area with service after they came over the border and back into Montana.

"Stop," she said with a wave of her hand. "I got service."

Casper pulled the car over to the side of the road. In the distance were the snowcapped mountains of the park.

She typed her query into the search engine: *Hells Keepers + crimes.*

The pages popped up with headlines from the local newspapers. Most of the headlines were about murders and thefts, and a few talked about drug deals gone bad. They had found themselves deep in a world of crime.

"Holy cow," she said in a single long breath. "Do you know who these Keeper guys are?"

Casper's hands tightened on the steering wheel,

almost like he knew exactly who they were but had been too afraid to tell her.

"What's going on, Casper?" she asked, dropping her phone into her lap.

"Nothing," he said, but his eyes were dark.

"Don't lie to me. What's wrong?"

He glanced over at her and, taking off his hat, set it on the dashboard. He ran his hands over his face and through his hair in exasperation. "I'm fine… I just think it's going to be better if you get away from all this—this investigation."

"What did I do?" she asked, trying to stop the hurt from leaking out into her voice.

All she had been trying to do for the last two days was solve this so they both could get their jobs done. Now, after a strange meeting with the Royal Canadian Mounties, she was on the outs. It didn't make sense.

"You didn't do anything, Lex. I promise," He sighed, but the sound only made her angrier and more hurt.

Was he tired of her?

She tried to remind herself they were only friends and maybe barely that. Sure, they had shared the kiss in the woods, but ever since they had gotten caught he had barely been able to look at her.

"Is this because of what happened…you know, back there?" She motioned in the direction they'd come from, but she was sure he knew exactly what she was talking about.

"Huh?"

She gnashed her teeth, but tried to control her anger. "You know. The kiss. Whatever it was back there. Did I do something wrong?"

He guppied, his mouth making tight "O" shapes while he searched for words.

"I agree. What happened back there—it was a mistake," she continued. "Won't happen again."

"Lex, no. That's not it. It's just that—"

"Just drop it. Let's both agree we can't make that kind of mistake again. We are both better off if we just get back to what we're good at." She thought about jumping out of the car and getting away from the tense air that simmered between them, but there was nowhere to go. They were miles away from the nearest town, which was no larger than a bar and a church. And even if she made it to one of those little rinky-dink towns, she still would need to make it home. There was no running away from this.

"Lex, I…that wasn't a mistake. I wanted that. I wanted you."

"You don't need to try to make me feel better. It was a stupid thing to do. What were we thinking? Tomorrow I have to go back to my regular job, and next week I will be in Apgar watching the winter snowshoers. You'll be… Where will you be? Do you even know? I mean, look, you don't tell me anything. Anytime I ask you anything real about yourself you repel from me like I'm asking you about your deepest, darkest secrets. I don't even know who you really are."

He leaned toward her and moved to take her hands, but she pulled back. "No, Casper. Don't touch me."

It was almost as if her words were a branding iron. He recoiled and his face was filled with pain. Maybe she had been wrong in coming at him as she had, but she wasn't wrong in her thinking. He hadn't been open with her, and if he couldn't be open he wasn't someone she wanted in her life.

She thought back to Travis. So much of their time together had been shrouded in secrets—late nights, unanswered phone calls and lies. He'd been cruel to her, telling her that she lived in a world built on unrealistic expectations when she asked him where he'd been or what he'd been doing. He'd never cheated on her—as far as she knew—but things between them had always been strained; that was, until she had started to pull away. It was strange how a man never wanted you too close until you were ready to walk out the door.

She never wanted to be treated like that again—not by any man, not even the handsome cowboy she had started to care about over the last few days. No matter what, she had to be careful, her heart was too fragile to be given to the wrong man.

"What do you want to know?" Casper finally asked, but there was still the same pained expression on his face.

"I don't want to have to force you into telling me anything. If you want me like you say you do, then you should *want* to talk to me. You should want to tell me your secrets—your past."

"It isn't that easy, Lex."

"If you care about me, then it *is* that easy."

"Damn it, Lex… I'm not like you. I haven't had an easy go of things over the last few years. My life has turned to complete crap. I lost the only job I cared about and now I'm stuck up here—at the most desolate place in the contiguous United States."

She prickled with anger. "You think I've had it easy, Casper? You think my life has been nothing but hiking and wildflowers?"

"You know what?" Casper rebuked. "You've accused me of not telling you anything, but has it occurred to you that you haven't told me anything, either? What happened between you and Travis?"

Fury roiled in her gut at the sound of Travis's name. "Do you really care?"

Casper's face softened. "No matter what you think, I do. Maybe we can't have a relationship—since that's not what you want—but at least maybe we can be friends."

A whisper of guilt filled her; his past caused him pain—he'd made that clear by attacking her and Travis's relationship—but that didn't mean that his past hadn't happened or that she could be kept in the dark. Yet she couldn't help the feeling that crept through her that told her if she kept pushing, the only thing she would achieve was making each of them more frustrated.

If he wanted this, he would talk to her. Until then, she couldn't risk her heart.

"Sure," she said. "Friends."

He seemed satisfied, like they had solved the problems that rested between them. Didn't he understand that she wanted him to fight for her—even if that battle was in himself? If he was the man she wanted, he would figure it out—if not, then things weren't meant to be. As much as she was attracted to him, as badly as she wanted to feel his kiss and fall into his arms again, she couldn't force a relationship to happen.

She clicked on her phone and stared down at the screen in an attempt to squelch her feelings.

"What did you find?" he asked, clearly oblivious of the turmoil inside her.

"These guys, these Keeper dudes, have an ongoing battle happening with the Canadian Parliament. There's a piece here about one of them being charged with attempted murder after he went after one of the local senators." She lifted the phone for him to see. "According to the article, the Keeper was only sentenced to three years in prison even though he managed to get a shot off on the Senator, hitting him once in the leg."

"Really?" Casper reached over and took the phone from her, his fingers grazing hers.

The touch made a surge of attraction pulse

through her, but she pushed the feelings aside. No matter what her body told her, she needed to focus on the investigation.

"Look at Gabrielle Giffords," Casper continued. "The shooter, the Loughner guy, got seven consecutive life terms in a federal prison. You can't tell me that the Canadian government would just let some guy off with a slap on the wrist for something like that."

"But that's exactly what they did."

Casper stared out the window. "That just doesn't make sense... Something has to be wrong. The media would have used this shooter and what he attempted to do as propaganda to stop something like that from happening again. Why would the justice system have just let him off?"

"What if he was meant to take a fall?"

Casper looked over at her. "You could be right. Or he was so deep into underworld politics that they were afraid of him. Somewhere there has to be something that explains it."

He tapped on the screen, moving through the article.

"From this, it looks like the guy's legal name is Peter Kagger, but went by 'Bug-Eye.' He's currently sitting in a Canadian prison."

She leaned close to Casper, so close that she could smell the rain and fresh air on his skin, a scent as intoxicating as his touch. She closed her eyes and took it deep into her lungs, pulling him into her like the simple action of growing closer could fix all of their problems.

On her phone's screen a picture caught her eye. There was a man wearing a black leather vest with patches sewn over it, who she assumed was the biker Peter Kagger, and standing next to him was a woman. Her eyes were tired and her face was taut and gaunt, merely skin stretched over bone. She looked like she had been to hell and back.

"Who's that woman?"

He enlarged the picture, making the woman look even more skeletal now that she filled the screen. Her eyes were dark and filled with what looked like even darker secrets.

"From the caption," Casper said, "it looks like her name is Lois Trainer. They said she was a friend of Kagger's. There's no mention of her in the article."

"Wait a minute," Alexis said, sitting back. "What do you think the connection may be?"

"I know Kagger isn't the guy in the woods, but with what few pieces we have to work with, I think looking into this is as good a place as any to start. If we can find this Lois Trainer, maybe she can give us a clue about anyone who has gone missing from the club." His eyes widened and his mouth moved as if he had just remembered something. "Wait, Steel said he was going to send me a list of the women associated with the MC that the FBI has been tracking. Maybe we can pull something from that."

He handed her phone back to her and took out his

to check his email. It was hot in her hands where he had been holding on to it. He had such passion for his work. No wonder he hadn't wanted to talk about losing his last position—the job he truly wanted. He was a man whose self-worth was built through his work—or wherever his passion lay. And, no doubt, when his work had been stripped away, he'd lost a part of himself.

As she looked at him, at the fine lines that were nestled around his gorgeous caramel-colored eyes, her anger at his inability to open up somewhat dissipated—though it didn't disappear. Sometimes loving someone meant talking about the failures just as much as the triumphs. True love could only be found in moments of honesty.

"I got it," Casper said, his voice sounding almost breathless with excitement.

"Huh?"

"The woman from the picture. Lois Trainer? She's from Columbia Falls. According to the FBI database, she's been in and around a series of major drug deals, but there's been no direct evidence linking her to the crimes."

"Do you think this is the woman we could be after? The woman from the shop?"

He exhaled, rubbing his hand over his face as he thought. "I don't know. I hope so, but knowing my luck, this lady probably doesn't know anything about it—and even if she did, she wouldn't tell us."

"You wanna try?" she asked, motioning toward

the open road in front of them. "We can make a stop at her place. It's out of the way, but maybe we can dig up something."

Was it a coincidence that this woman lived just outside the park and was connected to the gang?

He looked over at Lex, his face was tight, making the fine lines around his eyes deepen. "It's gonna be about two hours, and after the accident... Are you sure you want to go?"

Was this his way to tell her that he didn't want her in the car, or was he worried that she was still mad? Maybe he wasn't as oblivious as she had assumed.

"What do you want? I mean, as far as you and I go, Casper?" she asked, putting him on the spot.

"I know you think I'm being evasive, that I don't want to open up to you, but that isn't the truth. The truth is that I've never been great at relationships."

"Why? What do you mean?" Finally, they were getting somewhere.

He reached over and sat his hand down softly between them, palm up, as if he wanted her to slip her fingers into his. But she wasn't ready to forgive him. Not yet.

"My last relationship ended just over a year ago. It was hard... Really hard..." He spoke gently, as if he were pulling memories from the deep, dark, off-limits part of his psyche. "I loved her."

"What happened?"

"Her name was Elicia. She worked with me in the FBI."

An ache grew in her gut as she jumped to a million different conclusions, each one worse than the last.

"She got pregnant when we were working together," Casper continued.

"With your baby?"

His eyes darkened and the scowl she hated returned to his face. "She said so, but later I found out that I wasn't the only man who she had been seeing."

She slowly let out her breath in an attempt to hide her surprise as pity filled her. No wonder he was so closed off, his emotions so out of reach.

"It was hard when I found out, but truth be told, in the world of the FBI, sex can be just as powerful a weapon as any gun. Sometimes to make things happen, a person has to sacrifice themselves for the greater good—at least that's what she told me."

"Did you believe her?"

He nodded, his movement so small it was almost imperceptible. "Her job was really hard. It meant going undercover and putting herself in places where she had to make tough calls—finding herself in places where she had to have sex with random dudes. I didn't blame her, but it definitely made things harder when…" He stopped.

"When what?" She reached over and placed her pinky inside his hand, letting him know that she was there, present, listening—and in a simple way, thanking him for his honesty.

"She lost the baby. She was on a mission in northern Washington. The guy she was after was a militia member. They were trying to talk him down and he went berserk—she took a hard hit. I'd told her that she shouldn't go out there, that she shouldn't put her life—and the baby's—on the line. She wouldn't listen."

"I'm so sorry, Casper." She instantly regretted asking him to share. From the pinched look on his face, it was easy to see why he was always finding ways to avoid his past.

"Don't be sorry, Lex. I killed him. I killed the man," he said, his voice barely above a whisper. "When I got to him, he didn't even have a gun. He was defenseless...just like my baby had been. And I gunned him down."

"How did you..."

"Stay out of jail?" he said, finishing her question. "The FBI kept my name out of the press and me out of trouble, saying it was in self-defense. But in truth I was pissed. I meant to kill him. He had bombed people, he killed my child—but in the end, I was no better than him."

"Is that why you're here?"

He nodded as his eyes welled with tears he fought to keep in check. "They told me I was a loose cannon—a liability. Truth is, I am. I can't stand by and just let the people I care about get hurt."

"You didn't *let* her get hurt. She made a choice and tragedy struck. You can't carry that weight. It wasn't your fault."

"I can, Lex. I will carry that forever. I'm a monster."

"You're not a monster, Casper. You took a bad man off the streets. It may have been against the law, or outside what the FBI wanted you to do, but sometimes there's a gray area between what is right and what is legal." She moved her hand into his, stroking his fingers like they were those of a child. "You did what you thought was right. From what you told me, I think you were justified."

"Justified or not, you need to stay away from me. I don't want anything to happen to you. You have to focus on yourself. You don't want me in your life. I only bring pain."

"Lucky for you, pain is something I'm used to," she said, thinking back to her days when she'd lived with her biological parents. She could still see the crack pipes, stained with brown, on the only table in their house.

No matter how strong he was, she saw him for what he really was—a broken man. With each other's support and honesty, just maybe they could grow beyond their pasts.

Chapter Nine

The mobile home was tucked into the back of a park, out of sight from the road and hidden by a flurry of overgrown trees. If it hadn't been for a small white arbor, complete with the drooping, tired heads of the last-of-summer flowers, Casper wouldn't have noticed the house they were looking for.

Getting out of the car, they made their way up to the small porch, the steps sagging with too much age and too little care.

"Why don't you wait back here? We don't know what we're going to find. This woman has a reputation that could make her dangerous." He stopped himself from saying, *and I don't want you to get hurt.*

No doubt by now Lex had to know that he was always protective of the people he cared about, and the more time they spent together, the more he cared about her.

Lex moved to speak but stopped and nodded, staying at the bottom of the steps. "Be careful."

Contented warmth spread through him, the kind

that followed on the heels of realizing that someone cared and appreciated the way that he felt. Maybe there could be something more to what they had besides a simple friendship and passing work, but he hated to get his hopes up.

He knocked, the sound echoing through the thin, flimsy door. A dog started to bark from inside the place, followed by the sounds of a woman yelling for it to shut up. There was the metallic clang like that of a recliner being put down and then the steady thump of footfalls.

"Who in the hell is it? If you're selling something, I have a gun and I ain't afraid to use it," the woman yelled, her voice hoarse and raspy like that of a longtime smoker.

She threw open the door, letting it slam into the wall next to her. A small, mixed-breed dog that looked more like an overgrown ferret came running out and started to jump around Casper's feet.

He leaned down to pet the dog, and for a moment it was quiet as it sniffed him, and then it started its high-pitched bark again. The dog jumped on him, bumping his hand like it wanted to be pet, but it skittered away when he moved to touch it.

"Burt, leave 'im alone," the woman ordered, but the dog didn't listen. Instead it continued its dance between wanting love and wanting to defend.

The woman's hair was pulled up into a clip, wild with little brushing and infrequent washing, and as she stepped toward him he could make out the strong odor of cigarettes mixed with the stench of poor hygiene. He had envisioned the woman to be tough, but she looked tough for all the wrong reasons. The expression "ridden hard and put away wet" came to mind.

"Miss Trainer?"

"Who're you?"

"My name is Casper Lawrence. I was hoping I could ask you a few questions about a recent disappearance in Glacier National Park."

She frowned like she had no idea what he was talking about. "I don't know nothin'. Why're you here? How did you find me?" She stepped out onto the porch and closed the door behind her, blocking their view from whatever else lay inside. Her slew of questions made him wonder if she was the kind of woman who frequently had people looking for her.

"Like I said, we just want to ask you a few questions," he said. "Do you know of anyone who has gone missing in the last few weeks? A man?"

She looked toward the dog that had run down the stairs to sniff at Lex. For a minute the animal was quiet. "I don't know about no man and nothing about the park."

He nodded. "What do you know about the local motorcycle clubs?"

Her body went stiff and her nostrils flared. "Look, if you don't got no warrant, and I ain't under arrest, I don't gotta answer nothin' about the Keepers."

"That's true, Ms. Trainer, but the last thing we

want to do is come back and bother you again. We were just hoping you could be helpful and we could be back on our way. However, if you don't wish to help us, I'm sure that we could make a return visit—one that involves handcuffs. Don't you think we could avoid all that? I just have a few little questions. Nothing that's going to get you into any kind of trouble."

Ms. Trainer reached down and instinctively ran her hands over her wrists, like she was recounting the last time she'd been shackled. "I don't have anything to do with the Keepers."

The mere fact that the woman called the MC by its shortened moniker made it clear that she was lying. Very few people had heard of the club, and even fewer knew it by that name.

He took out his phone and pulled up the picture with her and Peter Kagger. "If that's true, Ms. Trainer, then why are you in this picture with the secretary of the club—a man who currently sits in a Canadian prison for his implication in a series of crimes involving the MC?"

She paled. "That…that was a long time ago."

He tapped on the date. "According to this, this picture was only taken a few months ago." He looked toward Lex, who was scratching away behind the ears of the now-quiet dog. "Lex, do you think a few months is a long time?"

She glanced up at him. "Well, Casper, it depends on what we are talking about. A few months isn't long in terms of a lifetime, but it's a long time if it's hours spent in prison."

"You haven't been in prison lately, have you, Ms. Trainer?" he asked, not even attempting to mask the implicit threat that lay just under the surface of his words.

"Do I need to call my lawyer?"

He waved her off. "Of course not. Lawyers only make things more complicated for both of us. When you lawyer up it's hard to say how things will go, but I can guarantee that it wouldn't be as friendly as it is right now. It's my hope that you can make this easy—on both of us."

"Fine. I dated that guy. It wasn't a major thing. When he came to town, we got together," Ms. Trainer said, but from the way her eyes lit up as she spoke about the man, he could tell she wasn't telling him the truth.

"How often did he come to town?"

"Well, he's from Alberta. I guess I saw him a few times a month. When he could make it down."

"Why was he coming to the United States?"

She clapped her hands, calling the dog, but the dog ignored her.

"Ma'am?" he repeated, though he knew full well that she was just trying to think up some kind of convenient lie.

"He came down to see me. It's what people do in a relationship. Isn't that right, Lex? Ain't that what people do when they are dating?" she asked, motioning with her chin toward Casper.

Lex jumped slightly at the sound of the woman

saying her name, or maybe it was the question, he couldn't be sure. "I'm afraid I don't know what you're talking about," Lex said, visibly taken aback at the woman's assumption that they were dating.

"You guys aren't an item?" She gave him an assessing glance. "You know, you can fake a lot of things, but you can't fake when you like someone. I see how you keep looking at her, Agent Lawrence."

He felt the warmth rush to his face, but tried to dispel it along with thoughts about how much he cared about Lex, and how she felt in his arms. He wasn't here to talk about his relationship or be interrogated by the woman they had come to question. She was the one under observation, not them.

"It's hard not being around someone you care about—which makes me wonder why you and Peter weren't together all the time." He attempted to steer the conversation back to the task at hand. "Based on this photograph I would guess that this man was someone who you cared deeply about. Why else would you have stood beside him on the court steps?"

Ms. Trainer studied her feet. "What does my relationship to Peter have to do with a missing person in the park?"

He smiled at her admission that there was more between her and the man than she'd wanted to say. "We believe that the man who went missing was a member of the same MC as Peter. We were hoping that perhaps you could help us shine a little more light on his identity."

"What do you want to know?"

Did that mean she knew the man whose remains currently resided at the Missoula Crime Lab?

"We took a picture of his bike. I was hoping you could tell me whether or not it belongs to him." He carefully sidestepped around the man's name, hoping that she would inadvertently take the bait and supply them with the information they needed. He pulled up the picture of the bike as it was being loaded onto the flatbed.

She sucked in a breath. "Son of a—"

"Is this his bike?"

She looked up at him with eyes wide with shock, and at their centers he was sure he saw the fires of anger. But why would she be angry at seeing the picture?

"Sure, that's Razor's bike. Where'd you find it?"

Razor? Was that the name of the man whose body they found? He needed more than the strange nickname to go on.

"We found it at the trailhead where it was believed Razor started his hike into the park."

He carefully avoided telling her that the man he was asking about was likely dead—he didn't want to create a situation that would raise alarm within the biker community any more than he was likely to already be doing. If they knew the man was dead, none of them would help their cause, but if they thought the man was simply missing, they were far more likely to aid in the investigation.

"Do you know why he was hiking through the

park?" Lex asked, stepping up onto the bottom stair. The dog was now in her arms and licking her face.

"Burt likes you," the woman said. "He don't like nobody but me—couldn't stand Peter. What did you do to him, feed him some uppers?"

Lex laughed, and the soft sound nearly made Casper forget what they were doing. He loved that laugh, that simple sound that made his heart reawaken.

"Wait—he did like Billy. One time he let him pick him up, but that was a couple of years ago," Ms. Trainer continued.

"Billy?" Lex asked with a confused look.

"Razor," the woman replied, but any softness she had shown when she looked at her dog was quickly replaced by an air of suspicion. "Who did you say you were?" she asked Lex.

"My name is Alexis Finch. I'm a park ranger and I'm working with Agent Lawrence on this investigation."

"I thought you were just looking into a missing person's case." The woman glared at him like she was trying to weigh and measure him for truth.

"Yes, ma'am," he said. "Missing person's case. We're hoping that this investigation will take a happy turn and we can return Billy to his family."

The woman's scowl deepened. "You say *his family*?"

"Why yes, ma'am." As he spoke he could feel the sand of her acceptance shifting under his feet.

"You need to leave," she said, charging down the steps and pulling the little dog out of Lex's arms.

"Don't you be coming back. If you got something to ask, you can ask my lawyer." She stomped up the steps, went inside and slammed the door behind her.

He could hear the click of the lock as she slid it shut. The dog started barking again, but instead of wondering if the dog was defending her, he suddenly wondered if the dog was really begging for them to take him home.

"Do you think the dog was named after Burt Reynolds?" she asked with a laugh.

"He was just furry enough to be him. But definitely the '70s version, not the current one," he joked.

He helped Lex into the car and took one look back at the vegetation-covered property before he got in and started to drive. He picked up his phone and dialed the medical examiner. After being handed off by a secretary, the medical examiner, Les Traver, answered.

"How's it going?" Casper asked as he steered the car back toward the park's entrance. "Have you had a chance to go over that Glacier Park body case yet?"

There was a rustle of fabric as Les must have moved the phone. "Actually, I was just going over the report. Interesting stuff."

"Did you find anything usable?" he asked, taking her hand. Her fingers were cold.

"There was a small imperfection on the man's right zygomatic arch. There was evidence of calcification, so he must have had some sort of injury to his cheek prior to his time of death."

Casper squeezed Lex's fingers. Between the

wound and what Lois Trainer had given them—now they would only have to track someone down who could give them the man's full name and a positive ID.

"Have you had any luck in identifying the man?" Casper asked.

"We've started to look into dental records, but so far nothing has matched. You?"

"I'm not sure, but we have a lead. We are thinking he went by an alias 'Razor,' first name Billy, possibly William. He was involved with a motorcycle club called Hells Keepers."

"Great." Casper could hear Les scratching something on paper. "We can use that."

"If I find out more, or have a positive ID on this guy, I'll let you know."

"'Preciate it," Les said. "By the way, did you get a chance to really look at the remains?"

"I was involved in the recovery, why?"

"Did you look at the skull, particularly the left orbital cavity, near the sphenoid bone?"

"His eye socket? What about it?"

"Yes, his eye socket, near what would have been his nose." Les gave a light chuckle at Casper's unscientific terminology. "Inside of it was a small hole."

He thought back to the grizzly prints that had littered the ground in and around the area where they had found the parts of the body. He had seen hundreds, if not thousands, of deaths and murder scenes, but Casper cringed at the thought of what this man's last moments must have been like with a bear possibly breathing down his neck.

"Is the hole consistent with an animal attack?"

"Based on the margins, it's clear that this was definitely a penetrating trauma of some sort, likely perimortem. At first, based on the coroner's report and how he documented the scene, I believed it was consistent with the type of injury that you would find in a bear attack."

"But then?" Casper pushed.

"When we looked closer, there were no other abrasions or marks on the bone—like what you would see caused by the animal's incisors. I ordered a set of X-rays of the skull and foot, and we found something interesting." Les paused. "We found what looks to be a fragmented bullet. Small caliber, in my humble opinion, something similar in size to that of a .22."

"Are you telling me that this guy didn't die from a bear attack?" He felt the air seep from his body as he thought about all the things that this could mean.

"Due to the amount of damage that was done to the brain by the round, I believe that it was the cause of death. However, I can't rule out that this man was attacked. It just may not have been the final blow."

A wave of chills charged down his spine. This man may have had a horrific death—the kind of death that they made movies about. Casper glanced toward Lex, who was staring at him with a horrified look on her face, as though she could hear exactly what was being said.

"Based on the fact that there was no exit wound, when this round penetrated the skull it didn't enter at a high velocity."

"Which means—"

"He didn't shoot himself. There had to have been someone else who pulled the trigger."

He stayed silent as the news sank in. "Our guy was murdered," he said, breathless at the thought.

"I'll continue looking over the remains and running tox screens," Les continued. "Maybe I can pull something else out of this, but I have to tell you, this is one of the more gruesome sets of remains I've seen in a while. This one time, we had a guy who'd died in his apartment, midsummer..."

The man droned on about the gory details of his former case, but all Casper could think about was the skull he'd held in his hands, the feel of the oil from the man's bones on his gloves. His stomach roiled, threatening to empty, and he forced the images from his mind. Sometimes the strong just had to muscle past the things that made the average man pale.

"Least this guy's death makes for one heck of a story," Les continued with a dismissive chuckle. "Would've hated to be in his shoes." Les laughed at his stupid joke. "Gunshot wound and a bear mauling... It's like the double whammy of deaths. Hell of a way to go. I guess the fates wanted this guy double-dead."

Chapter Ten

There hadn't been a single day that she had thought about playing hooky from work. Lex loved her job, and the fact that each day she could help people and the occasional animal. In her line of work, she never knew what was coming around the next corner, and that level of spontaneity always made her come back for more. It wasn't just the normal nine-to-five where she was stuck in some cubicle with a heinous boss coming down on her. In fact, today was the first time Dragger had really said something to her that was less than cordial.

Yet she was tempted to call in and tell him that she wouldn't make it in tomorrow.

She snorted at the thought. That would go over like a ton of bricks. By the end of the phone call she'd have no job, no place to live and no way to help Casper solve the case. She'd have nothing.

But there was a nagging feeling in her gut that told her she couldn't quit—she couldn't just let him take her back home for the night and leave things as up in the air as they were. She wanted—no, she *needed* to get to the bottom of this.

Maybe she could push the issue with Dragger that it was vital for them to figure out a way to stop the flow of drugs through their park—especially if it led to murder. They didn't need that kind of publicity. No doubt Dragger would simply tell her that nature would stop the drug running long before they could. And maybe he was right. Maybe this drug running had just been a one-time thing. Maybe she and Casper were doing nothing more than chasing rabbits.

He had to see that if and when the media got their hands on it, their office's role in the investigation would inevitably come into question. They'd have a royal storm on their hands if they didn't treat the situation delicately—there'd only been two other murders in the park's history. This would draw headlines. She had to make Dragger understand that this investigation had to come first.

She reached for her purse on the car's floor.

"What're you doing?" Casper asked, carefully keeping one eye on the road as they drove back toward the main park entrance.

"I'm going to call my boss. Maybe I can convince him to let me keep working on our investigation."

A look of concern flickered over Casper's face. "You can't. No, Lex. I don't want you to screw up your life over this. I want you to be at my side, but don't risk your job over this case. You're kidding yourself if you think calling in again is going to help anything—it'll only piss him off and put you on his radar."

"I don't get how winterizing is more important than letting me solve a murder. I just don't understand his thinking."

He reached over, putting his hand on her leg and slowly stroking her thigh. "Lex, I don't know how this thing is going to play out. For all we know, we might hit a dead end on this and never find who was behind this guy's murder—if that happened, would it be worth compromising your career? And don't get me started on your safety. You know how I feel about that. We're dealing with a biker gang here. If you want an idea of what they're capable of, all you need to do is take a look at Razor's body."

She hit the button on her phone that lit up its screen. They still had service.

"You're right, Casper," she said, staring at her wallpaper of the jagged Citadel Peak. "These guys are dangerous, but I'm not afraid. I'm not the kind of woman who passes the buck when things get hard. If I was, I wouldn't be working at one of the most rugged national parks in the United States. Instead I would have a safe little desk job. I want my life to be an adventure. I want to help people. Most of all, I want to make sure that justice is more than just lip service in this world. This is my way to make a difference."

She set her hand on his, stroking the lines that ran over the backs of his hands.

Casper nodded with a tired, handsome grin, the

kind that told her he'd known what she was going to say and wasn't surprised. "I love that about you, Lex. I do. But you need to know exactly what you might be walking into with this. I don't want you to have unrealistic expectations."

Her thoughts moved to Travis. He had always accused her of living with "unrealistic expectations," no more so than when she had tried to talk to him about their relationship and how she had wanted it to be. It wasn't that she had wanted the perfect marriage, but at the very least she had wanted a marriage based on honesty and enough mutual respect that they would talk and work together to make their relationship stronger. Instead he had pulled further and further away anytime she had asked him about anything beyond their four walls or the simple events of their work. In the end, her "unrealistic expectations" for a marriage that was something more than her waiting for him had cost her the man she had once loved. Yet she was glad she hadn't let it go on. She couldn't have suffered any more of the deafening silence and the complacency.

"Don't say that, Casper. I know what I want. I know what I'm doing. Trust me," she said, her voice flecked with old hurt.

His eyes widened slightly, as if her words had caught him off guard.

She lifted her phone and dialed Dragger. He answered on the first ring.

"Are you ready to go to the chalet in the morning?" he said, his voice gruff and unwavering.

She thought about avoiding giving him a piece of her mind, but after telling Casper how strong she was, how she believed in herself and in her boss's ability to accept this, she couldn't back down. "Mr. Dragger, so glad to catch you. I just wanted to give you an update on the situation."

"Unless it's to tell me that you're ready to hand off the investigation, I don't want to hear it."

"That's exactly why I'm calling, sir. I think it would be ill-advised to pass this to someone else at this juncture."

"It's nothing more than a bear attack. Let it go— Travis is supposed to be working up there tomorrow and he will take care of the last bit of cleanup as far as this case goes. It's time for you to move on. We don't have time or the budget to deal with this right now. You are aware that our tourism rate fell twelve percent this year? This is going to cut into our budget significantly if we're not careful."

Her mouth dropped at the sound of Travis's name. There was no way she would let him take this from her. He had already taken so much.

"Actually, sir, I was calling to let you know that we've just talked to the medical examiner who was handling the remains."

"What about them?"

"According to him, sir, we're no longer dealing

with an accidental death. I'm afraid to tell you he believes that this case is a homicide."

There was a moment of loud silence between them.

"Sir, I was hoping that, as this case has grown and the media will no doubt be involved, I could continue my work on furthering the efforts of the investigation," she said, stumbling over her words as she tried to make it sound as respectful but necessary as possible.

Dragger made a sucking noise. "I appreciate your enthusiasm and candor in this, Alexis. I do. However, that doesn't change the fact that I'm giving this to Travis and his guys. I want you to meet up with him in the morning at the ranger station. You can give him your notes and findings. He will do an adequate job, I'm sure. After your accident, I would hate for you to put yourself in harm's way any more than necessary." The tone of his voice was dry and threatening, a sharp contrast to what might have been caring words.

"I'm fine," she said, rolling her neck as if Dragger could see just how fine she was through the phone. "I'm not feeling dizzy. It was only a minor concussion."

"With that type of injury, you shouldn't be putting any more stress on your body." Dragger sighed loudly into the phone. "Don't fight me on this. No matter how this investigation plays out, this guy is dead—so don't risk harming yourself."

"You're right, sir," she said, "but the fact remains he was smuggling drugs across the border into our park and then was murdered. Who's to say something like this isn't going to happen again? If it gets out that we aren't doing everything in our power to stop murders within our borders, our tourism next year may drop even lower."

"This investigation isn't yours to worry about anymore, Alexis. Travis will get a handle on this, and winter waits for no one. If you don't have your butt up at the Sperry Chalet in the morning, I will consider that your resignation." He hung up the phone.

"That bastard," she said, throwing the phone into her purse. "He's giving this case to Travis... Travis. Can you freaking believe it?" She slammed her hand against the dashboard, making pain radiate up from her hand and into her arm.

Right now, he must have had his lips planted squarely on Dragger's butt in order to get this case. No doubt Travis begged him for it. He'd always been the kind of guy who wants all the glory.

This time she couldn't let him have it. She had to stop this from getting into Travis's hands, but if she didn't follow Dragger's orders she'd be fired, and then that was exactly where the case would end up. There was only one thing they could do—they had to get on top of this. They had to figure out who was behind the murder before she was supposed to meet up with Travis.

"Travis is going to be working with me?" Casper pointed at his chest as though he was as taken aback as she was by the information.

"Sounds like it. Aren't you the lucky one?"

Casper clenched the wheel.

"I have an idea," she said, sweeping through her memories for anything that could help their case. "There's a biker bar just north of us here in Columbia Falls. It's called The Pig Snout."

"The last thing you need right now, with your recent concussion, is to go tie a few on." Casper cocked an eyebrow as he looked over to her.

She smirked. "That's not what I was after, smarty-pants. It's a place where I've seen bikers hang out. I've never been in there. It may be nothing, but there're always Harleys parked out front. Maybe someone there will know something."

She was grasping at straws. Even if the bikers that hung out there were affiliated with an MC, there was little to no chance that they would give them any more information than Lois Trainer had, but she had to do something. She couldn't let Casper down, and she couldn't let her ex move in and screw up not only her investigation, but also whatever was happening between her and Casper. Nothing good could come of their budding romance if Casper was forced to work the investigation with her ex-husband.

BEFORE LONG, THEY were parked outside the bar. Its sign was missing some of its lights and it read nothing more than "Pig not." Its defunct sign matched the building perfectly, listing to the left as though it had seen a few too many drunken men stumble from its doors and was simply following their lead. The gravel parking lot was littered with a variety of bikes. She didn't know much about motorcycles, but a few looked like the ones that she always saw on the shows about choppers, with their too-long handlebars and their intricate detail work. One bike even had skulls machined into the chrome of its wheels.

She thought back to the paint job on Razor's bike. Two skulls. Was it possible that these guys were part of the same motorcycle club? Had Razor been here, at this bar, in the days before he was killed? Could one of these men be responsible for his death?

Her mind raced with unanswered questions, her gut roiling with nerves. If these men were involved with Razor in any way, she'd be walking into a snake's den. The men who made up the one-percenter motorcycle clubs were the type who didn't just think, but knew, that they were above the law. One word came to mind as she thought about biker gangs: hubris.

"Are you sure that you want to do this?" Casper asked, motioning toward the listing bar. "We could look more into the bag we found. Maybe it can tell us something about the guy and where he came from. Heck, maybe we can find the woman from The Prince and the Pea. Maybe she bought the bag or something."

It was a cop-out. He knew they wouldn't find anything from that bag. It was nothing more than a run-of-the-mill, every-survivalist-owns-one kind of bag. There had to be millions of those things in circulation around the country. It would be safer to go down that path, but she didn't have time for safe— she only had time for answers.

If nothing else, at least he hadn't warned her about her safety again. Maybe he was learning that she was tougher than she looked.

She opened the door and stepped out of the car. "You coming?" She hitched her thumb toward the bar. "I bet there's somebody in there who just can't wait to buy you a drink. Especially with that badge hanging from your waist." She nodded in its direction. "Just a suggestion, but you may want to leave that in the car."

He looked down with surprise, as if he had forgotten he'd put it on that morning. "Good idea. I'm sure we'd get a real warm welcome with me wearing it." He dropped the badge onto the dashboard and got out of the car.

"We may get one anyways." She led the way to the bar, keeping a comfortable distance between them in case any of the bikers saw them. As they approached the bar, she reached down her shirt and lifted her breasts so her cleavage could be seen just above her shirt line.

"What're you doing?" Casper asked, not taking his eyes off her hands.

"I'm going to get us the information we need one way or another. If anyone asks, you're my brother." She stopped. "Actually, why don't you hold back for a while, let me get a read on this place before you come in. While you're waiting, why don't you call your friend at the US Marshal Service and see if you can get more information on this Razor guy? Maybe they could at least get us his full name." She motioned for him to retreat and then opened the door and strode in, not waiting for him to respond.

Men were lined up at the bar. Most had beers in front of them, but a few had tumblers filled with dark amber liquid. Each had on a leather vest, or "cut" as she remembered them being called on television. On the back of the man closest to the door was a large patch. It was made up of the same image that had been on Razor's bike—two skulls and a snake wrapping its body beneath. Above the image were the words "Hells Keepers."

She'd found the right place. Now she just needed to find the right man.

As she started to make her way deeper into the bar, the conversations around her hushed.

There was a gray-haired man with a nearly white beard sitting at the far end, and he waved her over.

She looked back over her shoulder, but Casper hadn't come in. Maybe she had made a mistake in not having him with her. At least she would have been afforded some level of protection from the bikers. Then again, she couldn't be weak now.

She picked her way over to the older man, trying to saunter as she moved through pushed-out chairs and steel-toed riding boots.

A thin bead of sweat rolled down her back, making her feel even more afraid. If they noticed her acting nervous or *off* they wouldn't give her anything, and it would only put her further into danger.

"How's it going, pretty lady?" he asked, motioning for her to take the unoccupied stool next to him.

He had a patch that read "Madness and Mayhem," and above it was one that read "Hells Keepers." On the other side of the vest were two patches: "President" and "Montana Chapter." There were a series of diamonds and letters over the rest of the front of his vest, but she had no idea what they all meant.

"It's goin' real good," she said, trying to act as innocent and as acquiescent as possible. "How about yourself? Long day riding?" She slipped onto the stool and the man motioned to the bartender.

"You want a beer?"

Drinking was a terrible idea, but she couldn't fail now.

"Sure, I'll take a beer."

The man nodded toward the bartender, who grabbed a glass, filling it under the tap and then sliding it down the bar.

She grabbed it like she had caught beers a thousand times, instead of just having seen the movement in the movies. In a way, the action made her feel even more like an outsider.

"What's a pretty lady like you doing at a place like this tonight? Your man get mad at you?"

She took a long sip of the cheap and bitter beer and forced it down. "Nah, just saw you guys were here. Thought I'd stop by."

"We were here, huh?" He looked back at the man standing behind them like he was in on some inside joke. "I haven't seen you around here before. You looking for someone specific?"

"Actually, I met a guy a while back. He said his name was Razor. You know him?" She cringed inwardly as she thought of exactly how and why she had met the man.

The president looked down the bar to another of his comrades and motioned for him to come closer. The man answered in a second, stepping so close to her left that she could smell the oil on his vest and his day-old sweat. The patch on his chest read "Sergeant at Arms."

"This lady here says she's looking for Razor. You seen him?"

She tried to get a read on the president's windburned face, but she couldn't tell if he meant the question in earnest or if it was his attempt at getting the man's guard up about her. Either way it made her palms dampen with nerves, and she took another swig of her beer.

"I ain't seen Razor in a while. He's been up north so far as I've heard. Then again, I ain't his babysitter. You want me to look into him for you?"

The president looked to her. "The fine lady was looking for him. How did you say you met?"

"I didn't," she said, as the drink made her start to believe she had inner strength enough to go toe-to-toe with the bikers beside her.

The president started to laugh, the sound as raspy and hard as him. "I see why he liked you. He was always going after women who liked to throw their weight around." He leaned in close. "You know, he ain't around, and if you're interested in throwing your weight somewhere, my way's always available."

She glanced down at his wedding band. "Your wife know you talk like that?"

"What my old lady don't know won't hurt her." He laughed again.

A man who had been sitting at a table near them stood up and walked over. He leaned in and whispered in the president's ear as he pointed to something on his phone. Luckily, he spoke just loud enough so that she could make out his words.

"Our runners want to rendezvous tomorrow. Nine o'clock at the normal location. What do you want me to tell them?" the man asked.

The president turned away from her for a minute. "This about the Blue?"

The man nodded.

"Tell them we got their money, and this time they'd better not let us down."

The man walked back to his chair, texting as he moved.

She glanced over her shoulder, wishing Casper had been there to hear the men's exchange. They had to be talking about the Canadian Blue, which meant they must have been planning some kind of buy. These could be the men Casper was looking for, the men who had a role in smuggling the drugs over the border.

Then again, if these bikers were the smugglers, then why would they be buying and not selling?

She moved to stand up, but the president grabbed her by the arm and forced her to sit back down.

"Don't you be going nowhere. I'm sorry about that interruption, little lady. Sometimes business comes before pleasure, but both come in their own time." He gave her a nasty wink.

Pleasure from her wouldn't be coming his way, ever.

"I don't want to be interfering with any of your business," she said, motioning toward the man on his phone.

"Oh, don't worry about him. That was nothing. Already taken care of." He shrugged her off. "Now, about you and Razor... I know you ain't his old lady."

"Oh yeah, how's that?" she retorted, trying to sound cute enough to cover her genuine interest.

"Well, he's already got one of those. So do you belong to his chapter or are you general club property?"

She wasn't anyone's property, nor would she ever become something people could own.

"I ain't nobody's nothing. I've just been seeing Razor around. He told me to stop by this week. Said he'd be in town. If you ain't seen him, I should be goin'." She tried to pull her arm out of his vise-like grip, but instead he only held on harder.

"If Razor told you to come here and you listened, then you might just be the kind of girl this club is looking for." He stared at her with his cold, dark eyes. "We ain't desperate for women," he said, nodding toward the billiards area where a swarm of girls stood around with a few men as they played pool. Each of the women had Daisy Duke shorts and tank tops that rested so low a sharp breeze could have caused a nip-slip. A few of them wore the leather vests like the men of the club, but they simply said "Property of the Keepers," and a couple had specific men's names. She stared at them, looking for a woman who matched the description the shopkeeper had given her and Casper at The Prince and the Pea, but in the poor light of the bar, it could have been any one of the brunettes.

"We're good to our girls," the president continued. "If you're interested, I'm sure that we could bring you in. Make you club property."

"Why would I want to do that?" she asked, trying not to sound completely affronted even though she inwardly blanched at the thought of what he offered.

"Our girls want for nothing. You could travel the world on the back of anybody's bike you wanted. Money ain't ever an issue. Protection ain't a problem. If you're runnin' from something, or someone, we can be just the men you're looking for."

She was running from a lot of things, but most of them rested in her past—terrifying memories of her days in foster care, and nights spent hiding in the closet out of fear of being beaten once again. Right now the only place she wanted to go was out the door.

"What makes you think I'm running from something?" she asked, twisting the pint in her hands.

He chuckled. "If you are coming in here, looking

for a man like Razor, you have to be either looking for trouble or wanting protection. If it ain't protection that you wanted, then that only leaves trouble—and that, that's something I can give you plenty of." He leaned back and appraised her from behind. "I can probably give you more than you can handle."

That was it. She couldn't take it anymore. "Look, Pres," she said, standing up even though his fingers dug into her arm, "I don't want any of what you're selling. When Razor finds out what you are trying to do, he's going to come down on you like a ton of bricks."

The man threw his head back with a wicked, drunken laugh. "Lucky for you, I ain't worried about Razor finding out nothin'—it's awful hard to get mad when you're as cold as he is."

She pulled her arm from his grip and ran out the door. There was the sound of scraping bar stools behind her. Casper was in the car on his phone, waiting for her.

"Start the car!" she yelled, making the motion of a key turning.

He looked at her and frowned but started the car. His mouth opened as his gaze moved past her. She turned around just in time to see the president walk out the door.

She hurried into the car.

The president stood on the steps of the bar and stared at her, and then at Casper and his badge on the dashboard. The man pointed to her and then drew his fingers across his neck like a blade slicing through thin flesh.

Chapter Eleven

"What in the hell did you just do?" Casper seethed as he tore out of the parking lot and onto the highway.

"I didn't *do* anything. That was the problem." Lex looked back over her shoulder in the direction of the bar.

There was a group of men standing outside, watching them as they retreated.

"I thought you were just going in there to see if you could find anything out about Razor. How did you manage to get an entire group of bikers to chase you out of the bar?"

She turned back around and clicked on her seat belt. "Look, they didn't chase me out. I ran out. Entirely different thing."

"Okay, why did you have to run out, then?" He checked the rearview mirror one more time to make sure that there weren't any bikers following them. A thought struck him. "You think one of those guys is the one who followed us last night—right before the accident?"

She shrugged. "I don't know, but they were talk-ing about Canadian Blue. They were making some plan to have a buy…or whatever you call it."

"What do you mean?"

"I was sitting with the president, and another guy came up to him. They are having a rendezvous to-morrow where they are planning on buying the Ca-nadian Blue. At least I think so…"

"Do you know where?" The car lurched around the corner, the tires sliding on the wet pavement.

"You don't need to drive like a bat out of hell. They're not following us."

"Just like they weren't last time?" He readjusted the mirror. "I can't let you get hurt again."

"I'm not some fragile thing that you have to treat with gloved hands. I've lived this long on my own. I don't need you to protect me," she said, suddenly angry that once again they were having this argu-ment.

"Look, I know you're strong. Have you ever stopped to think that maybe I'm the one who's not?"

She stopped. The thought hadn't crossed her mind. "What do you mean, Casper?"

"I told you about the baby, my girlfriend, my past. I can't go through losing someone else that I care about." He glanced back again. "I shouldn't have let you go in there alone."

She fumbled for words.

He *cared* about her. He'd said it aloud. This changed everything. They were moving out of the safety of their friends-ish zone…well, friends-that-kissed zone. The thought of a relationship terrified her, but as she looked at his gold-flecked eyes and the concern for her that was strewn across his face, a sense of calm filled her. He wasn't one of the men from her past. He wasn't the type who was going to try and keep her in the dark. It would be a struggle for him to open up to her, but he was trying. He'd told her things that she doubted he had talked about in a long time.

She didn't know how to make him stop worrying, but one thing came to mind. He had opened up. Now maybe it was her turn.

"You know, before…you weren't wrong about me avoiding talking about things that really matter."

He glanced over at her as though he was wondering where this new line of conversation came from.

"I… I never lost a baby. I can't even begin to imagine how hard that must have been for you." She nibbled at her lip as she second-guessed herself. Maybe she should wait until things were more real between them, but if she avoided the truth any longer, it would only be that much harder to talk about when things got more serious—she didn't want to hide anything from him. He needed to know who she really was.

"It was hard… It didn't even matter whose baby it was. In my heart, it was mine. When she called me…" His grip tightened on the wheel. "There's no going back to the way things were before. You can't change the past."

"I know." She sighed. "I've tried."

"What do you mean?"

"When I was six years old, my birth parents were arrested. They'd been strung out for days. Neither of them had jobs. Most days I didn't eat and at night... nights were the worst." Memories of her mother and father screaming at one another filtered into her mind. "One night my mother tried to shoot my father. I ran to my neighbors and told them what happened."

Casper's mouth twitched with rage as he pulled his face into a tight scowl.

"I was taken by CPS and put into foster care. For seven years, I bounced around from one house to the next. Finally I landed on the Finches' doorstep and they were gracious enough to bring me in. For the first time in my life I had enough food, clothes and love. They changed my life."

He reached over and took her fingers in his and lifted their entwined hands to his mouth. Ever so gently, he kissed each of her fingers.

"For a long time, I fought back against their love. I didn't feel like I deserved it and I couldn't trust it. I couldn't accept that they wanted to just bring me joy and security—I'd learned early on that everything in life comes at a price."

"Do you still think that?" he asked, his hot breath caressing her fingers.

"I hate to say it, but I do." She twisted her mouth as she waited for him to chastise her for being so pessimistic.

Instead of disagreeing with her, he nodded. "Life makes us hard. Doesn't it?"

The truth was that she didn't want to be that way. She would give anything to be the kind of woman who could see the joy in other people just like she could see the true beauty of nature.

"Some prices are higher than others," she said. "And with some choices you have to continue paying for them for the rest of your life—even when the choice wasn't yours." As she said the words, it felt almost as if she was saying goodbye—as if no matter what happened between them, the vast plains of their pasts would be too immense for them to come together.

As they drove up to Lex's cabin, Ranger Grant was standing beside his truck, waiting for them. She was surprised to see the man, especially so late at night. Yet there he stood, leaning against the grille, arms folded over his khaki shirt that was pulled taut over his paunch belly. His hair was slicked down with too much gel in order to try and cover his balding top, but the attempt only made him look older.

In a way, she was relieved to see Grant—it meant that Casper couldn't just leave, he would have to stay and talk and he would be hers for at least a few more minutes.

She tried not to get her hopes up as she thought about her feelings of goodbye.

Grant walked up to the driver-side door and extended his hand to Casper as he got out. "Agent Lawrence?"

Casper looked confused and she realized that it was likely because he'd never actually met the man before. She rushed around to their side. "Casper, this is Ranger Grant. You spoke with him on the phone."

"It's great to meet you, Grant. Did you get a chance to look into the missing pills?"

Grant pushed his pudgy finger under the second button of his stretched shirt. "Actually, that's why I came here. I was hoping to catch you."

"How did you know I was going to be here?" Casper asked, an air of suspicion in his voice.

"Oh, I just took a guess." Grant gave him a knowing smile. "But about the pills. I got in touch with a detective friend of mine in Kalispell. It sounds like they have started to make their way around the county."

"How does he know that these are the same pills and not from another shipment?" Casper asked.

"Truth be told, we don't," Grant said with a shrug. "But from what the detective said, they had been going through a little bit of a dry spell. Not much was on their radar, but then within twenty-four hours of your heist, the pills started showing up on the streets. It has to be more than a coincidence."

"Could they have been coming in from anywhere else?" she asked.

Grant shook his head. "This isn't like meth. It can't be found everywhere. This is a localized epidemic, with a local—or somewhat local—source. The farthest these pills reach, on average, is Eastern Washington, in and around Spokane, and they had moved east into North Dakota, mostly in the dying roughneck towns."

"So you think that this smuggling operation is how the drugs are entering the country?" Casper asked, making Lex think back to the conversation they'd had with Steel.

"Without a doubt. If you drew a circle around where the drugs have been found, this would be the epicenter."

He'd been right.

Casper pulled down the brim of his hat, setting it tight on his head as he stood quietly. He looked at her with a questioning glance.

She nibbled nervously at her bottom lip. Until tonight, when they were in the middle of an investigation that was starting to pull them deeper and deeper into the shadows of society, Grant had never given her a reason not to trust him. But there was something about him, the fact that he knew where they were and when they'd be home, that made her nervous.

Chapter Twelve

Even though it was late summer, when they walked into her cabin the place was cold, and Lex was forced to start a fire. Normally this late in the season the weather was warm enough to keep the cabin heated, but a storm had settled into the mountain valley and had started to release its rain. Once again the place had started to take on the edge of cold that marked the onset of fall.

Time would slip by and she'd lose herself to the needs of the park. She looked out the window and watched as Casper stacked wood on his arm to help with the fire.

She sucked in a breath as he bent over to grab another log from the stack.

Casper stood up and, noticing her watching, gave her his provocative grin, the one that seemed to be only for her. His hat dripped as the light smatter of rain hit the surface and rolled off in small streams.

She'd never dated a man who wore a cowboy hat before, but watching him made her realize how sexy they were. They were the mark of a real man—a far cry from the bun-wearing men she often saw hiking through the park, or scattered across her social media feed.

Wait, were they dating?

No. She chastised herself. This was, in all probability, the last time they'd really spend together. She'd be handing her investigation off to Travis tomorrow and from there she and Casper would have no professional contact. She lived an hour and a half away from his post near Waterton—long-distance relationships never worked. Sure, they could see each other once or twice a week, maybe more in the beginning, but real life would take over, they would spend less and less time together, and soon there would be nothing between them but heartache and faded memories.

If they got together it would be doomed to fail from the very beginning.

She held open the door for him as he carried in the wood. He was breathing hard under the struggle of carrying all that weight.

"Thanks," she said, suddenly more aware than ever of the unwelcome feelings of desire that bubbled up within her. "It's nice to have an extra set of hands."

"No problem." He carefully set each piece of wood in the box a few feet from the potbelly stove.

He walked over to the fire and stoked the embers, even though they were fully alight with flames. "It should heat up in here in no time," he said, closing the stove and turning back to her. "But if you don't mind, I'm going to warm up before I go."

She couldn't help the smile that overtook her face at his lame excuse for wanting to be around her for a little longer. Was it possible that he was feeling the same confusing mess of emotions that she was?

"What about the bikers? What if they come here?" She nibbled seductively at her lip.

"I think you're okay. They didn't get your real name, did they?" he asked, almost as if he was oblivious to the fact that she was, in a way, asking him to spend the night.

He definitely wasn't a player, or there would have been no way he would have missed her pitch.

"I don't think so," she continued. "But I'd feel better if you stayed for a while. You know, just to make sure they don't come after me...or us."

Maybe his miss was a hit after all.

"About the bikers, why didn't you tell Grant about the rendezvous tomorrow?" He moved slightly so he could face his palms toward the heat.

Lex walked over and stood beside him at the fire. She shrugged. "I dunno. It just didn't feel right, you know?"

"Are you worried that if you tell him, word will get to Travis?"

She hadn't thought of that, but Casper might have a point. If she had given Grant the information, it would make Travis's work significantly easier. She wasn't vindictive or glory-seeking, but it ate at her that he was taking over, and no doubt would get all the accolades when he solved the case.

"I'm going to have to tell Travis about what we found anyway, I guess."

"If that's not it, then what do you mean by, 'it didn't feel right'? Grant didn't seem like a bad guy. If anything, he was pretty helpful going out and talking to the local cops for us, and he combed the wreck—twice."

A thought struck her. "You're right. He did comb the scene of the wreck." She rushed to the tiny table by the kitchen and grabbed a piece of paper. She jabbed her pen into the soft paper as she wrote down a series of names.

"Look," she said, lifting the note for him to see. "These are all the people who knew we were carrying the drugs that night. Travis, Hal, the other ranger—John—and you and I. We were the only people on the scene of Razor's death."

"We talked about this. I don't see how those guys could be behind us losing the drugs."

"Think about it... Who all have Travis and John been talking to?"

Casper shook his head, not following her.

"I'm sure they've been talking to Grant." She ran her hands through her hair with excitement. "When they were taking off in the helicopter from the crime scene, Travis was on the phone. He was probably telling Grant about what we had found and where we were going with the drugs. Maybe they set up the accident. Then maybe Grant just picked up the pills."

"Are you serious? You think that Travis and Grant have something to do with our drugs getting stolen? It seems a little far-fetched."

She paused, staring at the yellow legal pad and its list of names. He might be right, but then again, there was a little part of her that couldn't accept it. "How did Grant know we were here tonight? That you were with me? The last people who saw us together were the bikers."

"So now you think the bikers are in Grant's pocket?" Casper took off his hat and threw it on her couch, just atop the quilt her foster mother had made her. "This isn't some episode of *Law and Order*. Everyone isn't in cahoots. There has to be a more simple explanation to all this."

"Why are you being so dismissive of my idea?" she asked, trying to keep her annoyance from seeping into her voice.

"I'm not being dismissive. I just don't think the entire ranger district is involved with a biker gang. I mean, take yourself, for example. You were married to Travis. Did either of you have bikers stopping by? Was there anything at all before this started to make you think he, or anyone you know, has been working with the MC?"

She sighed, setting the pad back down on the table. "Maybe you're right. I'm getting ahead of myself. It's just... I want to get to the bottom of this."

"Everything's going to be okay, even if we don't solve this tonight." Casper walked over and stopped behind her. He started to rub her shoulders. It felt so good, the kneading pressure of his fingers in her taut muscles. She hadn't realized how stressed she was. "You know, at least something good came from all this."

She opened her eyes and looked back at him. "What's that?"

"I got the chance to meet you. You're the best thing that's happened to me in years." He leaned down and his lips met hers in one glorious kiss.

Her body flushed to life. It felt so right as his tongue brushed against her lower lip and she tasted the mint on his breath. She turned around, not breaking their kiss. Reaching up, she ran her fingers through his slightly-too-long locks.

His hair was so soft, it felt like strands of silk in her fingers. She pulled him harder against her lips. She wanted more. So much more.

Even so, there was a warning that sounded from the back of her mind. For a moment she paid it heed, but quickly doused the negative sparks with the euphoric wave of his kiss. She could have this. Him. Here. Now.

Consequences and the future be damned.

She was an adult woman. A woman with needs. A woman with wants. And right now the thing she wanted most was pressing against her, his body responding in a way that proved he wanted her as badly as she wanted him.

He pulled her into his arms. His shirt was wet and he smelled of pine and sweat all laced with the heady aroma of lustful pheromones. If she was forced to think of the sexiest scent on the planet, it would have been him, in this moment.

She trailed her fingertips down from his hair and over the rough stubble that riddled his cheeks. Drawing back, she ran her thumb over the slightly chapped skin of his lower lip. Playfully, he took her finger into his mouth and traced his tongue just over the tip. He nibbled it and she drew back at the surprising mix of pain and craving.

Lifting his hand from her waist, she mimicked his movement, sucking and pulling his finger into her mouth. Deep and long. Licking the length and stroking it with her lips. On his fingertip was a bump and he winced slightly as she swirled her tongue on the spot. She stopped.

"Are you okay?" she asked, looking at the place on his finger that she had felt with her mouth.

There was a small dot and the skin around it was raised and angry.

"Don't worry about it," he said, slightly breathless.

She smiled as she thought of how she had made him feel.

"What happened here?" she asked, attempting to prolong the agony of desire.

"I poked my finger when I was sewing your pants. It's no biggie. Really," he said, leaning in to take her mouth again, but she pulled back.

"You mended my pants?"

"Yeah, your work ones. The ones you ripped on the log."

"When?"

He sighed and stood tall, as though he realized that she was playing hard to get. "I mended them when you were asleep in the hospital."

She stepped out of his arms, going to the laundry basket in the bathroom and taking out the pants. There was a small series of stitches, perfectly aligned and set. It was better than she could have done. In fact, if she hadn't known better, she would have thought a professional had done the work.

He walked into the room behind her and leaned against the door frame. "Up to snuff?" He gave her that roguish grin she loved so much and she dropped the pants back into the basket.

"Even better." She took him by the hand and led him to her bed.

It melted her heart as she thought of him sitting beside her, setting to work on her pants. There was something so hot about this alpha-type man sewing. Thinking of her broken man taking care of her in such a selfless and domestic way made any last shred of doubt about him slip away.

He checked every box that she wanted in a man—strong, smart, sweet, caring, not afraid to speak his mind and not afraid to admit when he was wrong. He was the unicorn that every woman wanted. And he was hers.

She reached up and started unbuttoning his shirt.

"What're you doing?" he asked.

"You took care of me, now I take care of you." She gave him an impish grin. "We need to get these wet clothes off. I don't want you catching your death of cold."

He laughed. "I see…" He sucked in a breath as her hands moved to the lowest buttons of his shirt and she skimmed the rough fabric of the front of his pants.

She loved this game and relished the thought of making him long for her.

Slipping his shirt from his shoulders, he stood there, his body reflecting the orange flickering light of the fire. He had a thin patch of hair between his pecs, just enough for her to run her fingers through without being too much.

Stepping closer, she took his nipple into her mouth and sucked, making a popping sound as she moved to the next. His breathing intensified, and his hot breath slipped down her neck and under her shirt like a caressing touch, making her nipples as hard as those in her mouth.

He pulled her up to him, taking control. He fumbled with the buttons on her shirt, but in his state, his fingers seemed to be disconnected from his body.

He gave up and ripped it off, sending buttons flying throughout the room.

"It's a good thing you know how to sew," she joked.

His smirk returned, but this time his eyes were burning with red-hot desire that made her core clench and the dampness grow between her thighs.

He unbuttoned her pants and let them fall onto the growing heap of clothes. Gently he lifted her onto the bed, laying her head on the pillow. "Are you okay?" he asked, as if touching her hair had suddenly reminded him of their accident.

Some of the heat disappeared in his eyes and she longed for it to come back.

"Don't worry about me. Right now let's just be here, in this moment." She unbuttoned his pants.

His body arched around her touch as if he was shy, but wanted more. Ever so slowly, she lowered her hand, tracing her fingers down his length. The fire in his eyes raged once again.

She pushed his pants and boxers off.

He moved between her legs and lowered himself into her. Her body pulsed with life and she moaned at the beautiful torture of feeling him inside her.

If she had her way, this night would last forever.

Chapter Thirteen

As Lex arrived at the ranger station the next morning, her body ached with the pleasant pain that came after a long night of lovemaking. She smiled as she thought of their time together, him between her thighs, and the feeling of her head on his chest. Her mind swam in the warm thoughts of what the future could bring, until her friend Kelly stepped out from the back office and stopped at the front desk.

Her work friend was in her midthirties, petite but a bit on the heavy side, and on the cuff of her shirt there was peanut butter smeared where one of her kids had used her as a napkin.

"Lex, what're you doing here?" she asked. "I thought you were still recovering. I was going to stop by and see you after I got off work today."

"Dragger wanted me back—wants me to button up Sperry."

"Are you serious? Dragger called you back? He couldn't have meant it after what happened. Did they ever figure out who forced you off the road?"

Lex shook her head and, not for the first time that day, she wished Casper was still with her. She had made him stay behind and look further into the bikers.

"No one's come forward and we can't track down any witnesses. Grant's helping us." She paused. "By chance, have you talked to him lately?"

Kelly nodded. "He called me last night and asked me where you were. Apparently he was looking for you—did you guys catch up?"

So, Casper had been right. Grant had been telling the truth and had just luckily tracked them down. She felt silly for suspecting that everyone around her was guilty. Maybe she was just losing her mind; or maybe her past was conflicting with her present.

It was a wonder that Casper wanted anything to do with her and her baggage. Maybe he just didn't know what he was getting himself into. Or maybe last night had been his attempt at a one-time thing. A sliver of panic moved through her. Had last night been just that—a one-night stand?

"Are you okay?" Kelly asked, almost as if she could read her mind.

She plastered a fake smile on her face and nodded, but Kelly kept looking at her as though she didn't believe her.

Travis's voice echoed out from the back office, but she couldn't tell whom he was talking to.

She couldn't even fake a smile as she heard him. He was laughing at some unheard joke as he stepped out into the main office. He gave her a smug grin as he spotted her. "I thought you were going to quit."

So he'd been talking to Dragger at some point? She shouldn't have been surprised. Why had Dragger told Travis about his threat to fire her? Travis had no business knowing anything about her or her options.

"Oh, I'm sorry to disappoint," she said, trying to summon every bit of self-confidence that she could muster.

Dragger and John walked out from the back office. John, the blond ranger from the recovery, was strutting like a fat goose as he looked at her.

"What's wrong with you?" she asked as John stuffed his thumbs into his pockets.

"John here," Dragger said, motioning toward the man, "will be taking over the case."

"But—but you said it was going to be Travis who took over," she stammered as she stared in disbelief at her ex-husband.

"I changed my mind," Dragger said with a dismissive shrug. "He asked to go with you up to Sperry instead."

"What in the hell? Why did you do that, Travis?" Who did he think he was to push his way back into her life?

"Whether we are married or not, Lex, I care about you—not like that CBP agent you've been running with the last few days. There's no way that after your accident I'm just going to let you go up to the chalet and spend the whole day working all by yourself. It's a recipe for disaster."

Travis had never been the kind for grand gestures, and when they'd been together he'd never gone out of his way to make sure that she was okay. If anything, most things had revolved around him and his needs—especially when it came to "his time." There had to be something else going on, something that he wasn't telling her.

"First, Travis, you don't *let* me do anything. If I go up there, it's my choice to make and not yours. Second, why the sudden change of heart? You don't give two shakes about me."

Dragger stuffed his toe into the thin industrial carpet as he tried to look at anything but her.

Travis rolled his eyes, and the stupid adolescent response made her want to pitch her shoe at him. She had every right to get upset. He didn't love her. He hadn't loved her in a long time. Just like his showing up at the hospital, it was nothing more than a show.

"Lex, I've always loved you." He reached over and tried to touch her, but she batted his hand away in disgust.

"If you loved me, Travis, then why did you treat me like you did?"

Kelly smiled from behind the desk and gave her a little thumbs-up, as if she was enjoying the show that was happening in front of her.

"Knock it off, you two," Dragger ordered. "You

have plenty of time to hash out your private business on the ride up to Sperry."

She considered being petulant and telling Dragger that she refused to work with Travis, but from the sour look on Dragger's face, it would only end in her being reprimanded—or worse.

"I want you to take the pack horses and use Gunsight Trail. Check that all the hikers are out so we can close the trail," Dragger ordered, looking to Travis and giving a quick nod of the head like they had some private agreement. "Before you go, Alexis, you need to fill John in on all your findings with the case. Where's Agent Lawrence? I thought he was going to be here to pick up his new partner."

She was happier than ever that she had told Casper to cut and run.

"I have no idea where he's at, sir," she said, not entirely lying. All that mattered now was that he was making the most of what little time he had before John interfered.

Casper closed his eyes and leaned his head against the car's window as he let last night's memories flash through his mind. Their bodies entangled in a mess of arms and legs, wet with sweat and smelling of sex. His body shuttered to life, but he tried to ignore it. He was one lucky son of a gun.

He had imagined that a night with her would be hot, but she had been even better than his best fantasies. It had been one hell of a way to spend the night—and if he had his way, it was exactly where he'd like to spend the entirety of his life. If he did, he would die a happy man.

There was a knock on his window and he opened his eyes to see Deputy Steel standing outside the car, staring at him.

"Are we gonna work or just hang out and nap all day?" Steel asked, his voice muffled by the glass.

"Get in," Casper ordered, half laughing as he motioned to the passenger seat. "I've been waiting for you nearly all day. I thought you must have gotten lost. I know that's a problem for the Marshal Service."

"Sorry, your mom made me breakfast after last night," Steel ribbed.

Casper laughed. "It's just like old times. You're just lucky I'm feeling nice."

Steel thumped down into the seat next to him. "You're never this nice… Apparently you've been on your own too long in that little shack on the border." Steel leaned back and took out a notepad. "So, you told me about the bikers. Anything else I need to know?"

"Lex has been worrying about the people around her. I don't know if there's anything to the way she's feeling, or if she's being overly suspicious, but I think it's worth looking into."

"Lex?"

"Alexis Finch, the ranger I've been working with on the investigation, but her boss took her off today.

I'm supposed to be getting a new partner from them. That's why I'm out here waiting for your sorry butt."

"Why did she get taken off the case? Were you guys sleeping together?"

He couldn't help the heat that rushed into his face.

Steel glanced over at him and his mouth opened with surprise. "You were? You dirty dog."

"It isn't like that. I swear. There's no way they could have known. It just happened. They took her off the assignment before things ever heated up between us."

Steel raised an eyebrow. "So that's why you are feeling so nice?"

"This doesn't go any further than you and me. I don't kiss and tell."

"Good policy," Steel said. "My lips are zipped."

Casper gave him an appreciative nod.

"So your girlfriend—"

"She's not my girlfriend," Casper interrupted.

"Okay, so your not-a-girlfriend friend, Lex, is suspicious about her coworkers. Did you tell her that you thought there might be something to her feelings?"

"I'm not sure that there is something there. I mean, there's some other things involved that may be affecting her judgment."

"Like what?"

"Like she works with her ex-husband."

"They get along enough that they can work together?" Steel asked.

"Not really."

Steel nodded as if he finally understood why Casper felt the way he did.

"She just texted me. Sounds like she is going to have to spend the day with him deep in the park."

"Oh," Steel said. "I bet she's happy about it."

Steel leaned forward and pulled a laptop out of his bag. The thing was one of those huge computers that was equipped with industrial-strength plastic and a bulletproof shell. Secretly, Casper kind of wished that he had one like it. "I had my guys follow your friends, the Keepers, last night in an attempt to find out who, and where, they were going to meet today. I had to call in more than my fair share of favors on that one."

"Appreciate it, man. This will all come together, and you'll see that all your hard work was worth it."

Steel motioned for him to start driving. "Head toward Columbia Falls."

Casper pushed the car into gear. "What's up there?"

"It sounds like they had another shipment of the Canadian Blue come through."

"From where?"

Steel got a cheese-eating grin on his face. "The bikers are meeting up with someone at the back entrance to Glacier—the unmanned gate. We weren't able to make out who they were meeting, but—like you assumed—it's our belief that whoever is selling them the drugs is bringing the pills over the border and through the park."

"Do you want me to call in some backup so we're not on our own at this buy?"

"You don't like the ten-bikers-to-one-Fed kind of odds? Come on now, if there are any more of us it's almost unfair to them…"

Steel laughed, but the pit in Casper's stomach deepened. He'd never been afraid of facing bikers or any number of adversaries, but they had threatened Lex, and after what had happened last night with her…well, for once it felt like he had something—or someone—to live for.

"Don't you think it would be—"

"Hey now, Lawrence," Steel said, interrupting him. "I was just kidding. Three other marshals are going to meet us up there. We got a line on the president of the club. Three years ago he escaped the federal pen. According to our man, he's going to be at the buy. Hopefully you and I both get something that will help our careers."

Casper twitched. It wasn't a surprise that Steel knew he'd had trouble in the past, but he hadn't thought the guy would bring it up.

"That's why you're going after this like your ass is on fire, isn't it? So you can get your foot back in the door with the FBI?" Steel pressed.

Honestly, he hadn't thought of it in those terms, but Steel wasn't wrong. If he played his cards right— if he could take down an international drug-smuggling ring—it would look good on his résumé if he decided to go after his former job.

He sucked in a long breath as he thought about it. He wouldn't have to live in the middle of nowhere. His days wouldn't be an endless flow of checking bags and passports and the infrequent investigation. He wouldn't be the low man on the totem pole.

But if he went back to the FBI, he would likely be transferred out of Montana—and away from Lex.

There's no way they could make it work—the distance would be too far, and his life would fall back into the constant flux that came with a job in the FBI. His days would be filled with investigations and reports, and his nights would be filled with thoughts of what he could do better. He'd fallen into this trap before. He couldn't do it again—he couldn't give up his life, his chance at happiness, just to get a foot up at the Bureau.

As he drove, he thought back to the feel of Lex in his arms. Everything about last night seemed like a dream, every action a snippet held up in the surreal fog of too-good-to-be-real; her hair tickling his chest as she sat atop him, the feel of her hips in his hands, her feet entwined with his.

All this season, he had thought of the stand-alone station at Goat Haunt as his place of imprisonment, but maybe it wasn't a prison after all—maybe it was a chance for a new beginning.

It was all so confusing. He had thought he'd hated this place, but in the last few days everything had changed.

If he told Lex about the opportunity the case could

provide, would she want him to use it to his every advantage, or would she urge him to stay near her?

He imagined the look on her face if he told her that he wanted to go back to the FBI. It made something in his chest shift. He couldn't live with himself if he broke her heart. Hell, just the thought of leaving her broke his.

He shook the thoughts from his head. He was playing in the world of what-ifs anyway. Before he'd ever have to make any decisions, they would have to get a handle on the investigation. They needed to find direct evidence that tied these bikers to the drug trade, and they needed to find out exactly why and how they were running the drugs through the park—and they needed to find out who murdered Razor.

"Grant met up with me last night," Casper said. "He let me know that there was Canadian Blue hitting the streets in and around Kalispell. He thinks they're the drugs that were stolen from my truck."

"No crap?" Steel said. "He have any clue who stole them?"

Casper shook his head. "He's no closer to finding out, but my gut is telling me that the answer's right at our fingertips."

"What do you mean?"

"The night of our accident, there was a biker following us." He tapped his fingers against the steering wheel as he attempted to pick his words very carefully. "I know it's circumstantial, but everything about this case revolves around that MC and the men in it. I'd bet my bottom dollar that they set the whole thing up. Maybe they knew we had the drugs. Maybe they knew we were taking them back to Apgar to the evidence unit. So they picked a spot on that road and forced us off it."

"You think that they wanted to kill you guys?"

A wave of nausea passed over him as he contemplated the thought, but he swallowed it back. "If they wanted us dead, they would've killed us… They could have done it right then and there."

"Is there a reason they didn't?"

He thought back to that night. When they'd hit the rock wall, he'd lost consciousness. When he'd come to, they had been surrounded by bystanders. "There were a lot of witnesses."

"It sounds like you guys are lucky." Steel whistled through his teeth. "If these guys are as bad as I think they are, and they're behind the murder and the drug running, it would have been a win for them to take you and Alexis out. You were two of only a few people that could point a finger in their direction."

Chapter Fourteen

The chestnut mare's hooves clicked against the rocks as they climbed higher and higher up Gunsight Trail and closer to Sperry Chalet. The timber was intermittent as their elevation grew and, on the leeward side of the mountain, the horses had to fight through a thin layer of snow and ice on the trail.

Her horse pulled in a deep breath, making Lex's legs widen around her girth, and giving a long huff as if growing as tired of the hike as Lex was. Travis had been quiet most of the way, but as they drew nearer to their destination he had started to talk more and more.

"Do you remember that one time when we found the woman? You know, the one who died in the creek?" Travis asked as they passed by a small waterfall cascading out of a small crevice in the rocky hillside.

She tried to hold back the image that came to the front of her mind of the woman's blue lips and her clouded, sightless eyes. For a long time she had seen that face every time she had closed her eyes and tried to go to sleep.

"Travis, do we really have to talk about her?" she said, turning in her saddle slightly so she could look back at him over her shoulder.

He shrugged. "Just thought we could make conversation."

"Is that why you got me pulled off the case, so we could *make conversation*? Did it ever occur to you that I was *this close* to solving it?" She pinched her fingers together to emphasize her point.

"Trust me, you weren't that close, and besides, I'm not the one who got you pulled off the case."

"Then who did?"

Travis smirked. "You and your big mouth did that all on your own."

"What do you mean by that?" Rage steamed up within her.

"Nothing... I don't mean anything." Travis sighed. "Look, I didn't come with you to start a fight."

There was a strange inflection in his words as if he were holding back...or hiding something.

"This isn't your attempt to get back together, is it?" she asked, trying to finally address the elephant in the room.

Travis laughed, the noise echoing through the steep ravine and cascading down to the valley below—making it sound almost sinister.

"You and I were never meant to be, Lex. I know that now. You're too good."

"Too good? I've heard some stupid excuses before, Travis, but *too good*? That's a new one."

They came over top of a small rise and the cabin, made out of a collection of multicolored natural stones, came into view. It was encompassed by a stand of timber, making it look like something out of a Tolkien book instead of a real place.

"Remember the last time we were up here?" Travis asked.

Her horse nickered and its ears swiveled as if it was trying to catch a sound to its left. The horse didn't like something. She was becoming nervous, stumbling slightly as she grew more wary.

Lex reached down and patted the horse's neck. "It's okay, baby," she cooed, trying to calm the animal. "It's okay."

She looked around, trying to see what exactly had spooked the horse, but she couldn't see anything that would cause the animal to react like this.

She glanced behind them at Travis's black and white gelding sidestepping on the narrow trail as he tried to get him to keep moving forward.

"Stop, Travis. Don't push him. He's scared," she said, forcing her voice to be as calm and neutral as possible in an effort to keep the horses from getting more spooked.

Travis stopped moving the reins and sat still in the saddle.

Her mare stiffened beneath her, lifting her nose and drawing in a breath, trying to catch a scent in the air. She blew it out with a huff and nickered again, the sound high with fear.

"Was anyone supposed to be up here?"

Travis shook his head. "Everyone was supposed to be out. The last paying guest checked out yesterday."

She nudged the mare, trying to get her to move forward, but the animal refused to budge and instead started to scoot her feet backward toward the edge of the narrow trail.

"Whoa, baby… Whoa." She pulled up on the reins and the horse stopped inches from disaster.

Lex lifted her foot out of the stirrup, sliding her body out of the saddle and dropping to the ground, the motion slow and even. "It's okay, baby," she cooed, her full attention on the scared horse.

She moved around to the front of the mare, out of its way in case it decided to spook. "Come on, baby, move away from the edge," she said, gently tugging on the reins in an effort to get the horse to step forward and follow her.

They weren't far from the cabin. If she could just get the animal closer to the safety and protection of the structure, maybe it would calm down.

The mare moved after her a few steps and then its eyes grew wide with fear. She reared up and squealed, pulling back on the reins and tearing them from Lex's hands. Turning, she charged down the trail, disappearing from view.

Travis was fighting with his gelding, trying to get it from following after the loose mare. As he pulled on the horse's reins, it skittered sideways. It jumped, its back humping like a bucking bronco, throwing Travis to the ground in a heap. His foot caught in the stirrup and the gelding turned and started after the mare, dragging Travis a few feet, his leg in an inconceivable angle, before he broke free.

She held her breath as Travis lay motionless on the ground. His foot was at an obtuse angle from his leg, broken. There was a thin trail of blood where his body had been dragged over the angular, jutting scree that littered the trail.

"Travis," she said, her voice frantic. "Are you okay?"

She moved toward him, stopping as she came close. She didn't want to touch him too much. If he'd broken his back or his neck she couldn't risk moving him.

"Travis?"

He remained silent and unmoving.

What if he was dead?

She kneeled down and pressed her fingers to his neck. There was the slow, steady *thump, thump, thump* of his heartbeat, but he was seriously hurt. He needed help. Now.

She pulled out her phone. No service.

Maybe Travis's phone would have some bars. Ever so carefully, she reached around and flipped back the bottom flap of his jacket so she could reach in the coat's pocket. Her fingers brushed against cold steel.

There, just beneath his armpit in its holster, was a small silver revolver.

They had come up here to close down the cabin. Why was he carrying a gun? In all the time they'd been married, she'd never known him to carry a gun, except when he was on a call or when he was going to put an animal down.

Aside from their horses, she was the only animal here.

She pulled the gun from his holster and slid it into the back of her waistband.

Maybe she had this all wrong. Casper had told her that she was overreacting in being suspicious about everyone…maybe he was right. There had to be a legitimate reason for Travis to be carrying the gun.

Right now she just had to get him the help that he so desperately needed.

She reached back into his pocket, grabbing his phone. A plastic bag dropped on the ground as she took out the cell.

Inside the bag was a collection of blue pills—at least twenty, maybe thirty of them.

She gasped.

What in the hell was going on?

Someone grabbed her from behind and pulled the gun from her waistband. Their hand moved over her mouth, stifling her scream.

"Shut your mouth, Alexis," a man whispered in her ear, raising the barrel of the gun until the cold metal brushed against her temple. "If you want to live, you will shut your face and listen."

"PETER KAGGER, THE secretary for the Keepers' Alberta chapter, is willing to help us, but he wants extradition to the United States and to have his conviction expunged from his record once he arrives." Steel motioned toward the phone in his hands.

"What else does he want? A freaking gold star award? This guy shot a Canadian senator. We have zero jurisdiction there, and little leverage. How in the heck does he think we're going to be able to honor his requests?"

"He has two years left on his sentence and he says he's an American citizen."

"Oh, that's even better. How did an American shooting a Canadian senator not hit every newsreel from here to London? If he thinks that we are going to cause a possible international uproar by sticking our necks out for him just because he may or may not have information that will help our murder case, then he's got another thing coming."

Steel chuckled. "I hear you, but he's the only open door we got when it comes to finding anything out about the biker gang." He pointed toward the line of bikes that were parked outside Moose's Pizza Joint in Kalispell. "I don't see us barging in there and walking out with the information we need unless we make some sort of deal. I got friends in the Canadian Parliament. Maybe they can pull some strings."

Just on the other side of the windows, two bikers were standing guard at each side of the door. Since they had arrived the bikers hadn't stopped watching them.

They had to find out who was behind this mess and exactly what role the bikers had in all of it.

"Tell him we need some information to take to a federal judge. If he gives us something we can use, maybe we can see what we can do to bring him back to the old red, white and blue."

Steel went back to his phone. Inside the pizza joint, an older man with a black cut stood up and looked out the window, directly at Casper. The man had a goatee smattered with silver and black that made him look like a snarling dog as he spoke. The sinister look made every hair on Casper's arms rise, but he refused to look away. Just like a wild animal, the moment you turned your back was the moment they would attack.

Casper lifted his hand in an amicable two-finger wave.

"What in the hell are you doing?" Steel growled as he hung up the phone.

"Did you get us anything?"

Steel reached over and pulled Casper's arm down and out of view. "According to Kagger, that man you're making buddy-buddy with is the Montana chapter's president. He wouldn't give me a whole lot of details about the guy, but I'm sure that he isn't the kind you are going to be knitting sweaters with."

"Did Kagger know anything about Razor's murder?"

The chapter president walked over to the men by the door, and they kept glancing over their shoulders toward Casper's car.

"According to Kagger, their MC wasn't behind the hit. He said the gang wouldn't have touched him. From the word on the street, Razor was basically a made guy. He was the president's right-hand man did all his dirty business. If anyone touched him, there would have been a holy war."

"Then why is the gang sitting around having pizza if that's true?"

"Razor was in the Alberta chapter, not the Montana one, but Kagger said these guys are on the hunt for the killer, as well. He said that none of the clubs have a positive ID on the shooter—and they're willing to do just about anything in order to get a name. This could be our way in."

Steel slipped his cell phone into the breast pocket of his white button-up. "And if they get their hands on the shooter before we do, you better believe that it's likely we'll never know about it—or, if we do, it will be only because we'll be on clean-up duty."

The glass door opened and one of the guys who had been standing guard slowly sauntered out toward them. He had on the same leather cut as the other men in the restaurant, but instead of the normal rockers he only had one that read "Pledge."

So the president had sent an expendable. Casper

had a nagging feeling that things were about to get ugly.

"You wanna call for backup?" Casper asked, nodding toward the man who was making his way across the parking lot toward them.

"I think we can handle ourselves here. The last thing these guys want is a bloodbath in their backyard. These are one-percenters—they believe in the live-and-let-live ideal when it comes to law enforcement—especially Feds." Steel forced a smile as the man drew nearer.

Casper couldn't ignore the tension in his friend's voice and the way his hand instinctively moved to the holster under his left arm.

The man walked over to Casper's window and waited for him to lower it completely. He must have had a WWE wrestler as a father and an Amazonian as a mother. His neck bulged with muscles, and the leather cut he wore creaked under the strain of his wide chest as he breathed.

"Howdy, son," Casper said, greeting him as though the man was a lap dog instead of a pit bull.

"Son?" The man looked behind him and then turned back with a dangerous grin. "I ain't your son."

A thousand smart-assed rebuttals sprang to the front of his mind, but he bit his tongue. "No offense. How can we help you?"

The man readjusted his cut. "My friend in there—" he jabbed his thumb in the direction of the pizza joint "—he's wondering why you are following us."

"We're not following you."

"Bull," the man said, his voice taking on a steely edge that only promised problems. "Ever since your little girlfriend came in our club last night, we've had a tail—until you arrived it was the US Marshals. We ain't stupid."

Casper glanced over to Steel, who gave him an acknowledging tilt of the head.

"Is that why you guys called off your rendezvous with your buyers today?" Casper pressed.

The guy's eyebrow rose like a large, hairy caterpillar. "I got no idea what you all are talkin' about. We don't got nothing to do with no drugs. We just were hungry for the best pizza in town." He smiled, the action making his sunburned skin pull so tight across his chapped lips with the unaccustomed motion that they cracked. Little specks of blood dotted his lips. "In fact, you guys been out here a long time…watching us. I bet you're hungry. Why don't you both step inside?"

From the tone of the man's voice, it was clear that it wasn't a request.

"We're all good here," Steel said, either not picking up on the man's order, or else he'd chosen to ignore it.

The man put his hand up. "Just going for my phone," he said as he reached into his pocket.

Casper's hand tightened on the grip of his gun.

"Make sure to move real slow, or your vest will be air-conditioned."

Steel tapped his fingers on his holstered sidearm, and the man nodded.

"I ain't here to threaten you. Ain't in none of our best interests." He slowly pulled out his cell phone and opened up something on the screen. "Especially when we all just want what's best for your little friend."

He lifted the phone so they could see, and on the middle of the screen was Lex. Her hands were tied behind her back and her eyes were covered with a blindfold. A trail of blood dripped down the side of her face.

"What did you do?"

"I didn't do nothing. Someone's trying to make things right by killing your woman in our name." The man's smile disappeared, and he licked the blood from his lips. "I think it's best if you come on inside."

He turned around and started to walk toward the restaurant. Steel and Casper hurried to follow.

"Where was she supposed to be?"

"Her boss had her riding into a high-mountain cabin today. She left at six this morning."

"Would she have been there by now?" Steel asked.

She'd told him they were taking the Gunsight Trail, but that meant the trek would have been over thirteen miles. It would have been a long ride, maybe six hours. He glanced down at his watch.

"She could've made it to the chalet by now, sure. But how do we know that's where she's at?"

"Did you see her this morning?"

Casper nodded.

"And you are sure that she made it to work? These guys couldn't have gotten their hands on her?"

"I didn't escort her to the ranger station, but she texted me. She sounded fine. Nothing out of the norm."

"You mean other than the fact she was pulled off a murder investigation, just when things were heating up?"

Casper slammed the car door shut. "You make it sound like this is somehow my fault. Like I shouldn't have let her go to work this morning."

Steel shook his head. "You should know as well as I do that sometimes the best tool we've got in an investigation is our intuition. She told you that she felt she couldn't trust people, yet you just let her go. Now here we are. For all we know, she's a thousand miles from here... Hell, she could be in Canada right now. You should have stayed at her side."

"You don't know her at all if you think she was going to let me stand guard all day. Don't you think it killed me that I left her this morning? If I could go back and do this all over, I would. I love her, damn it. I thought I was protecting her by making her go back to work."

"If you love her, then you better make this right. You may be the only one who can save her life."

Chapter Fifteen

The president of the MC sat at the table in the corner of the restaurant, his fingers tented in front of him as if he grew impatient, waiting for them to sit down.

"Did my guy tell you what we have on the table here?" the president asked, his voice was hoarse with age and hard living.

"If you touch a damned hair on her head, I swear I will come down on you like you've never seen. Not only will you spend the rest of your life getting the full treatment in the federal pen, I'll make sure that no one in your entire club will ever sit on a motorcycle again. The only thing their butts will touch will be whatever gets to them at the various federal lockups across the country."

"Whoa now, man," the president said, putting his hands up in surrender. "You got me all wrong. We didn't do nothing to your little girlfriend. Though, I gotta admit she's a fine piece of work. You're a lucky man if you're tapping her."

"Don't talk about her like that," Casper seethed.

"Where in the hell is she? I want to know now, or every federal officer in the state of Montana will be here in a matter of minutes."

"Hey now, Agent Lawrence, don't make threats that your job can't deliver. We both know that you being a CBP brings about as much authority as a mall security guard."

"Shut up," Steel interrupted. "You're a damned idiot if you think that this is how you are going to go about getting us to see your side of things. If you're not careful, Agent Lawrence is right. You and your comrades here will be seeing the inside of your jail cells by nightfall. So keep talking crap if you got nowhere else to be, otherwise tell us where we can find Lex and who's got her."

The president threw back his head with a loud laugh. "Whoa, I thought we were out of the loop on this one. You do know the man up there, the body you all found, is one of ours, right? That's why you stopped by our place and played your Hail Mary last night, correct?"

Steel glanced over at him. It had been a long shot, coming into their bar, but they had been desperate to move the case forward. Now, looking back, Casper wished they'd done anything besides draw the gang's scrutiny. He'd screwed up and gotten Lex in trouble—all over a dead gang member and some drugs.

They were never going to stop the flow of drugs into the country, at least, not on their own. They had been naive to think they could handle this case—that they could actually make a difference.

He'd thought things were going to be different when he'd left the FBI, but here he was back at square one, the people he cared about getting hurt and being put in danger, just for some illusion that they could make a lick of difference.

A waitress walked up to their table, oblivious to the turmoil that was roiling through him. "Can I get you all something to drink?"

Casper shook his head, so upset that he could barely think, let alone speak.

"They'll both have Cokes. Put it on my tab, darling," the president said, giving her a quick smack on the butt as she turned and walked away. "And hurry up with my pizza…you don't want us to start eating you up."

The girl giggled at the terrible come-on and the sound made Casper's stomach sour. "Where is she? Where's Lex?"

"Sit down."

The president's guards pulled out the chairs for him and Steel and they both sat.

The president waited to speak again until after the waitress had disappeared back into the kitchen. "I want to make it clear—we didn't have nothing to do with your old lady's disappearance. If anything, we tried to talk them down. But they only see her as a bargaining chip. She got too close to the fire. There's only one way out for her."

"What are you talking about?" Casper asked, his mouth dry.

"She pissed off the wrong people. There's little we can do."

"Who did she piss off?" Steel pressed.

"If I talk, Kagger walks free, and we get full impunity. You don't get to come after us for what's happening to your old lady. We ain't responsible."

"Why would we agree to that?" Steel leaned back in the chair, using his body language to take the power position in their negotiations.

"Come on now, we all know that you are at my mercy. If you guys don't act fast, not only will every shred of your case disappear, but they're going to kill your woman. You guys don't want more blood on your hands, do you? Don't you think you've had enough in the past?"

"My past isn't up for discussion. Just tell us where Lex is," Casper ordered, his voice full of panic as he moved to stand up.

The guard behind him pushed him back into his seat. "You ain't goin' nowhere. Not until he says so," the guard said, looking at the man in charge.

The president nodded, turning to Steel. "Do you know what kind of man you work with? Your man here lost his job at the FBI over a woman. Apparently he lost it when the woman he'd fallen in love with had an affair, got pregnant and then lost the baby—he killed the guy responsible in cold blood."

Steel nodded. "I'm aware. It's a low blow to think

you can manipulate a federal agent. Besides, take a close look at how you live your life. Are you really in a position where you should be throwing stones?"

"I just want to make sure that you are aware that your buddy here thinks with his heart and not with his head—at least not the right head."

Casper jumped up, moving out of the guard's hands. "Where is she?" He reached down and grabbed his gun and pointed it at the president, taking aim right between the bastard's eyes. "Tell me where she's at, right now, or you're a dead man. You know I'm not bluffing." The gun was unwavering in his hand.

Steel moved behind him, pulling out his gun and flagging the men, moving them back and protecting Casper's six.

"If you shoot, Lawrence, you and Steel are going to be as dead as me in a matter of seconds. Then who's going to save Alexis? Use your head," the president said, not batting an eye.

"Tell us where she is, and we'll agree to your deal. You guys have impunity."

"You'll drop your drug charges against us and anything else you are brewing up?" the president asked.

"Drug charges? So you admit that you've been running the Canadian Blue over the border?"

The president snorted with derision.

"These guys are the ones who stole the Blue from my truck. They knew I didn't have enough proof or pull to come after them." Casper was numb. "Which one of you stole the drugs?"

The president tilted his head toward a guy standing to his right. The man looked hard, like the rest of his comrades, and wore a bandanna around his head.

"Don't forget, boys—full impunity here. You break your word…and, well, you don't want to know what we'll do to you and your friends."

"Who was the woman who helped Razor in Waterton? Was that Lois Trainer?"

"Lois? She told me you stopped by her place. Gave her a little scare."

"Was she the one with Razor?"

The president shook his head, but some of the color drained from his face. "You don't need to worry about that girl who was with Razor. She's young and innocent."

"But Lois isn't?"

The president didn't answer.

"Lois is your distributor, isn't she?" Casper shook his head as he thought back to the woman's trailer and the little dog. No wonder they had scared her. He and Lex had been at her house the day after the drugs had been stolen, and the pills were probably just inside Lois's door—it's why she hadn't wanted them to see inside, why she had been in the picture with Kagger and why they were all so desperate to have the guy out of jail.

If Casper's gut was right, Kagger wasn't just another member of the club, but only time would tell.

"Using these women is how these guys have managed to stay off the radar for so long," Casper continued. "They use their women to handle anything that might attract too much public attention. If everything had gone right, no one would have known anything about Razor or his involvement. Instead he got himself shot."

"Ding. Ding. Ding. We have a winner," the president said. "At least one of you knows his ass from a teakettle. You will not come after us—or Lois—with any charges. You got it?"

"Fine, you got impunity from any pending charges, that's it," Casper said. "But know this, if we catch you running drugs over the border again, we'll rain down on you with the full fury of the federal government. Do you understand?"

"Us, running the drugs over the border?" He laughed. "You really are in over your heads. No wonder Lex is up there at that chalet...you guys have no idea. You got no clue who your real enemies are."

THE FEAR HELICOPTER cut through the air, slicing around the ridges and valleys that surrounded Lake McDonald. It was a short flight to the chalet, but between getting the helicopter and working things out with the MC, Casper already felt like they had taken too long. Lex's life was in danger and no one in the world could move fast enough to comfort him.

"Tapping your foot isn't going to make the pilot move this piece of metal any quicker," Steel shouted into his mouthpiece, the sound echoing through the speakers in Casper's helmet.

"If we don't get there soon, I'm going to stick my feet out and Flintstone this mother," he said, but the joke was as rigid with fear and angst as the rest of him.

Steel laughed.

Every time Casper closed his eyes, the only thing he could see was Lex, her hands tied behind her back, the blindfold and that thin line of blood. Whoever had thought they could hurt her and get away with it had another thing coming.

"You thinking about the bikers?" Steel asked, pulling him out of the nightmare of his thoughts. "We're lucky they wanted to talk to us. It's amazing what happens when you're the highest bidder."

"Sure," Casper said, looking out the window as they flew over the crystal-clear lake. "I know I should feel lucky, thankful even…but it just doesn't sit right. We weren't that close to bringing down charges on them for stealing the Blue, or for selling drugs. It just wasn't enough motivation to drive them to work with us. There has to be something else going on here."

Steel gave him a knowing look. "Let's not look this gift horse in the mouth."

He was right, but that didn't make the knot in Casper's gut disappear. "This's going to come back and bite us in the ass—you don't need to lose your job over this."

"And neither do you."

"My job doesn't matter. The only thing that I care about right now is getting Lex back safe and unharmed. If she's hurt… You might have to put the cuffs on me yourself."

Steel drew in a long breath. "Whatever happens up there, Lawrence, we're in this together. Thick and thin, I got your back."

Chapter Sixteen

The world was black, and for a surreal moment Lex wondered if this was what it was like to be in the world of the blind. She drew in a breath, pulling the scent of pine and earth deep into her lungs. Wherever she was, it didn't carry the mineral-rich aroma of heated rock, or the leftover greasy scents of cooking that always seemed to permeate the chalet at the end of the season.

A damp chill wafted against her skin. Was she outside? No. She sat back slightly and her back brushed up against crumbling dirt. Sliding her foot to the right, it hit a wall. She had to be enclosed, but where?

Maybe in a place with an opening…somewhere that let in natural air. Perhaps a cave?

She racked her brain, trying to think of a cave that she knew of near the chalet, but nothing came to mind.

Her hands ached from being tied behind her back, and she tugged at the rough rope, but it only made slivers of the rope dig farther into her skin. Her wrists burned, but she kept moving, and the rope loosened incrementally.

"Sit still," a man ordered. She thought she recognized the voice, but she couldn't put a name to it.

A wave of light slipped through her blindfold as the man's footsteps shuffled on the dirt floor. He must have been standing in a doorway.

The pump house. They were keeping her in the chalet's pump house, but why? Were they hiding her? Was there someone coming, or was the place simply the first thing they had thought of to keep her out of sight?

She tucked her feet under her.

"I told you to sit still. If I have to tell you again, you'll get another lump on your head."

She stopped moving. Her fingers brushed against the edge of her pant leg. Running her fingers up the leg, she touched the L-shaped hole that Casper had mended. She pinched it between her thumb and forefinger and rolled it back and forth. In a strange way, the simple action calmed her and her thoughts wandered to Casper.

He couldn't possibly know what was going on here. She barely knew what was happening—or why. There wasn't a single chance that anyone was going to come save her. Whatever happened was up to her. She had to be strong. She traced the stitches. Casper was with her, at least in spirit. She could feel him there, just as if he was beside her.

"Why am I here?" she asked the man who was standing guard.

"Shut up. You're not here to talk. You're just making this harder on yourself."

She couldn't understand that in any way. He was the one making it hard on her. He was the one who had kidnapped her. None of this was her fault.

Waiting a few minutes, she spoke up again. "How's Travis?" The question was simple and decidedly safe—or so she hoped.

The man shuffled his feet as though he was trying to decide whether or not to answer her.

"Is he alive?" she pressed.

"Travis'll be fine, and a heck of a lot better off than you."

"Did you get him medical attention? It looked like he broke his ankle. He needs to see someone as soon as possible."

"Look, Lex, if you were smart, the person you'd be worried about here is yourself. Yours is the ass that's really on the line."

"Who are you?" she asked.

He snickered. "If you stopped to think about anyone besides yourself and the little melodrama you've had over the last few years with Travis, you'd know exactly who I am...and maybe why you're here. As it is, you and your stupid attitude have gotten you nothing but trouble. Now it's time you paid."

"My attitude?"

Normally, when it came to her job, she kept to

herself. It kept her out of the politics and away from the gossip mill. If anything, her attitude had been a healthy thing—especially when she and Travis had gone through their divorce.

"You always thought you were so much better than everyone. They all call you Wonder Woman behind your back, you know that, right?"

"What?"

"Yeah, if there's some amazing feat that needs to be done, we just call Wonder Woman. You always make a point of having all the answers. You're so self-righteous. You never screw anything up. It's freaking annoying."

She wasn't following his logic in the slightest. "If I'm so-called Wonder Woman, then why did Dragger pull me off the case?" As she spoke, a thought struck her. Had Dragger pulled her because he *didn't* want her to solve it? Was he somehow involved in all of this?

The man laughed again, the sound low and menacing. "You can ask him yourself when he comes back. From what I hear, it may be the last chance you'll get to talk to anyone, so you better make sure you ask any questions you want answers to 'cause the only person you'll be talkin' to is God himself when Dragger's done."

She couldn't think of anything that she'd ever done to make Dragger hate her. Why would he want to kill her?

"You guys don't have to kill me. I don't know anything. I won't talk to anyone." She hated begging, but panic filled her. "I promise."

"You are too much of a Goody Two-shoes to make me actually buy in to what you're saying. You couldn't even let the bear-mauling go." The man must have leaned against the door frame—she heard wood creaking beneath him. "Just think about it. If you'd just let things go and let our guys do what they do, the case would have been done and over with. You could be safe now. But no. You always have to go the extra mile. You always have to make the rest of us look bad."

"You look bad all on your own, John," she said, finally placing the man's voice.

"Screw you, Alexis." The man didn't deny his identity. He was the other ranger who'd helped recover Razor's body.

This must have had to do with her investigation, but how? What did he and Dragger have to do with it?

She rolled Casper's mend between her fingers. Silently, she wished he was here. He'd know how to get them out of this mess.

Outside, there was the sound of Travis's voice. He sounded upset, his tone deep and dark, but she couldn't quite make out his words.

"Is Travis okay?" she asked, hoping this time John would give her more.

"Your ex-husband is just fine. He just needs to

shut his damned mouth." John moved, the light shining through her blindfold again.

"Don't kill her. We already paid the MC—they got what they wanted. There has to be another way to get around this. There has to be," Travis shouted.

"What's he talking about?" Lex asked. She moved to her left, and her body rubbed against the cold rock wall.

"Don't worry about it," John growled. "Don't move. I'll be right back." He stepped out and there was the sound of a door slamming behind him.

She was back in the blinding darkness. Her only company was her nagging fear that the next time the door opened, death would be there to greet her.

THEY LOWERED THE HELICOPTER, the stone-sided chalet growing larger as they neared. A man stood out in the only flat area and raised a rifle. He shouted something, but they couldn't hear him above the sound of the chopping blades and the motor.

The pilot glanced down. "You guys know him?"

"No," Casper said, his voice grainy in the mic.

"Either he's going to have to move, or we're not going to be able to land. I did see another small clearing we could use, but it's about a mile back."

"No. We're not leaving her here with these men any longer than necessary. Land this sucker."

The pilot gave him a stiff nod, but even behind his sun visor, Casper could see the strain in his face.

The man beneath them motioned for someone

else, and another man, a taller one, with wider shoulders and a paunch belly sauntered out of the chalet. He took one look at them and flipped them the bird.

"Huh, so we're not going to get the royal welcome," Steel said, pulling out his sidearm and motioning for Casper to do the same. "If you want to save her, we may have to fight."

"With two of them out there in our landing zone, there's no way I'm going to be able to get any lower—and if they start shooting, I'm going to have to bug out. We can't put the bird at risk. Not if we want to make it out of this alive," the pilot said.

At their feet was a long rope, the type used for rappelling.

"You up for the ride of a lifetime?" Casper asked Steel, motioning toward the rope.

"I haven't done that since my training at Glynco. I guess it's about time to brush up on my skills," Steel said with a laugh.

They hurried to put on their rigging and Casper took his position at the door. "You got my six?"

Steel nodded. "You better hit the ground with a round in the chamber. Right now they are like trapped animals. It's going to be hard to tell what they'll do. They're desperate."

Steel hadn't needed to tell him. He was more than aware how deep they were in this. One mistake and none of them would make it to the end of the day. They would disappear, or become "victims of a helicopter accident," and no one besides the men responsible would be the wiser.

Casper jumped out the door. The rope whirred through his hands until he was far enough from the copter to slow his descent, but even then the rope burned his skin. He needed to get down there, get his boots on the ground and save the woman he loved.

A bullet zinged through the air and the copter pitched to the left, dragging Casper off course and forcing him to hang on to the rope for the lifeline it was. Steel was sitting at the copter's door, his legs out, taking aim at the men who'd tried to wing him.

His shot cracked through the air.

Casper slipped down the rope, taking the momentary cover that Steel was providing.

His feet touched the ground and he unclipped from the rope and pulled out his gun. There, just out of range, stood the man who'd been on the mountainside when they'd recovered Razor's body. John. The bastard pointed his gun at him, but the man next to him grabbed him by the arm and shook his head, motioning toward the helicopter and Steel. "Take them out first," the man yelled.

"You got it, Dragger!" The man took aim and his shot split through the air. There was a metallic tang as it struck the bird.

Dragger... Alexis's boss? He was in on this?

White-hot rage burned through him.

It made perfect sense. It was why he'd sent Lex up on the longest and most dangerous trail to the

chalet, and it was why he called her off the case…
Ultimately, everything came back to him.

Casper had been so stupid in letting Lex walk into
the trap her coworkers had created.

Sometimes your worst enemies were those you
thought were your friends.

Dragger took aim at the helicopter, but before he
could squeeze off a shot, the helicopter cut to the
left and whipped out of the hot zone. They moved
west, likely toward the safe landing area a mile away.
Casper was on his own. Alone with two gunmen.

Two men with guns were never going to be
enough to stop him, not when it came to saving Lex.

"Lower your weapons!" He raised his gun over
the top of the rock, taking aim squarely at Dragger's
center of mass. "I can guarantee that this isn't going
to end well for you if you don't put down your guns."

John looked over at Dragger like he was waiting
for an order, but Dragger didn't budge.

"Look, Lawrence, you don't have to get wrapped
up in all of this. This doesn't concern you."

"It does concern me. You don't get to kidnap the
woman I care about and then expect that I'm not
going to gut you."

"Gut us?" Dragger laughed. "In case you didn't
notice, you're outmanned and outgunned. You don't
have a snowball's chance in hell of making it out of
this alive. So why don't you play it smart and listen to what I have to offer… Or we can just kill you

now and get it over with. Your choice." He flagged
the gun in Casper's general direction as he spoke.

Casper was within his rights to pull the trigger
and kill Dragger, but he held back—this wasn't like
the last time he pulled the trigger. He only saw two
men, but that didn't mean that there weren't more
men in the wings…or with Lex. If he took the shot,
it wasn't just his life at risk—he might be putting
Lex even further into danger.

"What do you want from me?" Casper asked.

"See, I told you he'd come around, boss," John
said.

Dragger shut him up with the wave of a hand.
"Why did you come up here, Lawrence?"

He thought for a moment before he answered,
fully aware that the wrong answer could end up getting him killed. "I wanted to save Lex."

"It wasn't to cart us off to prison?"

It was, without a single doubt, but he held back
from saying so. "My main concern is Lex. I need
to know she's safe before we can discuss anything
else. Got it?"

Dragger turned to John. "Go get her."

John ran off in the direction of a small building
east of the chalet.

"You didn't really answer my question, Lawrence.
Don't think I didn't notice." Dragger lowered his
gun slightly, almost as if his arm was growing tired.
"How did you know we were here?"

"The tooth fairy told me."

"Told you what, exactly?" Dragger gave him an appraising look as if he were trying to understand how much trouble he was in.

There was untapped potential in his ignorance. For once, it wasn't Casper who was in the dark—and he could play this to his advantage and maybe get the confession he needed to bring this guy and his crew to justice.

"I heard all about your dealings, Dragger. You have one heck of a racket going. How much money did you pull in this summer running the Canadian Blue?"

"We would have gotten a whole lot more if you hadn't gotten in the way."

"How much did we cost you?" Casper continued.

"Close to 140k."

"That's just a drop in the bucket over the summer, isn't it?"

"Our Canadian friends charged us for the loss of their guy and they took our cut. They're threatening to take their business elsewhere. In order to make things right, we told them we'd take care of the loose ends—starting with Lex. Once she's gone, killing you should be easy."

"Assuming I'll let you hurt her is one hell of a mistake."

"Whether you believe me or not, I don't want to see her killed. She's a good ranger, but if we don't do something to make things right with our business partners, in the end it's the park that suffers. Half of that money goes into our budget."

Casper didn't believe him—Dragger was no Robin Hood antihero no matter how badly he wanted to convince himself he was. He was a criminal, and more than likely every cent they made landed squarely in his pocket. "Let's cut the bull. I know you're not giving the park the money. You're lining your own pockets."

Dragger smirked. "If you're capable of keeping your mouth shut, you could, too. You could make our whole process a hell of a lot easier. It'd be nice to have someone at the border helping us bring our supplies across. We could quadruple our business."

"Depends on what's on the table."

Dragger glanced over at the little building near the chalet. The front door opened and John dragged Lex out by her bound wrists. Casper rushed in their direction, putting himself directly in the line of fire— but he didn't care.

"Take your damned hands off her." He pushed John out of the way and ripped off Lex's blindfold. He fumbled with the knot of rope at her wrists, but finally managed to break her free. Her wrists were red and raw. "You had no right to treat her like this."

John stepped back, a look of fear crossing his face.

"Lex, are you okay?" Casper asked, wrapping her in his arms.

She pushed her face into his neck, drawing in a long sigh of relief. She smelled like dirt, sweat and fear and it made the fury inside him grow. The men she worked with and had grown to trust over the years had done everything in their power to break her spirit.

Every shred of him hated Dragger and John.

"I'm here. I'm going to get us out of this. Whatever you do, just play along," he whispered.

She leaned back and blinked a few times, unaccustomed to the bright light, and gave him a tiny, almost imperceptible nod.

"Where's Travis?" she asked, her voice hoarse.

"He's here?" Casper looked around for her ex, but he was nowhere in sight.

"He came up with me, but his horse threw him. I think he's hurt somewhere, but you need to watch out. He's a part of whatever *this* is." She nodded toward Dragger.

If he was hurt, he had to be here...unless there were other people who had been here to help carry him out. Casper shrugged off the idea. If the men had come up here with the intention of ridding themselves of Lex in order to appease the MC, they would have wanted as few witnesses as possible.

Casper ran his fingers gently over the bump on Lex's right temple where blood had seeped from a small cut and dried on the side of her face. "You're a real bastard, Dragger."

Dragger gave a dismissive laugh. "If you take the deal, we don't have to be death dealers anymore— I'm sure we could convince the MC to continue using our services if we had a CBP agent on our side. We could simply focus on the future. Together, we all could stand to make millions."

Lex tightened in his arms.

"Just think about it, Lawrence, you get everything you want—you'd be set for life and Lex…" Dragger looked to the woman in Casper's arms. "Well, Lex, you can just go back to your job. How 'bout it? I've always liked you. It tore me up thinking about what had to be done up here."

"It couldn't have been too bad for you," Lex spat.

"I know it's hard, but play along, Lex," Casper whispered into her ear. "We have to make it out of here, and our backup is still a ways away."

She looked up at him and closed her eyes, as if she hated what he asked of her.

"So, what exactly do you want Casper to do?" Lex pulled herself out of Casper's arms and winced as she moved. Her fingers moved to her inflamed wrists.

Dragger must have seen the damage, as well. "Damn it, John… I told you no rope. You were supposed to use zip ties. Now look at her."

John answered with a flippant shrug.

"Go get the first-aid kit out of the chalet and check on Travis."

John kicked the dirt as he walked away from them, clearly upset that he didn't get to be privy to their business dealings.

"I'm sorry, Lex. Sincerely. I didn't want you to get hurt," Dragger said, turning back to them. "As

I'm sure you are more than aware, Travis and John can both be a little oblivious sometimes."

Oblivious wouldn't have been the word he would have picked for those two scumbags. If he had his way, they'd both be sitting in a federal prison by the end of the year.

Lex snorted a laugh. "We can agree on that. Honestly, I can understand why you picked them as your guys, but what exactly were they doing for you? I mean, what is it that you want Casper and me to start doing?"

"Each week we meet someone on just our side of the border. It used to be the Mounties, who were helping the Keepers north of the border, but they were starting to draw scrutiny. So the last few months we've been working directly with the MC. They hike up from the Waterton side, skirting your border crossing," he said, motioning toward Lawrence.

A sense of impotence filled him. He'd been demoted from FBI to CBP and he couldn't even do that right—at least now he had the chance to rectify the problem.

"I had one of the rangers meet up with one of the bikers. They'd hand off the drugs, and then we'd bring them the rest of the way through the park. We couldn't get caught. We don't run the trade, we're only middlemen."

"So we're basically drug mules."

Dragger laughed. "Nothing as lowly as that. Think about it. We implement the laws here in the park. No one can stop us. Except for this little screw-up—thanks to your ex-husband and his trigger-happy finger—we're above the law. He should have just let the bear have the man. We could have avoided all of this"

"Why did Travis shoot him?" Casper asked.

Dragger shook his head. "No matter what Lex has told you, Travis isn't a bad man... A little private maybe, but in our business that's an asset. When the bear attacked, Travis decided to put Razor out of his misery instead of letting the beast eat him alive. It was an act of honor and pity."

The word *honor* fit Travis about as well as a cheap suit.

There was the sound of glass breaking and the crack of a gunshot. The men around them hit the deck, dropping down into the dirt, but out of pure instinct, Casper grabbed Lex and sprinted to his place behind the rock, setting her on the ground.

Casper turned. On the other side of the clearing, taking cover behind a tree in the dense stand of the timber, was Steel. Beside him was the pilot.

"Stay here. Don't poke your head up," Casper said to Lex.

"What's going on?" she asked, hugging her knees to her chest.

"Our backup just arrived." He leaned in and took her lips, more than aware that this could be their last kiss.

She let go of her knees and cupped his face, brushing her fingers over his skin.

There was another buzz and crack of a bullet as it cut through the air and struck the rocky side of the chalet. He hesitated but forced himself to break their kiss.

"Lex…" He sighed. "In case something happens, and this all goes to hell in a handbasket, I want you to know I love you."

She pushed a piece of his hair behind his ear. "I love you, too…and I miss your hat."

He hadn't even thought of his hat. He must have left it in the helicopter.

He stood up just in time to hear the crack of the bullet and watch as it ripped through Dragger's chest. He staggered back a few steps and reached up to the hole in his shirt as if in shock.

Blood seeped from the wound above where his heart rested. The gun dropped from his other hand and landed in the dirt. He collapsed beside it.

Even though he was some distance away, Casper could hear the rattle in the man's throat as he drew his last corrupt breath.

Steel and the pilot rushed over. "Are you guys okay?" Steel asked, nearly breathless.

"We're fine. You guys stay here with Lex, make sure she's safe. Travis and John are inside," Casper said.

"Be careful in there. They had to have heard the shooting. They might have laid a trap," Steel said, lifting his chin in the direction of the chalet.

Casper leaned down and gave Lex a kiss, hoping

it wouldn't be their last. She gazed up at him; the look in her eyes was that of a woman pleading for him to stay, to keep out of danger, but he couldn't. He had to finish what they started and bring down the other men who were responsible for this mess.

"I'll be back. Everything'll be fine." He turned away before she could ask him to stay. It was hard enough to leave her without hearing her speak those words.

He made his way to the chalet, running from tree to tree, making sure he had cover in case he came under fire. He ran up the steps and stopped beside the door, pressing his body against the cold rock beside it. "John. Travis. Come out with your hands up!" he ordered.

There was nothing. No movement. No sound.

They had to be inside. They couldn't have gone anywhere, not with Travis hurt.

It was now or never.

He stepped in front of the door and, with one swift motion, he kicked it in. The front room was dark. There was an empty table at its center, and Casper made quick work of clearing the room. A hallway ran down the length of the building toward a staircase, and on each side of the shiplapped hall were doors to the guest rooms.

He slipped down the hall. The first guest room was empty. As he moved to the second room, he heard the sound of footsteps inside.

"I know you're in there," he said, moving his body

against the wall, careful to keep a bit of distance between himself and the door in case John decided to come out firing. "Come out now. This doesn't have to turn ugly. Just come out with your hands up, and we can do this the easy way."

"There is no easy way—unless you die," John answered.

The door to the room opened, and John lifted his gun. Casper turned toward him. John's eyes were wide with fear and his finger trembled on the trigger.

"Don't do it, John." Casper lifted his gun and pointed it square at the man's chest.

John opened his mouth to speak, but instead his finger squeezed.

Casper dodged, just as the deafening roar of the gun permeated the narrow hall. He fired back. The gun recoiled in his hands, but he kept its aim squarely on John's chest. John stepped back in shock. He slumped against the wall. He closed his eyes as blood seeped from the hole in his chest, and as death took hold, his body slid to the floor with a thump.

John's eyes were open with the unseeing gaze of the dead.

"Travis?" Casper yelled. "Come out, Travis! You're the only one left. There's no other choice. Come along willingly."

"If you want me, you'll have to come get me," Travis answered from another of the chalet's rooms near the staircase.

Casper made his way toward the man's voice.

"Just come out of the room, Travis. Make this easy on both of us."

Don't make me kill you…

He couldn't bear the thought of what Lex would think if he killed her ex-husband. She might forgive him…or she might resent him for the rest of her life. Yet this man had hurt the woman he loved. Travis had intended on murdering her.

Rage filled him.

Casper had promised that he would never kill in cold blood again, but maybe Travis deserved to die.

The door leading to Travis's room was slightly ajar. Travis sat on the bed, his leg elevated on a pillow and his left arm wrapped in a towel that acted as a sling. On the bed, beside his battered body, was a small-caliber handgun. It looked like a .22. For a moment Casper wondered if it was the same gun that had killed Razor.

Casper aimed his gun at Travis's head as he pushed open the door the rest of the way and walked into the room.

Travis's hand moved toward the gun.

"Unless you want me to shoot, don't touch that gun," Casper said, his finger twitching on the trigger. "Don't give me any more of a reason to shoot your stupid ass."

Travis stopped moving, but his fingers were nearly grazing the black steel of the gun. "We both know that regardless of what I do, you're probably going to shoot me. I saw it splashed all over the internet about how you got kicked out of the FBI."

"You don't know me…"

"No, but I do know what kind of man you are. You're the kind of man who thinks he's above the law."

"I'm not above the law. But I'm going to do what I think is right," Casper argued.

"You keep telling yourself that. You killed a man who wronged you. I've wronged you. We both know you're going to pull that trigger. Your ego won't let you act any other way."

Travis wasn't wrong. He wanted to pull the trigger. He wanted the man to pay for what he'd done and the hurt he'd inflicted on Lex.

"You're a bastard. You'll always be a bastard," Travis said, egging him on. "You don't have self-control when it comes to women."

He pulled the trigger, lifting the barrel of the gun as he shot.

The bullet ripped through the wooden shiplap inches above Travis's head.

Casper's hand shook with anger. "If I didn't have control, Travis, you'd be dead… As it is, you're going to prison and I'm going to spend the rest of my life with Lex."

Chapter Seventeen

A month had come and gone, and Glacier National Park was buttoned up and ready for the winter—thanks to Lex's efforts as the new head ranger. Snow had started to fall and covered the mountains' tips in white. The cold air bit at her nose as she hiked the highline trail, but after Travis's trial and the events that had unfolded upon his arrival at prison, it felt good to be in nature and away from the stress that had followed them.

Casper was panting behind her.

"Are you okay?" she asked, stopping. "If you want, I can slow down." She gave him a playful smile.

"You're not going to beat me to the top," he said between heaving breaths.

Near the trail was a flat area. It was covered in scree, and between the bits of broken rock were a smattering of late-summer flowers, struggling to flourish in the chill of the fall.

He pointed toward the spot. "Why don't we take

a break?" He dropped his backpack and took out the picnic blanket and the lunch they had brought along.

She helped him set out two turkey sandwiches, grapes and a bottle of red wine. As they hiked, she hadn't noticed exactly how beautiful the world was around them. At their feet, the mountain dropped steeply into a valley. In the distance were the remainders of an ancient glacier and the fields of green that were fed by its runoff.

He poured the wine into little plastic cups. "Thank you," she said, taking a sip of the sweet red blend.

"Lex, are you happy?"

The question caught her off guard. "The last few months have been hard, but…" She set down her glass. "Having you at my side has meant everything. Especially after what happened to Travis."

"I'm sorry he's disappeared, Lex… Maybe the bikers had had a hand in it. Maybe they wanted payback for his screw-ups? Who knows. He could have been in deeper than we knew."

"I know. I just don't like the thought of him being out there somewhere. He has to be so angry—if he's alive."

"Don't worry, Steel will get to the bottom of his disappearance." Casper reached over. His hands were hot from their hike as he laced his fingers through hers. "Whatever happens, you need to know that none of this was your fault and I'm going to keep you safe."

"I can't believe I was so blind. I had no idea that

he was…what he was. I just thought he was quiet. I didn't know he was a criminal."

"It's not your fault. He was good at what he did— what he *does*."

He picked up a grape and lifted it for her to bite.

It squished, spreading its sweet juice through her mouth as she chewed.

"I'm not perfect, Lex," he said. "And over the last few months, more than anything, I've learned that we gotta take life with both hands." He smiled that half-lipped sexy smile of his and it melted her. "From the first moment I met you, Lex, I've only wanted you…as my wife. Forever."

He reached into the pocket of his jacket and pulled out a gray box. The hinges squeaked as he opened the lid. Inside was a white gold band encrusted with diamonds. Classic and beautiful in all the right ways.

She drew in a breath.

"I hope you like it. I wanted something that you'd love." He took it out and let the box drop to the ground. "Alexis Finch, will you… Will you be my wife?" He moved to his knee as though remembering the formality at the last moment.

The voice in her head that normally told her not to trust, to run away, to expect the worst—it remained silent; and in that moment of freedom, she gave her heart to the man who had taught her how to trust in love.

"Yes, Casper. Yes. I'll marry you."

He slipped the ring on her finger.

She lifted it and the diamonds reflected the world around them. "It's beautiful," she whispered.

"It's just like you. Strong. Bold. Perfect."

"I'm not perfect, Casper," she said with a soft smile.

"To me, you are."

He pulled her into his arms. Together they would have forever, forever to learn and grow, and forever to love.

* * * * *

MILLS & BOON®
INTRIGUE
Romantic Suspense

A SEDUCTIVE COMBINATION OF DANGER AND DESIRE

0217/46